**Rave reviews for Diana Rowland's
White Trash Zombie novels:**

"Angel continues to be a truly memorable character as she displays ample guts and determination when defending those she cares about. . . . With two stellar urban fantasy series running concurrently, Rowland expertly showcases the full range of her considerable talents. Awesome job!"
—*RT Book Reviews* (top pick)

"So far, this has been an incredibly fun series, and a breath of fresh air in an increasingly crowded field. While there's no denying that the basic premise is fascinating and entertaining, the real draw here is Angel's personal journey of growth and self-discovery. . . . Angel's a heroine worth cheering for."
—Tor.com

"If you haven't discovered this series, you're in for a treat. Angel is one of my favorite heroines in urban fantasy right now, and I can't wait to see what she's up to next!" —My Bookish Ways

"This spiraling roller coaster is as full of heart as blood (and brains and guts), exploring themes of love, sacrifice, guilt, and vengeance amid splattery action. This orgy of super science, roadhouse rumbles, and slapstick supernaturalism should satisfy readers searching for blood-soaked fun." —*Publishers Weekly*

"Rowland's delightful novel jumps genre lines with a little something for everyone—mystery, horror, humor, and even a smattering of romance. Not to be missed—all that's required is a high tolerance for gray matter. For true zombiephiles, of course, that's a no brainer." —*Library Journal*

"Every bit as fun and trashy as the brilliant cover. The story is gory and gorgeous with plenty of humor and a great new protagonist to root for." —All Things Urban Fantasy

WHITE TRASH
ZOMBIE
UNCHAINED

DIANA ROWLAND

DAW BOOKS, INC.

DONALD A. WOLLHEIM, FOUNDER

375 Hudson Street, New York, NY 10014

ELIZABETH R. WOLLHEIM
SHEILA E. GILBERT
PUBLISHERS
www.dawbooks.com

First Printing, September 2017

1 2 3 4 5 6 7 8 9

DAW TRADEMARK REGISTERED
U.S. PAT. AND TM. OFF. AND FOREIGN COUNTRIES
—MARCA REGISTRADA
HECHO EN U.S.A.

PRINTED IN THE U.S.A.

To Robert Neagle, for showing me it's okay to be weird.

ACKNOWLEDGMENTS

As always, there are vast multitudes of people who deserve my gratitude for their help in the creation of this book. This is where I try (and often fail!) to remember everyone. First and foremost, I have to thank Jack and Anna for being so utterly supportive despite my neglect, as well as my sister, Sherry, for being all-around awesome. Great glorious gobs of gratitude go to the real life Dr. Kristi Charish who told me how my zombies work and who really isn't all that evil. Huge heaping thanks also go out to Debbie Roma, David Hall, Jerry Bultman, Jennifer Boyet Harper, Nils Onsager, Joe Alfano, and everyone else who tolerated my odd questions and/or helped me survive my crazy schedule. My very deepest appreciation goes to Dan Dos Santos and his kick-ass cover art, and also to Josh Starr, Betsy Wollheim, and the rest of the amazing team at DAW, all of whom help me reach the finish line every single time. A very special super-thank-you is saved for Kat Johnson, for kicking butt and being brilliant. And, for everyone I ignored, blew off, disappointed, or forgot during the writing of this book, thank you from the bottom of my heart for putting up with me.

Chapter 1

Ten more measly miles. My index fingers drummed a happy beat on the steering wheel. I hadn't been home in three weeks—not since Mardi Gras, when a four-wheeler chase through the woods ended with me literally falling apart. Flying limbs. Rotting chunks. Not pretty.

Up ahead, a squirrel darted onto the road, then thought better of it and dashed back to the pines. My heart pounded stupidly hard, and I eased my death grip on the wheel. In theory, I was regrown, rehabbed, and ready to take on the world. In reality, this was my first time in the driver's seat since the accident, and I was still getting used to my new parts.

Thankfully, there was almost no traffic along this part of Highway 51—the rural, two-lane road between the zombie research lab and my house. Even with my extra-cautious driving, I was making good time.

I dug through the baggie on my lap for a desiccated brain chip—a get well gift from my friend Naomi. Perfectly freeze-dried and dusted with Cajun spices, it was the certified junk food of the zombie gods.

My phone buzzed the instant I stuffed the chip in my mouth, with the caller ID showing "Z.B." I rolled my eyes, unsurprised at the call. A little over a year ago, I'd been forced to turn badass operative Philip Reinhardt into a zombie, which I figured made him my Zombie Baby. In return, Philip had become a teensy bit protective of me. If I didn't answer, he'd no doubt come looking for his Zombie Mama.

I stuck in an ear bud and hit the answer button. "Hey Zee-Bee!" I chirped. "How's it going?"

"You snuck out of the lab."

"I didn't! You just happened to be in the bathroom when I left."

"Riiiiiight." Lucky for me, he sounded more amused than pissed. "Dr. Nikas recommended you stay another day."

"Yep. Recommended, not ordered. It's cool. I don't have to go back to work until tomorrow, so it'll be fine. I'm just gonna hang out with my dad."

"I could have driven you home. I'm not sure your reflexes are up to—"

"Dr. Nikas wouldn't have let me go if he was worried." He'd actually said I wasn't *quite* back to my normal self, but was likely no worse off than most drivers out there. That was good enough for me. "You did your zombie-baby duty and wheeled me around to my classes last week. You're off the hook."

He laughed. "I give up. Don't come crying to me when you have a fender bender."

"You'll be the first one I blame." I caught sight of a car in my rear view mirror. It was a good half mile behind but closing way too fast. "Let me call you later. Gotta focus."

My speedometer read sixty-two mph, which meant this asswipe was doing at least ninety. My contrary side dared me to slow down and straddle the center line, but the morgue tech in me had seen enough vehicular fatalities to put an end to that fantasy.

With one eye on the rear view mirror, I edged close to the side of the road and slowed to a respectable fifty. Despite my bluster to Philip, I didn't trust my reflexes a hundred percent yet. And I trusted the speeder's level of *stoopid* even less.

Especially considering the flash of blue lights in the distance behind him. The speeding car swerved into the other lane even as I eased my right wheels onto the narrow band of gravel between road and ditch. I stopped and waited. Three. Two. One.

Whoom!

My car rocked in the wake of the speeding silver Camry. I caught the barest glimpse of the driver as the car blew past. Male. Maybe. I stayed put and kept watch behind me, not about to move until the pursuit passed.

An unmarked midnight blue Dodge Charger flew by, though nowhere near as fast as Mr. McSpeedy. The driver had dark hair and a surly expression—Detective Mike Abadie. Not my favorite person, but a good cop. It looked like he was either backing off from chasing the Camry—since high speed pursuits risked civilians—or he was herding the guy into a roadblock.

Curiosity clamoring, I snagged the last brain chip from the baggie and pulled onto the highway. If it was, indeed, a roadblock, I'd find out soon enough.

Three miles later, I rounded a curve and slowed at a sea of flashing red and blue lights ahead. Two Sheriff's Office cruisers were parked along the right shoulder while Abadie's Charger and an unmarked dark green Chevy Impala blocked my lane. On the other side of the highway, the Camry rested with its nose in the ditch. The driver lay face down on the asphalt as a tall, black woman in plainclothes handcuffed him. Beside her, Abadie holstered his weapon.

Closer to me, a stick-thin deputy with scraggly blond hair packed away a set of spike strips. Beckett Connor. We'd been out on at least a dozen scenes together over the past year. Decent guy. Bad haircut.

The second deputy motioned for me to stop. Fit, muscled, hair shorn in a crisp high and tight. He'd been hired only a few months ago, and though we'd chatted on several scenes, I couldn't remember his name for the life of me.

I rolled down my window, trying to not be too obvious as I peered at his name tag. "Hey . . ." U. Blagojevic? How the hell was that pronounced? ". . . You!" I said brightly. "What's going on—whoa!" My train of thought derailed as my gaze lifted to his face. "That's an impressive sunburn."

"Hey, Angel." He managed a weak smile from his tomato-colored face. "Yeah, Connor and I spent four hours on the water yesterday."

"And you've never heard of sunscreen?"

Connor barked out a laugh, his face and arms darn near as red his partner's. "Our boy here brought the sunscreen, except turns out it was plain ol' lotion. But hey, my skin is as soft as a baby's bottom."

"Uh huh. If my baby's bottom looked like that, I'd take it back to the hospital."

"Wouldn't blame you," Connor replied with a wink then

turned away to load the spike strip case into the trunk of his cruiser.

"So, anything exciting going on here?" I asked U. Blagojevic, lifting my chin toward the man being handcuffed.

He shrugged. "Just another day at the office. You know how it is."

Well, that was completely unhelpful. But before I could ask a more probing question, Connor hollered that the road was clear.

"You can go on through now," Blaggy said. "But take it easy 'til you're past the vehicles."

I rolled up my window then took full advantage of my slow speed to shamelessly gawk at the spectacle. The Camry's tires were thoroughly shredded, and the airbag lay like a deflated jellyfish over the steering wheel. Abadie and the plainclothes woman had pulled the handcuffed guy to his feet, allowing me a good view of him. His nose was bloody, and he had on a tailored dark grey suit. Definitely didn't look like a typical car thief. Maybe he was an embezzler on the run? Or a serial killer? Whatever his crime, he looked pissed.

The woman glanced my way, and all thoughts of the bad guy's identity fled. Short-cropped greying hair and a distinctive scar that started beneath one ear and ran across her throat. FBI Special Agent Sorsha Aberdeen. Her eyes narrowed in recognition.

Crap. I yanked my gaze away and continued past the vehicles. I had plenty of questions, but no way in hell was I going to stop and ask them. Not while an FBI agent who I suspected knew zombies were real was around. I'd only met her once, right before Mardi Gras during her investigation of a short film that included footage of real zombies. I'd pretended the zombie rot on my cheek was part of a costume—but that woman was smart and suspicious, and my gut told me she wasn't fooled by my fib.

As soon as I was clear, I stepped on the gas and got my ass out of there. My paranoid side expected the FBI agent to come chasing after me, but my rear view mirror remained free of flashing lights and official vehicles.

I eventually turned onto the road that led to my house then slowed behind a FedEx truck, most likely destined for old Mrs. Grady, who lived across from us. Ever since her husband passed away last year, she'd taken to ordering nonstop from the shopping websites and got deliveries damn near every day. Sure enough, the truck stopped a few feet beyond my driveway.

The driver exited the truck carrying an Amazon box about the size of a sofa pillow. I hopped out to check the mail and gave him a wave. "Hiya, Chester! Another one for Mrs. Grady, I see."

"Nope. This one's for you, Angel. Good thing you're here. Can't release it without your sig."

"For me? Huh." Maybe my dad had ordered a welcome home gift for me. Or a new toilet seat. Knowing my dad, it could go either way.

I tossed today's bills and junk mail onto the passenger seat then exchanged my signature for the package. Definitely big enough for a toilet seat, but a bit too heavy.

While Chester delivered an unwieldy pile of four packages to the neighbor, I set the box on top of the mail and drove on up to the house. A warm, fuzzy feeling wrapped around me as I climbed out of the car.

Home.

An almost-new, two-bedroom prefabricated house with sky-blue siding and a tidy porch. Real gravel for a driveway, too, instead of the carpet of crushed beer cans it once had. The place wasn't much, but it was ours—replacing the rickety excuse for a house that got washed away in the flood last year. But even if it had still been the same old piece of crap house, I'd've been just as thrilled.

Box and mail in hand, I trotted up the steps and pushed the front door open. "Hey, Dad. I'm home—"

"Surprise!" my dad hollered and popped up from behind the sofa. All on his lonesome, but grinning wide enough for twenty people.

I grinned right back and placed the box on the coffee table. "You throwing me a one-man surprise party?"

"Sure," he chortled. "I thought about inviting all your friends and zombie pals and such, then decided, screw 'em. I wanted it to be just the two of us." He hurried over and wrapped me in a big, bony hug. "I'm so damn glad to have you home, Angelkins."

"I'm glad to be home, Dad." Tears stung my eyes as I hugged him. He'd done the best he could to raise me after my mom went to prison—where she killed herself a few years later. Unfortunately, my dad's best had been pretty rough at times. But that was all behind us now. He'd sobered up, and we were closer than we'd ever been.

He smelled of Aqua Velva, toothpaste, and . . . cigarette smoke, damn it. He'd told me he was going to quit. I suppressed the urge to grill him about it since it would probably end up with us fighting. Not only would that ruin the moment, but Jimmy Crawford was so stubborn there was a good chance he'd go out and smoke a pack out of spite.

He finally released me. "Whatcha got in the box?"

"No clue. I thought maybe you'd ordered something for me."

"I ain't ordered nothin'," he said. "Open it up and see what it is."

Armed with a box cutter, I made short work of what had to be half a roll of packing tape and soon opened the package to reveal a brand-spanking-new PlayBox game console.

My dad gave a low whistle. "That sure looks nice. Who's it from?"

"Hang on." I dug out the packing slip. It didn't show a price but had a gift note.

Angel, hope you're feeling better and get a chance to play soon. Your friend, Arnold Stein.

Huh? Who the hell was Arnold Stein, and why would he send—

A chill raced down my spine. What if someone was trying to plant a bug in my house? Lord knew I'd made plenty of enemies during the past year—Kristi Charish along with everyone involved in zombie research at Saberton Corporation.

Easy enough to find out, though. Tomorrow, I'd borrow the lab's listening-device scanner doohickey and do a thorough sweep of the house. Couldn't hurt to be smart and suspicious.

My dad peered over my shoulder. "Who's Arnold Stein?"

"No clue." I didn't want to get my dad worried in case it turned out to be nothing. "It has to be a zombie, though, considering this Arnold Stein knew I wasn't well, and no way would work send me anything." I kept my tone light as I lied through my teeth. "But I don't know everyone in the Tribe. He could be the Tribe guy who takes care of shit like condolence letters and Christmas bonuses, y'know?" The Tribe was a tightly knit organization of zombies and a handful of humans whose objective and purpose was to ensure the welfare and well-being of zombies—by any means necessary, at times.

That seemed to satisfy him. While he peered at components, I reread the note. What if "Arnold Stein"—A.S.—was actually Andrew Saber?

Philip wasn't my only zombie baby. Last fall, Andrew had been shot during a raid on Saberton in New York. I'd turned him—with his permission—to save his life, but becoming a zombie wasn't all sunshine and roses for him. First off, he was a Saber. His mother, Nicole Saber, was the CEO of Saberton Corporation, as well as the driving force behind their heinous abuse of zombies. If she ever found out Andrew was a zombie, he'd end up as a guinea pig in one of Saberton's special research labs. Zombie Hell.

Unfortunately, he'd come awfully close to exposure right before Mardi Gras, when Marla the cadaver dog indicated on him. I suspected one of Andrew's bodyguards had then tattled to Nicole about the dog's behavior.

Fortunately, Andrew had anticipated that kind of disaster, and with the help of his primary bodyguard, Thea Braddock, he'd executed his planned exit strategy. Now, as far as anyone could tell, Andrew was "visiting possible factory locations overseas." Whether there was any truth to that or not, at least he was out of his mother's clutches.

But why the hell would *he* give me a PlayBox? Sure, I'd saved his life but, to be honest, we really didn't like each other. Andrew was the last person who'd send me a get-well card, much less an expensive gift.

With that, my brilliant theory went kablooey. I'd have to do more digging to find the real sender.

My dad poked at the console. "Well, don't that beat all. I always wanted to try one of them things."

"I'll let you kick my ass in, uh"—I held up the included game cartridge—"*Swords and Swagger* later."

"Yep, later. Cuz I got another surprise for you. A cake!" He grabbed my hand and hauled me to the dining room. Set out on the table were two plates and a sheet cake, still in its plastic container with the grocery store sticker on top.

Dad bustled around the table to pull the lid off. "I thought about having the lady decorate one with zombies and the like but then figgered she'd wonder why we was doin' zombies in the spring 'stead of Halloween, and I sure didn't want to draw attention to you. So I went with what they had in the store." His nose wrinkled at the cake, where a plastic T-rex and palm tree were surrounded by raggedy green icing roses that were probably supposed to represent prehistoric plants. "They didn't have much selection."

"It's awesome, Dad." I hugged him again. "You even got them to write Welcome Home . . ." I held back a snicker. "Angle?"

"What? Jesus Flippin' Christ!" He flushed and spluttered. "I'm real sorry, baby. I shoulda checked. But how the hell d'ya mess up a name like Angel?"

"At least they spelled the rest of it right."

"Blind damn luck, I'm sure," he said and plopped down at the table. "Alrighty, *Angle*, how 'bout you go ahead and cut us some pieces."

Laughing, I obliged, then took a big bite. My phone buzzed in my pocket as I was trying to get through a weirdly crunchy icing-rose.

I grabbed a napkin and spat the mess out. "It's Allen. Probably about my shift tomorrow." Allen Prejean was the Chief Investigator at the St. Edwards Parish Coroner's Office, and my boss. Though he knew the truth about my medical leave, the official-but-fake reason was mono. Funny how "mononucleosis" looked better on paperwork than "dismembered and rotted."

"Hey, Allen!"

"Hi, Angel. Don't sound so happy to hear from me. It's unnatural."

"It's the new me," I said cheerfully.

"Well, cut it out," he grumbled. "Look, I know you weren't due to be back at work until tomorrow, but can you come in today? Jerry broke a tooth and has to go to the dentist, and we're a bit overwhelmed."

"What time do you need me?"

"I hate to say it, but as soon as you can be here. I'm heading out to pick up a body even now. Sorry about the short notice, but—"

"No, it's okay. Hang on a sec." I covered the phone with my hand and looked over at my dad, but he was already nodding and giving me a "go on" hand waggle. "I can be there in about forty-five minutes." It was a twenty-minute drive to Tucker Point, plus I needed to find my work uniforms—and hope like hell they hadn't been moldering in a pile of dirty laundry for the past three weeks.

"Perfect. I owe you one. See you in forty-five."

I disconnected. "Sorry about that, Dad."

"It's no biggie, baby," he said with a fond smile. "I know I ain't the only one happy to see you up and about again."

"You're the best." I kissed the top of his head. "I don't suppose you did laundry while I was gone?"

"Nah," he said to my dismay, but then his eyes twinkled. "Gina did, though."

I stopped. Blinked. "Who the fuck is Gina?" Oh god, not another trashy girlfriend. And yes, I was fully aware of the irony of *me* thinking that. But my dad's girlfriends took trashy to a whole new level.

He snickered at the look on my face. "You'll like her. Don't you worry. Your uniforms are all hangin' in your closet."

Hanging? Hell, that was more than I ever did. Still, I leveled a cool glare at him. "Are you dating her?"

He stuffed a forkful of cake into his mouth and grinned around it. Rolling my eyes, I continued on to my bedroom, only now realizing that the house was *clean*. Like, spotless. A peek into the bathroom showed that the tub was sparkling, and the yucky ring in the toilet had vanished. And my bed was made— with fresh sheets.

I could get to like Gina.

Chapter 2

Dressed in my *ironed* fatigue pants and uniform shirt, and with the scent of Springtime Fresh fabric softener wafting around me, I stepped through the back door of the Coroner's Office building thirty-eight minutes after Allen's call.

I drew a slow breath—formalin and bleach along with a hint of death no cleaning could ever erase—then let it out in a happy sigh. An aroma as welcoming to me as fresh baked cookies.

A deep and resonant baritone hum I easily recognized drifted from the cutting room. I stopped in the doorway and smiled in delight. Derrel Cusimano, protective gear stark white against his dark skin, deftly sewed up the Y-incision on a mottled corpse. A former linebacker for LSU, he was the first death investigator I'd ever been partnered with. And, one of the nicest people in the world.

"Yo," I said.

Derrel lifted his head, and a huge smile spread across his face. He made a final stitch, then shucked gloves, apron, and smock, and stuffed them into a medical waste can.

"One sec," he said with a wink. Once he'd scrubbed and dried his hands, he swept me off my feet and into The Hug to Rule All Hugs. "I missed you!"

"My . . . doze," I managed. Laughing, he released me. I made a show of making sure my nose hadn't been permanently flattened. "Missed you too, big guy. Are you my partner today?"

"No such luck. I'm done in five minutes. You'll be with Nick." He snorted. "Maybe now that you're working again, he'll stop being Old Nick."

"You mean . . ."

"Nick the Prick. Touchy as all hell." He cocked a sly smile my way. "Guess he missed you, too."

I kept my face composed despite the doubt that pulled at my stomach. Did Nick miss me? I sure as hell missed him. Or was he still freaked out that the girl he liked had turned out to be a brain-eating monster? One who'd rotted away before his very eyes.

He'd texted me only once, not long after I woke up.

Allen said you'll be off work for a week. Derrel and I are covering half your shifts. You owe me. I have your masks. Hope you're feeling better.

Painfully neutral, but less ominous than silence. I'd read that text at least fifty times, trying to find some nugget of reassurance that what I felt for him might still be reciprocated.

"Speak of the devil," Derrel murmured as Nick entered the morgue. Derrel placed a hand on my shoulder and gave it an encouraging squeeze.

Nick stopped dead. "Angel," he said, voice weirdly hoarse. His Adam's apple bobbed. "I thought you weren't scheduled until tomorrow."

Under any other circumstances, I'd have teased him with, "What, aren't you glad to see me?" But there was too much chance it might be true, and I couldn't handle knowing that right now. "Jerry broke a tooth," I said instead. "Allen asked me to cover."

A strained smile tugged at his mouth but didn't quite win over the uncertainty in his eyes. "That's . . . cool. I mean, not for Jerry. But, um, yeah. It's good to have you here." He lurched forward as if prodded and gave me a stiff hug. A shudder passed through him, and he pulled away.

Revulsion? Or relief?

"You're okay now?" He gestured awkwardly toward me then seemed to think better of it and dropped his hand to his side.

Holy crap, this sucked.

"I need to go," Derrel said. "Y'all play nice." To my surprise Derrel smashed me into a second hug and murmured into my ear, "Whatever's going on between you two, it'll all work out."

I nodded against his chest, but a hard knot filled my throat. No way would he be so encouraging if he knew about the whole incognito zombie thing.

He released me, grabbed his satchel, and headed out the back door, leaving me and Nick to stare at each other.

Three painful seconds later, the door reopened and Derrel poked his head in. "Allen's back with a body. And Ben just pulled in."

"I'll go help them," Nick blurted and sprint-walked out.

The instant the door closed, I let myself have a super-quick whisper-quiet third-grade-level flouncing why-me tantrum, complete with not-third-grade cursing. The tactic worked to improve my mood a teensy bit—enough that I was able to give Detective Ben Roth a genuine smile when he stepped in.

It helped that he was my favorite detective. Over six feet tall and burly, he could be plenty intimidating when he needed to be. But he'd always been friendly and chill with me.

"Hey, Angel." He returned my smile. "Weird. You don't look dead. Why'd you miss all that work if you weren't dead? Slacker."

"Har har," I said with a grin. If he only knew. "You know perfectly well I work harder than anyone else here. And damn, dude. You're looking pretty good. Have you lost weight?" The spare tire around his waist had shrunk considerably.

"Thirty pounds!" His smile widened. "I want to look good for the wedding."

I let out a squeal. "You're *engaged*?!"

Ben lifted his left hand to show a slim gold band on the third finger. "Sure am. Neil proposed to me this past weekend." He wisely didn't resist as I seized his hand and did a proper scrutiny and *oooh pretty!* over the inset of four dark red gems. "Total surprise," he continued. "He told me we were going to a movie, but instead he took me to Romero's Steak House. I was clueless, even though the place was about as romantic as you can get. He had a table reserved by the water with candlelight and everything. Didn't click until he did the one knee thing." He chuckled. "My detective skills must've taken a vacation."

"I'm so happy for you," I gushed, relinquishing his hand. "Y'all are going to be the most gorgeous couple *ever*."

"Well, you can see for yourself June twentieth," he said. "Invitations should be going out next week."

The back door opened before I could start happy-weeping. Allen held it while Nick pushed in a gurney bearing a black body bag.

"Take him straight to the cutting room," Allen told Nick. "I'll get him logged in."

I snatched gloves and followed Nick. Together we hefted the body bag from the gurney onto the metal autopsy table.

"Douglas Horton," Ben said, flipping open his notebook. "A hunter whose boat overturned sometime early yesterday. Search and rescue found the body this morning and are still looking for his buddy." His expression soured. "Lifejackets were in the boat. Fat lot of good they did there."

"You don't think it was a murder?" I asked. "Maybe his buddy whacked him and took off."

Ben's eyes crinkled. "I'm not ruling anything out yet. That said, the boat definitely hit a log and overturned. Plus, if his buddy did decide to murder him, he picked a lousy spot to do it. He wouldn't get far in the swamp without a boat of his own."

"Maybe he had an accomplice," I offered. "Someone who put the log in the way and waited nearby in a second boat, and the murderer whacked Douglas and then jumped out of the boat before it hit the log . . . Okay, yeah, it's a stretch."

"Yes, it is," Ben said. "But I like the way you think."

Allen stepped in, clipboard in hand. "Dr. Leblanc wants us to get our boy here opened up to save time. Nick, why don't you take care of the pics."

"Gotcha." Nick unzipped the bag then retreated as an eye-watering stench of shit and rot flowed out. Within the bag lay the corpse of a pasty white middle-aged man with skinny legs and an impressive beer gut. Part of a beer gut, at least. A sizable chunk was gone from the left side, exposing mangled bowels—the source of most of the stink. Ugly punctures covered his thighs, and the meat had been stripped from his right arm, shoulder to elbow, the bone marred by deep scrapes. "Jesus," he muttered and moved off to retrieve the camera.

Ben's phone buzzed. He glanced at the screen and grimaced. "Hate to leave the shit-fest here, but an FBI agent I've been working with wants to meet up. Allen, if you could forward the report to me when it's done, I'd appreciate it."

"Will do," Allen replied.

I stomped down the urge to ask if his meeting was with

Special Agent Sorsha Aberdeen and if it had anything to do with the roadblock this morning. Now wasn't the time or place.

Ben departed, and I returned to my perusal of the corpse. "Propeller didn't do that damage," I said with a frown. "Those are bite marks."

Allen leaned close. "Yep. Alligator. At least two of 'em." He pointed to a distinct bite. "See, this one has a snaggle-tooth in the front. The one beside it doesn't. My guess is Mr. Horton drowned after the boat flipped and was then feasted upon."

"How d'ya know a gator didn't drown him?" I asked with a frown. "Isn't that how they kill their prey?"

He twitched a shoulder up in a shrug. "Gators aren't usually aggressive enough to go after a full-grown man."

"Maybe the gator had a buddy who told him he was big and bad enough to take down a pot-bellied hunter too cocky to wear a life jacket."

Allen rolled his eyes. "Fine. There's a dastardly duo of man-eating gators lurking in the swamps of St. Edwards Parish." He waggled his fingers at me. "Go get your gear on. Some of us have shit to do."

I stuck my tongue out at him but headed to the prep room with a spring in my step, humming under my breath as I grabbed a gown and apron from the supply cabinet. I felt like I was back home. Made sense considering it *was* my home in a lot of ways. I'd held this job for over a year and a half, ever since Marcus Ivanov saved me from dying by turning me into a zombie. He'd arranged for this job and informed me—anonymously—that I had to take it, or I'd go to prison. Where I would *die*. Dramatic, but it worked. I'd hauled my head out of my ass, got my shit together enough to keep the job, and along the way discovered I was a zombie and liked—*needed*—to eat brains.

But the job turned out to be more than a buffet. This was where I'd learned how to be a grownup. Responsible even. I made friends. Real friends who didn't hang out with me only to score pills or pot.

A shout of alarm from the cutting room jerked me out of my reverie. *Nick.*

I dashed in then stumbled to a stop as my brain struggled to process the scene. The body of Douglas Horton was on the floor. *He fell off the table,* I thought then stared in horror as Douglas staggered to his feet, right arm dangling uselessly, and small intestines trailing. *But . . . he's dead!*

Douglas lurched toward Nick.

"No!" I ran full out and tackled Douglas as hard as my skinny little ass could manage. The guy wasn't exactly a lightweight, but I had enough momentum to send us both crashing into a steel storage cabinet.

Douglas gave a wet, warbling moan that raised the hairs at the nape of my neck then clamped his good hand onto my upper arm. I yelped in surprise, even more surprised when my body remembered a fragment of *jiu jitsu* and twisted against the grip to free myself.

"Angel, move!"

I stumbled aside just in time as Allen and Nick jammed the rolling table against Douglas to pin him against the cabinet. The dead man let out another eerie wail, shoved at the table, then swiped his arm out. Nick jerked his head back and managed to merely get clipped on the jaw instead of walloped. He hissed a curse but held his ground beside Allen. But it was clear they wouldn't be able to keep Douglas pinned much longer.

"Heads up!" I snatched the fire extinguisher from the wall then swung it at Dougie's skull as hard as I could. Except he was over a foot taller than me, and with the table in the way, I only managed to graze his shoulder and smash the extinguisher into the cabinet, leaving an impressive dent. To add insult to injury, the rebound ripped the fire extinguisher from my hands and sent it sailing across the room.

However, my masterful shoulder graze had riled Douglas up. He let out a spluttering roar and overturned the table, knocking Allen and Nick off balance, then took a lumbering step in my direction, hand reaching toward me like a claw.

I was cornered, and I wasn't brained up enough to have super-zombie powers. Sure, I could take a lot of damage but, dammit, I'd just recovered from being in pieces. No way was I going through that again.

I ducked his swipe and lunged at the tray of autopsy tools. My hand closed on a pair of scissors right before he smacked the tray and sent the contents flying.

Thunk.

Douglas staggered. Behind him, Allen stood with the fire extinguisher, poised to deliver another blow. Douglas pivoted with a wet growl and flung his arm up. Allen danced away barely in time. The back of Douglas's head had a dent like the cabinet's, but clearly it wasn't enough to slow him down.

Like Judd. My mouth went dry. Judd Siler had turned into something horribly similar to this—and that was *after* I'd removed most of his brain for a desperately needed snack. But I'd left behind the medulla and most of the cerebellum—the parts that made everything work.

And then I'd defeated him by destroying those essential bits.

With a fierce shriek, I leaped onto Douglas's back, wrapped an arm around his neck and my legs around his waist. Fist tight on the scissors, I wedged the point into the base of the dent in his skull. Jammed them in and down, hard. Douglas howled and arched his back, but I shoved the scissors deeper and sawed them in messy circles, as if mixing a really thick milkshake.

Douglas went slack, then crumpled, face down. Breathing hard, I released my death grip on him and clambered to my feet. Nick stood a couple of yards away, shoulders heaving and fire axe in hand.

Still brandishing the canister, Allen eyed the prone man warily. "Is he . . . neutralized?"

"God, I hope so," I said. "But he will be for sure once we get the brain out. *All* of it." I clenched and unclenched my hands, fighting the worry that threatened to swallow me. "Where was this guy found? *Which* swamp?"

"Upper Mudsucker Swamp," Allen replied. "Northeast end, near Pauvre Bayou." Questions crowded his eyes, but Nick spoke before he could voice them.

"What the hell do we do with him now?"

All three of us looked down at the caved-in skull with the scissors sticking out of the dent. We couldn't simply get rid of the body. Not when he was supposed to be autopsied then sent to the funeral home.

"Maybe Dr. Leblanc will believe the damage happened in the swamp?" I offered weakly. "Post-mortem injuries?"

Nick sucked in a sharp breath. "Dr. Leblanc. He's due back from court any minute now."

Allen cursed and yanked the scissors free. "Do the pics. Fast. We'll get him opened up. Angel, you need to get that brain out ASAP."

Together, we wrestled Douglas onto the table. Nick grabbed the camera and took pictures as fast as humanly possible. The instant he finished, Allen started the Y-incision on the chest while I sliced through the scalp and peeled it away from the skull. Nick stowed the camera then hurried to get the room cleaned up so it wasn't *quite* so obvious we'd battled a zombie.

Definitely a zombie. Except it wasn't "my" kind of zombie. *A shambler like Judd*, I thought with a shiver and added "panic about the implications" at the top of my to-do list.

I took the bone saw to the skull, forcing myself to focus on the task at hand and not look at the clock. Or at Nick as he frantically cleaned up blood, shit, and scattered instruments.

"Samples," I breathed. "Allen, I need samples. For Dr. Nikas."

Dr. Ariston Nikas was the Tribe's research scientist and the go-to person for all things weird. The ideal scenario would be to deliver the entire body to him so that he could use the resources in the zombie research lab to figure out what the hell had caused Douglas to shamble. But the family no doubt wanted to do the whole funeral thing and would probably notice the lack of a body, so tissue and blood samples would have to do.

Allen gave a curt nod. "Understood."

A distant sound of a door cut through the air. "Hallway," I croaked. We had less than a minute, even if Dr. Leblanc took his sweet time down the long corridor from the front of the building. I pulled the top of the skull off and tossed it onto the table then slipped a scalpel between brain and skull to slice through the brainstem. As I tipped the brain out into my hands, my gut dropped at the sight of the mangled cerebellum and medulla. No way would Dr. Leblanc believe a blow to the head had caused that damage.

Allen glanced at the brain as footsteps approached. "We're fucked," he muttered.

Behind me, the door opened. "Good afternoon," Dr. Leblanc said.

Go big or go home, Angel. Faking a startle, I fumbled the brain and deliberately let it slip through my grasp to *splat* on the floor like a balloon full of Jell-O.

I whirled, wearing the best horrified expression I could pull off. "Oh my god! I'm so sorry, Dr. Leblanc!"

A grimace flitted across his face, but in the next instant it was replaced by his usual kind smile. "It's all right, Angel. It's not as if the cause of death is a mystery." Before I knew it, he'd crossed to me and pulled me into his arms to give me an utterly lovely and heart-melting squeeze, clearly not caring about my gore-covered gloves. "Welcome back. You have no idea how happy I am to see you doing so well."

Guilt tugged at me, but I mentally kicked it aside and let myself wallow in the wonderful embrace—as much as I could while holding my yucky hands away from him. Dr. Leblanc's hug was as comforting as a warm cozy blanket on a cold day.

I gave him a smile as he released me. "Yep, I'm all better."

"To my eternal delight," he said. "Mono can be tough to recover from. Kudos for being young and healthy."

"'Scuse me, Angel," Allen said. He scooped the mangled brain into a plastic tub then tilted his head toward the body. "He's all ready for you, Doc." He set the tub on the counter beside me then stepped to the autopsy table with Dr. Leblanc.

Nick casually slipped an empty plastic baggie into my hand before joining the others. I glanced over to confirm he and Allen were holding Dr. Leblanc's attention. Within seconds I had four small chunks of brain in the baggie, and the baggie in the pocket of my cargo pants. With any luck at all, that would be enough for Dr. Nikas.

Because if my suspicions were correct, we were going to need all the luck in the world.

Chapter 3

While Dr. Leblanc remained occupied, I mumbled an excuse about needing to potty then shed my yucky gloves and slipped out. The brain sample bag squished and shifted in my pocket as I walked. *Yech.* I'd been carrying human brains around for over a year and a half, but this was the first time I was even a teensy bit grossed out.

I ducked into the restroom, locked the door, then texted Dr. Nikas.

<Corpse in the morgue woke up on the cutting table. Just like Judd!! Hunter drowned in Mudsucker Swamp. Bit by gators!!! I disordered his medal> Scowling, I fixed my phone's damn autocorrect. <Scissored his medulla so no threat now. Have samples of brain but Dr L doing autopsy now. Dr L didn't see. Only Allen and Nick>

I hit send and waited anxiously. The reply came less than a dozen seconds later.

<That is very disturbing.>

Despite everything, I had to smile at his unflappable manner. <What should I do?>

I waited nearly a minute, then: <Rachel is in your area. Can she pick up the samples?>

Bleh. Rachel was one of the top security people for our zombie Tribe. I didn't care for her, and she couldn't stand the sight of me.

<I have to go back in for autopsy> Which was true. <Will leave the baggie on right front tire of my car> That way I wouldn't have to actually deal with her.

<Excellent. If at all possible, I would appreciate it if you could obtain other samples from the decedent. Bring them when you come here after your shift.> He proceeded to list what he needed: tissue samples from every organ imaginable, scrapings from beneath the fingernails, and samples of blood, vitreous, bile, cervical spinal fluid, urine, saliva, and even fecal matter. Ew.

<I'll do what I can>

<Of course. I'll see you this afternoon.>

I flushed the toilet in case anyone was listening, then hurried to the parking lot to place the baggie on the tire.

Allen glanced up as I returned to the cutting room then continued with his removal of the liver. At the counter, Dr. Leblanc sectioned a lung. Nick placed a kidney in the scale and recorded the weight on the white board. My eyes went to a red mark on Nick's jaw where Douglas had clipped him. Damn it, that was going to bruise.

Tugging on fresh gloves, I moved to the other side of the table from Allen and held skin and fat out of the way while he worked. The normal chatter was gone, held at bay by what we wanted to talk about but couldn't until Dr. Leblanc left. Fortunately, the pathologist seemed to be too absorbed in his work to notice we were uncharacteristically quiet.

"Cause of death appears to be drowning," Dr. Leblanc murmured, setting aside the lung and moving on to the heart.

The crushing silence descended again.

I cleared my throat. "So. Whatcha all been up to lately?"

"Nick is in a play," Dr. Leblanc said as he made tiny slices in a vein.

"No shit?" I swung my attention to Nick. He loved theater, but had given it up years ago to meet his dad's strict academic expectations. "Is that the Less Miserable thing you said you were going to audition for?"

His mouth twitched. "*Les Misérables*. I got the part of Marius Pontmercy." At my blank look, he rolled his eyes. "Marius is one of the main characters."

"That's awesome!" I paused. "Soooo, what did Bear say about it?" Bear was his dad, and hadn't always been a fan of Nick's love of theater.

One shoulder jerked up in a shrug. "He said he'd come see me. The show opens next month."

"I'll be there!"

He looked away and placed the liver in the scale. "How's school going? Did you miss a lot of classes?"

"It's going pretty good," I said, only lying a little. My first semester of college was trying really hard to kick my ass. "I started back last week. My doctor said I was okay to attend classes as long as I took it easy." Actually Dr. Nikas had said, since my mind hadn't suffered, and I'd recovered enough strength to sit without exhaustion, there was no reason not to return to school—*if* I let my zombie baby Philip handle the driving and cart me around in a wheelchair. "Plus, it was Mardi Gras break when I got sick," I added, "so I ended up only missing one week of school."

Nick jotted the weight of the liver on the whiteboard. "You keeping up in English?"

"Yeah," I lied a lot. "Holding onto a C." And by C, I meant the lowest C minus possible. I was seriously considering dropping the class, but I didn't want to tell Nick and risk him feeling obligated to tutor me again—or awkward for not offering. Not to mention, I wasn't sure how well I'd handle us being alone together. "Biology is fun, even though the professor is a real tool. We have quizzes every damn day, and I think he stays up nights to think of the hardest questions. He's also not even remotely nice. But he knows his shit, and it's super interesting. We just finished learning about bacteria." I grinned. "Found out poop is mostly water and dead bacteria. Our bodies are teeming with bacteria, and for the most part that's a good thing." I cocked my head. "Which I guess means we're covered with corpses of bacteria, too? Yuck."

Nick placed the liver on the counter. "They break down and get et by other bacteria. The problem comes during stuff like surgery. You can sterilize a scalpel, but the dead bacteria are still there. The body's immune system works by identifying certain chemical triggers in bacteria, and the corpses—including the toxins they release when dying—trigger the same response as living bacteria."

"That's why the dead bacteria are called pyrogens," Dr. Leblanc said without looking up.

"Wait, I know this," I said. "Pyro means fire or heat. So a pyrogen is something that causes a fever?"

He flicked an approving glance my way. "Yes. They cause fevers, among other issues. Even death, sometimes. That's why heart surgery scalpels go through a process called depyrogenation, which removes all the dead bits."

I shuddered. "That's nasty."

Allen snorted. "You're elbow deep in a body, and you say *that's* nasty?"

"At least I can *see* this nastiness."

Dr. Leblanc set the heart aside and lifted the somewhat-smushed brain from the tub to the counter. I watched, barely daring to breathe as he frowned and peered more closely. At least his focus was on the frontal lobe and not the medulla. So far.

"Allen, will you get a spinal fluid sample as well?" Dr. Leblanc gently prodded the brain.

"Will do," Allen replied. He gave me a speaking glance then added to Dr. Leblanc, "Do you see something?"

"I won't be certain until I can look at the samples under a microscope," Dr. Leblanc said. "But I believe there's inflammation. I maintain drowning was the cause of death, but he might have been suffering from some sort of encephalitis when he died."

Or after *he died*, I thought grimly.

Allen retrieved a sample of cervical spinal fluid, squirted it into a vial and sealed it, then placed it with the rest of the samples. The fluid was cloudy—which even I knew wasn't normal.

While Dr. Leblanc finished, Nick and Allen did cleanup, dawdling over every task. Meanwhile, I took my sweet time sewing the body up, using big, looping stitches since I was going to have to pull them out anyway to get the samples Dr. Nikas wanted.

After what felt like an eternity, Dr. Leblanc shed his gloves, gathered up his notes, and left the cutting room. Unfortunately, we could still hear him moving around by the computers.

I retrieved a cold pack from the first aid kit, cracked it, then thrust it at Nick. "Put this on your face." He let out a quiet scoff but obeyed.

Allen lifted an eyebrow. "What, no ice for me? Maybe I got a booboo, too."

I smiled sweetly. "You already have the chill of your ice-cold heart."

Nick smothered a laugh. Allen heaved a long-suffering sigh.

A chair scraped in the other room, and we froze. *Finally*, footsteps retreated down the hall, and the door at the end creaked open and banged shut.

Immediately, Allen pivoted to face me. "Okay, what the actual fuck *was* that?" He flung an arm out toward the body. "I've never seen a zombie act that way. Was he just really brain-hungry?"

I frowned at the corpse. "I'm not sure what his deal is, but he definitely wasn't brain hungry, considering he came after *me*. My kind of zombie goes after real human brains. The times I've been really crazy hungry, I could smell a human a block away."

Allen's brow furrowed. "You can't eat a zombie's brain?"

"I suppose I *could*, but it's about as appealing as eating a human brain was before I got zombified." I shrugged. "A lack of brain scent is one way to tell if someone's a zombie." I stopped. "Hang on." I yanked the top off the tub with the mangled brain and took a deep whiff. "Huh."

"Enlighten us?"

"It has a brain scent, but it's kind of not quite right. Like how lunch meat smells a bit off a day after its expiration date." Yet Judd's brain hadn't smelled or tasted odd when I ate it. Then again, I'd smashed his skull open less than a minute after he died. Still warm and fresh.

Nick swallowed. "Do you, ah, have a desire to eat that?"

"No. Not in the slightest." I replaced the lid, unsettled and not sure why. The smell of the brain wasn't repulsive, but the *idea* of eating it was. "It's definitely not a normal human brain. Or a normal zombie brain. Hell, he's not a normal zombie, period. I mean, my kind doesn't mindlessly *shamble* like that dude."

But Judd did. I held back a shudder.

"Why did you want to know where the hunter was found?" Allen asked, watching me closely. "Do you have a theory about why this guy shambled?"

I hesitated, torn about how much to share. Screw it. They needed to know. They were allies, right? "More like a hypothesis. Y'all remember Judd Siler?"

"His face was all over the news right after Mardi Gras," Nick said. "Wanted for murder and kidnapping. Big manhunt, but he's still at large."

"Well, they ain't gonna find him," I said, "'cause he's dead.

Twice. He tried to kill me out by Lock Three, and I bit him—just a regular old bite on his arm. The next day, west of Mudsucker Swamp, he attacked me and ended up getting shot dead. Not by me," I hurried to add. "I, uh, needed the fuel, so I busted his skull and ate his cerebrum. But later that night he came after me as a shambler—even though he was missing the top of his head. I had to rip out his cerebellum and medulla to kill him for real."

Nick's throat worked. "That's how you knew to attack the medulla."

"It made the most sense." I grimaced and rubbed the back of my neck. "Thing is, I left Judd's body deep in the swamp. So if an alligator or three snacked on him . . . I dunno, maybe they turned zombie, too, and a couple of them chomped our guy here."

Allen stared at me. "That's ludicrous."

I threw up my hands. "The whole thing is insane! But what if there *are* zombie gators out in the swamp? What if there are more shambly-zombies out there? Here I am, trying to work out how my zombies can safely come out of hiding and go public, but if a whole bunch of . . . of *shamblers* start showing up, that's going to fuck over the real zombies!"

Nick and Allen exchanged an oddly significant glance.

My eyes narrowed in a glare. "What?"

"Allen and my dad and I have been talking about this going public stuff," Nick said. "We agreed that you can't let the world know zombies are real. Even if there wasn't a shambler complication."

I folded my arms over my chest. "We are *not* going to stay in hiding forever."

"Not forever. You just can't reveal yourselves anytime soon. There are serious drawbacks to coming out."

"I know. We'll have all sorts of people deciding to become zombie hunters, and—"

"No," Nick interrupted. "I mean, yes, you'll have amateur zombie hunters. Maybe even military. But more importantly, your legitimate brain sources will dry up."

"I *know*," I said then smiled. "And I was about to say that. Trust me, I had a lot of down time to think about it. It's not like we need blood, where people can donate some and still live. To donate a brain to my dinner, that person pretty much has to be dead. And since no one wants to worry that Uncle Tommy might get eaten, the instant the news hits that brain-eaters are real, every morgue and funeral home will start keeping an eagle eye on each brain that comes through their door."

Nick's forehead puckered. "Exactly. So how can you still be thinking of going public?"

"Because of you guys. And Marcus."

Allen and Nick took on identical looks of confusion.

"What did we do?" Allen asked cautiously.

"You're human," I said, "and you don't think all zombies are monsters that need to be destroyed. Human allies will make a huge difference. Like how Nick and his dad helped me keep zombies from being exposed, and how you skimmed brains for me and told Dr. Nikas about the *goule gris* salve." Allen had stumbled upon the secret world of zombies during a medical aid rotation in the Central African Republic. His disclosure of the components for a zombie-only wound salve had triggered new developments in Dr. Nikas's research. "We still need to figure out more ways to reduce our need for real brains, but it's a *humongous* start."

"All right," Allen said. "What did Marcus do?"

"He inherited a chain of funeral homes," I said. "Okay, so they were already zombie-owned, but my point is we *can* safeguard some of those brain sources. Maybe get more allies in the morgues." I wrinkled my nose. "But it'll take time, and we need to safeguard those sources *before* the general public gets freaked out by a shambling zombie horde."

"Let's deal with the problems we know of," Allen said. "What samples does Dr. Nikas need? Better get them now while we can."

"I'll text you the—" I stopped as Allen's phone buzzed.

He heaved a sigh as he read the message. "Crappy timing. Body up in Bideau. Possible heart attack. Texting the address to you both now. Don't worry, Angel. I'll take care of getting the samples."

I thanked him fervently and forwarded the list to him. It would take a lot longer for Allen to do it on his own, but he didn't seem at all put out.

Because he knows how important this is, I realized as I followed Nick out to the parking lot. Allen was an ally. Maybe even a friend?

Nick peeled off toward the Durango and I climbed into the

van, snickering to myself. Never thought I'd see the day I was *friendly* with Allen Prejean, much less consider him a possible friend. What next? A rain of puppies? *Dr.* Angel Crawford?

With a snort for the ridiculous mental images, I plugged the address into my GPS and left to get a corpse.

Chapter 4

Once upon a time, when I first started working at the Coroner's Office, I'd thought it a waste of gas and money to have the death investigator and the "body snatcher"—me—in two separate vehicles. After all, why couldn't we both ride in the van? It didn't take me long to realize the death investigator did more than simply help babysit the body. They often had to stay at the scene to speak to next of kin and hunt down paperwork and medical records long after I headed back to the morgue. Not to mention, it was the investigator's duty to give death notifications to the decedent's loved ones—something I had absolutely zero desire to ever do. I knew damn well I'd break down crying right then and there.

And I was never more grateful for separate vehicles than right now. Bideau was at the very north end of the parish—a twenty-five-minute drive with no traffic. If Nick and I had been trapped together in the van, it would've been twenty-five minutes of torturous silence broken by occasional stilted conversation. And then twenty-five minutes back—with a corpse who was unlikely to be talkative.

I'd only been to Bideau a couple of times, and I murmured a prayer that the GPS would be up to the task of getting me there again. On a map it looked easy—highway, then another highway, then another highway, then yet one more highway. But in reality, each highway was smaller and less traveled than the last, with wickedly easy-to-miss turnoffs.

Yet it wasn't the GPS that helped me find the first turn. It was the brand-spanking-new billboard at the junction with *Saberton* splashed across the top in enormous letters.

I pulled to the shoulder and glared up at the sign.

Opening soon
Saberton Agricultural Equipment Manufacturing
Now hiring all positions
Turn left here then head south on Old Haybarn Road

Interesting. And odd. A couple of years ago, Saberton Corporation bought the tractor factory that had been up and running for near fifty years, and they'd immediately laid off all the employees. They'd promised to hire everyone back once they nailed a juicy defense contract and started production on some sort of new tank. But the defense contract had fallen through, and therefore so had the jobs.

Now, it seemed they'd decided to return to making tractors. Though it wasn't a complete surprise, I wasn't quite sure how to feel about this turn of events. Saberton had a nasty bent for unethical research on zombies, and no good would come of them having a stronger toehold in the zombie Tribe area. Yet I couldn't help but be relieved for all the people who'd get their jobs back.

Naomi might know more about how this crap came about, especially since she was the daughter of Saberton's CEO. I made a mental note to ask her when I next saw her, most likely later today since she worked for the Tribe, and I'd be taking the Douglas Horton samples to the lab as soon as my shift was over.

I snapped a quick phone pic of the billboard then pulled back onto the highway.

At the scene, Nick's Durango and a Sheriff's Office vehicle were parked on the street in front of a snug house with missing shingles and a tidy yard. I joined Nick inside where a Mr. Carlton Prince lay in his bed. Sixty-seven years old, skinny as a rail, no muscle tone, a history of heart disease, and a pack-a-day smoking habit. Dr. Leblanc might not even autopsy him, especially considering the dead man's skin was flushed red from mid-chest up—a strong indication of a heart attack. Most likely the doc would simply check for signs of suspicious wounds and run a tox screen to make sure Mr. Prince hadn't been hurried off to the afterlife with a little physical or chemical help.

I laid out the body bag while Nick interviewed a middle-aged woman with generous curves and kind eyes—the neighbor who'd found the body. She'd spoken with Mr. Prince the previous evening and agreed to give him a ride to his doctor's office today. After he didn't answer the doorbell, she let herself in and found him still in bed and clearly deceased.

"Went to sleep and never woke up," Nick murmured after she left. "Not a bad way to go, I'd say."

"Only if you know it might be coming," I said. He gave me a quizzical look, and I added, "What scares me the most about dying is dying unexpectedly. I want to be able to say goodbye to people. Tie up all the loose ends. That sort of thing."

His eyes met mine briefly before his gaze darted away. "Yeah," he said, voice oddly rough. He'd seen me come close to dying a few weeks ago. "Here, I'll help you."

Together we got Carlton Prince into the body bag—though the guy was so light I could have managed it easily on my own, even without any sort of zombie-aided strength. A shiver of unease trailed up my spine as I wheeled the gurney out of the house. My dad had a similar scrawny and unexercised build. An image of a body bag zipper closing over my dad's lifeless face burned itself into my brain.

Blinking hard, I continued to the van, oddly grateful the uneven sidewalk meant I had to concentrate on keeping the gurney upright, with no mental space free to worry about my dad dying.

Yet once I got the gurney loaded up and started toward the morgue, the unsettling image returned full force. I swiped at my eyes then turned the music way up and sang along, making up my own lyrics when I didn't know the real ones. By the time I passed the Saberton billboard, I'd shaken the worst of the morbid thoughts, and my spirits had recovered somewhat. It was silly for me to compare the body in the back of the van to my dad. Carlton Prince was fifteen years older than Jimmy Crawford. And my dad didn't have heart disease. Not that I knew of, at least.

Ugh. I didn't even know when he'd last seen a doctor. Somehow I needed to convince him to get a physical. *And* quit smoking for good.

I sighed. Or maybe I could reverse climate change. That would be easier.

*   *   *

My half-shift was all but over by the time I made it to the morgue with Mr. Prince. Allen helped me get him entered into the system and tucked away in the cooler then let me know he'd collected the samples Dr. Nikas needed.

"They're in your lunch box," he added. "I put another cold pack in there as well, to keep them fresh."

"My *lunch box*?" I shuddered. "Ew."

Allen looked at me askance. "You're kidding, right? You keep human brains in that thing."

"Yes, *brains*. Not fecal samples." I shuddered again.

He rolled his eyes. "The container is sealed. I promise you won't get any BM on your brains."

I gave him a challenging stare. "That's the best alliteration you can come up with? Bowel movements and plain old brains?"

Allen chuckled. "I'd like to see you do better with the material at hand."

"Let's see, there's 'poop on your pons' or 'crap on your corpus callosum' or 'doo-doo on your dura' or—"

"Stop." He lifted his hands in surrender. "You win."

"Damn straight," I said, preening. "And I'm going to leave now so you can cry about how sad your wordplay game is."

"Sad indeed," he said. "I think I liked it better when you hated me."

"Well, how's this for old time's sake then," I said, grinning as I flipped him off.

"You've never flipped me off before."

"Not to your *face*."

He groaned. "Go. Depart. I'll see you tomorrow."

I was smiling as I snagged my lunch box, but my mood had dimmed considerably by the time I reached my car. It was fun bantering with Allen about the grossness of the samples, but they were a reminder of the gigantic problem known as Douglas "Shamblin' Man" Horton.

The Tribe's zombie research lab was over twenty minutes away, giving me far too much time to fret about zombie gators on the loose in Mudsucker Swamp. Then again, Dr. Nikas already had several bits of Mr. Horton's brain. It was *possible* he'd already examined them and instantly realized why the man had gone all Walking Dead on us. And perhaps he'd even come up with a way to make sure it never happened again.

Totally possible. I grimly clung to that optimism for the rest of the drive.

Eventually, I arrived at the Tribe's zombie research lab: an utterly nondescript, faded blue, windowless, cinderblock building, squatting in a desolate field surrounded by thick pine forest in the middle of nowhere, Louisiana.

I parked in the gravel lot and sauntered up to the single door that marked the front. There were other exterior doors, but they were carefully concealed and *massively* secured. So much so that the one time the lab had been infiltrated, the Saberton aggressors had no choice but to make entry via the front door—and that was no walk in the park unless you were welcome.

Though everyone referred to this building as "the lab," it was much more than a research facility. A medical area served both zombies and humans, permanent quarters housed the handful of personnel who lived at the lab, and nicely furnished dorm-like rooms accommodated temporary guests. There were even cells for unwilling guests. *Plus* an emergency bunker that could supposedly survive damn near anything but a direct nuclear strike. Moreover, Dr. Nikas was a key member of the Tribe and part of the inner circle, and since he rarely left the building, the lab also served as the de facto headquarters for Tribe operations.

After clearing all three security doors, I passed through the central hub and into the research wing of the building. In the chemical assay room, a pale, thin, ponytailed man sat hunched on a stool as he calibrated a spectrophotometer. Jacques Leroux—Dr. Nikas's right hand man. Though I was fairly sure he didn't have any medical or science degrees, he knew Dr. Nikas's methods and moods inside and out and was a skilled medic and research assistant. Of course, he probably didn't need any degrees considering he'd worked side by side with Dr. Nikas since the Franco-Prussian war.

Jacques glanced up, expressive hazel eyes startling, as always, given his otherwise wan appearance. Those eyes flicked to the box in my hand. "You have the rest of the samples?"

"Yup. Everything Dr. Nikas asked for."

"That's good news," he said, returning his attention to the calibration. "Dr. Nikas is still working on the brain pieces Rachel delivered. If you could prepare slides for what you brought, it would be very helpful."

"Got it covered." I tamped down my disappointment that Dr.

Nikas hadn't already solved the shambler-mystery, then tugged
on gloves and worked on getting slides set up. Dr. Nikas knew
everything there was to know about the zombie parasite and how
zombies worked. If there was an answer to be had, he'd find it.

Or would he? I despised the whisper of uncertainty that crept
in. Only a couple of weeks ago, Dr. Nikas himself confessed his
self-doubt and told me that despite his *centuries* of experience,
there was still only so much one man could do to tackle the mass
of needed research. For several months last year, Dr. Kristi
Charish had been an "unwilling guest" of the Tribe. Though she
was an evil psychopath, she was also an utterly brilliant neurobiologist. During the short time Dr. Nikas worked with her, he'd
made more progress in all of his research and development than
in the past *decade*. Two incredible minds working together had
produced far greater results than either could have managed on
their own, even with all the time in the world. The sad truth was
that Dr. Nikas and Kristi were perfect research partners, each
able to expand and extrapolate upon the other's ideas.

But Kristi had only helped because she had no choice—
though she'd surely filed away juicy research results in her
twisted brain the entire time. Considering she now worked for
Saberton Corporation, it was unlikely she and Dr. Nikas would
ever be brainstorm buddies again. I fucking hated Kristi Charish
with the fiery heat of a thousand suns, but not having her brain-
power flat-out sucked for our current situation.

I finished the slides and put the rest of the samples in the
fridge. "Is there anything else that needs doing?"

"Not at the moment, thanks to your recent industry," Jacques
said, eyes crinkling with a rare display of humor. My "recent
industry" had been an effort to keep from dying of boredom
during my recovery. I'd quickly grown sick of browsing the internet and watching TV, and so once I had the strength, I wheeled
my little butt over to the lab and took on all the low priority tasks
that tended to pile up.

I skimmed a glance around the room. "Maybe I should see if
Reg needs anything? Or inventory the reagents?"

"Angel, you have inventoried, cleaned, organized, and labeled everything in this lab that can be seen without a microscope." He paused. "And a few things that can't."

Damn.

A faint smile tugged at his mouth. "Don't worry. You haven't inventoried yourself out of a job. We're simply in a holding pattern while Dr. Nikas works. You know how he can be."

I snorted. *Utterly absorbed* didn't even begin to describe Dr. Nikas when he was working through a problem. He would ignore everyone and everything, muttering to himself in languages no one spoke anymore, filling whiteboards with formulas and symbols and whatnot, and forgetting to eat or drink until Jacques gently pushed one or the other into his free hand—and even then surfacing from his deep focus only enough to chew and swallow.

"I'll go check the heads and Kang," I said.

"I'll call you when I need you."

Not *if* he needed me. When. That felt nice. I'd never be as kickass brilliant as Dr. Nikas, or even Jacques, but I could be the best damn assistant ever.

Chapter 5

"Kang" was John Kang, the first zombie who'd admitted to me he was a zombie. He'd worked at Scott Funeral Home, and not long after I started working at the morgue, he confronted me about brains missing from body bags—brains I'd harvested from autopsied bodies for my own consumption. Turned out he'd been running a side business providing brains for zombies who didn't have any reliable sources. Lucky for me, once Kang was satisfied I wasn't going to cut into his business, he helped me adjust to becoming a zombie. After all, he'd been one for seventy-something years. And though we never really became *friends*, we'd been fairly friendly associates who had a common goal: survival.

I'd warned Kang a serial killer was hell-bent on collecting zombie heads, but he didn't bother to take precautions and ended up getting his own head chopped off. Several months later, I discovered Kristi Charish had orchestrated the zombie murders because she wanted the heads for her own depraved research. After a shitstorm of shenanigans and downright unpleasantness, the Tribe recovered seven heads, including Kang's, from her private lab. Dr. Nikas then began the uncertain and monumental task of regrowing zombies from their heads alone.

And the regrowth lab—a.k.a. the Head Room—was my current destination.

I passed through the lab's central rotunda and down a corridor with walls decorated in colorful tile mosaics. Near the end, I punched my code into the number pad on an unmarked door. The lock clicked, and I stepped into the room. Cold air sent goosebumps racing over my skin as I paused to let my eyes adjust to the dim lighting that was ideal for regrowth.

An empty, coffin-sized glass tank dominated one side of the room, and a counter along the far wall held four stainless steel crock-pot-looking vats. Each contained a zombie head and fifteen gallons of nutrient medium—an amount I knew all too well since one of my weekly duties was to change the snot-like goop.

Taped to the front of each vat was an index card bearing the name of the occupant. I peered through the glass cover of the vat marked "Adam Campbell." Sightless white-filmed eyes stared up from the grey, shriveled flesh of his face—exactly the same as when I checked on him yesterday. Absolutely zero sign of regrowth.

The parasite activity indicators on the side of the vat were also the same as yesterday. The parasite was dormant but still viable—in stasis, according to Dr. Nikas. A quick check of the other three vats revealed the same: dormant but viable. Two of the recovered heads hadn't fared as well. Peter Plescia's parasite bit the dust a couple of days after arriving at the lab, and Timothy Kaye's died while Dr. Nikas was in New York.

I dutifully entered the parasite activity data into the tablet on the counter then left and locked the room. Kang had been the only one to show any sign of progress. He'd spent the last few months regrowing his body in the coffin-tank, and four days ago he'd finally been transferred to a hospital bed in the lab's medical wing.

Which was where I headed next—though it wasn't so much a *wing* as a hallway with a half-dozen hospital-type rooms. Two of the rooms were for prisoners or hostiles—equipped with constant surveillance and steel doors that required a code for both entry and exit. To my annoyance, Kang was in one of the secured rooms. The reasoning was that, since he was coming back from a frozen head, no one knew what he'd be like when he woke up. He might be brain dead or Normal Kang or possibly even Violent Psycho Kang. Better to have him locked down, just to be safe.

But I'd seen him in the tank during the first attempt to resurrect him a couple of weeks ago. I'd met his eyes. I *knew* he was totally Kang and not some brain-warped crazy thing. Unfortunately, no one was willing to take my gut feeling as proof of his Kang-ness.

His door was half-open, and a woman's voice drifted into the hall.

> ". . . *Poor prey to his hot fit of pride were those.*
> *And now upon his western wing he leaned,*
> *Now his huge bulk o'er Afric's sands careened,*
> *Now the black planet shadowed Arctic snows,*
> *Soaring through wider zones that pricked his scars"*

Within, a dark-haired woman with a slim, athletic build sat beside the bed, reading aloud from a book with a tattered green cover. Naomi Comtesse—one of the few non-zombies who worked for the Tribe. She was actually Julia Saber, twin sister to Andrew Saber and daughter of Saberton's unscrupulous CEO, Nicole Saber. Julia had worked in corporate espionage until she discovered the atrocities committed against zombies by her own company. Since she knew her mother wouldn't hesitate to have her killed in order to protect Saberton, Julia had fled. After a rocky start, the Tribe took her in and helped her change her identity to Naomi—though unfortunately a surveillance device had blown her cover a few months back.

Kang lay motionless in the bed, wrapped in gauze from neck to ankles like a zombie-mummy. On the wall, an origami dragon perched atop a monitor, where squiggly lines crawled across the screen, tracking vital signs, brain activity, and heart rhythm. Kang was definitely alive, and all of his various parts seemed to be in order. Except, apparently, his eyelids, 'cause he sure as hell hadn't opened them since he came out of the tank.

Naomi had read or talked to him every day he'd been in this room. A half dozen other origami animals lurked, crouched, or perched on the nightstand—swan, bear, horse, elephant, bird, and frog. Naomi did origami when she was stressed or bored. And she stayed far too busy to be bored.

She flicked a glance my way, lifted a "hang on a sec" finger, and kept on reading.

> *"With memory of the old revolt from Awe,*
> *He reached a middle height, and at the stars,*
> *Which are the brain of heaven, he looked, and sank.*
> *Around the ancient track marched, rank on rank,*
> *The army of unalterable law."*

She let out a sigh of satisfaction then gave me a smile. "Look at you, standing upright and all."

The last time she'd seen me, I was clinging to a walker for dear life as I staggered down the hallway. "Haven't fallen on my ass yet today. Knock wood." I rapped my knuckles on the door-frame, producing a dull metal thud. "What on earth are you reading to him?"

"'Lucifer in Starlight.' It's one of his favorites." She turned her gaze to the silent figure in the bed. "I think I saw an eyelid twitch, but that might have been wishful thinking."

"Wishful and maybe a teensy bit impatient." I moved to the bed and peered at Kang's face.

Her brows drew together in a frown. "I'm not impatient. I'm worried. *You* woke up the day after you came out of the tank."

"I wasn't regrown from just a head. Plus, Dr. Nikas had the new and improved regrowth formula, thanks to Allen's information. I got dunked in the good stuff from the very beginning. Not to mention, I was nice and fresh when I went into the tank. Kang and the others had been sitting in a freezer for a couple of months. *And*, by the time I fell apart, Dr. Nikas had over a year of experience from working with the heads."

Naomi made a face. "All right, that makes sense. Damn it."

I couldn't blame her for worrying. She and Kang had been friends long before I ever met him. In fact, their friendship had been the seed for her "divorce" from Saberton. Because of Kang, Naomi had understood that zombies were *people*, not monsters.

"He's going to be fine," I said with all the reassurance I could muster. "At least Dr. Nikas laid down the law to stop Pierce from trying to *make* Kang wake up."

Her nose wrinkled. "Pierce was in here earlier. Checking if there'd been any change."

The original Pierce Gentry had been a Saberton security

badass—until Tribe leader Pietro Ivanov killed him to escape Saberton's prison-lab in New York. But he hadn't just killed him. Pietro had eaten Pierce's brain and used a mature zombie ability to mimic his DNA, and thus physically became Pierce. For the sake of security, as well as to keep Saberton from learning about mature zombies and their abilities, it was decided Pietro Ivanov would "die" in a plane crash, and everyone would be told that Pierce Gentry had simply been a Tribe operative the whole time and would rejoin the Tribe now. Only a handful of people knew the truth: the Pierce Gentry who'd returned with us from New York was in fact Pietro Ivanov.

"Did Pierce *do* anything?"

"Nothing other than sniff Kang and scowl a lot."

I snickered. "Yeah, because Dr. Nikas would have *his* head otherwise." Ever since Kang started regrowing, Pierce had pressured Dr. Nikas to hurry the process and pestered him with questions. *How quickly will Kang recover?* and *Will he have all of his memories?* and others along the same line. It was obvious Pierce desperately wanted to know something only Kang could tell him, but Dr. Nikas had put his foot down. He didn't care what Pierce wanted from Kang. His first priority was to his patient. Period. Finally, during a particularly heated exchange, Dr. Nikas pointed out that if Pierce insisted on rushing the regrowth and recovery, Kang might not be in a condition to answer any questions. Ever. That stark truth backed Pierce off.

Naomi blew out her breath. "Yeah. Dr. N is the best. I should have more faith in him." She summoned a smile. "Have you heard from Andrew?"

For a fraction of an instant I considered telling her about the game console, but immediately discarded that idea. I didn't know if it was from Andrew, and Naomi could get pretty emotional when it came to her brother. It would be way worse for her if I told her about the package and then it turned out it really was from some long-lost cousin named Arnold Stein.

I shook my head. "He was on CNN last night, talking about some trade agreement and its impact on something or other. My eyes glazed over after about thirty seconds, but he sure looked alive to me."

"I saw that one, too. Alive and in India." A slight crease formed between her eyebrows.

"You don't believe he's really there."

Her eyes snapped to mine. "Do you?"

"Not for a second," I said. "I think he's been doing interviews and stuff like this to make it *look* like he's there."

"Exactly!" Naomi cried, relief washing over her face. "And he's probably video-conferencing for board meetings and other matters. Heck, over half the board attends remotely. And if Andrew has a tech person on tap, he could appear to be connecting from anywhere he wants."

"He has Thea Braddock," I said, referring to his bodyguard and the former head of security for Saberton New York. "She's super competent, and I bet she found someone to do that for him."

"But he's so new to being a zombie. What if he's not getting enough brains?"

"He didn't look at all brain-hungry on CNN," I reassured her. "Plus, I trust Thea to get whatever he needs."

The tension in her shoulders eased. "Right. Of course. So he's okay."

"That's right." I mentally crossed fingers it was true then decided to shift the conversation to a less worry-filled topic. "So, are you going to stay Naomi or go back to Julia? I mean, your cover is totally blown and everyone including your mother knows you're really Julia Saber."

Her expression turned fierce. "I don't want to be a Saber. I'm a completely different person now, both inside and out."

"You never seemed like a Julia to me."

"Exactly! I've never felt like a Julia."

"I feel like an Angel, but I sure as hell don't act like one!"

"You do in all the ways that matter," Naomi said with unexpected warmth then glanced at her phone when it buzzed.

"Duty calls. Let me know if Kang does anything interesting." She closed her book and set it on the nightstand then stood and leaned close to his face. "Hey! Wake the fuck up, you lazy shirker."

Kang remained utterly still except for the shallow rise and fall of his chest. Naomi straightened with a sigh. "Worth a try." She flashed me a cheery smile that didn't fool me one bit. "Catch ya later, babe."

She was out the door before I realized she hadn't asked about the shambler incident at the morgue—which meant she didn't know about it. Was it being kept from her because she was human? Or was the info restricted to the Tribe's inner circle?

Or, in a less paranoid world, maybe she'd simply been busy and hadn't heard the latest gossip yet.

I plopped into the chair and picked up the book. *Victorian Poetry from Clough to Kipling.* On a whim, I opened to a random page and started reading.

Come, fill the Cup, and in the fire of Spring
Your Winter-garment of Repentance fling;
The Bird of Time has but a little way
To flutter—and the Bird is on the Wing.

"What the shit?" I made a face and set the book aside. "She's trying to torture you awake, Kang. Why else would she read you *this.*"

"Kang likes to style himself an autodidactic polymath," Pierce drawled from the doorway.

The fit, broad-shouldered, thirty-something Pierce Gentry was a far cry from his old Pietro Ivanov form, but I was used to it now. Helped that his personality hadn't really changed.

I had no idea what an automatic polymorphy thing was, but I also didn't care about looking stupid in front of Pierce. "A whatsit whosit?"

"An autodidact is a self-taught person, and a polymath is one whose expertise covers a wide variety of subjects." He closed the door behind him. "*I* style Kang a pompous ass."

I tensed as Pierce approached the bed. He smirked. "Don't worry. I'll abide by Ari's wishes."

More like Dr. Nikas's *commands*, I thought, but kept my expression bland.

He folded his arms over his chest. "Tell me everything of what happened at the morgue."

My eyes flicked toward Kang. "Er, here?" Couldn't some coma patients still hear what was going on around them? I definitely remembered bits and pieces from my time regrowing in the tank.

"He's not awake, Angel," Pierce said, misinterpreting my hesitation. "I would know if he was faking unconsciousness. Even Kang can't control himself to that extent. Now, tell me what happened."

"I didn't think he was *awake* awake," I muttered then went

ahead and launched into the stirring tale of Angel and the not-really-zombie. When I finished, I slouched in the chair and eyed him. "What did you mean by 'even Kang'?"

Pierce didn't answer for several seconds, still mulling over my story. "His great age affords him certain . . . advantages."

"Great age? But he's only seventy-something, isn't he? I mean, he told me his parents died in the Korean War." That was old, but not *oooold*. Hell, Jacques was pushing two hundred.

Pierce gave me a slow blink, then he tipped his head back and roared in laughter. "My god, Kang is such an asshole. Yes, his parents died in *a* Korean war. But not the one in the twentieth century."

My face felt ready to break from the confused expression. "There was more than one?"

"That area has known many wars," Pierce said with way too much delight. He leaned down and placed his hands on the arms of my chair. "As does any country with a long history. Gojoseon was Korea's first kingdom, founded in 2333 B.C. by Dangun Wanggeom. Gojoseon lasted for many many centuries, until Emperor Wudi of the Han Dynasty invaded. It fell after a year of war and disintegrated into fiefdoms and confederacies which later came together to form new kingdoms and wage new wars."

"I assume you're telling me this for a reason," I snapped then fought the urge to shrink away as he brought his face close to mine.

"Kang's parents died when Emperor Wudi's forces invaded," he intoned, ". . . in the year 109 *beeee ceeee*."

I gulped. *Kang is over two thousand years old? Holy fucking shit.*

Pierce straightened and cast a mocking glance at Kang's still form. "He's a bit older than seventy, I'd say."

"How old are you?" I blurted.

He slid a look to me. "I was born in the Emirate of Cordoba. I don't know my exact birth year, but my best estimate is somewhere around the Year of Our Lord 760." His mouth crooked. "I was an old man of perhaps four decades when Kang turned me."

He pivoted and strode to the door, leaving on a perfect dramatic note.

Until I ruined it. "Hang on, Pierce. Something doesn't make sense."

Pierce stopped, then slowly turned back to me, a thin smile on his face and annoyance in his eyes. "Yes, Angel?"

I stood and folded my arms over my chest in a mock-Pierce pose. "If Kang is so old, then he has the mature zombie super senses, right?"

His head dipped a couple of millimeters. "Kang is indeed a mature zombie."

"Then how did Ed Quinn get the jump on him to chop his head off? Kang would've smelled him coming and known he was up to no good." A rush of exultation flooded me. "That's what you want to know, isn't it! You want to ask him how Ed managed it so you can defend against it!"

The amusement returned to Pierce's eyes. "Kang was tranqed first, just enough to dull his senses."

My exultation popped like a soap bubble. "Oh."

His smile widened. "I'd wondered the same thing, so I asked Quinn."

"Right." I fought back a scowl. Of course he would ask Ed. Want to know how someone was murdered? Ask the murderer.

"He informed me Kang was staggering down the corridor and didn't hear him come in." Pierce looked positively elated as he stomped my theory into dust. "Quinn thought he was drunk. I knew that wasn't possible and believed a tranq was to blame. Dr. Nikas confirmed my hunch by finding traces of zombie tranquilizer compound in Kang's neck tissues."

"You're enjoying this way too much," I said sourly. "But that's cool. I'll let you have this one. Still, if Ed didn't tranq him, who did?"

Pierce's smile spread into a grin. "My guess is Kristi Charish. That woman is devilishly clever."

I snatched up the book of poetry. "I swear to god, I will bean you right in the head if you don't stop gloating."

Whistling "You Can't Always Get What You Want," he turned and strolled down the hall.

I stuck my head out the door. "Y'know, you could just tell me what the hell you need from Kang."

Still whistling, he lifted his right hand to give me the finger, keeping it raised until he turned the corner.

I chuckled despite myself then glanced at Kang. "And he has the balls to call *you* an asshole? Then again, you made me believe you were only seventy. Guess it takes one to know one." I returned to the bed and leaned close. "Y'know, Kang . . . whatever it is he wants to know, just think how much it would piss him off if you told *me* first."

No reaction. Not the slightest blip on the monitor. Damn it.

"All right. Be stubborn. But I'll be back." I watched him for a few more seconds then left, locking the door behind me.

Chapter 6

I returned to Jacques only to learn that Dr. Nikas had finished with the samples Rachel delivered but was now absorbed in analyzing the stuff I'd brought.

"Fine," I said, not bothering to hide my frustration. "I'll be in the media room."

"I'll let him know," Jacques replied, unruffled as always.

Grumpy and frustrated, I retrieved my school backpack from my car then made my way to the media room. Personally, I thought it should be called the living room since it looked and felt like one, with comfy sofas, recliners, an arm chair, and a gigantic flat screen TV.

Reg, Dr. Nikas's other lab tech, snoozed in a recliner that looked a size too small for his long and lean frame. A half-full glass of brain smoothie sat on the table beside him, and a sheaf of lab printouts rested on his chest. His head was cocked toward one shoulder at a painful angle. I had a feeling he hadn't meant to fall asleep.

"Hey, Reg?" I said softly.

He startled awake, sending papers sailing. "Angel. Damn."

I dropped my backpack on the sofa and hurried to gather the printouts. "Sorry. I thought maybe you'd want a nudge awake."

"Yeah. Thanks." Reg shoved the recliner footrest closed and sat up. "I have puh-lenty of work to do. My boss is a real hard-ass, y'know?"

I rolled my eyes and shoved the gathered papers into his hands. "Uh huh. Riiiight. Dr. Nikas is a certified meanie pants."

Reg chuckled and ran his fingers through unruly red curls in a futile attempt to tame them. A few months back, he'd decided a buzz cut wasn't his thing anymore and opted for more of a "shaggy poodle" style. I'd never tell him in a million years, but I preferred the curls simply because he was so tall and skinny the buzz cut had made him look a bit too much like a matchstick.

He downed the smoothie, stood, and stretched. "You know what we need around here? Cats."

"Um."

"Sure! We have a dog in the lab now. Would be cool to have a couple of cats to make things homey."

"I've never had a cat." I shrugged. "Or any pet, for that matter."

"Oh man, Angel. You're missing out! Nothing like kicking back with a good book and a cat on your lap." A whisper of nostalgia touched his voice, but then he winked. "And one chewing on your hair. And one knocking breakables onto the floor just to watch them fall."

I gave him a dubious look. "Hair chewing and property destruction. Sounds great. I've really been missing out."

"Animals are the best." He then whinnied, quacked, and croaked, all very convincingly.

When I stopped laughing, I said, "Why stop with a cat? Might as well bring in a bunny rabbit and a pony while we're at it. Maybe an iguana."

"Why the hell not?" he said with a mischievous sparkle in his eye then sauntered out, whistling "Old MacDonald."

What a goofball. Sharp and dedicated and nice as hell, but still a goofball.

"Never change, Reg," I murmured then settled on one of the sofas and pulled a composition notebook from my backpack. The required reading for my English Comp class was a pain in the butt, even with the mod Dr. Nikas gave me to help with my dyslexia. But the true bane of my existence—and a quarter of my grade—was the personal journal. We were supposed to write daily entries about the events of the day and how we felt about them, our personal struggles, hopes, dreams, accomplishments, fears, worries, blah blah blah. Everyone in the class agreed it was a dumb waste of time, but I was fairly certain no one else was forced to make up most of their journal entries. The professor was nice and all, but I knew damn well if I turned in a journal entry of, "Dear Diary, today I finally finished regrowing my body after my legs and arms fell off," I would earn a swift F.

After a moment's consideration, I started an entry about changing an old lady's tire. Seriously heart-warming shit, and way more plausible than tending heads in crock pots, or fighting the mindless dead.

"Angel." Dr. Nikas stood in the doorway, a German Shepherd by his side—Marla, a cadaver dog who'd been used to track zombies.

My heart dropped to my toes at Dr. Nikas's troubled expression. "I caused it, didn't I. The shambling zombie."

He sat in the chair near me. Marla settled at his feet and rested her head atop his shoes. "You frame it as if you made a deliberate choice." He lifted a hand to stop my protest. "I beg you not to give me some pap about how you chose to take the drugs that damaged your parasite. It happened. It's past. That line of thinking is of benefit to no one." A smile brushed across his face as I closed my mouth. "Analysis of the tissue samples you collected show Douglas Horton and Judd Siler had remarkably similar, ah, we'll say 'infections' for lack of a better word, with the pathogen being an aberration of the normal zombie parasite. And, considering Mr. Horton was found in the same swamp where Mr. Siler met his end, it is safe to hypothesize that the disease transferred from Judd Siler's remains to Mr. Horton by some means. And that you are, indeed, the source of the mutation."

"I bit Judd *once*. How could that—" I straightened. "Wait. When I was a prisoner in Kristi Charish's lab, after I turned Philip, and after she screwed him up with bad fake brains, he bit those two guards. And then *they* turned into screwed up zombies—fast—from just one bite. They weren't shamblers, but they were unstable. Bitey."

Dr. Nikas nodded. "His bite caused a rapid turning. Your bite on Judd Siler took over a day to make him turn. But you and Philip both had very damaged parasites at the times of those incidents. I have been seeking the mechanism for the aberration and accelerated effect of the mutation." Frustration and weariness shadowed his eyes. "I continue to search for answers."

He didn't have to add *without the benefit of another re-*

searcher. I found my voice. "Are Philip and me still dangerous that way?"

"No," he said, firm and reassuring. "Your parasite has recovered to a significant degree, as has Philip's. Every test I've conducted on you two indicates nothing out of the ordinary for one of our kind."

"Whew." I managed a smile. "Okay, so Judd didn't bite Douglas Horton. But an alligator did. I took most of Judd's brain, but left his body out in the swamp. Could a gator turn zombie from eating Judd?"

He spread his hands. "Occam's razor."

"Wait, I know that! The easiest explanation is most likely the right one?"

"Indeed. The more assumptions you have to make, the more unlikely an explanation is. The easiest explanation in this scenario is that an alligator consumed Judd's remains and then transmitted the infection to the hapless Mr. Horton. The alligator itself could have turned zombie, or a variation thereof."

"That's possible?"

"With a normal parasite, no. But there's nothing normal about this shambler infection. I shudder to think of this dreadful mutation passing to animals. Until contrary evidence surfaces, I will hold onto the hope the alligator was simply an unafflicted means of transmission."

"A vector. Like mosquitoes and malaria."

"Precisely."

"Search parties are still looking for the other hunter," I said. "And those alligators are out there." I shifted, worry rising. "What if a whole bunch of gators chowed down on Judd? What if there's an army of zombie-making gators out there. We need to find them!"

"That is being discussed," he said, exuding calm. "But there are quite a few alligators in those swamps. Pierce believes it would be a futile search unless we have a way to identify them."

"What does Marcus think?" Marcus was the publicly recognized head of the Tribe, though Pierce-Pietro still secretly held the real power. However, Pierce couldn't openly contest Marcus without blowing his cover. If Saberton ever found out that certain zombies had unique and heightened abilities, such as changing physical form, they wouldn't stop until every mature zombie had been hunted down and locked in a lab for heinous experimentation.

"Marcus agrees with Pierce," Dr. Nikas said, "though he is more open to the idea of at least making an onsite assessment in the swamp."

"I can work with that," I said sweetly, triggering a quiet snort from Dr. Nikas. "Alligators don't usually go looking for trouble, and tend to avoid people tromping through their territory. We'd be searching for aggressive gators. And the other hunter, too. I don't know what condition he's in, but if he's a shambler, we don't want him attacking whoever finds him."

"Agreed, but the—"

I sucked in a breath. "I think I know how to find the hunter. And maybe the gators as well." I scratched Marla's ears. "*She* knows what zombies smell like!"

Dr. Nikas winced. "Yes, she does. But she's been living with us for nearly a month and has most likely gone noseblind."

"Oh." I slumped and considered for a moment. "But Judd and Douglas were mutant zombies. And Douglas's brain smelled funny when I sniffed it at the morgue. What if it's distinctive enough for Marla to zero in on it?"

Dr. Nikas pursed his lips in thought. "Interesting. We have the samples and could test the theory with Dante Rosario's help." He met my eyes and gave me a conspiratorial wink. "And if your theory pans out, we'll take your idea to Marcus."

I'd met Dante Rosario a week or so before Mardi Gras, when he was involved in a number of anti-zombie plots dreamed up by Dr. Kristi Charish. After a variety of hijinks and disasters, I managed to stop him from revealing zombies as monsters to the world, but during the resulting four-wheeler chase through the woods, he'd crashed and been critically injured. He'd also crashed emotionally when he finally *finally* realized Kristi had ruthlessly duped him, thrown him under the bus, and laid the blame for everything on his shoulders.

After quite a bit of discussion—and with my very insistent input—the Tribe inner circle had agreed that Rosario could be a valuable ally and asset, and gave him protection. Even better, Rosario was Marla's handler, which meant we got a sweet package deal.

Dr. Nikas and I soon found him doing careful stretching and

calisthenics in the weight room. Rosario had been in peak physical condition before his injury, and with the help of surgery to stabilize the mess of his ribs, followed by kickass physical therapy, he was almost fully recovered.

Unfortunately, determining whether Marla could indicate on the shambler samples was a shitload tougher than I expected. First we had to get past Rosario's "Are you crazy? You expect me to train her on a new scent in just a few minutes?" Once we convinced him to at least *try*, it ended up taking nearly three hours for Marla to recognize the shambler tissue's distinct scent and another three for her to consistently indicate on it. Even then we had to put up with Rosario's dire warnings as to how it couldn't possibly be reliable with so little training and that this sort of thing usually took weeks. It wasn't until Dr. Nikas told Rosario his position with the Tribe was safe even if Marla failed to find the shambler scent that I realized the source of his anxiety: If the Tribe cut ties with Rosario, Saberton would take him out in a permanent fashion at the first opportunity.

Convincing Marcus to organize a gator hunt was a far easier hurdle. He agreed with Dr. Nikas that, for the safety of the Tribe *and* the public, a search should be mounted for the other hunter and any infected alligators. He then surprised me with praise for the insight into gator behavior and the idea to use Marla.

"I hated the thought of doing *nothing*," Marcus said. "But Pierce—" He stopped and smiled tightly. "Using Marla gives us an edge, however slight. Chances are low we'll find anything. But chances are zero if we don't make an attempt." He glanced at the clock and frowned in thought. "Early in the morning will be best. That'll give us time to make arrangements. Plus we need to return no later than noon to allow Angel to get to work at the morgue."

I blinked. "You know my work schedule?"

"And your school schedule." As I fumbled for a reply, he chuckled. "I'm not psychic, Angel. You gave all of that info to Dr. Nikas to schedule your shifts here, and I just happened see it this afternoon when I was going over payroll and scheduling."

"Stalker," I teased, but I was impressed. "You said 'we.' Are you coming, too?"

"That's right," Marcus said with a determined set to his jaw. "I'm ready to get out into the field and do something *real*."

The frustration in his voice tugged at my heart. He wasn't

really the head of the Tribe, and he knew it. Pierce still called the major shots. Even worse, Marcus had given up law school to be the Tribe figurehead. It was doubly galling that he was more than competent enough to run the Tribe, if Pierce would ever give him the chance.

"What if Pierce doesn't agree to this?" I asked reluctantly.

Dr. Nikas spoke up. "I will make certain he does."

A whisper of relief passed over Marcus's face. "I appreciate the help."

I cleared my throat. "How early will we be leaving?"

"Sunrise is around seven," he said. "But it starts getting light before six, and since alligators are nocturnal, I'd like to be on the water and searching well before dawn. With travel and prep time, I'd say plan on a 4:30 departure."

"Uh huh. Just to be sure we're on the same page here, you want us to leave at 4:30 in the *morning* which, by the way, is technically still night?"

"Correct."

Ugh. It was a thirty-minute drive from my house to the Tribe lab, which meant I'd have to leave home by 4 a.m., which meant I'd have to *wake up* around 3:30 . . .

"Yeah, I think I'll just crash here tonight, if that's okay." Besides, I already had extra clothes stashed at the lab. I'd learned the hard way to keep a few changes here, including a spare Coroner's Office uniform, since shit could go sideways at any moment and a change of underwear—or more—might be needed.

Dr. Nikas's eyes crinkled in a smile. "A wise decision." He shifted his attention to Marcus. "Shall we go beard the lion in his den?"

Marcus blew out his breath. "Sure. This will be fun." But he shot a grin my way before the two headed off to double-team Pierce.

Once they were gone, I texted my dad to tell him not to wait up for me. Even though staying the night at the lab made the most sense, I felt bad about being away from home again so soon.

Yet to my relief, he replied that he'd scored another job doing cleanup at one of the local bars and didn't figure he'd be home 'til darn near four in the morning himself. For once, the universe seemed to be cutting me some slack.

Maybe in return I should be responsible and study biology?

After all, I had a test on the digestive system next week. On the other hand, if I went to bed in the next ten minutes, I could score six and a half hours of sleep.

The buzz of a text message saved me from grappling with the decision. I smiled as I saw it was from Justine Chu, who'd starred in *High School Zombie Apocalypse!!* I'd met her during the Zombie Fest when I rescued her from a fan who was being way too handsy, and we'd quickly struck up a friendship.

<Well????? How was your first day back?!! Can you video chat?>

<gimme 5 mins!> I texted then dashed to my room.

Chapter 7

"My room" was the same one I'd occupied for the past two weeks, after coming out of the regrowth tank. Though similar in size and layout to Kang's, it was *far* homier, especially since it lacked both steel door and surveillance.

The bed had been made up with fresh sheets since I'd left this morning, and my clothes were still in the dresser. Best of all, the laptop I'd been using for the past few weeks was on the table where I'd left it.

I shucked off my shoes, made myself comfy on the bed with the laptop, and fired up the video chat program. I'd told Justine the same fiction as everyone else who didn't need to know the truth—that I'd come down with mononucleosis right after Mardi Gras. Since then, we'd texted or video-chatted darn near every day.

After a moment, the video chat icon blinked. Justine's face popped up on the screen—Asian-American with pretty, delicate features and dark eyes that practically snapped with determination.

"Hey! You survived your first day back at work! Go you!"

"Go me!"

She peered at my face. "You don't look tired, which is good. You don't want to overdo it."

"I promise I'm not." I made a show of crossing my heart.

She nodded sharply in approval. "Did you get anything good and gruesome today?"

"Kind of. A hunter drowned and got chewed up by alligators." That much was true. No way could I tell her the rest.

"Ew!"

"At least he hadn't been in the water long," I said. "I remember one time we picked up a body that'd been in the bayou for over a week. His skin kept slipping off as we pulled him in."

Justine listened in morbid fascination as I related the disgusting details. I'd come to enjoy her friendship way more than expected. Maybe because I'd never really had a female best friend before? I mean, I was friends with Naomi, and I could totally hang out with her, but somehow it wasn't on the same level. Justine was fun yet able to be serious and understanding. Plus, she gave every indication of enjoying my friendship just as much. I had a feeling part of it was because I didn't suck up to her, even though she was kind of famous. She could be straight-up honest with me and vent about Hollywood and the jerks she had to deal with. And while Justine didn't know I was a zombie, I could still share my triumphs and woes on a purely human level.

"How did your audition go?" I asked once I finished describing bloated corpses.

"Oh, they totally hated me, and I'll never work as an actor again." She cracked up at my stricken expression. "I'm kidding. That's what I always say. It feels like a jinx to say I thought it went well."

"You are so weird."

"Ha! I'm not the one who works with dead bodies." She cocked her head. "So, are you going to be a pathologist?"

"Me?!" I scoffed. "No way. I can barely handle my two measly community college classes. And I'm probably going to drop English anyway."

"What? Why?"

I shifted, grimaced. I'd shared a lot with Justine, but had skimmed over a few things. She knew I was an addict, but didn't know my mom went to jail for child abuse. She knew I'd dropped out of high school, but didn't know I had a learning disability. I'd kept stuff to myself because a stupid little seed of uncertainty refused to leave. Justine was cool and hot and smart. What if she decided I wasn't worth the trouble?

That's stupid, I told myself and stomped that little seed to dust. "Okay, well, you see, I'm dyslexic, so it takes me forever to read the assignments, and I just . . ." I stopped and gulped as her eyes went wide. "What's wrong?"

"This is crazy," she breathed. "I *just* registered for the fall semester at UCLA to finish my degree." She leaned close to the camera. "In English education!"

"Wait. You're going to college? But you're an actor. You starred in a movie!"

"The acting is how I'm *paying* for college," Justine said. "Don't get me wrong, I absolutely adore acting, but I can't count on it lasting forever as a career. You never know what life will throw at you, so I want to get my degree under my belt." She drew a deep breath. "Look, the only experience I have with dyslexia is a special needs course I took two years ago, but I could probably help with everything else. Give you a little leg up at least. I mean, if you want. I don't want to pressure you." Her mouth quirked. "Too much."

"That would be great," I said then winced. "But it's not just the dyslexia stuff. I'm supposed to write a narrative essay about a birthday party I had when I was a kid. But I've never had a birthday party. My mom . . . well, let's just say my childhood sucked. I dunno. I guess I could make something up."

Her dark brows pulled together in a frown. "Why would you make something up?"

"I don't think the prof really wants to read about the time my mom busted my lip and burned all my toys in the back yard because I was singing 'Happy Birthday' too loud."

Instead of looking shocked or pitying, Justine gave her head a firm shake. "Your prof wants you to write about what happened to you. If you make it up, he'll know it's bullshit, because there won't be any real emotion in it. Besides, he knows damn well he's going to get a bunch of essays about bad shit. The only birthdays anyone remembers are the ones where stuff went wrong."

I let out a sigh. "Yeah, it's always easier to remember the bad shit."

"That's how our brains are wired. Damn stupid design, but I guess it was good for survival at one point." She lifted her chin. "Anyway, I've written a godawful number of essays in my life. I know all the tricks. I'll help you."

"Thanks," I said fervently. And even if she couldn't help me, I still had a couple of weeks to drop the class.

The conversation shifted to lighter subjects, like celebrity butts and boob jobs. Yet after we finally disconnected, my thoughts returned to her question about being a pathologist. Jeez, after chatting damn near every day for the past two and a half weeks, I'd've thought she knew me better than that.

I closed the laptop and checked the time. I'd lost out on half an hour of sleep, but it had been totally worth it. After finding my toothbrush and de-gunking my teeth, I changed into a night shirt, set my alarm for 4 a.m., and snuggled between sheets that smelled of lavender.

I startled awake at a hard rap on the door. "What?"

"You're needed in the conference room." That was Brian Archer—longtime head of Tribe security, but now second to Pierce. "We're planning this alligator expedition."

I fumbled for my phone. Wow. I'd managed to sleep for a whole twenty minutes. "Okay. Be there in five."

"Make it three," Brian said, then his footsteps retreated down the corridor.

I shot the door my middle finger then scrambled out of bed.

I changed back into my work clothes and speed-walked to the conference room, only to find it empty. Weird. I was sure Brian had said conference room. Maybe I'd misheard him and I was supposed to go to the media room? I turned to leave and ran right into the broad chest of the man himself.

"I didn't expect you to be so fast," Brian said as he steadied me. "I was joking about the three minutes."

"Jerk." I aimed a light punch at his abs.

He blocked it with a swift move. "You'll have do better than that."

"You definitely deserve worse. I could've slept another five minutes!"

Naomi pushed past us into the room. "Save your punches for Kyle. *He* deserves them."

"What happened?" I asked, registering her bedraggled appearance and red eyes and nose. "Oh no. Have you been crying?" My fists clenched. "What did Kyle do?!"

"No, I haven't been *crying*," she snarled. "And by the way, you should never ask someone if they've been crying, because if they *have* been crying—which I wasn't—it'll only embarrass them and make them cry more." She paused, held up a finger, then turned her head to deliver a mighty sneeze into her elbow.

Now the red eyes made sense. "So noted. But my question stands: what did Kyle do to deserve punches?"

"He forgot that *some* of us have human immune systems." Naomi pulled a tissue from a pocket and wiped her nose. "All I can say is, we were working an op that required us to hide for nearly an hour in a water-filled ditch. *Cold* water."

I gave her a wince of sympathy. "Yeah, I gotta say, I don't miss getting colds."

"Well, I haven't gotten this one yet," she declared then spoiled it by blowing her nose. "I'll be fine by morning. Lots of vitamin C and fluids. Works every time."

Before I could question her confidence, Pierce strode in, with Marcus a second behind him carrying a tube of rolled paper.

Pierce took up a position where he could see everyone. Playing the part of the security chief and definitely not the actual Tribe leader. No sirree.

Marcus went to the table and unrolled a detailed map of Mudsucker Swamp and the surrounding area. He glanced up as Rosario entered. "Close the door, will you, Dante? We're all here now." He waited for the latch to click then addressed the room. "Everyone here has been briefed on the situation with the drowned hunter who reanimated in Angel's morgue. At her suggestion, tomorrow morning we're going to the swamp with three goals: to search for the other accident victim, to locate any possibly infected alligators, and to avoid drawing attention." He lifted his chin toward Rosario. "Marla will hopefully give us an edge in finding the body. I've figured out some details that should help as well."

He gestured for everyone to gather around the table then angled the map so we could see it. "That's Bayou Pauvre on the right side of the map. The blue dot marks the inlet where the overturned boat was found wedged between a couple of cypress knees." He traced his finger up along the bayou until it reached a red dot several inches away. "Here's where Mr. Horton's body was found. Search and Rescue is operating under the assumption the boat hit a submerged log and overturned in this immediate area, then drifted nearly a mile with the current before getting stuck in this inlet." He dragged his finger back downstream to the blue dot. "It makes a degree of sense because, when someone drowns, they tend to sink right where it happened. Plus, the direction of the current supports it. *But*, at the estimated time of the accident, the tide was coming in which would all but cancel out the current. Moreover, winds were from the south last night, so I don't believe it's possible for the boat to drift so far."

Naomi turned away to sneeze then peered at the map. "If all that is true, where do we find the second body?"

"We're going to search the area where the boat was found." Marcus tapped the blue dot. "The *real* accident site. With the tide, the wind direction, and how this waterway curves, the only way for the boat to get stuck in the inlet is if the accident happened very close by. The boat didn't move. The victim did."

"Because the *gator* dragged Douglas Horton to where he was found," I said. "And Search and Rescue would never consider that a possibility."

"Especially because that's not normal behavior for an alligator," Marcus agreed. "But of course we're not dealing with normal alligators."

Brian rubbed his jaw. "We already know from the bite marks there was more than one alligator. How do we know the second body didn't get dragged off, too?"

Marcus spread his hands. "We don't. But the accident site is the most logical place to start. I expect when Search and Rescue continues to come up dry, they'll look at the issue with the wind and tides and realize their error. However, my intel says that hasn't been discussed yet. We should have a good chunk of the morning to search without interference. That said, I want to be there on scene and ready to search the instant there's enough light."

"I'm making arrangements for boats and gear," Pierce said. "We'll put in at the Tribe training ground. It's west of Mudsucker and quite a bit farther from the accident site than the public boat launch, but it avoids unwanted attention. Not to mention, Angel can show us where she killed Judd Siler."

"Um. I'll *try*," I said with a heaping load of uncertainty.

He smiled winningly. "I have all the faith in the world in you."

"This is no time for jokes, Pierce."

Naomi sniffled again. "Do we have a cover story? Or are we just going to meander around the swamp and pretend to also be looking for the dead guy?"

Pierce shook his head. "That could draw attention we don't want. Easiest cover story is we're hunters."

I frowned. "Turkey is the only thing in season right now."

"Then we'll be turkey hunting," he replied with a glare.

Marcus grimaced. "But no one in their right mind would hunt turkeys from a *boat*."

Pierce glowered as I nodded agreement. "Well, if that's the only thing in season right now, we don't seem to have much of a choice."

"No, it's all good," I said. "Y'see, nuisance animals are legal to hunt year-round. And because of the floods last year, feral hogs are a huge problem. Coyotes, too. It's totally plausible to be hunting those in the swamp, from a boat."

Pierce's glower vanished. "Okay. Good. That works." He paused. "Thanks."

I inclined my head in acknowledgement.

Marcus made notes on a pad. "Everyone needs current hunting licenses, in case we get stopped by Wildlife and Fisheries. We can buy them online and print out the E-licenses."

"I have a lifetime license," I said, hiding a smile at Marcus's look of surprise. Back when Randy and I were dating, his dad had taken us deer hunting. I was eighteen and had never gone hunting for a darn thing in my life, but obediently froze my ass off in a deer stand and then insisted to Mr. Winger I'd had fun, because it was clear he'd really wanted me to enjoy it. Not long after that, he went ahead and spent the several hundred bucks on a lifetime permit for me, because he knew me and my dad couldn't afford even the basic annual license. I went out several times more with him and Randy, and though I never developed a *love* for hunting, I found a respect for it. I even made sure to get a replacement license after I lost the original in the flood. Seemed wrong not to.

"I have one, too," Naomi said then grinned. "Never know when a hunting license will come in handy during an op."

Marcus laughed under his breath. "Well, the rest of us will have to settle for cheap and basic." He jotted down the names of everyone who needed a license. "All right, that should do it. We'll meet in the garage tomorrow at oh-four-thirty. And yes, Angel, that's still in the morning."

"Damn."

Chapter 8

My alarm went off at 4 a.m., and when I finished cursing, I flipped on the lights. That sparked another round of cursing, but it kept me from falling asleep again. When my eyes finally adjusted, I found a pair of boots and a pile of neatly folded clothing on the chair by the bed. Kinda freaky to realize someone had crept into my room while I was sleeping, but hey, new threads!

Ten minutes later, I was clothed and booted in the camo hunting gear—xx-small that actually fit me. With teeth clean, bladder emptied, and hair shoved into a mostly neat ponytail, I took a detour to the kitchen for a ham and egg sandwich and still made it to the garage by quarter after.

The *enormous* garage. Large enough to hold a dozen vehicles with room to spare, and secured by a double set of heavy security doors. Halfway across the garage, Marcus and Pierce conferred near the back of a dark blue Chevy Tahoe. Not far away were Brian, Rosario, and Marla. I hustled over to them. At least Naomi wasn't here yet, which meant I wasn't last.

Rosario crouched to adjust Marla's harness, black tactical pants stretching tight over his scrumptious ass. Yep, that right there was why I'd dubbed him "Tactical Pants Man" before I even knew his name. Sexist as hell, but damn. It was truly a work of art.

The door from the lab opened behind me, and I spun, ready to gloat at Naomi for beating her here. But my salty comment died away at the sight of the tall black woman striding in. Rachel Delancey, wearing camo pants and a black t-shirt. A jacket was draped over one arm, and her long braids had been pulled back into a tight knot.

Ugh. If Rachel was here, it meant Naomi was too sick to come. Which sucked. Naomi was fun and cool. Rachel hated my guts. And now it looked like I was going to be stuck in a boat with her for hours.

I summoned a bright smile. "Hi, Rachel. Is Naomi coming, too?" If the universe really loved me, Naomi would be totally recovered, and Rachel would simply be a last-minute addition. A girl could dream, right?

"Dr. Nikas scrubbed her from the op for medical reasons," Rachel replied coolly then continued past without waiting for a reply.

Through sheer force of will, I managed to resist the urge to flip her off. She walked up to Marcus, and I braced myself for a show of affection between the two. About a month ago, I'd discovered they were an item. Sure, Marcus and I had broken up quite some time ago, but that didn't mean I couldn't get my back up if he decided to be with someone who disliked me so intensely.

Yet, to my surprise, the expected kiss didn't happen. No clasped hands or lingering touch. Hell, not even a sultry look. It didn't seem as if they were simply being professional, either. Nope, that flame was gone. Interesting.

"Is everyone ready?" Pierce asked.

I raised my hand. "What about food and lifejackets and stuff?"

"Food, weapons, brains, and other necessities have already been loaded up." He gestured to the Tahoe. "Boats and lifejackets and special equipment will be waiting for us at the training ground. Any other questions? Good. Let's roll out."

The Tribe's wetland property was only twenty minutes away as the crow flies, but when the crow instead had to navigate a series of remote highways and decrepit back roads, it took closer to forty minutes.

At long last we turned onto the dirt road that, in another two miles, would end where we trained in paintball tactical exercises—and where Judd had come after me for the second time. But after only half a mile, Pierce hung a left onto a deeply rutted lane that bounced us around for several more minutes before ending in a gravel lot.

A white pickup sat waiting, headlights casting stark shadows across scrub grass and slash pines and smooth water. Pierce didn't seem surprised it was there, which told me it probably held the rest of the equipment we needed.

I climbed out of the Tahoe with the others, stretching after the less-than-gentle ride. Stars glimmered in a moonless sky, and a low breeze brought the scent of stagnant water. A damp chill came as well, and I hurried to pull my jacket on. Fortunately for me, mosquitoes weren't attracted to zombie blood. Rosario wasn't as lucky though, and moved quickly away to douse himself and Marla in repellent.

The driver of the pickup stepped out—a stocky, brown man of middle-eastern descent, smiling brightly despite the early hour.

Pierce gave him a chin lift in greeting. "Hey, Mo."

"Hey, Pierce. Got everything you asked for." Mo dropped the tailgate and lifted the cover on the truck bed. "Flatboats are already in the water. Twenty-footers, gassed up and ready." He jerked a thumb behind him where two low shapes rested at the edge of the gravel. "I added the special compartments you wanted, too." He thrust a box at Pierce who in turn passed it to Brian. "These are the good automatic life vests that inflate when you hit the water. Easier to move in. Almost like wearing a pair of suspenders. Got a regular one for the puppy, though."

"Good deal. And the sampling devices?"

Mo flipped open a long case and pulled out two very odd-looking rifles. "Modified a couple of the taggers marine biologists use to get biopsies from whales and sharks. Shoot your beasties and then pull the line back. Tissue sample'll be in the dart. I stuck plenty of extra darts in the case."

Marcus examined one of the taggers. "Will these penetrate alligator hide? I imagine it's way tougher than whale skin."

"Uh huh, and I thought of that," Mo said with a touch of pride. "I worked up sharper darts, then tested it on the gator who hangs out in the canal behind my house." He chuckled. "He didn't like it none, but I got a sample."

Pierce nodded in satisfaction. "Excellent work as always, Mo."

While Rosario adjusted the doggy life vest for Marla, the rest of us loaded the boats. In addition to gear and food, each boat had a satellite GPS, a cooler of brain packets labeled "protein gel," and a gator tagger and darts—stowed in a cleverly hidden compartment of Mo's design. And, of course, weapons: a 12-gauge shotgun and two Remington Model 700 .308 bolt-action rifles per boat, as well as a number of handguns concealed beneath clothing. Even I had a sweet little Glock .380 in an ankle holster, both on loan from Marcus.

"I'm sure I don't need to warn everyone to be on their toes," Pierce said once we were ready. "But I'm going to anyway. Not only are we looking for a body and alligators who might be more aggressive than usual, but we also need to keep an eye out for search and rescue teams, and Wildlife and Fisheries agents. Our radios are tuned to the Sheriff's Office frequencies, and with luck that'll give us an idea where they are. We have over an hour until civil twilight, so first we're going to where Angel finished off shambler-Judd, locate and sample as many alligators as possible, then head to the accident site for first light. Yes, Angel?"

I lowered my hand. "Gator season has been over for months, and these boats don't exactly have a lot of storage space. How are we supposed to hide a zombie-gator if we find one?"

"We won't," Marcus put in before Pierce could reply. "Hide one, that is. Since we're not sure if infected alligators appear any different than uninfected ones, Dr. Nikas suggested we take tissue samples from as many alligators as we can. But if we have clear indication an alligator is infected, we'll dispatch it and remove the brain."

"Probably safest," I agreed with a sigh. I felt oddly sorry for the poor zombie-gator, but it helped knowing Dr. Nikas was on board with the plan.

"Let's get moving," Marcus said. "Angel, Rosario, and Marla will be with me. Rachel, Brian, and Pierce will take the other boat."

I clipped on the life vest and climbed into the indicated boat, masking a smile at the brief look of annoyance on Pierce's face. He'd probably wanted the dog in his boat, but he could hardly override Marcus without raising questions. *Ha! Suck it!*

Marcus moved to the rear and started the motor, shattering the velvety peace. Rosario and an eager Marla took the front, while I settled in the middle.

Mo untied the lines then gave us a cheery wave and a "Happy

hunting!" I returned his wave with a chipper one of my own, and then we were off, with Pierce and the others a short distance behind.

Though the boats had spotlights, Marcus kept our pace slow—a decision I heartily approved of. Any one of the numerous submerged obstacles in the marsh could end this mission before it even began. Since it was too dark to see much beyond the spotlit area, I sat back and watched the sky progress to deep indigo. The last time I'd seen it that color was after I spent a hellish night in this very swamp. I crossed my fingers that today's mission would turn out a whole lot better.

Once the waterway widened a bit, Pierce's boat pulled alongside us. The indigo sky shifted to a dark purple, with a handful of stars standing their ground against the approaching dawn. The trees remained little more than black shadows, but one in particular drew my attention.

"I think that's the bald eagle nest," I said, pointing. "It's one of the landmarks I used to find my way out of the swamp. We should be getting close to where I finished off Judd."

Pierce nodded sharply. "Let's switch to the trolling motors. Rachel and Angel, get the taggers out and ready."

But twenty minutes of slow patrols produced exactly zero hyper-aggressive alligators. Twice I caught sight of eyes shining red in the spotlights, but we couldn't get close enough for the tagger to be effective. And though Marla seemed to be having the time of her life sniffing the breeze and watching wildlife, she gave no indication she detected shambler-scent. I thought for sure Pierce would be frustrated by our lack of progress, but his face remained impassive as he scanned the water.

"So much for hyper-aggressive gators," I grumbled.

"Maybe they're *shy* hyper-aggressive gators," Rosario said.

Pierce flipped a cooler open. "Well, we need samples from any gators we can find, so let's chum the waters." He hauled out a bag of bloody beef lung chunks and tossed several overboard.

The floating bait lured two alligators close enough to be darted, but no others found the lungs so enticing as to risk getting jabbed.

"Time to start working our way east," Marcus said after a glance at his watch. "We'll see if we can lure any others along the way."

Lavender and orange painted the heavens, and apparently

lulled the alligators into a blissfully trusting mood. By the time we crossed Bayou Cher and the Tribe property line—marked with prominent PRIVATE PROPERTY NO TRESPASSING signs—I'd managed to get samples from seven alligators, and Rachel had edged ahead with eight.

Tree frogs chirruped and a bullfrog boomed in the distance, while birds hidden in the cypress and scrub sang their hearts out to the impending dawn.

Yet still no sign of anything that might be a zombie-gator.

As I reached for my water bottle, movement from the other boat caught my eye. Rachel was lowering a 35mm camera, soft smile on her face as she gazed at the brilliant pre-dawn display. The smile vanished when she saw me watching.

"Too pretty not to capture it," she said with a small, defensive shrug.

"Yeah, it's gorgeous," I replied then pulled a face. "I can't take decent pictures."

She ignored me as she took several more shots. I looked away, silently cursing myself for giving her more ammunition for insults.

Pierce lifted his head. "Boat. Stow the taggers."

As if choreographed, Rachel and I slipped the taggers into their hidden compartments, then sat and acted natural.

The sound of an engine grew louder, and a sleek white patrol boat with a dark green stripe rounded the curve up ahead.

"Crap. It's Wildlife and Fisheries," Marcus muttered, though he kept a pleasant expression on his face.

Any hopes they'd continue on past died as the boat slowed. One agent stood near the front of the boat, a deeply tanned man with sun-bleached hair cropped short. The second, a slim, black woman who looked younger than me, worked the wheel and throttle with a deft touch. She eased the boat to within a few feet and idled the engine.

The male agent had "Z. Carbo" stitched above his left front pocket. To calm my nerves, I tried to guess what the Z stood for. Zeus? Zuul? Zebulon?

"Mornin', folks," Agent Z. Carbo said with a friendly but official smile. His eyes flicked over both boats, most likely counting people and life jackets, and taking careful note of the weapons. "What're y'all hunting today?"

"Wild hogs," Pierce drawled with a shockingly convincing

redneck accent. He turned and spat over the side of the boat, even though he didn't have any dip in his mouth. "And coyotes," he added, pronouncing it to rhyme with "pie-oats," just like god intended. "Hogs're tearing up my fields, and the coyotes done kilt two of my barn cats."

Agent Carbo nodded. "Uh huh, they're a real problem this year. And don't forget the boat has to be at a full stop before you shoot." He paused as if trying to get a point across. "Y'all mind showing me your permits?"

It was nicely asked but an order all the same. I dug my permit out of my vest pocket and handed it over along with everyone else.

Except Rachel.

Shit. Naomi had a lifetime pass, so Marcus hadn't bought a permit for her. And apparently no one thought of that when Rachel replaced her.

The agent handed the permits back then rested that very official smile on Rachel. "Ma'am, if you're going to hunt, you need a permit."

To my utter shock, Rachel gave an airhead-worthy scoff and made an *ew* face at the guns. "I canNOT stand hunting," she announced, packing the words with enough vocal fry to rival a Kardashian. "I'm only here because my boyfriend wanted me to come along." She simpered over at Pierce.

I bit the inside of my cheek to keep from cracking up. Pierce affected a put-upon expression and heaved a sigh. "Yeah, you don't have t'worry about her downing a hog. I ain't never seen her touch a gun unless it shot t-shirts." He grinned up at the agent. "She used t'be a cheerleader. Ain't she cute?"

Agent Carbo pursed his lips. "That sure is interesting. See, you may not realize it, but this waterway curves back on itself, and a little while ago, my partner and I were taking a break not even a hundred yards away from y'all."

My gaze went to the spit of land, and my heart sank. The grass was tall but not terribly thick. How much had they seen?

"Thing is," he continued, "I could've sworn I saw this former cheerleader here standing up—while the boat was in motion, mind you—and aiming at something on the bank."

"It was a camera!" I blurted, thinking fast. If they'd seen us from around the bend, Rachel would have been facing away from them with the tagger. "She likes taking pictures."

Rachel seized her camera and held it up. "It's true!" To my amazement, her lower lip trembled, and her eyes welled with honest-to-god tears. "It wasn't a gun," she said with an utterly believable quaver in her voice. "I *promise*."

The agent's expression softened. "All right, sweetheart. You don't need to cry. It's okay. But if y'ever change your mind and want to take a shot at something, you gotta get you a permit, y'hear?"

She sniffled and nodded. "Ok-kay."

Agent Carbo returned his attention to the rest of us. "You folks should also be aware that search and rescue is still looking for the body of a man who went missing and is presumed drowned," he said in a grave tone. "Y'all are several miles from where they're searching, but I'd hate for these pretty ladies to get themselves a bad fright."

Somehow I managed to not roll my eyes and instead did my best to look suitably anxious about the possibility of encountering a dead body. Oh, the horror.

"Where are you searching?" Marcus asked. "I mean, so we know to avoid it."

"Piney Waters area," the agent replied. "If you stay south and west, you should be fine. And best not to do any swimming either. Alligators have been known to bite people who get close to their nests." He offered Rachel and me a nod of apology for offending our delicate sensibilities with the topic of wildlife acting wild, then he gave his partner the thumbs up. She nudged the throttle, and they motored away.

"That's good news for us," Marcus said once the agents were well out of earshot. "They still haven't twigged to the other possible location."

"Then let's get moving before they do," Pierce growled.

Chapter 9

Since the encounter with Wildlife and Fisheries had been such a close call, we all agreed the taggers would remain in their hiding places until needed. No sense tempting fate.

Of course that meant I had nothing to do now except stare at the scenery.

Grass. Water. Trees. Bug. Frog. Water. Algae. Fish. Bug. Grass. Trees. Water. Grass.

I swiped Marcus's map from beside his seat then scrutinized the route he'd marked. "Do any of these waterways have names? Besides the bayous, of course."

"I don't know of anything official," Marcus replied. "That's why I have this." He lifted the satellite GPS.

"Then I'm naming them. We're currently on Medium Squiggle. Next we cross Blob to Small Squiggle and then we hang a left onto Yet Another Squiggle and finally reach Biggish Squiggle."

"Biggish Squiggle is Pauvre Bayou," Marcus pointed out.

"It's a terrible name. Pauvre means poor. Biggish Squiggle has much more character."

"I can't think of a single counter-argument to that."

We picked up a bit of speed as we crossed the patch of open water known as Blob. In the other boat, Brian had the sheriff's office radio pressed to his ear, and Rachel snapped more pictures. Rosario sat with his arm draped around Marla while he scanned the area.

I glanced at Marcus. "How much longer?"

"Fifteen minutes, tops. We'll get there a bit after sunup." He glanced down at the GPS. "And in another hundred feet we're going to take Small Squiggle, so keep your eyes peeled."

But Small Squiggle turned out to be Shitty Squiggle. We were barely a quarter of the way through when the engine on Pierce's boat stopped.

"Hydrilla," Brian said through clenched teeth as he helped Pierce hack the snaky weeds off the prop. "It's an invasive. Not too many things here eat it, so it grows out of control and clogs up the water." He tipped his head to the left where tiny white flowers dotted an expanse of green. "And that's alligator weed. Those big mats block the sun. Kills off native fish and screws up water quality."

Pierce muttered something filthy and continued yanking at weeds until the prop was clear.

Five minutes later it was me and Marcus's turn to hack and curse.

"The whole channel is filled with this shit," Pierce fumed. "Is there any way around?"

Marcus gave a sharp head shake. "It would take twice as long. Another quarter mile and we'll be in clearer water."

"We'll burn out the motors if we keep this up," Pierce said. "Best break out the paddles."

"Paddle," Brian said, holding one aloft. "We only have one."

"Same here," I said after a bit of rummaging. "To be fair, I don't think they're required in this kind of boat."

Pierce looked anything but mollified by that bit of helpful info.

With only one paddle per boat, it was slow going, with plenty of splashing and switching from one side to the other. Pierce cursed nonstop, while Marla stood with her front paws on the bow, tongue lolling and big doggy grin on her face as she sniffed the air.

By the time we propelled ourselves out of the weed-choked channel and into Yet Another Squiggle, we'd lost over half an hour, and the sun had cleared the trees. I put the paddle away while Marcus and Pierce started the trolling motors. Smooth, steady, and quiet.

I dug sunscreen out of the gear bag and slathered it on.

Rosario gave me a puzzled look. "Zombies get sunburn?"

"Yup," I said, making sure to get my ears and the back of my neck. "The parasite'll heal any damage, but I'm so stupid pale it would be a criminal waste of brains."

He chuckled. "I'm glad I don't have to rely on brains."

After several more minutes, Marcus cut the motor and signaled Pierce to do the same. "See those twin pines up and to the right? This waterway joins Pauvre Bayou there."

A hundred yards ahead, the two pines stood at the end of the strip of brushy land that ran alongside us, the final divider between Yet Another Squiggle and the larger bayou. I looked from the map to the brush and the hint of water beyond. "Not far to go now, right?"

"We'll head past the pines then turn downstream on the bayou. The hunters' boat was found about fifty yards further on. Once we get there we'll—" He held up a hand for silence.

A breeze riffled the surface of the water, bringing with it a shout of *"Fuck! Watch what you're doing!"* accompanied by heavy thumping.

"That's coming from near the accident site," Marcus said, jaw tight. "At least the wind is in our favor."

As if in agreement, Marla tensed then sat.

Rosario straightened. "She's indicating."

I craned my neck to peer without success through the thick brush. "What's she got?"

"Funky zombie or regular decomp. No way to know yet."

Pierce jerked his head to the right. "Let's hug the bank along the spit. There's enough cover to shield us, and we can get in position to see who's over there."

Using the paddles, we made our way quietly over then let the current pull the boats along. The underbrush thinned to tall grass and scattered scrub as the spit narrowed. When we were a dozen yards from the pines, Marcus waved for us to stop.

"Damn it," he growled.

"What is it?" I scrambled to kneel on my seat for a better vantage. The spit was barely ten feet across at this point, with steep banks, but the grass was sparse enough to allow a partial view of the bayou beyond. A light grey patrol boat with "Sheriff" stenciled on the side in big blue letters lay anchored some forty feet away, on the far side of the bayou. Two deputies stood at the back—one a carrot-top and the other bald as an egg. A scuba diver broke the surface by the stern and gave them a thumbs up, then the deputies crouched and hauled something into the boat. No, some*one*.

"Shit," I breathed. A very obviously dead someone, with sickly pale skin and a partially severed hand dangling by a single tenacious tendon.

Pierce muttered a curse. "Looks like Wildlife and Fisheries was wrong about the search area."

Rachel flicked a glance my way. "The body will be taken to the morgue, right? Angel can still get samples, so it's not a total loss."

"Yeah, but it's nowhere near as useful as having the whole body. And it's risky, especially if it turns out to be a shambler . . ." I trailed off, brow furrowing. "I thought all of the Sheriff's Office boats were white."

"Might be a new one," Marcus said, but a sliver of doubt crept into his voice. He fished a set of binoculars from beneath his seat and peered at the grey boat. "I don't recognize any of those guys. Doesn't mean they *aren't* deputies, but it's only been a few months since I left—and they wouldn't have a pair of newbies out on their own for a search."

"May I?" Rosario extended a hand for the binoculars. After Marcus passed them over, he examined the boat and its occupants then let out a weary sigh. "The bald one is a Saberton security bigshot."

Pierce narrowed his eyes. "Are you certain? How the fuck could Saberton possibly know—" He cut himself off with an angry shake of his head. "We'll have to figure that out later. We absolutely cannot let them get away with that body."

"We outnumber them two to one," Rachel pointed out. "Using both flatboats, we can do a flanking maneuver."

I shook my head. "We shouldn't put the non-zombies in the line of fire."

Rosario frowned. "Now, hang on—"

I stopped him with a fierce glare. "You die a lot more easily than our kind. And so does Marla."

He flicked a guilty look at the German Shepherd and subsided.

"Enough," Pierce said, voice low yet no less commanding. "It's a non-issue. We could put Rosario and the dog on the bank to wait, but there's no need. Rachel, Brian, and I will use the 'dumb hick' ploy to get us close enough to take them out. You and Marcus will remain here as emergency backup."

"Hold on," I said. "That won't work."

Pierce scowled at me. "It served just fine earlier."

"With Wildlife and Fisheries, sure, but this is *Saberton*."

"What the hell does that have to do with—"

"Just because you don't recognize them doesn't mean they won't recognize *you*," I snapped.

Finally, a flicker of realization in his eyes. It had to be tough pretending 24/7 to be Pierce Gentry, ex-Saberton security honcho, all while not giving himself away to colleagues—like Rosario and Rachel—who weren't allowed to know he used to be Pietro.

"Angel's right, Pierce," Marcus said. "I should go, and you should stay."

Pierce dug a faded Saints ball cap from under the seat and jammed it on his head. "You were a good cop, but I have ops training and experience." He shoved on sunglasses and drawled, "They ain't gonna see city slicker Gentry in this here boat."

I regarded him then shrugged. "Yeah, I guess they won't be expecting a New Yorker to go full redneck."

Marcus lifted his rifle. "That works. I'll cover from here."

"Still a crack shot, I take it?" Pierce asked with a hint of Uncle Pietro pride in his voice.

Marcus quietly chambered a round then brought the rifle to his shoulder and sighted through the grass. "I can get my point across."

In less than a minute, Pierce, Rachel, and Brian had readied weapons, agreed on a basic plan, and downed a packet of brains each. In the bow of the flatboat, Brian lounged as if half-asleep. Rachel pretended to read a book, pistol hidden beneath the jacket draped over her lap. Pierce set his shotgun close at hand, pulled a beer from the cooler, and cracked it open.

"Why do you have *beer* in the brains cooler?" I asked, perplexed.

He chuckled and took a sip. "It's good cover. Besides, I happen to like beer." He took a longer swig then started the motor and headed down toward the bayou.

Marcus climbed partway up the bank, put his eye to the rifle's scope and waited.

"You want a spotter?" I asked, half-expecting him to tell me to stay behind cover.

"Wouldn't mind at all," he murmured.

Pleased, I snatched the binoculars from Rosario then scrambled up the bank to where I could watch events unfold.

Pierce rounded the twin pines and turned downstream on the bayou—into plain sight of the "deputies." The diver had climbed into the boat and was facing away as he shed gear, but the other two tensed, hands twitching to weapons.

"G'mornin'!" Pierce hollered, lifting his beer in salute as he steered toward them. "How y'all doin'?"

Rachel lowered her book and shot Pierce a withering look. "Oh my *god*, Cooter. They're *cops*. You're gonna get busted for drinking while boating!"

The Saberton men exchanged a glance, then Baldy leveled a stern look at Pierce. "Sir, you need to stay back. We're conducting an investigation."

"Woowee!" Pierce grinned widely. "Listen to our boys in blue, darlin'. They soundin' all official. Least I can do is offer 'em a beer!" He guided the flatboat closer.

"They can't have beer on duty," Rachel scoffed.

"But they can save it for when they're off!"

Carrot-top glowered as the flatboat came within a couple of feet of the patrol boat's hull. "Get the fuck away from our boat, asshole."

Pierce donned a hangdog expression. "Well, gawddamn. I guess when you put it that way—" He snapped the shotgun up. A split second later, Rachel and Brian had their guns trained on the Saberton trio.

Carrot-top and Baldy froze, hands on their weapons and very obviously assessing how best to handle the turn of events. Behind them, the diver stood motionless, gripping his mask.

"Hands off your guns and up where we can see them," Pierce said with no trace of the redneck accent. "The diver, too. I need to see his hands. There's a rifle trained on you."

Baldy's eyes narrowed. "You're full of sh—"

I jerked as Marcus fired the rifle. Water poofed up a few feet behind the patrol boat.

"Jesus," I hissed. "Warn a girl next time!"

Marcus smiled and chambered another round.

Expression murderous, Baldy slowly put his hands on his head. The other two followed suit.

Rachel and Brian swarmed onto the boat and began disarming the three men. Pleased, I panned the field glasses down to the flatboat where Pierce sat with a lazy, deadly smile on his face, shotgun never wavering. Something splashed in the bayou. A fish, most likely. Or perhaps an alligator was watching the whole show from beneath? Hard to tell since I couldn't see the water between the flatboat and my vantage on the backside of the bank.

Two quick gunshots split the air, startling me again. But not from Marcus.

"Who's shooting?" Marcus demanded.

"I don't know—" I sucked in a breath at the sight of the slumped figure in the flatboat. Red stained the back of his shirt. "Pierce is down!"

As the flatboat began to drift downstream, a third shot cracked. Rachel cried out and staggered. Carrot-top seized his opening and slugged her hard across the jaw, dropping her.

Heart pounding, I stood up to get a better look, right as a dark figure disappeared beneath the water, halfway between the patrol boat and the spit. "There's another diver," I said in growing horror. This was bad bad *bad*. Both Saberton men grappled with Brian now. What if the second diver shot him next? Or decided to finish Pierce off with a bullet to the brain?

Or, just as bad, what if they captured one of our zombies?

"I've got to help them," I gasped, lurching up the embankment.

"Angel . . . wait! We can plan a—"

"No time!" I took off, pouring on the zombie speed for a good hard sprint across the bit of land. As I reached the far side I let out a ululating war cry and launched myself into the air. Every head turned my way. Brian mouthed something I hoped was "You're so awesome!" but was more likely "Are you shitting me?"

Though I barely avoided a belly flop, the momentum of my ungraceful dive carried me toward my target. The dark shape of the diver moved ahead and below. I kicked hard, reached for him.

Then popped right back to the surface as the automatic life vest inflated. Shrieking a curse, I struggled with the clasp, all the while looking for a shadow that marked the human shark swimming below. I finally squirmed free of the vest and threw the stupid thing aside, then shrieked again as a hand seized my ankle.

I barely had a chance to suck in a partial breath before the diver yanked me under. I was a lousy swimmer—and my heavy boots sure didn't help—but I was one hell of a scrappy fighter.

Though my gun was holstered on my other ankle, I didn't waste effort trying to get to it since the drag of water slowed bullets down too much. I stuck to the basics and kicked and twisted until I broke free of the grip, but instead of making for the surface as the diver no doubt expected, I turned on him and ripped at hoses and mask.

I had no luck pulling the hoses free from the tank, but I managed to yank his regulator out and mask off.

Her mask, I realized with a start as the mask dropped to the bottom. Even through the murky water, it was pretty clear this was a woman.

She jammed her regulator in her mouth even as she pulled her gun and tried to shove it against my side. Point blank was the only way an underwater shot would be effective, but a hard kick to her gut solved that problem. Though the stupid boots weighed me down, they delivered a lot more punishment than her flippers ever could. I followed up with a zombie-power snatch and ripped the gun out of her hand, only to have it slip through my fingers and sink. Pissed, I kicked her again for good measure.

Not hard enough, apparently. She yanked a long knife from a sheath and slashed at my midsection. I barely managed to twist away then bit down on a yelp as she sliced my thigh on her backswing. I grabbed her arm, but my nifty *jiu jitsu* moves didn't work worth a shit underwater. With her tank in the way, I couldn't even try and get her in a chokehold. Going for a point-blank shot with my own gun was also out of the question as well since she'd move in for the kill the instant I tried to draw it.

My lungs strained for air as we battled for the knife. I gasped, sucking in water that burned in a new and horrible way, and flailed as panic slithered in. Hands grabbed and held. My body acted without me, took another breath of water. Parasite. Compensating. Like being submerged in the nutrient goo at the lab. But without the nutrient. Couldn't sustain long, but it was enough for now.

Yet my brief distraction was all the diver needed. She kneed me hard in the gut then wrestled free of my grasp and jammed the knife between my ribs.

Pain jolted through me. Triumph lit her face.

Baring my teeth, I grabbed her hand on the knife and held it firm between my ribs. In a glorious water ballet cartwheel, I flipped to my right, propelling myself around with my boot on her face.

As I spun, her hand slipped from the hilt. I yanked the knife from my chest then rammed it into her throat.

Her entire body spasmed. I shoved away from her, knife in hand. Eyes wide, she clawed weakly at the wound, blood billowing out in a dark cloud. Her hands dropped away, and she drifted from sight, limp and unmoving.

I'd won. And it felt like shit.

I slit the laces on my boots, kicked them off, then swam for the surface.

Chapter 10

I broke the surface and puked water. Coughed. Heaved in air. Puked some more.

With every violent move, pain radiated from the knife wound in my chest, and brain hunger twisted my gut. The vibrant green of the grass and trees dulled to grey. The pain faded to the background, and the distant birdsong grew flat and toneless. *Shit*. My parasite was shifting all resources to the task of keeping me alive.

The current had carried me at least a hundred feet, to where the bayou widened and the banks sloped gently down to narrow beaches. Treading water and hacking up mucky phlegm, I turned to make my way upstream—just in time to see Brian sail over the side of the patrol boat with Rachel tucked under his arm.

He surfaced and stroked one-armed toward where Pierce's flatboat had wedged itself in brush along the bank. Pierce shifted a little, though sluggishly, and a teensy bit of my worry eased. He was alive, and Brian would get him and Rachel the brains they needed.

A rifle cracked, then again. Water sprayed up a few inches from the Saberton boat. Marcus was shooting right below the waterline, trying to hole the vessel enough to sink it, or at least slow it down.

The shots sounded muffled and distant to my dulled senses. I needed to get my ass to land and brains in my mouth before I lost too much blood, but my feeble doggie paddle barely held me steady against the lazy current.

A powerful motor roared to life, and the Saberton boat leaped forward, heading upstream—away from me, thank goodness. I was still screwed but not as quickly.

A grey plastic bag floated by a couple of feet away. No, not grey. Yellow. And not a plastic bag. *My lifejacket!* I seized it with a groan of relief and looped my arm through a strap. Getting it on all the way wasn't going to happen, but at least it kept my head above water. I doubted the water-breathing trick would work if I went under for good.

The sound of another, smaller, motor reached me as our other flatboat came racing around the spit of land with a grim-faced Marcus at the tiller. Rosario crouched in the bow, with Marla right beside him.

"Angel!" Rosario called out, scanning the water frantically.

"Here," I croaked then realized he'd never hear it in a million years. Plus, he wasn't looking far enough downstream. With every ounce of effort I possessed, I lifted my hand and waved. "Here!"

Marla's ears perked up, then she started a frenzied barking. Marcus angled the flatboat in my direction, and in no time at all, the guys hauled me into the boat.

I slumped across a seat. "Drowned." I coughed. "Sucks."

"Dante, grab two brain packets," Marcus said, taking in my injuries.

"I killed her. The diver," I managed, throat tight, then focused on draining the first packet dry. I knew it had been self-defense. Didn't matter.

His eyes darkened with sympathy. "I'm sorry that it was necessary," Marcus murmured then jerked his head up at the sound of a quickly approaching boat.

I struggled upright, only to see the damn Saberton fake Sheriff's Office patrol boat racing around the curve and toward Pierce's flatboat.

Gunfire spit from a Mac-10 in Baldy's hands, even as Pierce and the others threw themselves flat. The patrol boat zoomed past them then veered straight for us.

"Get down!" Marcus shouted. He snapped the rifle up then dropped it and crumpled, blood blooming on his chest.

"Marla!" Rosario threw himself over the dog to shield her,

and I threw myself on top of him. I could survive most bullet wounds, but Rosario didn't have that luxury. His head was right beneath my crotch, which meant *my* head was right by his very excellent ass, affording me the perfect vantage to see a bullet whiz past my nose and hit his gorgeous glute. Too damn close to a fatal headshot for me.

Rosario jerked and gasped a curse, but kept himself wrapped around the dog. A bullet punched my thigh, but I stayed glommed onto Rosario. A wave rocked us, then something big slammed into the boat and everything went sideways. As we all went flying, I had an instant to realize the Saberton assholes had deliberately sideswiped us. Then we hit the water, and I had to focus on not drowning all over again.

I'd lost hold of Rosario but by some miracle still had an arm looped through my life vest. Marla bobbed in her doggy life jacket a couple of feet away and gave me a single excited bark. Marcus popped up a second later as his vest inflated, with Rosario right behind him.

Rosario spluttered. "They . . . gone?"

"For now," I said with a glower.

Together we helped Marcus to the narrow beach. Of the three of us, he seemed to be the worst off, with blood frothing from a sucking chest wound. Since he was still mostly conscious, I grabbed his hand and slapped it over the wound.

"Hold that there," I ordered then stripped off my sodden jacket and shoved Rosario onto his side. "And you, hold this on your ass."

Hunger rolled over me in a slavering swell at the scent of a fresh, warm brain. Rosario's brain. I gritted my teeth and backed away, then did a quick personal inventory. The one packet of brains I'd managed to down had taken care of the godawful burning in my lungs and slowed the bleeding from the stab wound, but now I had a bullet hole in my left quadricep. No visible exit wound, which meant the damn thing was still in there. But at least I'd successfully stopped it from hitting Rosario's vitals or Marla.

Upstream, the other flatboat remained wedged in the brush. No sign of movement within. I swallowed the worry and focused on our own situation. We needed brains, which meant I needed to find our cooler.

Only one teensy weensy problem. Our boat was nowhere to

be seen. I stared in horror at a spot ten yards downstream where bubbles lazily popped on the surface.

Muttering all sorts of filthy words, I stripped off the life vest, waded toward the bubbles until the water reached my chest, then swam-flailed the rest of the way. One thing was for sure: as soon as we were done with this bullshit, I was going to take some goddamn swimming lessons.

After a deep breath, I dove under and found the boat about a dozen feet down where, by some blissful miracle, it had settled right side up. No way would I be able to pull the thing to the surface on my own, so I groped around the interior until I came across the cooler. It took some tugging and desperate kicking, but I managed to free it and reach the surface before my parasite decided to turn me into a wannabe fish again.

Now the hard part: getting back. The current wasn't as strong along the edges of the bayou, but swimming one-handed with my already pathetic stroke meant I'd most likely reach the others sometime next year. Switching tactics, I veered closer to the bank until my toes brushed the bottom then made my way toward the little beach with a combination of tiptoe-wading and spastic semi-freestyle. The mud squished through my toes in the most disgusting way, and I tried hard not to think of the many icky things that might be lurking in it. Broken bottles. Giant water moccasins. Man-eating squid.

The body of a diver.

I shuddered and forged onward. I'd progressed to where the water was only chest deep, with maybe twenty feet to go. Marcus had turned his head to watch me and offered a weak thumbs up with the hand that wasn't pressed over his chest. Marla gave an encouraging bark and started toward the water, clearly ready to help play this fun game.

Rosario's eyes widened. "No!" he gasped. "Marla, *halt*. Angel, watch out!"

The dog stopped then growled, hackles rising as her gaze fixed on the reason for Rosario's sudden alarm.

A puce and snot-green log with a pair of milky yellow eyes slid soundlessly through the water toward me. A *big* log.

I froze, heart pounding as the alligator approached. The *zombie*-gator. Absolutely no doubt in my mind. Not with those blank eyes and odd coloring. In my periphery, I saw Rosario pull his gun, hand tremoring as he brought it to bear.

"Don't," I said, gulping. "You might piss it off." Plus, the gator was only a few feet away from me at this point.

I remembered enough of my high school science to know its kind had been around for millions of years. Apex predator. But I'd been a southern chick all my life, and I knew this wasn't normal behavior for an alligator. They were known to attack humans, but mostly when they felt threatened. *Or when they think they have vulnerable prey?* Here I was, bleeding into the water. I could almost certainly survive an attack, but it would really hurt. And, dammit, I did *not* want to be regrown all over again.

The zombie-gator stopped with the tip of its snout barely a foot from my chest. We stared at each other while its breath ruffled the water between us. One big sweep of its tail, and it could lunge forward and grab my face in those toothy jaws.

Noooo, I didn't need to start thinking about horrible shit like that. "Nice gator," I squeaked out. "N-now shoo. Go home."

In reply it lifted its snout and let out a weird croaking growl, water vibrating around its midsection. What the hell was that? A challenge? A mating call?

Shhhthook.

I barely had time to register the dart in the gator's hide before it reared up, thrashing. I scrambled back, fully expecting it to attack me in retaliation, but instead it dove to the side and swam away, powerful tail churning the water.

Trembling with relief, I looked over to see Brian pulling in a sampling dart while Pierce lowered his pistol. Between them, Rachel sucked on a brain packet and scowled down at the hole below her sternum.

"Sorry to chase off your new friend," Pierce said. "Couldn't shoot it without risking hitting you, though." He angled his boat to run aground near Marcus and Rosario. Brian leaped onto the bank and pulled it further up then waded out and helped me in. And "helped me" meant he wrapped an arm around my weak-kneed body and hauled me and the cooler to the bank.

Pierce shoved an already-opened brain packet into my hand. I greedily wolfed the contents down and two more after that. Color and sensation seeped back into my world. The bullet popped from my thigh and fell to the ground. By the time my wounds closed and my hunger returned to manageable levels, Marcus was healed. While he, Brian, and Pierce discussed how to retrieve the sunken boat, Rachel worked on field-dressing Rosario's hole-y ass.

"Lucky bitch," I murmured without thinking. She jerked her head up and gave me a narrow-eyed glare. I gave a slight chin lift toward the bandage then turned my hands over and made the universal sign for squeezing a butt.

The glare vanished, to be replaced by a quick conspiratorial smile. She affixed the last piece of tape then pushed to her feet and angled her head toward mine. "I almost shoved Pierce into the water so I could get to Rosario first," she said under her breath.

"I can hear you," Rosario muttered good-naturedly.

I smothered a laugh then had to act all serious as Marcus glanced our way.

"We lost all the weapons and supplies in the flatboat," he said, expression dark. "And even if we could raise it, there's no way we'd get the motor working." He turned to Pierce. "I take it Saberton got away with the body?"

"They did," Pierce replied, much less grimly. "But all is not lost. Not only can we fit in the one boat, we have a tissue sample from the body, thanks to Rachel's quick thinking."

Brian lifted a baggie with a severed hand in it. "When Rachel went down, she finished pulling the hand off and stuffed it down her shirt."

Rachel gave a mock-shudder. "Definitely not the way I want a hand on my boob."

"Excellent work," Marcus said with a relieved smile.

"That's the good news," Brian said. "The bad news—besides the fact Saberton was here at all—is that they also had a live, trussed up alligator on board. Looked a lot like the one we chased off."

"Let's discuss the Saberton angle after we get the hell out of here," Pierce said. "That much shooting is sure to draw attention. We have samples, Angel had a heart to heart with a gator, and Rosario can't catch a break."

While Brian and Rosario rearranged gear in the remaining flatboat to make room for everyone, Marcus dove down to the sunken boat and recovered the shotgun, tagger, darts, samples we'd collected, and the—thankfully waterproof—GPS. "We'll come back later with a metal detector," he said then muttered something about fucking expensive rifles.

The flatboat rode a bit low in the water once we all piled in, but Pierce insisted it was rated for six passengers. "And Angel plus the dog equals the weight of one person," he added with a smirk.

We headed downstream for about a quarter mile then, at Marcus's direction, took a medium-squiggle-sized channel to the west.

Not even five minutes later, Pierce lifted his head. "Boat." His mouth thinned. "Wildlife and Fisheries."

"Are you sure?" I asked with a touch of skepticism. Even tanked up on brains, I couldn't hear anything but the usual swamp noises.

Ignoring me, Pierce guided our boat around a cypress tree and stopped behind a stand of tall grass. "Everyone get down and stay perfectly still," he ordered then hopped out of the boat and into the waist-deep water.

I didn't see how the clump of grass could possibly keep us from being seen, but I hunkered down with everyone else.

Pierce moved quickly, grabbing seemingly random tree branches and plants. Some he draped around the boat, and the rest he arranged between us and the channel. Apparently satisfied, he crouched in the water and watched. After a couple of minutes of waiting in silence, I picked up the noise of a boat motor, and not long after that, Agent Carbo and his partner cruised on by without a glance in our direction.

Pierce remained motionless for several minutes after they passed. Finally, he stood and waded to the boat.

"We're good now," he said as he climbed in.

"Damn, Pierce, you win the Hide and Seek trophy," I said. "Where'd you learn to do that?"

He met my eyes, expression utterly devoid of humor. "The Vietnam War."

Note to self: Don't ask Pierce anything that even remotely resembles a personal question. Sheesh.

We rode the rest of the way back in near silence, watching and listening until we crossed Bayou Cher and were safely in Tribe territory. Only then did Pierce relax.

"Can we discuss the Saberton-sized elephant in the room now?" I asked. "Why were they there? How the fuck could they have known anything about that body and the gators?"

"They had to have found out about the shambler at the morgue," Rachel said, expression murderous.

"They were collecting alligator samples, too," Brian said. "I saw a container of beef lungs, and several large hooks on cables."

Ugh. And being assholes about it. Hook and release was far more damaging to the gator than our method.

A muscle worked in Pierce's jaw. "There's no possible way the lab is bugged. It's been swept numerous times, by different personnel and with different equipment. Everyone who enters or leaves is scanned. And everyone who stays there permanently has been scanned, repeatedly."

"Even the dog?" Rachel asked.

"Even the dog."

"The morgue?" I gave a helpless shrug. "There must be a bug somewhere in it. It's the only thing that makes sense. Saberton could have heard us fighting off that shambler, and maybe even heard me when I called Dr. Nikas to tell him about it." I frowned. "Wait, what if my phone is tapped?"

"We'll check it," Pierce said. "We'll check everything." He tugged a hand through his hair in a rare show of frustration. "I'll arrange with Allen Prejean to have the morgue swept for listening devices."

"I'll borrow the bug scanner thingy and go over my house again." I planned on checking the PlayBox for bugs as well, but I didn't want to tell Pierce about the game console—yet—in case he decided to do something crazy, like blow it up the way the bomb squad did with suspicious packages.

"Good plan, Angel," he said. "Get it from Raul when we return."

With the subject exhausted, we fell silent, lost in thought. A hawk wheeled overhead, graceful against the bright, clear sky. Water rippled as a snake swam past, and a great blue heron stalked through the grass in search of prey. The swamp was beautiful and dangerous in any number of ways. Environment. Weather. Wildlife.

People.

My thoughts veered back to the diver. I'd killed people before, but never a woman. It shouldn't have made a difference, but . . . it did. At least I knew without a doubt she was no innocent bystander. She'd shot Pierce and Rachel, then tried her best to take me out of the game.

Now the swamp held a new threat: zombie-gators. It sucked that we couldn't simply cordon off Mudsucker Swamp so no one else got infected.

However, I *could* warn people who might come out here, such as Bear Galatas and his survivalist group. I made a mental note to call him once we made it to the lab, then returned to mulling over how Saberton could have known about the shambler.

"Kristi Charish is involved," I said after a moment. "She has to be."

"Dr. Charish is in Chicago," Pierce said flatly. "I've had eyes on her ever since she took Saberton's offer. Her daily movements are monitored closely. If she's doing more zombie-related R&D, she's doing it while she's taking a shit."

Marcus scratched the back of his head. "Still, she could be calling the shots, even from Chicago. That Saberton operation today had her stink all over it."

Pierce gave a grudging nod. "Maybe so, but it's a stretch to assume she's responsible for Angel's shambler."

I winced. "Yep, that one seems to be all on me." I paused. "And on Judd. And the gators. And, well, those hunters who didn't think they needed life jackets."

"Could be worse," Brian said, mouth crooked in a smile. "That gator could've bitten your face off."

Pierce snorted. "Please. Gator face-biting is nothing. What's abysmal is being the one who has to explain to Mo why we're one boat short."

"Maybe he won't be as mad if you tell him there are some really nice rifles down there—ow!" Laughing, I ducked away from a second swat from Marcus.

"Stop helping, Angel," he warned.

"But I'm just so good at it!"

Marcus rolled his eyes heavenward in mock-despair. "The world isn't ready for Angel Crawford in charge."

"What?! Say you're sorry." I launched into an acapella version of the *Charles in Charge* theme song, using my own name instead.

"For the love of god, he's sorry!" Pierce exclaimed. "Aren't you, Marcus?"

Marcus held up his hands in defeat. "More than you can possibly know."

*   *   *

As predicted, Mo lost his shit when we arrived at the launch without the other boat. But after Pierce pulled him aside for a low conversation, he was all smiles again.

"Did you tell him about the rifles?" I asked Pierce as we climbed into the Tahoe for the return trip.

"Nah," Pierce said, mouth curving in a wry smile. "Marcus will send some people out to retrieve the Tribe weapons and equipment. I simply told Mo where to find the boat *and* that I was doubling his payment. Money is the way to Mo's heart."

"Y'know, that works for my heart, too," I pointed out, then settled in for the ride back to the lab. To my surprise, I fell asleep almost instantly and didn't wake until we were in the lab garage.

After we unloaded, I started toward the door to the lab proper, but Rachel stopped me with a touch on my arm.

"When you're taking pictures, composition makes all the difference," she said after I gave her a questioning look. "I mean, it's how you position the elements in your viewfinder and the angle of your shot." She hesitated a moment then let out a breath. "Maybe when we get some free time I could show you a couple of tricks."

"I'd like that," I said, accepting the enormous olive branch. I doubted we'd ever sit over coffee and actually talk about photography, but that didn't diminish the gesture one bit. "Thanks."

She gave me a short little nod then strode over to Rosario and helped him and his injured butt onto a stretcher.

I watched her head off toward the infirmary with Rosario. "What a weird fucking day."

Chapter 11

I had an hour before I needed to leave for my biology class, and I used more than half of it for a steaming hot shower to boil away the swamp funk. When I returned to my room, I found three syringes and a note penned in Dr. Nikas's elegant handwriting.

Angel,

Here is your refill of V13. The second syringe is a stay-awake mod. With it, two hours of sleep will feel like ten. There are adverse effects if activated after less than two hours sleep. I only supplied one dose as it should be used infrequently, but in these challenging times, you may have need. The third syringe is four doses of a mild combat mod. You have been off V12 long enough for there to be no interference. After the events at the swamp, I am uncomfortable with your being without access to emergency augmentation.

Stay well,

Ari

Hot damn. My first legit combat mod. Standard human drugs didn't work on zombies, but Dr. Nikas had developed his own line of parasite-modifying pharmaceuticals—mods for short—for a variety of purposes. A basic combat mod heightened senses and improved speed and reflexes.

During my regrowth, Dr. Nikas had installed a mod port in my chest—a syringe access point to an implanted receptacle for storing and dispensing up to four different mods, unnoticeable unless you knew where to look. In one compartment, I had V13 on auto-dose—the Angel-only formula Dr. Nikas had come up with to counter my addiction to V12, with the bonus effect of helping my dyslexia.

I stuck the first syringe in the port and refilled the V13 reservoir, then added the stay-awake mod to the second compartment. The combat mod went into the third. I sure could have used this kind of enhancement with the diver this morning.

Maybe I wouldn't have had to kill her.

Sighing, I pushed down the guilt and grabbed my phone to call Bear Galatas.

Bear was Nick's dad and, after one hell of a rough start, an unlikely ally to the Tribe. A savvy businessman, he'd built Bear's Gun Shop and Indoor Range from the ground up into a hugely successful venture. He was also widely considered to be an expert on survival and disaster preparedness, and ran a well-organized group of like-minded survivalists.

Unfortunately, Bear's determination to survive any apocalypse had long ago caused a deep rift between him and Nick. Bear had been forcefully insistent that, for the benefit of the survivalists, Nick would go to medical school and become a surgeon—which Nick hadn't wanted at all. After I finally managed to make Bear see the error of his ways, their relationship improved. Slightly. But that was before my rotting-away "setback" and recovery. I had no idea if they were getting along any better, but at least Nick hadn't flinched at the mention of Bear's name.

No, he only flinched around me now.

I flopped onto the bed and gazed morosely at the ceiling. How could Nick—or anyone—get over watching me rot away? Maybe it would be better for everyone if I pulled back and gave him some space. Spare us both a whole lot of grief.

The idea sent a horrible pang through me. It would probably hurt less in the long run, though. Rip the bandage off.

I shook myself out of the black funk and called Bear's store.

A deep male voice answered. "Bear's Den."

"Is this Bear?"

"Nope, he's . . . with a customer. This is Clark."

"Hey, Clark, this is Angel. I really need to talk to Bear. It's important. Won't take long."

"I'll buzz him. Hang on a sec."

Hold music came on the line. Eighties pop. For a gun store in the middle of redneck country? Seriously, Bear?

The music clicked off. "This is Bear. With whom do I have the pleasure of speaking?"

The cultured reply left me briefly at a loss for words. "Er, it's Angel."

"Hey, Hank. I'll have to get back to you on that Brockman rifle. I'm still waiting to hear from the company rep."

"Um, I think you're on the wrong line. This is Angel."

"Nope, I'm not wrong. I'll give you a call when something changes. Have yourself a good day now." He hung up.

That was either the weirdest conversation in history, or he didn't want whoever was with him to know it was me on the phone. I didn't like the thought of that.

I hunted down Raul and got one of the listening device scanner things then left the lab. I was almost to Tucker Point Community College when my phone rang. Unknown number, which usually meant either a telemarketer or someone insisting they could fix my computer over the phone if I gave them my credit card number. I declined the call, but a few seconds later it rang again from the same number.

Hmm. Telemarketers and scam artists didn't usually call right back. "Hello?"

"Angel. It's Bear."

"Dude. What was that all about when I called the store? And are you using a burner phone?"

"Yes, I am. There was an FBI agent here. Sorsha Aberdeen. Asking questions about you and Dante Rosario and your dad."

"My dad! What was she asking?"

"Fishing around mostly. Like if I'd ever noticed anything unusual. I told her I hadn't seen you or Dante since Mardi Gras, and I wouldn't know your dad from Adam."

"Well, shit." I scowled. "I saw her out on Highway 51 yesterday arresting some guy. I wonder if there's a connection." I needed to tug some strings and find out why she had him stopped.

"Worth looking into," Bear said. "What did you call about earlier?"

"To tell you to keep your people out of Mudsucker Swamp. Hell, stay clear of any place with alligators."

"Yeah, Nick told me."

"Oh. How much did he say?"

"That there are some screwed up gators who can make people sick. Like you. But mindless."

I blew out my breath. "That about covers it."

"You need any help dealing with it?"

"I might," I said, grimacing. "I'll let you know."

"Do so. And be careful."

I loved biology. Loved it. It was fascinating and cool and right up my alley.

The professor, not so much. Mr. Dingle seemed vitally interested in making sure everyone knew precisely how very smart he was and how fortunate we were to be in his class. Meanwhile, I was like, Dude, this isn't Harvard. You're teaching at a community college in bumfuck Louisiana.

It probably didn't help my attitude that I worked every day in a *real* lab.

I plopped my backpack on the floor by a lab bench and parked myself on the stool. We'd already dissected formalin-preserved earthworms and grasshoppers, but during our last class, Mr. Dingle had said he was going to have a surprise for us on lab day. Gee wow. Yawn. I dissected *people* for a living. I doubted his surprise would thrill me.

Most of my classmates chatted or played with their cell phones. One woman at the back bench frantically flipped through notes. Isabella Romero, or something close to it. About my age. Raising a kid on her own.

The instant the clock ticked to the hour, Mr. Dingle strolled in—a gangly man with a wispy, mouse-brown combover. He placed a covered, clear plastic bin the size of a shoebox on the table. Inside, a live frog hunkered, looking lonely and pitiful.

He called the class to order and held up an instrument with a wooden handle and metal pointy end, like a mini ice pick. "This probe," he said as if announcing an Oscar winner, "will be used as a pith tool."

I sucked in a breath. "You're going to *kill* that poor little frog?" I blurted, aghast.

His lips separated to show teeth in a godawful abortion of a smile. "First off, *you* will pith your frog. Second, if you double pith the frog exactly as I instruct, you will destroy the brain and spinal cord. The creature will be mindless and pain-free, but very much functionally alive. Third," he said, before I could point out how much worse that was, "I'm not going to *make* you do anything." His mouth widened. "However, anyone who does not follow the proper procedures—which happen to include pithing your frog—will simply receive a grade of zero for this lab."

Groans and mutters rippled through the class.

A curly-headed guy I didn't know raised his hand. "Are we all going to dissect that one frog?"

A whisper of existential ennui flashed over the professor's face. "No, Mr. Jenkins," he said through his teeth. "The rest of the frogs are in a tank in the supply room at the end of the hall. After I lecture, we will all walk down there, and I will—yes, Ms. Sanders?"

A girl nearly as scrawny as me lowered her hand. "Why do we have to learn about frog guts anyway? It's sooooo stupid."

"Comparative anatomy, Ms. Sanders," he bit out. "Though I don't expect you'll take much away from the exercise."

I hid a scowl. If the dude wasn't such a tool, I might almost feel sorry for him having to deal with students who either didn't appreciate or didn't really *want* an education. But anything a bunch of newbie biology students could learn from a pithed frog could just as easily be learned from frogs pre-killed and nicely packed in formalin. And yeah, they'd end up dead either way, but there was no way this group would get the pithing right on the first try. And the gleam in Dingle's eyes told me he wanted us to pith the fucking frogs ourselves because he was an asshole. Assssssshoooooole.

But mostly, I didn't want to kill a frog. Sure, I'd killed humans—when they were trying to kill or hurt me or my friends. Even when it was "justified," it still sucked. Besides, the frogs weren't trying to kill me.

"Ms. Romero!" Dingle snapped.

Isabella fumbled her phone, and it crashed to the floor. "Yes, sir?"

"Some of us are trying to learn." He whacked his workbench with the flat of his hand. The poor frog flinched. "Phone. Here. Now."

"But my kid's sick. I was just check—"

"Now, Romero."

I fisted my hands to keep from flipping Dingle off as Isabella slunk to the front and deposited the phone. Dingle-the-Dick got off on embarrassing people. He'd tried that crap with me once, but this small-minded asshole couldn't touch me. I'd been through hell and back.

After she returned to her seat, Dingle droned on about the differences and similarities between human and frog internal anatomy. I felt safe enough tuning out since I'd seen more human organs than this guy ever would. Much more important was the issue of the frogs. If anyone could liberate them, it was me.

My gaze went to the door. The science building had been built in the fifties and never been modernized—which meant there were still transoms for ventilation.

The plan came together in my head. I shot my hand up.

Dingle glared at me. "What is it, Ms. Crawford?"

"I need to use the restroom."

"You should have taken care of that before class."

"It's a female problem!"

His eyes narrowed while I put on a desperate and horrified expression. But since I was undeniably female, he could hardly insist I was lying.

"Go." As he snarled the word, I activated a dose of combat mod.

It slammed through me, charging every cell with hyper-potential. The hardest part was walking at a normal-hurry speed to the door while the modified and concentrated parasite stimulant coursed through my body. But the instant I closed the door behind me—and made sure there was no one in the hall—I used every fucking molecule of that mod.

I sprinted to the end of the corridor, breaking every Olympic record for the next twenty years. At the supply room door, I jumped and caught the top of the jamb, then did a one-arm pull-up and held myself there while I propped the transom open with my other hand. With the ease of breathing, I pulled myself up and through the transom, twisting in midair to land in a crouch. I was winning *all* the Olympic medals.

I'd been in here before, so I knew there were several five-gallon buckets in the corner. At super-speed, I grabbed one. Uncovered the tank. Scooped frogs and water. Placed the lid on loosely. Opened the window. Set the bucket against the wall outside. Closed and locked the window. All in the span of about fifteen seconds.

Getting out was simple—jump up, make sure the coast is

clear, dive through, twist and land, another one-arm pullup to close the transom. Then sprint like hell back.

I stopped before the lab door and slowed my breathing, ran my hands over my hair to smooth any scraggly bits, then walked in nice and calm-like.

Dingle broke off mid-word and narrowed his eyes at me. My pulse quickened in response. Did I have frog goo on me somewhere? Had he heard me running?

"That didn't take very long," he said. "I thought you were having *female troubles*."

"False alarm," I said with a cheery shrug. "You know how it is. You feel a bit squishy, and you're not sure if it's just crotch sweat or—"

"I do *not* require an explanation," he gritted out. Someone tittered, and his scowl deepened. "If we are quite finished learning about Angel Crawford's reproductive system, perhaps we can commence the lab portion of this class. Everyone follow me."

I summoned a placid expression and dutifully marched after him to the storage room. Dingle pulled a set of keys from a pocket, unlocked the deadbolt, and marched into the room. "You will enter one at a time and take an empty container from the shelf," he announced. "I will place your frog in your container and then the next student . . ." He trailed off as he came into view of the tank and its distinct lack of frogs. "What the *fuck*." He whirled, scanning the room as if hoping they'd taken up residence elsewhere. "This . . . this is impossible. I checked the tank right before class." His mouth tightened. "Crawford! Did you do something to the frogs?"

I widened my eyes in shocked innocence, but the rest of the class leaped to my defense.

"She was only gone a minute," Curly-headed Guy said.

"The door was locked," another student pointed out.

Dingle slowly turned. "The transom. You could have climbed in over the transom!"

I scoffed. "Do you see how short I am?"

"She's right, prof," a guy said who was at least a foot taller than me. "And even if she could jump that high, she doesn't have the muscle tone to haul herself up."

"Um, thanks?"

Dingle moved to the window and checked the lock. I

watched, tense. If he got close to the glass and looked down, he'd see the bucket.

But Dingle apparently decided the intruder would have a hard time locking the window behind him, and the bushes outside were deterrent enough. He stepped away from the window, subdued. Dejected, even. If he wasn't such a flaming turdblossom, I wouldn't have been forced to ruin his day.

"Very well," he said, all trace of arrogance gone. "We shall return to the lab and," he sighed, "do a virtual dissection online."

As we filed toward the lab, Curly-headed Guy leaned close. "I don't know how the hell you did it, but I owe you a beer."

I masked a grin, but an instant later my breath caught. I'd forgotten all about the frog on the front table. I needed to find a way to save him, too. Knowing Dingle, he'd take his frustration out on the poor thing. Unfortunately, the only rescue plan I could think of involved liquid nitrogen and a tub of peanut butter. Not terribly feasible.

We shuffled into the room, and I cast a forlorn glance at the container on the front workbench.

The *empty* container. Still covered. Hot diggety damn, someone else in the class had risen to the challenge.

Dingle entered last then stopped dead as he registered the frog's absence. His shoulders sagged.

"You have five minutes to go over your notes," he muttered. "I . . . need a moment."

He turned and slumped out of the room. I bit my lip against a laugh and sent silent thanks to the unknown hero who'd rescued the last little froggy.

Chapter 12

After the class finally let out, I dawdled outside the building, pretending to be on my phone as I made sure Dingle was indeed headed to his office in the next building over. I carefully checked my surroundings for possible witnesses, pausing as I caught sight of Isabella striding briskly toward the parking lot. When she reached the sidewalk, she stopped and set her bag down, then crouched and peeked into her lunch box. Apparently satisfied with what she saw, she closed it, stuffed it into her bag, and hurried off.

"Oh, Isabella, you sneaky little minx," I murmured with a mixture of delight and admiration. If that wasn't a frog in her lunch box, I'd eat my backpack.

With that particular mystery solved, I slipped behind the bushes and retrieved the bucket of frogs with—crossing fingers—no one the wiser. Getting them to my car was a bit more challenging, especially since the only available parking had been somewhere near the rings of Saturn. Halfway there I had to stop and secure the lid after nearly sloshing a frog out. But the gods must have been smiling upon me, because no one seemed to notice or care that I was lugging a heavy bucket across the parking lot. Arms aching, I eventually reached my car and jammed the bucket behind the passenger seat—securely enough, I hoped, that it wouldn't tip over and turn my car into a traveling pond. Of course then I worried about them suffocating with the lid closed. After all, there were a lot of frogs in there.

I solved the problem by digging a pocket knife out of my console and cutting a fist-sized hole in the lid. There. Frogs could breathe, and sloshing water and frogs would still be contained.

Whistling "Rainbow Connection," I got the hell out of there.

Though I'd never performed a heroic frog rescue before, I knew the very best place to give them their freedom. A few months ago, I'd picked up a body in Belle Maison Estates, about ten miles north of Tucker Point. On my way out of the subdivision, I got lost and ended up driving around the prettiest pond I'd ever seen. The frogs would love it. And with nearly an hour before I had to be at work, I might even have a bit of chillout me-time after I liberated the captives.

Belle Maison Estates was a gated community, but like darn near every other gated community I'd been to, the gates stood open during the day. Made me wonder what the point was. Did they think Bad People only came out at night? Plus, did they realize how laughingly easy it was to get in, even with the gates closed? All you had to do was follow another car in. I snickered as I sailed through the impressive, open, and pointless gates. Security theater. Make things *look* safer and more secure, without actually being so.

Other than the silliness with the gates, there was a lot to like about the place. I made my way down peaceful, winding roads, past lovely, large houses on lovely, large lots. Walking trails wound throughout the neighborhood, and there were trees everywhere. It was obvious you had to have a lot of money to live here, but it wasn't obnoxious and in-your-face about it. Classy. Like a genteel Southern lady.

After several turns, I took a road that circled the pond and rejoined itself, like the eye of a needle. About a third of the way around, I parked in a space nestled in a grove of flowering trees, then unloaded the bucket, relieved to see that only a little water had splashed out.

I followed a path through the grove and to the water's edge. The pond was sort of a squished oval shape, measuring about a hundred yards at its longest point. Wildflowers bloomed along the banks amidst reeds and cattails, turtles sunned themselves on a partially submerged log, and butterflies flitted everywhere. A shaded walking trail offered exercise with a lovely view, and every thirty or forty yards a wrought iron bench rested beneath mature oaks.

It was gorgeous. I seriously needed to get rich so I could live here.

A woman with sleek, salt-and-pepper hair caught up in a tidy bun strolled down the trail toward me. A shaggy, mixed-breed dog padded by her side, tongue lolling.

She waved. "Hello there!"

Crap. Suddenly the bucket felt very conspicuous. I hadn't planned what to say if asked why I was dumping frogs in the pond. "Hiya!" I replied with a bright smile. "Nice day, huh?"

She approached and peered into my bucket. The big dog sat without command, ears perked.

"Parish project," I blurted. "Um, repopulating local habitats."

"I wasn't aware local frogs were on the decline," she said, accent smooth and midwestern. She tilted her head, amusement dancing in her eyes.

I scrambled to come up with my next line, but there was something disarming about this woman. "You know I'm lying through my teeth."

She laughed. "You have a passel of *Rana pipiens*—all the same size, so probably raised in captivity—in a bucket stenciled TPCC, not St. Edwards Parish."

"Oh. Crap." I squinted at the frogs then at her. "Wait. You know what species of frog they are?"

"Only because it's the most common one used in labs." She chuckled. "And I have a PhD in conservation biology with a specialty in riparian environments."

"Well, I could not be any more busted," I said ruefully. "Our jerk of a professor wanted us to pith these guys." I made a face. "It just didn't seem right to let them be killed by a bunch of students who don't give a rat's ass about learning. And what does 'riparian' mean?"

"The area between land and a river, stream, or bayou," she said without the slightest hint of condescension. "The banks, to put it simply." Her smile warmed. "In other words, I completely support your rescue of these frogs. Besides, with all the new video tech, there's no need for undergrads to work on live animals. Some states don't allow it." She grabbed the bucket handle with me. "We'd better be quick before someone from the homeowners association comes through. They'd raise a ruckus over your little relocation project."

Together, we lugged the bucket to the edge and scooped frogs into the water. They swam quickly away, leaving only ripples behind. "Buh-bye, froggies." I gave them a cheery wave, stupidly pleased at the success of my scheme. I had no delusions about what would happen to them now. Some would end up as dinner for various wildlife. Others might meet their maker beneath a car tire, or get sick and die from some dread froggy disease.

As if reading my thoughts, the woman said, "Old Blue will likely spot some of them." She nodded toward the far end of the pond where a stately heron stood motionless among the reeds.

I shrugged. "That sort of thing would happen wherever I took them. My hope is for a few to survive and go on to make happy froggy families. Either way, they're better off than if I'd left them in that storage room."

"No argument from me!"

"I'm Angel Crawford." Now that we were partners in crime, it couldn't hurt to give her my name. "Thanks for the help."

"Portia Antilles, and this is Moose." She nodded toward the dog.

"Nice to meet you both." I emptied the last of the water from the bucket. "You're a biologist? That's so cool."

"I enjoyed my work tremendously," she said. "I retired last fall."

I didn't think she looked old enough to retire, but then again I wasn't the best judge of age. Besides, maybe she had a good retirement account. "Nice place to retire."

"Yes, it is." Portia's gaze traveled over the pond before returning to me. "So tell me, do you often pilfer amphibians?"

I laughed. "No more than the average biology student, but who knows what the future holds?"

"Good to leave your options open." She nodded in approval. "How long have you been taking classes at TPCC?"

"This is my first semester," I said then winced. "I'm only taking two classes, though. I work full time as a morgue tech at the Coroner's Office."

"You must find that absolutely fascinating," she said, watching me with interest.

"I do," I said, pleased she understood. "It's *really* awesome."

"I'm very glad to hear it. And don't fret about your course load. I didn't start college until I was twenty-five."

"Well, I dropped out of high school when I was fifteen and just got my GED last year."

Portia cocked her head. "Yet here you are."

I grinned. "Yeah. Here I am. An accomplished frog thief."

She laughed then dropped her eyes to Moose as he leaned against her leg. "My assistant here is reminding me I need to get home. It was very nice to meet you, Angel. I do hope our paths cross again someday."

"It was nice to meet you, too," I said. "And ditto."

Portia gave me a parting smile then headed back the way she came, Moose trotting happily at her side.

As I watched her leave, my gaze fell on a dark blue Tahoe cruising slowly around the pond. I went still, watching and ever-so-slightly wary. There were plenty of Tahoes just like the one Pierce drove.

But not that were actually being driven by Pierce. Dark hair, powerful build, strong jaw. Yep, that was him in the driver's seat. Why on earth was he here?

I grabbed the bucket and hurried up the path to the relative concealment of the trees. Once there, I crouched and watched as the vehicle rounded the far end of the loop. Was he following me? And if so, why? I couldn't think of a single reason that made sense. Not to mention, I'd been here for several minutes already, so either he'd been pretty far behind me, or he was being impatient and looking for me now. Which *really* didn't make sense, since my car wasn't exactly concealed.

My bafflement increased as Pierce pulled to the side of the road just shy of making the full loop. Definitely not in a position to be watching me. I suspected he had zero idea I was here. He had some other goal in mind.

Wildly curious, I dashed to my car, stuffed the bucket into the trunk, then grabbed a pair of field glasses. As soon as I returned to my semi-concealed vantage in the trees, I trained the glasses on Pierce. I had a silly instant of worry that I'd see him looking straight at me through his own field glasses, but his attention appeared to be on a house up the street, the second one from the pond.

My curiosity increased about a billion percent, and I scrutinized the house in question. It wasn't a mansion like some of the houses here, but it was definitely *nice*. Two story, pale brick, with pretty landscaping full of flowers, and a half-circle driveway where a white Audi was parked.

"Vewwy intewesting," I murmured. Interesting and ever-so-slightly annoying. I needed to be at work in twenty minutes, and I had to drive past the house Pierce was watching to leave the neighborhood. He'd paid no attention to my car in the little parking lot, but he'd certainly recognize it as mine as I went by. And even though we were each here on completely separate errands, I knew damn well he'd give me grief of some sort, because . . . Pierce.

If I had to wait him out, I might as well be nosy. I took note of the address then pulled up the property tax website on my phone and did a search.

Owner: Pennington, Jane Alexis.

"Holee shiiiiit," I breathed. Pierce was stalking his ex. Or rather, Pietro's ex, who was also known as *Congresswoman* Jane Pennington. She and Pietro had dated, but Pierce had told us *no one* was to inform her that he was Pietro, zero exceptions, full stop. And clearly he hadn't spilled the beans to her, or he'd be knocking on the door instead of skulking around. I bit back on a laugh. Talk about unexpected. Pierce was always so serious and careful and focused, and here he was clearly *pining* for his lost love.

I glanced at my watch. He needed to *pine* a little faster, or I was going to be late to work.

The minutes ticked by as Pierce watched the house. Right when I was about to say to hell with it and zoom past him, he lifted his phone. After a conversation that lasted maybe half a minute, he drove off.

I checked my watch. Barring disaster, I'd make it to work with minutes to spare. Add that to freeing the frogs and meeting Portia, and this was turning out to be a damn fine day.

Chapter 13

Allen called when I was less than a mile from the morgue. "As soon as you clock in, head out to Highway 1268 near the parish line. Traffic fatality. Nick's already on his way in his own car."

"Gotcha." I held back a sigh that I'd be working with Nick again. *Yes, please, let me have more tension in my life.* But I couldn't really complain since Allen was great about scheduling my shifts around my classes. "By the way, did the, uh, exterminators ever come?"

"Wait, what? Did you see a roach?"

"No! I mean . . . *bugs.*"

"What kind of—Oh. Yeah, they came. No roaches."

"You do know I'm talking about listening devices, right?"

Allen huffed. "Yes, Angel. I get it. No bugs."

After he hung up, I muttered a few choice curses. If the morgue wasn't bugged, then how the hell had Saberton known about the gators and the shambler?

Baffled, I clocked in, snagged the van keys, then got on my way.

Louisiana State Highway 1268 was a long, two-lane stretch of nothing, giving me plenty of time to think about my life choices.

Too bad it took only about three minutes for me to accept my choices as a lost cause—for now at least. With another twenty minutes left to kill, I started the audiobook of the essay collection I was supposed to read for my English class. *Listening* to my required reading not only made these long drives bearable, but since my reading speed was about as fast as a snail on Xanax, it also saved me hours and hours of time that could be better spent doing important stuff. Like sleeping. Or watching funny videos online. Unfortunately, a legit and legal audio recording of the collection—which I'd've gladly paid for—didn't exist. Instead, I pirated a PDF copy, found a program that would read it to me, and also bought the paperback so I wouldn't feel guilty about the piracy.

The robotic tones of the e-narrator droned on as I left what passed for civilization in St. Edwards Parish. After several miles of pine forest, I crossed an ancient drawbridge where rust-covered struts supported two counterweights that would lift the entire roadway to let boats pass.

By some miracle, I made it to the other side without the bridge collapsing into brick-red dust. The pines gave way to water oaks and tallow trees, and wildflowers bloomed madly along the shoulders in a frenzy of gold and magenta and purple. I crossed yet another decrepit drawbridge, and the trees thinned, interspersed with low scrub and grass. A few miles farther, red and blue lights flashed just beyond a sharp curve.

A helicopter rose from the highway and zoomed off, heavy *thwup-thwup-thwup-thwup* vibrating my van. As I neared the line of emergency vehicles, a Fire and Rescue ambulance drove away from the scene, lights dark. I exchanged waves with the driver, then did the same with the driver of the passing fire truck.

Since I didn't know what I was dealing with yet, I left the gurney and body bag in the van and trekked up the highway past Nick's Hyundai and two Sheriff's Office cruisers. Up ahead, a gnarled oak tree hunkered twenty feet or so from the shoulder, bark gouged with old scars. Forty feet beyond the oak, a black Camaro rested upside-down like a dead insect. Halfway between the tree and car, Nick stood beside a human-shaped lump in the grass, clipboard in hand.

An odd sense of *déjà vu* tugged at me as I trudged toward him. There was something familiar about this area, but I couldn't put my finger on it for the life of me. Didn't help that I'd never been to this part of the highway. Then again, it was a desolate stretch of cracked pavement in the middle of nowhere, and there were at least a thousand similar settings in St. Edwards Parish.

A rake-thin deputy with a familiar, sunburned face rolled a measuring wheel down the centerline. He stopped at a faint skid mark and wrote something in a pocket notebook, then gave me a chin lift and smile. "Hey, Angel. Are you stalking me?"

"Hey, Connor. If I was, you'd never know it." I gestured toward the wrecked car. "Don't the State Troopers handle accidents on state highways?"

"They do, but they're dealing with an overturned chicken truck west of Longville. The Troop asked the Sheriff's Office if we'd work it until someone can break free. Since I usually do the accident reconstruction for our jurisdiction, the Captain had me come out."

I nodded sagely. "Makes sense. Who's with you?"

"Blag." Connor hooked a thumb behind him. "He's taking pictures at the other end."

It took me a second to realize he was referring to Blagojevic. "How the hell do you pronounce his name? And . . ." I stopped and peered at the oily sheen covering his sunburn. "*What* do you have all over your face?"

He chuckled. "I think it's Blah-goy-yah-vich, but my rule is I don't gotta learn any newbie's name until they've been here six months. And it's coconut oil." He pointed at his face. "My mom swears by it for sunburns. Next time, though, I'm bringing my own damn sunscreen!"

"Could've been worse," I said, expression serious. "You might've been wearing a speedo out there."

"Yeah, at least I only got burned bad on my face and neck."

"No, I meant it would be worse for everyone *else* if you'd been wearing a speedo." I danced back as Connor swung a mock-punch at me.

"Good thing you're cute," he growled.

"Aw, I'd kiss you, but I'm afraid I'd slide right off."

He winked. "You can owe me."

I blew him a kiss then continued to where Nick crouched in the wildflowers. As I got closer, the lump resolved into the badly mangled body of a white male. Blood stained the ground, but not a big pool of it—most likely because his entire torso had been crushed, instantly stopping his heart.

"Spencer Leigh. Thirty-four years old." Nick tapped a driver's license on his clipboard. His jawline bore a shadow of purple from where Douglas Horton had clipped him.

My gaze lingered on the bruise then shifted away. "Is he the only fatality?"

"So far." His mouth thinned as he straightened. "The driver has multiple compound fractures and a tenuous airway. He's being airlifted to Baton Rouge—the closest level-one trauma center."

I took in the deep gouges in the turf. "What happened?"

Nick sighed and lifted his chin toward the mangled vehicle. "Connor says it looks like the driver took the turn way too fast, overcorrected, and flipped three times. Neither occupant was wearing a seatbelt. The passenger here was ejected and crushed by the vehicle. Driver got bounced around inside." He scowled as he looked down the road. "This is a bad curve. It's supposed to be marked, but an accident a couple of years ago took out the signs, and they've never been replaced." He returned his attention to his notes. "That was a fatality, too."

My entire body went cold, as if I'd been dunked in ice water. *Glass and twisted metal. Dark blood and jagged white bone. Grey brains.*

And hunger. So much hunger.

My heart began to pound. That oak. The curve. I knew this place. I knew it because I'd been here before. A year and eight months ago.

I worked spit into a mouth gone dry. "That fatality was Herbert Singleton," I said, amazed I could keep my voice steady. "He died the day before I started working at the morgue. You told me you'd autopsied two, and neither one had a head."

"Damn, I'd forgotten all about that." Nick glanced up with a slight smile. "You have a really good memory." His smile faded as he registered my stricken expression. "What's wrong?"

I swallowed. "That was the night I . . ."

His forehead puckered. "The night you what? Angel?"

"Nick." I took a shaking breath. "I was in that car. With Herbert."

"Huh? How could you . . ." His eyes widened, and he took a step back. "Oh Jesus. The driver was decapitated. You . . . did you—"

"No! I-I didn't kill him. I wasn't a zombie then. And Herbert was already dead. That's what I was told." I hugged my arms around myself and looked away from the horror in his eyes. "I was fucked up bad that night, dying even before the crash.

Herbert had roofied my drink but didn't realize I was already high . . . I think when I started having trouble breathing, he came out here to dump my body."

Nick didn't speak for several seconds. When he finally did, his voice was brittle. "He intended to rape you?"

I let out a short, humorless laugh. "That's usually the next step after you roofie someone." A shiver crawled down my spine. "I don't remember most of that night. But I woke up in the emergency room without a scratch on me, and with a note saying I had a job waiting at the morgue." I dared a look at him, but his expression was unreadable. "Forgot you didn't know any of this." I sighed. "I mean, you found out the hard way what I am. But not how. Or why."

Nick remained still and silent for several agonizing seconds, then he glanced toward the highway as the sound of an approaching car reached us. "State Police are here," he said, tone betraying nothing of his thoughts. "You should be able to take the body in a few."

"Right." I couldn't think of anything else to say, so I returned to the van and busied myself with getting the body bag unfolded just right.

By the time the State Trooper gave me the go-ahead to remove the body, I'd perfectly spread out the body bag, organized the loose change in the console, and regained my composure.

Nick and I transferred Spencer Leigh into the bag, then Trooper Hoang helped us carry it to the highway where the gurney waited. While Nick and Hoang conferred, I wheeled the gurney to the van, teeth clenched as the cracked and pitted asphalt sent jangling vibrations through the stretcher.

Blagojevic was on his phone in his cruiser. Connor glanced up from his notes as I drew close then leaped to open the back of the van for me. He was even nice enough to help me load up the gurney, though I didn't really need the assistance since it was designed to be pushed right into the van, with the legs folding up neatly beneath it. But I had a feeling hefting a dead body for me was Connor's way of flirting.

"Thanks for the help," I said then stifled a gasp at how pale he looked despite his sunburn. "Dude, are you okay?"

Sweat covered his oily face. His throat worked as he swallowed. "Feel weird all of a sudden." His hand trembled as he pressed it to his stomach. "Must've eaten something . . ." His eyes rolled up, and his knees buckled.

"Shit!" I dove forward barely in time to keep his head from smacking the pavement. A shudder passed through him, and he began to convulse. "Nick!" I shrieked then tore off my jacket and stuffed it under Connor's head.

Blagojevic bailed out of his car. "Oh fuck!"

"Ambulance left maybe ten minutes ago," I gasped. "See if you can get them back!"

"Got it." He keyed up his radio then barked stuff about officer down and paramedics.

Connor jerked beneath my hands, face impossibly pale, with frothy spit oozing from the corner of his mouth. I rolled him to his left side into recovery position.

Nick sprinted up, tugging on a fresh pair of gloves, and dropped to his knees beside Connor. Hoang followed, speaking urgently on his cell phone.

"What do we do?" I asked.

"We keep him from hurting himself," Nick said tersely as he checked Connor's pulse.

Blagojevic lowered his radio. "ETA two minutes on the ambulance."

"How the hell could they—never mind," Nick muttered. "Doesn't matter as long as they get here fast. Good job using the jacket to cushion his head, Angel. What happened?"

"He helped me get the gurney into the van but all of a sudden looked pale. And was sweating buckets. Then bam, he dropped." I shook my head. "How can he be a cop if he has epilepsy?"

"I don't think he does, but that's not the only cause of seizures." Nick exhaled as Connor stopped convulsing. "His pulse is slow. Really slow."

Blagojevic shifted from foot to foot in consternation. "I spent all damn day with him yesterday and the day before. He was *fine.*"

"Maybe it's from the sun," I said. "Bad burn and more sun today?"

"Could be," Nick said. "Get his shirt open and a sleeve rolled up. Paramedics will probably want to start a line."

I didn't bother fumbling with buttons and simply ripped Connor's shirt wide open and the front of his ballistic vest off, revealing a fish-belly-pale chest. I tore his sleeve along the seam to his bicep—and exposed a four-inch square of gauze taped onto his forearm. A tiny spot of old blood stained one side where a scratch extended beyond the edge of the bandage. Cold dread filled my gut as I stared down at the tiny line of scabs. *No. There's no way.*

I peeled the gauze up, heart pounding at the sight of three deep scratches trailing from a pair of ugly bruises. Nick glanced over and breathed a curse.

"How did he get this?" I demanded, eyes on Blagojevic.

"Huh? Oh, alligator." He offered a strained smile. "It was the damnedest thing. Connor was working a drag line, and out of nowhere this fucking gator comes out of the water and goes for his arm. But my boy's got good reflexes and snatched his hand back before the fucker could bite down. Got grazed instead of chomped."

"He's tough," I managed to say. Leaning close, I took a good sniff and picked up a whiff of the Douglas Horton shambler smell, confirming my suspicion. Shit shit shit. This couldn't be happening. Judd and Douglas had both been dead and come back to shambler life. Connor was most definitely alive. A whole new and awful pattern.

The ambulance raced up and stopped with a squeal of tires. Two paramedics leaped out, grabbed their monitor and jump bag, and ran to us. I backed away to give them room.

"Good thing Barney wanted to stop and take pictures of that drawbridge," the driver said.

"Good thing Howard let me," Barney replied even as Connor let out a weird moan that lifted the hair on my arms.

"Whatever he has might be contagious." I wished I could come up with a way to say, "and don't let him bite you," without sounding weird as hell.

Barney simply gave me a nod and tugged on gloves. In under a minute, the paramedics had IV access and the cardiac monitor hooked up. Howard took a blood pressure then manually checked Connor's pulse at the wrist and neck. He let out a low whistle. "Bradycardia. Twenty-four beats per minute. BP fifty over palp. How's he even conscious?"

"Dunno," Barney said. "But he is, so let's roll."

Without warning, Connor lunged and clawed at the paramedics, teeth clacking unnervingly, eyes wild and cloudy.

"Shit! Restraints," Howard gritted out.

It took all of us to wrestle the slavering Connor onto the stretcher and restrain him, and then both medics and Hoang to get the stretcher loaded.

Blagojevic strode toward to his car, face filled with distress. "I'm going to follow them to the hospital."

"I'll be there as soon as I can," I said. "Keep me posted if anything changes, please?"

"Will do. Thanks, Angel."

The ambulance took off, lights flashing, with Blagojevic right behind them.

Fuck. I yanked the van door open then felt a hand on my arm. Nick's.

"I just talked to Allen," he said. "Take my car and go to the hospital. I'll take the van and check the body in." He held the keys out for me.

"Thanks." I resisted the urge to throw my arms around him in a hug of gratitude. We exchanged keys, then I paused as a stupid little worry leaped out. "Who's going to drive Connor's unit?"

"Sheriff's Office is sending someone out," Nick said, voice gentle and reassuring. "Hoang has to stick around anyway until the tow truck comes for the Camaro."

"Okay. Right." I wanted to stay right here with Nick, worrying about little shit like minor logistics—things I could handle. But I couldn't. Not with the horking shitstorm stirred up by Connor's collapse.

I quick-timed it to Nick's Hyundai. As soon as I was on the road, I called Dr. Nikas. "We have a problem."

Chapter 14

The call to Dr. Nikas didn't last long since there wasn't much to tell: Connor collapsed and started acting shambly a day after being teeth-grazed by a gator. A few minutes after I hung up, Dr. Nikas sent me a text asking me to meet up with Allen at the hospital to obtain samples from Connor. No words of reassurance or hints at a simple explanation.

Over a dozen cop cars lined the street near the emergency room, and I recognized another half dozen unmarked units in the parking lot. Connor was their brother in blue and they were here for him.

I found a spot for the Hyundai on the last row and hiked to the ER. The instant I walked through the waiting room door, worried deputies mobbed me for details of the accident scene events. I related the shambler-free version, then had to repeat it for Connor's sergeant and lieutenant, then again for the chief deputy and the sheriff himself. With every retelling, the sick feeling in my gut grew. Was Connor even really alive and himself anymore? I clung to hope since he'd never *died* like both Judd and Douglas Horton. But if he was alive and mentally whole, what then? We had no "cure" for the normal zombie parasite, much less for a mutated version.

I finally slipped away from the sheriff and found Allen scanning the crowd for me.

"This way," he said tightly. We ducked through the double

doors that led to the treatment area. The noise level dropped away, the worried hum receding to background tension.

"How'd you get access when everyone else is stuck out in the waiting room?" I asked.

"Connor's mom is on her way here from Longville." He started down the corridor with long strides, and I trotted to keep up. "I know her, and the ER doc's a friend. Between the two of them, I wrangled my way in."

"How's Connor doing?"

"Restrained. He almost bit a nurse who was trying to put in a catheter. A patient care assistant yanked her back in the nick of time."

I tensed. "Did Connor get his teeth on her at all?" If it was like his minor gator encounter, any break in the skin would do it.

"Not even close, thank god. That PCA was on the ball. I need to remember to tell his boss." Allen opened a door to our right. "In here."

I followed him into a treatment room where Connor writhed on the bed, wrists and ankles bound with padded leather restraints. A lanky black man in sky blue scrubs stood with his back to us as he made adjustments to a torso restraint. Connor's head swiveled my way, milky eyes fixed on me and tongue lolling. "Uuuuuggggguuurrraaaah."

I couldn't control my startle when the "PCA" turned to face us.

"Angel," he murmured.

"Dude, I'm so glad you're here," I breathed. Kyle Griffin. A former Saberton operative, he was now one of the Tribe's best and most loyal combat and infiltration specialists. "Allen, this is Kyle. He's, um, like me."

Allen gave a soft snort. "No wonder you moved so fast. Good work there."

Kyle inclined his head in acknowledgment. "The nurse was fortunate I was here."

I peered at his name badge. It looked totally real, with Kyle's name and picture. "Connor hasn't gotten his teeth on anyone, right?"

"Not since he arrived," Kyle said in his usual mild tone, "but his presence is an ongoing threat."

Allen's mouth tightened. "He should be in quarantine, but even that might not be sufficient."

"Maybe we should try brains," I suggested. "See if that helps."

Kyle shook his head. "Already did so at Dr. Nikas's request. Connor won't eat. Just bares his teeth or snaps. We're to hold off on any further attempts for now."

I edged closer to the bed. "We need to get him the hell away from the hospital altogether, but I have no idea how we could pull that off."

A nurse entered, clipboard in hand. "Any changes, Kyle?"

"No, ma'am," Kyle said. "Vitals are still depressed. Restraints are holding."

She gave Allen and me a professional harried smile. "I'm sorry, but I have to ask you to leave while I—"

"Dr. Renley signed off on my staying per family request," Allen said then casually flashed his badge. "Also, we're with the Coroner's Office. I was hoping to have a word with the parish infectious disease doc if he comes down."

Her brows knitted. "I haven't seen Dr. Ingram today, but a doctor from the Louisiana Department of Health and Hospitals met the ambulance as it came in. She and her assistant wanted to get samples processing ASAP. They were in here with Mr. Connor but must have left right before Kyle came in."

Kyle and I exchanged wary glances. How could they have known about Connor in the first place?

Allen didn't waver for an instant. "Well, isn't that a crying shame, Miss"—he peered at her nametag—"Patricia. I sure would've liked to speak with her. Do you happen to know what samples they took?"

Patricia gestured to the blood draw tube rack on the counter. "Four red tops and a gold, along with an opaque tube they brought with them. Saliva, cheek swab, mucosa scrapings, and even earwax, of all things. I'm not sure what else, but they may still be in the building."

"Would you be a lamb and see if you can spot them?" Allen flashed a charming smile. I'd never known Allen was even capable of being charming.

Her smile brightened. "Sure thing!"

"You're the best. And, if you don't see them, would you mind checking the log for their names? I'd be ever so grateful."

"My pleasure, Mr. . . ."

"Prejean. But please call me Allen."

She cast a coquettish look over her shoulder and bustled out.

"What the hell?" I said as soon as the door closed.

"That was awfully fast for the health department to show up here," Kyle growled.

"No, I was talking about Allen turning into some sort of seductive sex god just now."

Allen's mouth twitched. "Let's get the samples before she gets back." He unslung his messenger bag and pulled out a syringe and blood vials. "Kyle can help me. Angel, run interference."

"You got it." I leaned against the door, hard. "If that doc wasn't from the health department, I'm betting Allen's paycheck they're from Saberton. But how the hell did they know about Connor?"

"Same way they knew where and when to go alligator hunting," Kyle said.

"A damn bug." I scowled. "Even with all the sweeps."

With Connor gurgling and snapping, Kyle and Allen went to work gathering the needed samples—including earwax, in case Saberton was onto something. As they were finishing up, someone shoved the door.

"Out of time," I said in an urgent whisper, holding the door as whoever it was shoved again. Trusting the guys to scramble, I counted to five then pulled the door open. "Sorry! Dumb place for me to lean." I made a show of step-stumbling back as a stocky, brown-haired man in maroon scrubs entered and gave me a tight smile. Brad Renley MD, according to the name embroidered above the pocket. At least his attention remained on me, which meant the guys weren't in an obviously compromising position.

Allen zipped his messenger bag. "Brad, this is the colleague I told you about. Angel Crawford."

"Ms. Crawford," Dr. Renley said, face relaxing. "A pleasure. I heard you were with Deputy Connor when he went down."

"It was pretty awful. Do you know what's wrong?" Of course he didn't, but it was the expected question.

"We suspect meningoencephalitis, but don't know the cause yet. I'm starting him on broad spectrum antibiotics. They won't hurt anything if the etiology is viral, but if it's bacterial, better to initiate treatment ASAP. We'll have more answers after a CT scan and lumbar puncture."

I nodded, anxiety rising. What would a CT scan and lumbar puncture show? From what I'd gathered while working with Dr.

Nikas, the zombie parasite couldn't be detected with ordinary medical tests. It required specialized equipment, along with a knowledge of precisely what to look for. But what about the mutated parasite? For all I knew it might jump up and down and wave at the microscope, yelling, "Hey, look! I'm really fucking weird and like nothing you ever studied in med school!"

Patricia hurried in, IV bag in one hand, and a handwritten note in the other. "Dr. Renley, the EMR system is still down, but Mr. Connor's primary care physician called back." She passed him the note. "That's the medical history. No known allergies."

"Thanks. Go ahead and hang the Paxi." He glanced at Allen. "Pain in the ass. The entire electronic medical records system crashed hard about fifteen minutes ago. Couldn't even get into our backup."

"That happen often?" Allen asked.

"First time since this system was installed." He shook his head. "You don't realize how dependent you are until you don't have it."

While Dr. Renley examined the monitor readings, Patricia cautiously approached the bed. Connor let out a howl and lunged, teeth snapping, but the restraints held, and Kyle stood ready to intervene. Would she dare get so close if she knew she was dealing with a zombie and not simply an unusual case of meningitis?

She hung the IV bag of Paxibiotic alongside the larger bag of normal saline already on the pole, then ran the tubing through the pump. "Mr. Prejean?" Her tone was cool and professional, probably because Dr. Renley frowned upon staff openly flirting with visitors. "The LDHH doctor is Linda Garrison. She was on her way out just now. But she said you can give her a call later."

"Ah. Okay. I have her number." Allen glanced my way, forehead creased in puzzlement that echoed my own. Did that mean the people who took the samples really had been from the health department and not Saberton?

"I'll be right back," I muttered and ducked into the corridor. Whatever the deal was with Dr. Garrison, we needed to know for sure.

I dug my phone from my pocket as I headed out the ambulance entrance. A black Humvee sat in the physician's parking area barely twenty feet away. A bald man opened the passenger door for a heavyset woman with a long braid of auburn hair. I didn't recognize her, but the man was unmistakable. Baldy from the Saberton boat.

I raised my phone and took a photo. *Zhu-zhik!*

The woman climbed into the vehicle, apparently oblivious to the stupid little sound. But Baldy's gaze snapped my way, eyes narrowing in recognition.

Busted. He'd very likely seen my face out in the swamp, plus Saberton security no doubt had my picture plastered up on their most hated list. Not that I cared, since he was just as busted.

I scratched my nose with my extended middle finger. He closed the passenger door and sauntered around to the driver's side, locked eyes with me and grabbed his crotch before climbing into the driver's seat and slamming the door.

If there hadn't been security cameras, I'd have mooned him, so instead I settled for a good ol' Italian chin flick followed by a full-fisted "up yours."

Baldy must have realized he couldn't compete in the obscene gesture game with this white trash chick, and pulled out of the parking lot without a comeback. As soon as he drove off, I called Dr. Nikas and filled him in on the Saberton involvement then sent him the photo. "We have to get Connor out of here."

"Pierce is looking at options."

"He'd better look fast. They're doing a CT scan and lumbar puncture soon."

"Oh dear. That is unfortunate."

"And Connor is bitey as hell. The longer he's here, the more chance of someone else getting infected."

"I will inform Pierce," Dr. Nikas said, voice tight and stressed. "Keep me apprised, please."

"Wait. Sedatives aren't working on Connor, so that fits the normal zombie model, but they're starting a Paxibiotic drip right now. Is that bad?"

"Antibiotics shouldn't cause a problem, even with a mutated parasite."

"Whew. Thank heaven for small favors. I'd better get back in there. Thanks, Dr. N."

By the time I reached the room, Patricia and Dr. Renley were gone. Connor still struggled against his restraints but seemed a touch calmer. Kyle and Allen had their heads together in quiet but intense conversation.

"Pierce is working on options to get Connor out of here," I told them. "But it can't hurt to brainstorm from this end, too."

"Removing him from the hospital is one of the options," Kyle said, voice unusually grave. "The threat may need to be eliminated."

"Right, that's what I just said . . ." I trailed off as his meaning sunk in. "You're saying Pierce is thinking of outright *killing* him?"

"It's on the table."

"Fuck that. Not *this* table. Connor has a mom who loves him. There are a few dozen cops out in the waiting room hoping and praying that he's going to be fine. Pierce can't do that to Connor or to *them*."

"I'm with Angel on this," Allen growled. "No one is killing anyone."

"Not yet, no," Kyle said. "It is a last resort contingency, but Connor is dangerous."

"We'll figure out how to make him undangerous!" I all but shouted. "We don't even know if he can infect someone else since it's a mutated parasite. Surely Dr. Nikas can learn more from a live subject! We can say he's being transferred to another facility." I shot a desperate look to Allen, but his gaze was on Connor.

Kyle released a low sigh. "A fictitious transfer to another facility would raise suspicion. His family, friends, and colleagues—*cops*—wouldn't simply forget about him. There would be a hue and cry over his disappearance, which would engender the sort of attention our kind must avoid."

"But it could buy us time. Buy *him* time."

"Angel is right," Allen said, expression somber. "And even though the Connor we knew may already be gone, I won't condone murder. But if this infection spreads . . ." He rubbed his eyes. "Maybe it's time to put another option on the table. Turn this over to the CDC."

"No!" Kyle and I said in unison. Kyle eyed Allen warily as if assessing whether or not he would take that step on his own. Allen was a solid ally to zombie-kind, but we were staring at the kickoff of a potential zombie apocalypse. I couldn't blame him for thinking beyond our need to keep zombies secret.

"Look," I said, "there's no need to get radical with the CDC just yet—"

Connor turned his milky-eyed gaze on me. A sound rattled deep in his throat before it gurgled out. "*Annnnnnggggggellll.*"

A chill shuddered through me and settled in my chest. Kyle didn't flinch, but Allen backed away from the bed, eyes wide and face pale.

"It's okay," I forced out, not feeling the least bit okay. "Judd did the same with his entire cerebrum gone. It doesn't . . . mean anything." Like whether there was a chance Connor was still Connor somewhere in there.

Allen's shoulders relaxed a bit, but he stayed well away from the bed.

My lower lip began to quiver. "Connor wouldn't be in this mess if it wasn't for me. I bit Judd and—"

"Angel." Kyle snapped my name out like a whip. "Cut the shit. That's like blaming a person who transmits the flu for not keeping their immune system up to snuff."

It wasn't the same thing at all, but I couldn't marshal an argument. "Fine," I said, voice cracking.

To my utter shock, he reached out and pulled me into a hug. I'd never ever seen Kyle hug anyone—or even give so much as a pat on the back. He was the absolute last person I would have ever described as affectionate or soothing or remotely cuddly.

But, damn, he had hug superpowers. The tension and anxiety flowed away. It only lasted a few seconds, but when he released me, I felt less as if the world was about to crumble.

"Thanks," I whispered.

Connor moaned long and low then lay motionless, cloudy eyes fixed on me. I edged closer to the bed. "This is the first time he's been still?"

"Since I've been here," Kyle said.

Allen gestured toward the IV pump. "Might be the antibiotic affecting him."

"Dr. Nikas was convinced it wouldn't," I said. "But it sure fits the timing."

Kyle frowned at the monitor. "His heart rate's dropping."

Before I could ask what that might indicate, Connor wailed in what could only be agony. He went rigid, back arched and hands curled into claws by his sides.

Dr. Renley burst in followed by Patricia.

Kyle snapped out a status report as if he'd been born to his

PCA role. Renley shouted an order for IV lora-something, but called it off as Connor went limp, head lolling to the side.

"Angel?" Connor's voice barely had breath—thin, weak, and . . . scared.

A chill swept over me. That was no mindless babble. "I'm right here, Connor."

His eyes met mine, milkiness diminished to a mere haze. "Ange . . ." He let out a long sigh, and his body went so limp it seemed to sink into the mattress.

"Asystole!" Kyle barked.

Dr. Renley cursed. "Call a code."

Allen rushed out of the room with his messenger bag that contained the covertly obtained samples. Four more staff hurried in, and a flurry of activity commenced under the direction of Dr. Renley. *Intubate. Compressions. Ventilate.*

I backed into the corner by the door and watched in helpless anguish. For that brief moment, Connor had been himself. And now he was dying.

Maybe death was inevitable if the mutated parasite affected a living person? But Connor had seemed so stable earlier—in a shambler sort of way.

Earlier. Before the antibiotic. If the treatment itself wouldn't hurt the mutated parasite, what was up with the timing? I trusted Dr. Nikas's judgment. I did *not* trust Saberton. What if Baldy or Dr. Garrison had tainted the bag of Paxibiotic? They'd still been in the building when Dr. Renley ordered it.

I eased toward the IV pump where it had been shoved out of the way. Kyle flicked a glance toward me as I reached it then gave me a micro-nod, as if gleaning my purpose. Everyone else's attention was fixed on Connor, and with a smooth and super casual move, I disconnected the tubing, slipped the bag from the hook, and stuffed it under my shirt.

I quietly left the room, arms crossed over my chest to hide the lump, and found Allen by the nurse's station.

"Unzip your messenger bag," I murmured while trying to look worried rather than guilty. He obliged, and I tugged the Paxibiotic from beneath my shirt and shoved it in.

"What's that for?" he asked.

"Just a hunch. Might be tainted." I broke off as the sound of activity from Connor's room ebbed away. Dr. Renley's voice carried clearly. "Time of death . . ."

Numbness crept over my face and hands. No. This wasn't happening. This wasn't right. "I need to make a call," I gasped and lurched off down the corridor without waiting for a response.

The cops were still in the waiting room. Feeling like a coward, I exited through the ambulance doorway. I didn't want to be around when they got the word Connor had died. Couldn't.

I leaned against the wall, cool brick mildly soothing against my back. Stared at my phone.

"Angel?" Dr. Nikas's voice. I must have called him.

I swallowed past the knot in my throat and lifted the phone to my ear. "Connor died. I think the Saberton people might have poisoned him with something in the antibiotic. That's when he started going downhill." I took a shuddering breath. "Connor was *there*, Dr. Nikas."

"What do you mean?"

"In the seconds before he died, it was him. Or a part of him at least. He was scared. He knew me. It sounds stupid, but . . ."

"Not stupid at all, Angel," he said gently. "We don't have enough information about the mutation to know what's possible."

"Is he going to go dead-shambly now? Like Judd and Douglas Horton?"

"Kyle is taking post-mortem samples. I won't know until I can check them for parasite activity."

I rubbed my eyes, and my fingers came away wet. "Okay. You'll keep me in the loop? Please?"

"Of course I will, Angel. You can count on me."

I lowered the phone. The doors *shooshed* open, and Allen exited. He put a hand on my shoulder. "Angel, I was going to have Nick take care of transporting Connor to the morgue, but I need to send him on a call. I'm sorry."

"It's okay," I said. "I . . . I want to be the one to bring him in."

He gave my shoulder a squeeze. "I told Nick to meet you at the boat launch to swap vehicles. It's going to be a while before Connor's body is released to us, so I'll text you when you need to come back."

I gave him a grateful nod then returned to Nick's car and made my escape.

The boat launch wasn't exactly a halfway point between morgue and hospital, but I suspected Allen knew I liked it out there. I parked facing the river then sat on the hood. Sunset cast shimmering streaks of pink and orange across the water. Soon this day would be over. Hard to believe it had started at 4 a.m. No wonder I was exhausted. And hungry—in more ways than one, especially since I'd left my bag of brain chips in the van. I could use a burger with a side of brains right now.

Nick pulled up a couple of minutes later. I hopped off the Hyundai.

He climbed out of the van, sympathy in his eyes. "I'm so sorry, Angel." He hesitated then wrapped his arms around me. I returned the embrace, ready to open up, share the grief with him.

The scent of his warm, fresh brain made my mouth water. A shudder went through me, and I pulled away. I was a monster. No changing that. I wasn't hungry enough to try to crack his skull open, but it might happen someday.

Nick gave me a puzzled look. "Angel? Sorry, I didn't mean to—"

"It's not you. I promise. Keys are in the console." I took a step back. Safer for us both if I kept my distance in every way that mattered.

Nick gave a single nod, eyes on mine, then tilted his head toward the van. "Okay. Ditto." For an instant he looked uncertain, as if he wanted to say more, do more. But then he turned away and climbed into his car. "Call if you need anything." He hesitated again, then shook his head and drove off.

"Fuck," I said then said it a few more times. I grabbed the bag of brain chips and stuffed four in my mouth, which kept me from continuing to say Fuck until the heat death of the universe.

The van didn't have a hood I could sit on, so I leaned against the bumper and finished the chips while the sun slipped below the horizon. I tried to think of anything but Connor—biology notes, the morgue inventory, the fate of the frogs—but the mental image of his eyes floated before me, and his voice endlessly whispered, *Angel*?

My phone rang as the first stars made their appearance. Dr. Nikas.

"Kyle arrived with the samples," he said. "I've only performed the test for parasite activity on the post mortem sample thus far, but I wanted you to know that it was negative. Deputy Connor is truly deceased."

"Oh." I swallowed. That was good, right? As if anything could be good in this whole situation. "Okay. Thanks for letting me know."

"I'm very sorry, Angel. I will call again when I have more information."

I hung up. A few seconds later my phone buzzed with a text from Allen.

<It's time>

Allen helped me roll the gurney out to the van. Even using the ambulance door, I couldn't escape the grief and shock of the cops. It flowed out like a black wave, enveloping everything in the vicinity. I caught a glimpse of the sheriff holding the hand of a freckled, middle-aged woman wearing a grief-stricken expression. Connor's mother.

Averting my eyes, I loaded up Connor's body, closed the doors, and headed for the morgue.

The morgue. With Connor. Dead. My palms grew sweaty against the steering wheel.

After a year and eight months at the Coroner's office, I'd picked up more bodies than I could count, and never been bothered in the least. But this was different. This was *Connor*. Saberton had murdered him, but I was still responsible.

I pulled into the empty parking lot of a strip mall, shut off the engine, and climbed into the back to sit on the wheel well beside the gurney. Hands shaking ever so slightly, I tugged the zipper down then pushed the heavy plastic of the bag aside to show his face, the sunburn ashen now. At least his eyes had been closed. I couldn't do this if they were open.

"I'm sorry, Connor," I whispered, clenching my hands together. "I'm so sorry. It's my fault. Those motherfuckers murdered you. You weren't dead yet. I know it." A sob welled up, and I let myself bawl, gasping out the truth about the zombie situation. Of what I was. What I'd done. He deserved to know. Even like this. Even . . . dead.

Eventually the torrent subsided. I fumbled a tissue out of one of the supply bins and blew my nose. Calmer now, I placed a hand on his shoulder. Cool, not yet cold. "I'm going to do everything I can to make this right, Connor."

I reverently zipped the body bag then climbed into the driver's seat and continued on my way.

Dr. Nikas called less than a minute later—perfect timing, since I'd've been incoherent any earlier.

"My testing of the samples is in progress, with no new revelations yet. Dr. Leblanc will autopsy Deputy Connor in the morning, and Allen will run interference with any issues that might arise in the process."

"What about after the autopsy?" I asked. "I mean, is Connor still, er, a biohazard?"

"Fortunately for all, Deputy Connor's mother has decided to have him cremated which eliminates any risk."

I exhaled in relief. One tiny worry in a sea of worries taken care of.

"Allen told me that your shift is over once you transport Deputy Connor—"

"It is, and don't worry. I'm heading straight for the lab as soon as I'm done."

"No," he said, quiet yet commanding. "You are to go home and get a good night's rest. Can you be at the lab for 10 a.m.?"

I wanted to protest, assure him I could be there a lot earlier, but I knew I'd only receive another firm No. "Yeah, ten works fine."

"We'll get through this, Angel. I'll see you tomorrow."

I mumbled a goodbye and hung up. At the morgue, I placed Connor's body in the cooler and logged him into the computer.

Then I clocked out and cried all the way home.

Chapter 15

In a turn of events that would surprise absolutely no one, I slept like total shit. By 6 a.m., I was awake and staring at my ceiling—which had far less character than the one in the old house. That ceiling had been cracked and stained, and if I was lucky, a roach would skitter across as entertainment.

But this ceiling was new and white and smooth. A blank space that a piece of me envied.

My alarm was set for eight, but I stubbornly refused to turn it off, even though I knew damn well I wasn't going to fall back asleep. But shutting it off somehow felt like giving up.

I stared at the ceiling and tried to go numb. When the alarm finally beeped, I forced myself out of bed and got my pathetic ass in gear.

The route from my house to the lab was a series of scenic and mostly empty back highways. The part of me that wasn't sad, stressed, and exhausted could recognize it was going to be a pretty day and that the drive was even lovelier than usual. Patches of fog swirled along the edges of the road and wrapped around the trees. Sunlight pierced through the mist in beams so tangible it seemed as if I could reach out and grab one. Azalea bushes were in full pink and fuchsia bloom, and the occasional dogwood offered a burst of white amidst the lush green of spring leaves. Gorgeous. And wasted on me.

Okay, maybe not *totally* wasted. I'd have been a lot more miserable if the scenery was dreary. And my mood wasn't completely at rock bottom. I had enough mental energy to tell myself to pull it together. I was going to help Dr. Nikas find a solution. Or at least find out what the hell was going on and how bad it might get. Because yeah, I knew it could be a whole lot worse.

My phone buzzed with a text from Reb, the Coroner's Office receptionist. I pulled over to read it.

<Ms Portia Antilles wants you to call her. No reason given>

Delight and worry rushed through me in a confusing emotional cocktail. I'd really enjoyed talking to Portia, but what if she was simply calling to give me a heads up because the homeowners association had seen us dump the frogs? Or to tell me that the frogs had mass-suicided in the maw of the great blue heron?

I got back on the road and dialed the number Reb had included, trying not to think of even more dire reasons Portia might want to speak to me.

"Hello?"

"Hi, this is Angel Crawford—"

"Oh! Thank you so much for returning my call so quickly." She gave a warm chuckle. "The instant I left the message I realized how odd this might be, but I knew that calling back and saying never mind would be even creepier. However, I enjoyed talking with you yesterday, and since I have to be in town this afternoon, I was wondering if you'd like to grab coffee together?" She said it all in what felt like a nervous rush, which of course made me like her all the more.

"I'd love that," I said and thought I heard a relieved breath on the other end. "I have class at one today, so would noon work?"

"That's perfect. Is Dear John's Café all right? It's not far from the campus."

"I know it well," I said. "That totally works."

"Excellent! I'll see you then."

I hung up, mood improved about a billion percent.

As I made the turn onto the road that led to the lab, I caught movement out of the corner of my eye. A quick glance toward the passenger seat revealed nothing, though. Probably a trick of the light. The dappled sunlight cast shifting patterns, making it easy to think there was—

Something furry and rat-sized launched itself at my face. I reacted in the only possible way—shrieked, batted it frantically away, and slammed on the brakes. The instant the car stopped, I threw it into park then bailed out and didn't stop running until I was a good twenty feet away. Only then did I turn and warily peer at the car. The driver's door stood open, but I couldn't see any sign of a rat or bat or whatever the hell had tried to attack me.

Jesus, Angel. You've gone up against trained mercenaries. And you're acting like a weenie about a rodent?

Yeah, well, I'd yet to come across a mercenary who was weird and squirmy and jumped at my face out of nowhere.

I squared my shoulders and crept toward the open door. The Thing jumped onto the passenger seat, and I backpedaled—fast—in case it decided to lunge for my throat. But it remained motionless.

I eased closer. Not a murderous rat-bat at all, but a *frog* covered in hair and fuzz and dirt and god knows what else it had picked up from the floorboard of my car.

"Oh, you poor thing!" I scooped it up, wincing at all the stuff that clung to its skin. "You escaped the bucket only to spend the whole night in my car? I wouldn't wish that on my worst enemy." I looked around for a ditch or some other froggy-friendly body of water, but it hadn't rained in a while, and the ditches were all dry. And no way could I let the frog go by the side of the road.

"Well, Mr. Fluffy, how about I take you someplace I can clean you up?" I didn't have anything in my car I could put him in, so I set him gently on the passenger seat. "But don't jump at my face again, 'kay?"

The frog simply stared at me, which I took as a solemn promise to not cause any trouble.

A couple of minutes later, I pulled into the lab parking lot, scooped Mr. Fluffy up and headed inside. Once we were both cleared through security, I took the frog to the nearest procedure room and washed him off in the sink, then left him there while I hunted through cabinets for a suitable froggy container.

Pierce stepped in. "Angel, I need you to—" He startled as the frog let out a deep crooooooak—made even more impressive by the resonance of the metal sink. "What the hell?"

"That's Mr. Fluffy," I explained. "My biology prof is an ass and was going to have us kill our own frogs before we dissected them, so I rescued the frogs and set them all free. But this one must've escaped the bucket in my car, and I found him only a few minutes ago."

He scoffed. "Mr. Fluffy? It's a frog."

I smiled sweetly. "Yeah, well, it's kind of like how I sometimes think of you as Mr. Happy."

A flicker of amusement passed over his face, but then he sobered and stepped close. "Have you ever knowingly passed information relative to the Tribe or operations in this lab to Saberton or other potentially hostile outsiders?"

An indignant reply sprang to my lips, but I held it back as his nostrils flared. He was scenting me. My outrage dissipated. Old zombies like Pierce and Dr. Nikas were walking lie detectors— better than any polygraph. Everyone was getting this treatment. It wasn't personal.

"No," I said.

A pause, a sniff, and then, "Are you aware of anyone else doing so?"

"No."

"Where does your loyalty lie?"

This one was a little annoying. If he expected me to pledge my allegiance to the Tribe, he was going to be sorely disappointed. I folded my arms over my chest. "To the preservation and protection of all zombies."

A low snort escaped him before he stepped back. He didn't seem upset by my answer, though. "Once you've finished with your new pet, I need you in the north conference room. Meeting starts in five minutes."

"Got it. Thanks," I said and kept the bright smile on my face until he left the room. Gah. The north conference room was where the inner circle held their super private closed-door pow-wows. Even with all the stuff I'd done for the Tribe, I'd never been invited to one of those meetings. Never really wanted to be, either.

Pierce asked me to come because I'm patient zero, I told myself, but logic didn't help my overactive imagination. What if they had more information about how Douglas Horton and Connor became shamblers? And what if that information drove them to prevent more shamblers by getting rid of the source—me?

Which would be totally stupid since surely they'd want to keep me alive in order to use my unique parasite to find a cure. Besides, if they wanted to get rid of me, they'd hardly call me into their inner sanctum to do the deed. The carpet was really nice in there.

One thing was for sure, though—if they had plastic drop cloths on the floor, I was totally out of there. I'd seen enough mobster movies to know what that meant.

I transferred Mr. Fluffy into a suitable ventilated container, stuck a note on top that read "Property of Angel," then gathered my courage and proceeded to the meeting room.

About half the size of the main conference room, this one had a good deal more elegant comfort. An enormous whiteboard took up most of one wood-paneled wall, and a screen dominated another. Eight leather executive chairs surrounded a burnished walnut table, with a pad of paper and pen at each place. Best of all, there was no plastic to protect the luxurious cream carpet from blood stains.

Marcus occupied the seat at the head of the table, flanked by Dr. Nikas and Kyle. Brian sat near the other end, and across from him was a woman I didn't recognize. Mid-thirties or so, wearing a deep blue hijab. She had serious dark eyes that flicked up to me before returning to the tablet before her.

Marcus gave me a nod of greeting. "Angel, I don't believe you've met Shideh Rajavi yet. She's our accountant and financial advisor."

And she was human, too, with a brain that smelled just right to my still teensy-bit-hungry parasite. How did a human get to be part of the inner circle of the local zombie mafia? I held my questions and did the polite smile and nice-to-meet-you, which she did right back, then I took the conspicuously empty seat between Brian and Kyle. Brian was Kyle's zombie daddy, but there was no love lost in that relationship. Several years ago, Kyle had been a Saberton operative, in the final stages of aggressive lymphoma caused by an experimental combat stimulant. He'd welcomed death for long-standing personal reasons and was ready for it. But Brian stole death away from him, turning him zombie against his will—on Pietro's orders to recruit him.

Pierce entered and closed the door firmly behind him then sat at the opposite end from Marcus. Suddenly *that* was clearly the head of the table.

"Let's cut right to the chase," Pierce said, placing both hands flat on the polished surface. He launched into a quick and dirty briefing about the shambler in the morgue and how it related to me and Judd, the suspected gator involvement, the decision to go to the swamp in the hopes of retrieving the body and getting tissue samples from alligators, and finally our encounter with the Saberton thugs and all that we discovered.

My presence was justified when the topic moved to Connor, and I was asked to relate what happened before, during, and after his collapse, up to and including the hospital and his death. Once I finished, I fielded questions, even from the accountant. Kyle gave his report next—with about a thousand percent more detail than I had on the hospital events. He even rattled off Connor's heart rate and other vital signs at varying stages of the ordeal. Damn, the dude was a pro.

At long last, the others seemed satisfied that they'd wrung every scrap of information from me and Kyle.

"Angel killed Judd Siler a little over three weeks ago," Pierce said. "Then two days ago this drowning victim, Douglas Horton, decides to go for a fucking walk in the morgue. And yesterday Deputy Beckett Connor appeared to succumb to the same malady—and then died in the hospital under suspicious circumstances." He frowned at Dr. Nikas. "What have you found out?"

"I'll begin with the alligator samples," Dr. Nikas said. "All but one were normal. The tissue of the off-color gator was rife with a parasite mutation identical to the one found in Mr. Horton."

I shuddered. "What happens if an infected gator bites another animal? Will the prey go shambly?"

"I wish I knew the answer," he replied, eyes haunted at the implications. "I have some preliminary tests running, but resources are thin, and my priority *must* be the development of a cure."

"Get on with it," Pierce growled. "The samples?"

Amazingly, Dr. Nikas didn't flip him off, as I would have done in his place. "The severed hand Rachel retrieved from the Saberton vessel carried the mutated parasite, as well."

Marcus muttered something foul. "Saberton got away with

the rest of the body, which means they're in possession of the mutated parasite now."

Dr. Nikas exhaled. "I'm afraid so."

I made a hmmfing noise. "We'll be here all night if we keep calling this thing the mutated parasite. I vote we name it Eugene. Two syllables instead of six. Easy peasy."

Pierce let out an annoyed grunt, but Dr. Nikas gave me a curious smile. "Why Eugene, Angel?"

"Because it messes with *you genes.*"

Brian groaned, and Kyle almost smiled. Dr. Nikas simply inclined his head. "Eugene it is then."

"What about Deputy Connor?" Pierce snapped.

"My testing shows that Beckett Connor was infected with, ah, Eugene."

I raised my hand. "Connor is being autopsied today. Will there be a problem with lab tests and stuff? Will they find Eugene?"

"Based on the samples taken, I would say not," Dr. Nikas said. "Eugene is as cagey as the normal organism, and detection requires specialized equipment and the knowledge of precisely what to look for."

At least our secret was safe. Though it also meant we were on our own to find a cure. "Did you test the Paxibiotic?" I asked. "Was it poisoned?"

"It was untainted." The lines in his face seemed to deepen. "But he was, indeed, murdered."

"By Saberton," Pierce said. "Why?"

"I don't know for certain, but it is well within Saberton's methodology to kill for no reason other than to give themselves an advantage. My guess is they acquired the samples they needed, then killed Connor so I would not have access to a live patient."

Pierce scowled. "Why do they care? What's their game?"

"Exploitation is ever their underlying motivator. I wish I knew more."

"If it wasn't the antibiotic, what killed him?" I asked.

"The earwax sample contained an extremely high concentration of"—Dr. Nikas rattled off a long chemical name—"which is the primary ingredient in Saberton's zombie tranquilizer. The compound had been encased in a wax with a melting point close to body temperature. This delayed the toxin's delivery long enough for the murderer to be clear of the scene—and coincidentally corresponded to the administration of the Paxibiotic. I suspect what the nurse interpreted as taking an earwax sample was, in truth, the insertion of the tranq capsule into the ear canal, where it would not likely be noted on autopsy. Further testing revealed that, while the tranq merely slows the healthy zombie parasite, this particular compound is fatal to Eugene . . . and host."

Silence fell as we digested the ugly news.

"How did Saberton know about Connor?" I finally asked. "Allen said the morgue isn't bugged, but they were at the ER not even twenty minutes after we called for the ambulance."

"We swept the entire Coroner's Office building and vehicles thoroughly," Brian put in. "I don't know of any surveillance devices that could avoid detection by our equipment."

"Perhaps the phones are tapped?" Shideh asked, voice a gravelly alto.

"Calls to and from the lab are encrypted and secured," Pierce said. "Angel's phone has been checked, and neither Ari nor I have sensed a mole among our people."

Marcus tugged a hand through his hair. "We're missing something."

"Maybe we need to have a chat with Kristi Charish," I said, lip curling on her name. "Baldy must be working for her."

Pierce pressed a button on the remote, and my cell phone picture of the health department doctor and Baldy appeared on the wall screen. "We haven't confirmed Dr. Garrison's ties to Saberton, or determined whether she was coerced into assisting them. But Angel was right about her assistant. He's Harlon Murtaugh, the Saberton operative from the boat incident. But even with that connection, I'm not convinced Kristi is pulling the strings."

"We monitor her every movement," Brian said and pulled up the message app on his phone. "This morning Kristi woke at 5:40 and went to the 6 a.m. yoga class in the studio at the end of her block. She returned home at 7:10, had a cup of coffee, showered, had another cup of coffee, and ate a boiled egg and half a grapefruit. At 7:45 she called for her car, and she arrived at her office at 7:58."

I slouched in my chair. "Okay, I get it. She's probably not being a horrible psychopath in *this* situation."

"Actually, that brings me to my next point." Pierce leaned back in his chair and laced his fingers across his stomach. "Kristi Charish is a brilliant scientist who has considerable research experience with our *unique* condition." His mouth tightened into a smirk. "But, as we know, she would love nothing more than to fuck over all zombies and see to it that we become her test subjects. It's only a matter of time before she takes radical action against us, especially if she finds a way to weaponize the mutated para—*Eugene*. Personally, I'd rather not wait for the axe to fall."

"You want to take her out?" Brian asked.

"No. I want to turn her into a zombie. Make her work for us." Kyle tensed beside me.

I stared at Pierce in undisguised horror. "Are you fucking kidding?"

His gaze snapped to me. "I'm not fucking kidding. She is a potential asset and an existing threat. We remove her from Saberton and cut them off at the knees."

"But *turning* her? No," I said with heat. "That's *wrong*."

I swung around to look at the others. Kyle sat with hands clenched and expression dark. Brian was as unreadable as always, while Shideh could have given him lessons in "inscrutable." Marcus looked tense and unhappy, but then again, he looked like that a lot lately. Dr. Nikas sat with his head bowed so I couldn't see his face. Was he relieved that he might be able to work with Kristi again? He'd certainly been frustrated by his lack of progress while working alone.

I dragged my attention back to Pierce, the smug asshole. "There's no guarantee that Kristi would help us under duress. She's Kristi Fucking Charish! She's killed, kidnapped, mutilated, and tortured for her own twisted purposes. If you bring her into our midst, she'll find a way to take us down from the inside."

"Your opinion is duly noted, Angel," Pierce said with a mocking incline of his head. "Not that you have a vote in this matter."

"However, I do." Dr. Nikas lifted his head, face pale and eyes haunted. "It is but one vote of those gathered here, but I cannot support such an abhorrent and deeply offensive plan."

Kyle stood, expression hard. "Another voice of dissent here." His gaze bored into Pierce. "Not that my dissent mattered to you when you ordered me turned, but at least we had a common enemy in Saberton. I had a reason to work with you after I was . . . saved." He spat the word.

Brian's mask of inscrutability slipped, and he looked away.

Dr. Nikas cleared his throat as Kyle sank to his chair. "I know I have thus far failed to find the answers we need, but this . . . this is not the solution. If you force Dr. Charish into our service, I will not work with her."

Pierce snorted. "Come on, Ari. Do you expect us to build a second lab for her to use?"

"No. There would be no need for a second lab." Dr. Nikas stood. "What you propose is an abomination. If you move forward with your heinous proposal, I will leave this lab . . . and the Tribe."

I sucked in a sharp breath. Leave the Tribe? Dr. Nikas had been with Pierce for *hundreds* of years and had a crippling phobia of crowds.

Shock washed over Pierce's face. "You can't possibly mean that. You're overreacting. You of all people know how much we need her on our side."

"It is slavery," Dr. Nikas said, biting the words out. "We trod too close to that line when she last worked with me. Your current proposition eradicates the line altogether." He planted his fists on the table, eyes locked on Pierce. "You would deny her freedom and bind her to the Tribe through need of brains. Much like human traffickers hook their victims on narcotics in order to better force their compliance. Would Dr. Charish also be required to spread her legs for any man who desires her?"

A horrible and tense silence fell. The outrage flowed from Dr. Nikas, thick and palpable.

"You're absolutely right," Pierce said, jaw set. "But what if she agreed to be turned?"

"Without *any* coercion?" He held Pierce's gaze, and it felt as if communication beyond my perception crackled between them. Ancient zombie mojo. "You cannot be serious."

After a long moment, Pierce looked away. "I was, but I was wrong. I withdraw the proposal."

The tension vanished from the room, probably blown away by the many relieved sighs.

Dr. Nikas sat, hands trembling ever so slightly. "Thank you."

Pierce spread his hands. "I'm fortunate to have such wise counsel."

I rolled my eyes. Hadn't I said flat out it was a stupid idea? But at least Pierce had no real choice but to listen to Dr. Nikas. I couldn't imagine the Tribe—or Pierce—without the doctor. Hell, if he left, I'd be right there with him.

"What if we found someone else?" I asked. "Someone willing, I mean. Kristi is an amazing neurobiologist and researcher, but surely she's not the only person who knows that crap. And yeah, there's still the whole 'zombies are secret' thing, but what if we found someone who *wanted* to be turned? Y'know, maybe there's a scientist out there who has cancer or ALS or something equally awful who'd be willing to come work for the Tribe in return for getting their life saved by being turned into a zombie."

Dr. Nikas gave me a look of such appreciation and regard that I damn near started crying right then and there. "I believe such an avenue would be worth exploring, at the very least."

Heads around the table nodded, paired with murmurs of assent. Even Pierce looked relieved that I'd shifted the subject away from his fucked up human trafficking proposal.

Shideh tapped the screen of her tablet. "I can put out discreet inquiries."

"Very well," Pierce said. "Does anyone have anything else they wish to discuss? No? Then I believe we are adjourned." He pushed his chair back, inclined his head to everyone, then swept out of the room.

The others followed him out, but I caught Marcus's arm as he started toward the door.

"Are you okay?" I asked quietly.

His brow furrowed. "What do you mean?"

I waited for the last person to leave and close the door. "We might not be dating anymore, but I know you pretty damn well. You're miserable."

Marcus offered me an unconvincing smile. "I'm not *miserable*. I'm just . . ." The smile dropped away, and he sighed. "Disappointed, I guess. I spent so many years wanting so fucking badly to be a part of the Tribe, while wondering what the hell I'd done wrong to make Uncle Pietro exclude me." Hurt shimmered across his face. "And now, not only am I in the Tribe, I fucking lead it. Except I don't. You saw that meeting. I sure as hell didn't run it. I have minimal say in anything that matters, and it has nothing to do my skills or what I can offer." Bitterness sliced through his words. "I'm a goddamn puppet. It's worse than being kept out of the Tribe. At least back then I had a life of my own." He scrubbed a hand over his face. "And there's not a goddamn thing I can do about it. I can't even quit. It would affect everyone—Aw, shit, Angel, no no no. Don't cry."

My lower lip quivered as the tears poured down my cheeks. "It's all my fault you're the head of the Tribe," I wailed. "Which means it's all my fault you're miserable!"

"What on earth are you talking about?" He pulled me into a hug. "None of this is your fault."

"It is. It *is*." I sniffled against his chest. "When we were in New York, after we rescued you and Kyle, I told Pierce how much you hated being excluded. He said he'd made a promise to the original Pietro Ivanov to keep his family away from all the zombie dealings and drama and danger and stuff, but then I pointed out that he'd turned you to save your life, and it was really stupid to cling to that promise now especially since it hurt you to be shut out, and he said I was right and then all of a sudden he said you should become Tribe head in his place."

He tightened his arms around me. "It's still not your fault, you goose. Pietro-Pierce laid everything out for me before I agreed to it. I knew I was going to be a figurehead." A sigh escaped him. "I just didn't expect to be so . . . powerless. Useless. I suppose I had this idea of him grooming me to take over for him someday—teaching me how to lead the Tribe, or something along those lines."

I tipped my head back to look at his face. "But that's the sort of thing mortals do," I said. "Pierce was born over a thousand years ago. He's basically immortal. Why should he ever worry about training a replacement?"

A corner of his mouth tugged up. "And I've been thinking like a mortal." He took a deep breath then reluctantly released me. "Thanks, Angel. I think I needed to vent."

I cocked my head. "You don't look as unhappy." He didn't look *happy* either, but it seemed as if a bit of the weight had lifted.

"Well, other than traumatic brain injury, I'm basically immortal too, right?" Marcus crooked a smile. "So, for the sake of the Tribe, I can put up with a few years of being a puppet."

It still sounded sucky to me, but I didn't want to shatter his newfound morale. "You're tough and smart," I said instead. "You'll come out on top and be happy and fulfilled. I'm sure of it."

But, immortal-ish or not, no way was I going to sit back and watch Marcus waste years of his life feeling useless.

Chapter 16

My thoughts broke off as Raul stuck his head in. "Marcus, there's a problem." His eyes flicked my way then back to Marcus. "There are more cases. And it's on the news."

"Oh fuck," I breathed. Marcus echoed my curse.

Raul nodded grimly. "I have it paused on the TV in the media room." He departed at a jog, and we followed on his heels.

Pierce arrived the same time we did. "Dr. Nikas and Brian are on their way," he said. On the TV, a dark-haired news anchor was paused with her mouth open and eyes in mid-blink.

Less than a minute later, the other two stepped into the room, with Marla pacing beside Dr. Nikas. Marcus picked up the remote and unpaused the TV.

"—ennan Masters with a new development on the health front."

The scene cut to a clean-cut, sharp-eyed reporter standing in front of Tucker Point Regional Hospital. Brennan Masters. I'd met him about a month ago near a murder scene. I'd lent him a towel to wipe off mud, and he'd left me a note inviting me to coffee. Nice guy.

"The medical community is grappling with a new and deadly health threat looming over St. Edwards Parish. Earlier today, one person died from a currently unidentified form of encephalitis, and five more patients have been admitted with symptoms of non-standard encephalitis marked by blind aggression."

The report cut to a grey-haired, white-coated woman inside

the hospital. The crawl at the bottom of the screen read Dr. Maureen Bauer, epidemiologist.

"What we know is that the deceased and the five new patients contracted a form of meningoencephalitis. We're working in close coordination with other epidemiologists and the CDC to determine the cause."

Masters smoothly queried, "Do you know yet how this disease was transmitted?"

"We have reason to believe this form is transmitted via bites."

"Mosquito?"

"Mosquitoes can't be ruled out yet, but we suspect human-to-human bite transmission is currently the primary means. The infected patients are aggressive, and there's strong evidence that human bite wounds were the source of infection in at least three cases."

The scene returned to Masters outside the hospital. "If you come across anyone exhibiting symptoms, including extreme pallor accompanied by sweating, convulsions, or radically heightened aggression, call nine-one-one immediately. Please do *not* engage with any possible victims."

The news anchor thanked Masters for his report. "And now Dana with the weath—" She froze with her tongue between her teeth.

Marcus lowered the remote.

"I'll call Allen." I left the room and hit his number with shaking hands.

"I was just about to get in touch with you," he said. "You saw the news?"

"Yeah." I swallowed. "Connor and five more patients."

"The report left out some details. Patient One is the nurse we saw in Connor's room. Patricia."

"Oh no. He managed to bite her."

"Maybe just grazed her, or maybe the shambler pathogen is transferred by other means as well. We don't know."

"Shit. What about the others?"

"Patients Two and Three are brothers. They're not sure how the twenty-year-old contracted it, but he works in the hospital cafeteria. The parents were on the way to the ER with him last night when he bit the seventeen-year-old. Less than an hour later, little brother became aggressive, and both parents were bitten and infected." He paused. "It's bad, Angel."

"I know," I choked out. "It's awful."

He sighed. "Let Dr. Nikas know he can call me twenty-four seven if need be."

"I will. Thanks."

He hung up. I returned to the media room and related what Allen had told me. "Pierce, have you ever seen anything like this before?" I asked. Desperately.

"No, but that doesn't mean much. Before the twentieth century and rapid communication, I had little knowledge of events beyond my local area."

Dr. Nikas pinched the bridge of his nose as if he had a headache. "I will speak to Allen," he said then left with Marla. Pierce did a come-with head nod to Marcus, and they departed, leaving me alone with the news anchor and her weirdly bared teeth.

I sank to the couch, stomach a tight knot of acid. I wanted to be numb, too shocked and upset to feel anything. But I didn't deserve that luxury, not when I was the one responsible for this catastrophe. There was absolutely no denying this was all my fault. Horton and Connor. Dead. And now five more people were infected. Connor had been murdered, but what if the disease itself was fatal?

If I hadn't abused the V12, I wouldn't have damaged my parasite, and I couldn't have infected Judd, which meant the alligators that ate his remains wouldn't be all zombified. And sure, even as normal gators, they might've chowed down on the hunters, but Douglas Horton wouldn't have turned into an undead monster.

And Connor would still be alive.

I forced myself up off the couch. Enough wallowing in misery. Sure, I'd fucked up bigtime with the V-12, but who the hell could've anticipated it would result in contagious *zombie-gators*? All I could do now was look for ways to put out the dumpster fire I'd started. Dr. Nikas was hard at work on the issue, and he knew more about zombies than any other zombie alive.

Or maybe there was someone who knew zombies even better. Maybe a certain someone who was a couple of thousand years old.

I made my way to the medical wing and Kang's room. The door was closed, so I quickly punched in the code then slipped in and shut it behind me.

Kang lay gauze-wrapped in the bed exactly as I'd seen him

the other day. Squiggly lines continued to crawl across the monitor screen, but his eyes remained stubbornly closed.

I sat on the chair, propped my elbows on the bed, and planted my chin in my hands. "Kang, it's Angel. Again. I really need you to wake up. Please. There's some bad shit going on, and I'm hoping you might know a way to fix it or help us out with your ancient zombie mojo smarts. People are . . . shambling. I don't know what else to call it. And it's all my fault. I got addicted to the V12 mod, and it really fucked up my parasite, and then I went and bit a guy named Judd who was trying to kill me but then he got wasted by another dude and so I ate Judd's brain but I didn't eat all of his brain 'cause I was in a hurry and had to escape into the swamp, but later that night Judd fucking came into the swamp and found me even though most of his brain was gone. And he was all *Night of the Living Dead* and shit. But I killed him again for good, so I thought everything was okay. But a couple of days ago a hunter got in a boat accident and drowned, then got bit by an alligator, or got bit by a gator then drowned, either way he woke up in the morgue and came after me all *urrrrrrrrrr* so we figured some gators must have eaten Judd and got infected. And then yesterday a really decent cop who'd been grazed by alligator teeth collapsed and started going shambly. But then some Saberton fuck *killed* him. He didn't deserve to die. And now we have zombie-gators out there, and Dr. Nikas is trying to find answers, but we don't know jack shit about curing a shambler and . . . we're so screwed."

I massaged my temples. Kang remained frustratingly unconscious. I couldn't even annoy him awake with my unchecked blather.

"Wake up," I snapped. "Wake the fuck up. I need you." I pressed my middle knuckle in the center of his sternum and twisted.

Nothing.

"Goddammit, Kang. I know you can hear me. Please." I gulped back a sob. "What the hell do I have to do? Bribery? Barter? Blackmail? How's this: if you don't wake up, I'll post pictures of you looking like a mummy all over the internet."

Was his steady breathing a teensy bit faster? I yanked my gaze to the monitor. The pulse had climbed two whole beats per minute. Didn't seem like a lot except for the fact it had been steady at fifty-two since he came out of the tank.

I clenched my hands together as adrenaline set them shaking. "That's right," I said. "If you don't wake up, I'll upload a pic of you to one of those Photoshop battle sites. Next thing you know, there'll be pictures of mummy-Kang getting ass-fucked by bin Laden."

Kang's chest shifted as he drew a deeper breath. I froze, certain that if I so much as twitched, I'd scare him back to the safety of his coma.

"Would . . . break . . . internet," he whispered, eyes open a crack.

I leaped to my feet and punched the air several times. "Is it too bright in here?" At his infinitesimal nod, I rushed to the wall and dimmed the lights to about quarter strength. "Better?"

"Much," Kang rasped, opening his eyes more. He cleared his throat, wincing a bit. "Angel. I . . . saw you. In the tank. A dream?"

"Nope, it was me," I said. "I had a little problem and had to be regrown, so I know a bit of what you were going through."

"A problem . . . such as mine?"

"No, not the serial killer. I, uh, had trouble with one of Dr. Nikas's parasite supplements."

Questions swam through his eyes, but he merely gave a nod. "Has the killer been stopped?"

"Yeah. It was Ed Quinn—the paramedic. But he's in Costa Rica now since it kinda wasn't his fault. He was coerced and brainwashed by Kristi Charish to kill zombies. It's a long story, but Kristi had your head—frozen—then Pietro got it back, and Dr. Nikas here did the work of regrowing you."

"How long has it been?"

"Ed attacked you about a year and a half ago."

He wheezed something in a language I didn't recognize. "So much time lost due to my own hubris. I should have listened when you warned me of the threat."

"Yeah, well, I can be smart sometimes."

"I have little doubt." A faint smile flickered across his mouth then faded as if it was too much effort to maintain it. "You look well."

"I am. Now, at least." I winced. "You've missed a lot."

"You'll catch me up—" He broke off, eyes flicking to the door. A half second later the sound of running footsteps reached my ears.

Crap. I darted to the door and punched in the code, yanking it open just as a red-faced Pierce reached it. "Kang's awake!" I announced with a cheery smile. "I was about to come tell you!"

The red darkened a shade. "You should have notified me *immediately*," he snarled and pushed past me. He stopped at the foot of the bed, crossed his arms and gave Kang a fierce smile. "And now we can finish our *conversation*."

Kang gave a slow blink. "Who . . . the fuck are you?"

I stifled a giggle. "Oh yeah, that's another thing you missed. This is Pietro! Though now he's known as Pierce Gentry."

Pierce shot me a furious look.

Kang began to make an odd gasping sound. Alarm shot through me until I realized he was laughing.

"I wondered how long you . . . would tolerate that aged form, forced to watch others fight your battles, itching to wade into the thick of the action."

"The Pietro identity was a necessary sacrifice for the good of my people," Pierce said through his teeth. Though he kept his arms folded over his chest, the muscles stood out like cords. "I didn't abandon it for selfish reasons."

"Of course not. You are an ever-suffering saint."

Pierce bristled. "There are only a select few who know Pierce Gentry is the same person as Pietro Ivanov. It's best if we keep it that way." He stabbed a dark glare at me.

I was immune to them by this point. "Jeez, I know! But this is *Kang*. Like your zombie daddy wouldn't know you?" I glared right back at him. "And surely Kang would need to know you're a Pietro-Pierce mashup if y'all were going to finish some super special *conversation*."

Before Pierce could squash me like a bug, Dr. Nikas stepped in, breathless. I gave him a triumphant grin. "Dr. Nikas, look who's finally awake!" I gestured brightly to Kang then let out a sour *hmmf*. Kang's eyes were closed, and the activity on the monitor was back to his pre-waking levels. "Well, he *was* awake."

Pierce rounded on Dr. Nikas, face suffused with rage, and hands tightening into fists. "Wake him up, Ari. *Now*."

"I will not," Dr. Nikas replied, voice as calm as a crisis counselor on Valium. I started forward to defend him, shocked by Pierce's sudden fury, but he gave me a micro head shake.

"I've waited long enough already," Pierce growled. "Wake. Him. Up."

Dr. Nikas remained icy cool in the face of Pierce's heat. "No."

For an instant I was certain Pierce would strike Dr. Nikas, but then he spun away with a guttural cry and slammed his fist into the wall, penetrating the heavy plywood. Teeth bared, he yanked his bloody hand free and stormed out.

Silence descended.

I gulped and tore my eyes from the hole in the wall. "What the hell was that about?"

Dr. Nikas let out a small sigh. "It's all right. The rage will pass soon enough."

Frowning, I peered at him. "You've seen him like this before."

He let out a longer sigh. "Too many times. It's rare to see him thus lately, but the unchecked anger still occasionally surfaces when he grows deeply frustrated." He turned away and busied himself checking Kang's vitals, giving me the distinct impression he didn't want to talk about it anymore.

I held my burning questions and instead replayed the incident in my head. Pierce's blowup had been startling, but Kang's behavior had been odd, too. He'd been awake and coherent and talking. And then . . . not.

Dr. Nikas gave me a slight nod then quit the room, closing the door behind him. I returned to the chair and took Kang's hand. It remained limp and cool, but he wasn't fooling me. He was faking being asleep. I was positive. There were plenty of reasons he might do so, and one stood out neon-bright: He didn't want to answer Pierce's questions.

Yet eventually Pierce would find a way to wring the answers from him. I didn't know whether Pierce or Kang was in the right, but it felt *wrong* to force Kang to reveal a secret he'd prefer to keep.

"Pierce has been itching for you to wake up ever since he got your head back from Kristi's lab," I murmured, shifting my grip so we were palm-to-palm, with my hand beneath his. "I sure hope you'll tell me what the big deal is. Soon." My pulse quickened as I used my middle finger to trace four numbers in his palm. I was trusting my gut, even though it had steered me wrong a time or three. *"Sure, it's okay to get back together with Randy. For the fifth time."* Or *"I'll try OxyContin just this once. Can't get addicted on only one pill."* Or, more recently, *"Dosing myself with V12 is a good idea and worth the risk."*

But this felt different. I hoped.

After a brief pause, I traced the numbers again. If he was awake, he'd understand what I was doing. If he wasn't awake, then I was worrying over nothing, and no harm, no foul.

"All right, dude. I have a coffee date with someone a whole lot livelier than you." I withdrew my hand and stood. "Catch you on the flip side."

I punched my four-digit code into the keypad by the door and left.

Chapter 17

Though Tucker Point had a number of coffee shops and cafés, Dear John's was my hands down favorite. Not only did it have excellent coffee and pastries—baked fresh on the premises—but it was also in convenient walking distance from the morgue. Not to mention, the place had a cool origin story. A decade ago, John Hickey had received a literal "Dear John" letter from his then-wife after she left him for his brother's ex-wife. Hickey decided it was time for a change, quit his job, and invested everything in the café. Last month he'd opened another café in Longville, and rumor had it he was looking at commercial property in Baton Rouge for a third location.

Meanwhile, I was happy to support his ambition by indulging in his super yummy hot chocolate at every opportunity.

There was no sign of Portia when I arrived, but that was forgivable since I was early. The café was at the end of its lunch rush, and after ordering my hot chocolate—extra chocolate, extra whipped cream—I snagged a table by the window that also allowed a view of the door. I had Mr. Fluffy's container with me, though I'd stuffed it into a paper grocery bag, since I suspected the café workers would be less than thrilled at the frog's presence. I warned him quite firmly to not make any croaks, then placed the bag under the table and savored my super excellent hot chocolate.

Portia arrived a couple of minutes later, managing to look

elegant in jeans and a simple pale green shirt. She scanned the room, face breaking into a smile when she spied me. After making her purchase, she settled into the chair across from me with a cup of herbal tea. "I hope I haven't kept you waiting long."

"Not at all. And I have a bit of a surprise for you." I motioned for her to look under the table then unrolled the top of the bag. "*Rana pipiens*, right?"

Portia chuckled. "Excellent memory! Did you pilfer more?"

"No, this one escaped the bucket. I found him hiding out in my car, and I was hoping you might take him to join the others?"

"It would be my pleasure," she replied with zero hesitation and set the bag by her purse.

"I'm really glad you called," I said. "The past twenty-four hours have been kind of shitty." I hesitated. "Dunno if you heard about the deputy who died yesterday."

Her brow furrowed with concern. "I saw it on the news. Was he a friend of yours?"

"Not close or anything, but we'd worked a bunch of scenes together. Kinda half-ass flirted with each other but nothing serious." I curled my hands around my mug, wishing I could draw all of its warmth into me. "But I was with him when he collapsed . . . and in the ER with him when he died."

"Oh, Angel. I'm so sorry."

Tears stung my eyes. I grabbed a napkin to blot them away. "Sorry."

"Don't be," she said, warm and firm. "You're more than justified, and it's far healthier to express your grief."

"It's just *bullshit*, y'know? He was a really nice guy." I crumpled the napkin in my fist. "I've seen a lot of death. So much of it is stupid and pointless, but this . . . he didn't deserve it." My throat clogged, and I covered by turning away to blow my nose. I wanted so badly to share my sense of guilt over Connor's death. I couldn't help but feel she'd understand. But opening up would reveal too much.

"No, he didn't deserve it," Portia said, emotion rippling through her voice. "And the fact that it was sudden and unexpected makes it all so much harder."

I met her eyes. "You've lost someone suddenly?"

"My husband," she said and gave me a soft smile. "Last October. Massive heart attack. And then a few weeks later, my friend and neighbor lost her fiancé in a plane crash."

"Ah, shit."

Portia chuckled. "I used that word and many others. As did Jane. The two of us went through a truly profane amount of ice cream together in the following month."

Something clicked into place in my brain. "Jane? You mean Jane Pennington?" How many other Janes could there possibly be who lived near Portia and whose fiancé had died in a plane crash? Or, in her case, *pretended* to die in a plane crash.

"Yes. The Congresswoman."

"I know her," I said. "Actually, I met her through Pietro, her fiancé. I dated his nephew for a while."

Her face brightened. "What a small world! I liked Pietro quite a bit."

"Yeah, he was cool." Then, since I felt like I needed to add something nicer, I said, "He helped me out a bit with tuition." Technically, the tuition had been covered by the bonus the Tribe had paid me for helping rescue zombies from Saberton's New York lab, but "helped me out a bit" was a tetch more discreet.

"And now you're an expert frog rescuer."

"Go with your strengths, right?" I grinned and took a sip of hot chocolate. "You told me you didn't start college until you were twenty-five. Why so late?"

"I got pregnant when I was sixteen," she said with a wry twist of her mouth. "My parents sent me to live with my grandmother in Atlanta, and I was kept out of school—to avoid embarrassing the family." She shook her head. "I was angry at my parents for sending me away, and furious when they told me I had to put the baby up for adoption or be cut off completely."

"Wow, they sound like assholes."

She grimaced. "It was a different time, and they did what they thought was best for everyone. I didn't have a choice. But after I gave up my baby, I refused to return home. I lived with my grandmother and finished high school in Atlanta." Her nose wrinkled. "I was nineteen by the time I graduated, thanks to missing a year of school. Then I was too proud to ask my parents for college money"—Portia rolled her eyes at her foolish younger self—"so I stayed with Grandma and found a job that helped pay the bills."

"What happened at age twenty-five?"

Her expression softened. "I met Korbin Antilles. A lawyer, eight years older than me, and already on the fast-track to partner in the firm where he worked. We were married barely six months later, and I was in college the following semester with his unwavering support."

"That's a seriously cool story," I said fervently. "Do you know anything about the baby you gave up?"

"I do," she said, smiling. "About a decade ago he went looking for his birth mother and found me. He's an engineer. Had a great childhood." She turned her hands over and examined them. "Part of me wished I could have watched him grow up. But letting him go was the right choice."

"You and your husband never had kids?"

"We tried for years with no luck." Portia chuckled. "According to the doctors, my husband had slow and scarce swimmers. We discussed alternatives but finally decided having children simply wasn't a priority for us."

I can't have children, I realized, and it felt like a blow. I'd never really thought about it before, but no way could a zombie carry a baby to term. And now that it was off the table, it had a lot more emotional weight.

Portia must have sensed my downward spiraling mood, because she steered the conversation to lighter topics, such as the new movie theater and the never-ending construction on 7th Street. By the time we got to the latest scandal involving the Chief of Police, I'd shaken off the brief funk and giggled with her about the goat and the alien sex doll found in his office.

All too soon, Portia glanced at her watch and sighed. "I have to go, and so do you."

English class. Bah. "I really enjoyed this. We need to do it again."

She glanced away, and for a godawful second I was sure I'd misjudged everything, and she was going to make an excuse about how busy she'd be for the next year painting her toenails and reorganizing her sock drawer and washing her hair. But when she looked back, there was only a gentle, faraway sadness in her eyes. She reached across the table and squeezed my hand.

"I hope we can," she said, her voice ever-so-slightly rough. "I'd like that."

Before I could say another word, she gathered up her purse and Mr. Fluffy and hurried out. It felt like fog had rolled in and masked her sunshine, and I wanted to chase her down to give her a hug and tell her everything was going to be all right. But, I didn't. She'd think I was crazy, and besides, my gut was probably wrong.

I dropped a dollar in the tip jar and headed out. Portia waved as she pulled out of her parking space. I smiled and waved back—and kicked myself.

Dammit. I *did* trust my gut. I didn't know why, but that lady needed a hug.

Too late now.

Unlike Dingle, the English instructor was a nice guy. Young, sorta cute in a nerdy way, but very unforgiving when it came to spelling errors or comma splices. I was starting to get the hang of punctuation, but spelling was my nemesis thanks to my dyslexia.

Fortunately, the universe gave me a break, and Mr. Worthing didn't assign one of his dreaded in-class writing projects. I had too much on my mind to focus, plus I never earned better than a C minus on those stupid things because there was never enough time for me to make it coherent.

Instead, we launched into a class discussion about how to write a clear thesis statement and come up with logical support for assertions. I threw myself into the conversation since not only would it pump up my class participation grade, but it also served to distract me from the impending shambler epidemic.

Yet as we talked about the oh-so-important freshman-level essays, something clicked for me. The principles could easily carry over to my science-y work at the morgue and lab in the form of clearer and more concise reports of observations. For the first time, I saw English Comp as something besides a total pain in my ass.

Before I knew it, class was over, and everyone was gathering up their stuff to leave. As I headed for my car, I dug my phone out of my purse and turned it on. The only thing Mr. Worthing wasn't nice about was cell phones. They had to be off and stowed away. If he caught sight of a phone during class, the offending student would be marked absent and get zeroes on any in-class assignments.

I had no messages from the lab—which I hoped meant no new shamblers—but there were back-to-back missed calls from an unknown number, followed by a voicemail from Reb at the Coroner's Office.

"Hey, sweetie. A lady called for you. Said it's urgent. The name is Dr. Charish, and her number is . . ."

I didn't hear the rest due to the blood roaring in my ears. Kristi Fucking Charish.

Of course then I had to replay the whole thing since I'd zoned out. Reb gave the number and finished with, "She was real nice and polite, but sure seemed to want a callback ASAP, hon. I'll text the number over, too, so you have it right there."

My hands went icy, and a lump of undisguised fear settled in my gut. I found Dr. Nikas's number in my favorites but paused with my thumb hovering above the screen.

ASAP. Kristi had left the message with Reb nearly an hour ago, and no way would a call about this to Dr. Nikas be short and sweet. What if Kristi already had some horrific plan in motion? Or what if she had my dad or someone else close to me in her crosshairs? She'd ordered my dad kidnapped once before. Nothing was off the table where she was concerned.

I punched in Kristi's number before I could dither any longer. Time was ticking away, and I'd have more info for the Tribe if I knew what her game was. I forced myself to breathe deeply and evenly. The last thing I wanted was for Kristi to know I was rattled.

On the fourth ring, she picked up. "Hello, Angel," she purred. "What took you so long?"

"I was in class." I throttled back the snarl that hovered behind the words. "What do you want?"

"Class?" Amusement colored her voice. "Sounds fascinating. Are you learning to cook? Knit? Or are you finally making a go at finishing high school?"

"It's *college*," I spat, instantly annoyed at myself for letting her goad me.

"That's absolutely *adorable*. Kudos to you for pulling off the con. It doesn't say much for the college's standards, of course, but it fools people into thinking you're just a teensy bit smarter than you really are."

Ugh. Nope. Not gonna rise to that bait. "What the fuck do you want that's so goddamn urgent? And I swear, if you've fucked with my dad or any of my friends, I'll rip you apart with my bare hands."

She made a tsking noise. "I'm utterly wounded you would think that. No, darling. I'm calling to offer my help."

"Help?" My brain fumbled for purchase. "With what?"

"With that tragic little homage to *The Walking Dead* you have going on down there. You lot have a serious problem on your hands."

That was the understatement of the year. "Why would you help us?"

"You truly are thick. Your zombie epidemic needs to be stopped before it gets completely out of control. I'm offering my help because a) I'm the best goddamn neurobiologist in North America and the only one with knowledge of the zombie parasite. Those CDC morons will spend years simply trying to determine what the hell they have. And b) I have no desire to become one of the shambling horde, so it behooves me to do my part to put a quick end to it." She gave a low chuckle. "Besides, Ari and I have worked together before. With our combined intellectual resources, we'll make short work of this disaster."

Shit. Her reasons were more than plausible. "I can't answer for Dr. Nikas or the Tribe. Why didn't you just call them directly?"

Kristi let out an impatient huff. "I don't have the lab's number. I do have yours. And, now, you're wasting precious time. Contact Ari and pass along my offer. I can be reached at this number." She disconnected.

I made several obscene gestures at the phone then called Dr. Nikas.

"Angel. What is it?" He sounded harried and stressed, but that was normal lately.

"Kristi Charish." I quickly told him about the conversation and her offer. When I finished, he heaved a sigh.

"While I am understandably wary of her proposal, I confess to a generous amount of relief. Though I doubt Pierce will view it in a favorable light, especially right now."

I frowned. "Right now? What happened?"

"Kang is gone."

Chapter 18

Marcus paced the length of the north conference room while Brian pulled up the surveillance video. Dr. Nikas sat at the table across from me, and I silently counted to a thousand to keep any hint of guilt off my face. Not that I felt the slightest bit of remorse about helping Kang escape, but no sense being obvious about it.

Brian clicked a button. "Here's Kang's room right before he makes his move." The wall screen lit up with a view of the gauze-wrapped Kang lying motionless on the bed, the closed door visible beyond him.

For nearly half a minute nothing happened. Then, moving almost too fast to follow, Kang leaped from the bed and to the door, punched a code in, and slipped out.

"How did he have a code?" Marcus demanded.

I shrugged. "If he was really awake the whole time, he could've watched any of us put it in."

Marcus scowled, but appeared to accept my hypothesis. It was a darn good hypothesis, too, especially considering I wasn't *stupid*. I'd given Kang Pierce's code—which I knew because I'd watched him use it more times than I could count.

Brian played it again at half speed, giving a nod of appreciation at Kang's economy of movement. When it finished, he switched to the feed from the hallway outside Kang's room, side by side with the view of the corridor that intersected it. He glanced at us and winked. "Pierce would kill me if he heard me say it, but I could watch this next part a million times."

He hit play. On the left, Kang exited his room and broke into a sprint toward the main corridor. On the right, Pierce strode with grim purpose down said corridor toward the intersection.

Marcus groaned as he realized what was coming. I bit the inside of my cheek to hold back a laugh.

As Pierce rounded the corner, Kang—without breaking stride, and with timing so precise it would put the space program to shame—leaped at him, somehow twisting in midair to seize Pierce in a chokehold from behind.

Kang sank his teeth into Pierce's trapezius. Pierce shuddered and let out a low moan then went quiet.

Marcus stepped forward. "What the fuck just happened?"

"Kang did a control bite," I said in awe. I'd instinctively done the same thing to Philip a year ago to keep him calm, but with nowhere near the pizzazz Kang had shown.

Dr. Nikas gave a reluctant nod. "He did indeed." On the screen, a glassy-eyed Pierce walked to the far end of the hallway with Kang on his back like a gauze-wrapped tick.

Brian stopped the video. "Pierce walked him all the way to the garage and out—after first giving him a cooler of brains and a set of scrubs."

"Pierce could not have hoped to resist," Dr. Nikas said. "Not against Kang."

"Because Kang is his zombie daddy," I added sagely.

"So that's it then?" Marcus asked, frowning. "Kang has escaped, and we're not going after him?"

"How could he *escape* if he wasn't a prisoner?" I asked sweetly, earning myself an exasperated look.

"What do you hope to gain from his recapture?" Dr. Nikas asked.

Marcus opened his mouth then closed it again. "Fuck if I know. Pierce never saw fit to tell me what he wanted from Kang." He threw up his hands. "Fine. Kang is gone. More power to him. Now we can focus on the Kristi Charish shitstorm. Brian, will you catch me up on the latest intel?"

Brian and Marcus retreated to the far side of the room. I took the seat beside Dr. Nikas, wishing I knew how to erase the lines of stress on his face. "You want Kristi's help."

A sad smile touched Dr. Nikas's mouth. "I cannot deny that

her insight would be exceedingly valuable. And her point about having a personal stake in this is compelling. She wouldn't want to risk the contagion spreading such that she herself might become infected, nor do I see her as genocidal via inaction." At my blank expression, he clarified. "Not helping when she could unlock the answers."

"I totally hate her, and I don't trust her, but this is too important. I'll support whatever you decide." I tapped my nose. "You and Pierce can tell if she's lying, right?"

"Alas, it's quite difficult with her, unless she is caught off guard. She is comfortable in her lies, meaning there's little change in her body chemistry through guilt or fear or anxiety, thus rendering our senses unreliable."

The door banged open, and Pierce stepped in with Kyle right behind him. Pierce looked even grumpier than usual, which was no surprise considering Kang had made him into a Pierce-puppet.

His untamed eyebrows drew together in a glower. "There've been three new cases, according to my contact at the hospital." He and Dr. Nikas exchanged a long look that practically shouted, *We may not have a choice about accepting Kristi's offer.*

Kyle cleared his throat softly. "My contact in Chicago has informed me that Dr. Charish asked her assistant to ensure the Saberton private jet would be available this evening."

I frowned. "She sure is confident we'll welcome her with open arms."

Dr. Nikas pushed to his feet. "No. Confident that *I* will." The lines in his face deepened. "I'm sorry."

Pierce moved to him and took his arm. "There's nothing to be sorry for, my old friend. You've saved us a thousand times over already. I won't fault you for failing to be omnipotent."

"None of us will," I said.

Dr. Nikas's gaze traveled the room, resting briefly on each face before he dipped his head in acknowledgement. "It has always been my privilege and honor to serve the Tribe thus," he murmured, though his eyes still looked bleak, and he didn't smile.

"Are we doing this?" Marcus asked, forehead creased. "Allying with Charish?"

"We are," Pierce said, voice resolute. "Angel, give me the number she called you from." Then added, "Please."

Slightly mollified by the attempt at courtesy, I found her number in my previous calls and held it so Pierce could dial it on the conference room phone.

"Marcus, you'll need to speak for us," Pierce said. "Tell her we welcome her here, but she'll still have to submit to our security screening." He dialed the number and pushed the speaker button.

I held back a derisive snort. Sure, Marcus would speak for the Tribe, but Pierce would feed him the words.

The ringing filled the room. Everyone stared at the phone. Five rings. Six. Didn't the bitch have voicemail?

On the ninth ring, Kristi picked up. "This isn't Angel's number," she said, voice silky and filled with confidence. She had the upper hand and knew it.

Marcus straightened. "Dr. Charish, this is Marcus Ivanov. I speak for Angel and the rest of us when I say—"

"How wonderful to hear your voice, Marcus! It's been ages. I think the last time we chatted was at a party at your dear departed uncle's house."

Marcus cut a sharp look at Pierce. "Yes, it's—"

"But if you've called to discuss my *very* generous offer, it's Angel with whom I'll speak."

Pierce rolled his eyes.

"Angel's right here," Marcus said, giving me a helpless shrug.

"Ready and waiting," I said with a heap of false cheer.

"Lovely. Take the damn thing off speaker. And everyone but Angel can leave the room."

Marcus stepped back as if more than happy to relinquish this bullshit. Dr. Nikas squeezed my shoulder as he passed. Pierce looked ready to chew nails and didn't budge.

I gave him a nod and picked up the handpiece. "Okay, it's off speaker, and everyone else is gone. Though I'm not sure why you bothered with that. You know damn well the phone lines here are all monitored and recorded."

"Oh, I know. Call it performance anxiety." She trilled a laugh. "Besides, this feels friendlier, don't you think?"

"Like hugging a cactus," I muttered. "Anyway. You're invited to the lab, and Dr. Nikas will share what he's done so far."

"That won't do. A few too many unpleasant memories at that lab."

"I know all about unpleasant memories," I said through my teeth. "Abandoned factories, animal cages, that sort of thing."

"I will use the facility at NuQuesCor," she said, blithely ignoring my comment. "It has everything I'll need, and Ari can consult there just as well as in his own lab. It's as close to neutral ground as we're likely to get."

"Um. Sure." NuQuesCor was the biotech company that Pietro had been part owner of and where Kristi had begun her zombie research. "You do know I can't make these decisions, right?"

"Of course *you* can't. But I doubt your superiors will be able to come up with a better option. Using the Tribe lab is off the table."

"Fine. Whatever. I'll pass it along."

"Whatever," she mimicked. "Now call the grownups back in so we can hammer out the details."

"NuQuesCor should serve well enough," Pierce said after Marcus hung up with Kristi. He glanced at Dr. Nikas. "Are you all right with that?"

"No, not personally," he said, expression placid. "However, from the larger perspective it is a win-win. She won't work in the Tribe lab, and I do not want her there. The NuQuesCor facility has most of the equipment and supplies we need. The rest can be transported." He let out a soft sigh. "I will curb my fear."

Pierce regarded him for a long moment. "Ari . . ."

Dr. Nikas held up a hand. "Dr. Charish—understandably— left no other option, and short of remaining at my lab, there is no better alternative for me. NuQuesCor is a smart choice for a neutral research base. I can do this."

Pierce dipped his head in acknowledgement. "As Pietro's heir, Marcus has an ownership share in the facility, which means we have full access. Moreover, we can easily manufacture a reason to clear out personnel and have privacy."

Marcus crossed his arms. "We should send some people over now to make sure there are no nasty surprises lurking. Just in case."

Pierce looked briefly surprised at Marcus's input then nodded in approval. "Good call. We'll get moving on that and make security arrangements for the facility."

Everyone departed except for Dr. Nikas who had a thoughtful look on his face.

I put a hand on his arm. "Are you going to be okay?"

He covered my hand with his. "There will be only a few
people there. My irrational fears shouldn't hinder the work."

"That's not what I mean." I met his warm brown eyes. "A
year ago, Kristi tried to kill Philip in the cruelest way she could
manage, by brain-starving him. When you found out, you said
you'd made a huge mistake trusting her and that you would
never do so again. I don't deny that we *have* to accept her offer.
And I know you'll be on your toes. But you never . . ." I groped
for the right words. "You never stopped admiring her abilities as
a scientist. And that's okay," I hurried to add. "I mean, even I
have no trouble admitting she's brilliant. I just worry about you."

Dr. Nikas exhaled a long breath and folded to sit again. "I do
admire Kristi—her knowledge, her skills, and the facile ease
with which she draws conclusions and discovers new paths to
explore. I have seen her at her very best, and for so long I could
not help but feel as if there was still a chance to reach what
might be left of her soul, bring her to care for how her accomplishments could aid others rather than how she would benefit,
whether from power or money." He passed a hand over his face.
"I *despised* having her imprisoned here, coerced to work toward
our ends. I know she is a murderess and kidnapper and worse,
yet it never ceased to feel vile to *use* her. It was not justice. It
was convenience. And after that incident with Philip, when I lost
my temper and commanded she be starved as she starved
him . . ." Self-loathing crawled over his face. "I returned to my
rooms and wept. The next morning, I rescinded the punishment." He looked at me with heart-breaking sorrow. "How can
one blame a slave for striking out against her masters?"

"Do you think she can still be . . . saved?"

He shook his head. "I am neither foolish nor blind. She was
a self-serving narcissist long before she encountered our people.
But we destroyed what little hope there was for her to rein in her
antisocial proclivities. I grieve for the woman—the person—
Kristi might have been, but I have accepted that she is who she
is. I will take full advantage of what she offers, and I will not
waste efforts or energy attempting to redeem the irredeemable.
And I will *never* trust her."

"I'm sorry," I said. "I can't imagine how agonizing it must be to give up on someone." I surrendered to the urge and hugged him. There were certainly people who'd had given up on me, back when I was in full-blown Loser Mode.

"Thank you, Angel," Dr. Nikas said softly. "Putting voice to my angst has loosed its stranglehold upon me. I am grateful for your insight and empathy."

"I learned from the best."

Chapter 19

I headed home, sick and unsettled about Kristi being back in our lives, despite my reassuring words to Dr. Nikas and despite our desperate need of her expertise.

But what if it wasn't enough? What if animals other than alligators could get infected? What if mosquitoes really were transmitting the "zombie encephalitis" and this mess turned into an outright pandemic?

A shiver crawled down my back.

My dad. I needed to get him someplace safe. Out of town, preferably, until this all blew over and the danger was past.

If it ever blew over.

And what about the other people who mattered to me? The Tribe zombies were safe and immune, but not the cops I'd become friends with. Or my classmates. Or co-workers at the Coroner's Office. Allen and Nick knew what to watch out for, and the other death investigators and morgue techs knew the basic procedures around bio hazards. But Reb, the secretary, might not. She was so kind-hearted that if someone shambled up to her, she'd give them a hug and buy them a hot meal. And get infected in return.

Yet I couldn't warn everyone without coming off as batshit crazy.

So warn the ones you can.

I plugged my earbuds into my phone then dialed Randy's

number. The last time I'd seen him was after I kicked him and Coy Bates out of my car, told them to walk to the gas station, call the cops, and tell them everything they knew about the murder of movie producer Grayson Seeger. Not long after that, my arms and legs had decided to fall off, and Randy had been the last thing on my mind. Until now.

"Angel?" Surprise filled his voice.

"Hey, Randy. Look, I think maybe you should leave town."

He sucked in a sharp breath. "Oh, fuck. Am I in trouble?"

"No! Sorry. No, it's nothing like that. I promise. It's just . . . I dunno if you've been watching the news, but some people have been getting sick."

"Yeah, saw that." He barked a laugh. "The 'zombie seff-lite-us,' right?"

I winced. "Yeah. Zombie- or necro-meningoencephalitis is what they're calling it. I have an inside track on this kind of stuff since I work at the Coroner's Office, so I know this thing is contagious."

"Oh shit." All humor left his voice. "Like how bad? In the air or sex or fluids or what?"

Well, how about that. Randy had more of a clue than I thought. "Right now it's fluids. The people who have it like to bite, which transmits it. But it could get worse. I mean, there's some talk that it might even be spread by mosquitoes and, well . . . I know we're not dating anymore, but I don't want to see anything bad happen to you. I was hoping that maybe you could get away from here for a while, at least until there's a vaccine or treatment." *Please god let us find a treatment. A cure. Anything.*

"Thanks, Angel," he said with unexpected warmth. "That's really sweet. I feel the same way about you. I'm finishing up a repair job on a private jet out at the Tucker Point Airport tonight. It came in Monday, but we've been waiting on a part for two goddam days and just got it. Once that's done, I suppose I can take a road trip over to Houston and drop in on my dad."

"That's terrific," I said, feeling a bit of the worry ease. It was one strand of a zillion, but every little bit helped. "Since when did you know how to repair planes?" Randy had fixed cars for as long as I'd known him. Maybe the occasional motorcycle, but that was about it.

"Since two weeks ago when I started apprenticing with the

main aviation repair guy out there," he said with a note of pride. "Figured it was 'bout time I got a proper job, y'know? Luke says I'm a natural. I guess I pick up that mechanical shit real easy. Like, I can just *see* how it's supposed to work."

"This is going to sound corny as all hell, but I'm really proud of you."

"Well, you kinda inspired me. I mean, if a good-for-nothing like Angel Crawford can get her shit together . . ." He snickered.

"I can still kick your ass," I warned, but I couldn't help but grin.

"Oh, I know it. I'm gonna slather on some DEET then call my old man and let him know I'm heading that way tomorrow. He'll either be thrilled or pissed."

"I know your dad, and he'll be thrilled," I said. "Take care, and let me know if you run into any trouble."

"You got it. Thanks, Angel."

He disconnected. I stuffed my phone back in my purse. Now to talk a certain Mr. Jimmy Crawford into getting the hell out of town.

I expected to find my dad either napping or kicked back on the couch watching reality TV. What I did *not* want to find was my dad out smoking in the back yard.

Turned out it was none of the above. Instead, I walked in to find him sitting cross-legged on the floor in front of the TV, game controller in hand and a gaming headset with mic holding down his wispy hair. On the screen was a busty blonde wearing a skimpy fur bikini and armor that barely covered her nipples. Dad jabbed a button, and the woman swung a fire-wreathed sword at a dog-sized beetle, slicing it cleanly in two.

My dad hooted in glee. "Yeah, take that, you little shitlickers!" His thumbs smashed buttons with fierce intensity as a silvery wasp-thing dove toward the bikini barbarian. Her arm jerked forward, skewering the bug. It exploded in a shower of sparks, and a giant "4" glowed briefly on the screen.

"Hot damn!" He whooped in delight. "Another level!"

"Hey, Dad," I said then repeated myself at twice the volume.

He jerked around then yanked the headset off and scrambled to his feet. "Hey, Angelkins! Man, this thing is a real treat." He gestured to the TV with the headset. "Um, I hope you ain't mad that I cracked it open, but Libby down at Kaster's called and said they was getting fumigated so they didn't need me to come sweep up 'til tomorrow when they'd have all the dead bugs. So I was kinda bored, and the box was just sittin' here . . ."

"I'm not mad," I said, mouth twitching. "I *am* impressed you were able to get it set up."

His chin went up. "I ain't as dumb as I look, Angel." Then he grinned sheepishly. "Plus, that Arnold Stein character who sent it included step-by-step directions that were written so easy a squirrel could follow 'em. Even got it hooked up to the internet. Directions said that was important."

"That's pretty cool. But why are you a porn star?" I cocked my head toward where the woman stood with her sword raised high, chest thrust forward, and back arched to show off her overly curvy ass.

His face scrunched. "Well, the directions said this character was all set up and ready for you. I tried to make me a man-type fighter, but I couldn't figger out how to get him clothes and gear. I finally settled on it bein' less weird to play a lady fighter than to be a guy struttin' around with nothing but a hankie covering his junk."

I choked back a laugh. "That sounds reasonable," I managed then stepped closer to the TV and peered at the corner of the screen. "You named her Momzombique?"

"Nah. Came with that name. I'd've picked a name that wouldn't twist my tongue all up. Like Beth. Somethin' easy."

"Beth the Barbarian. I like it." Plus, now I was certain the game was from Andrew. But *why*? "I'd like to play it some," I said, "but first you and I need to talk."

I couldn't bring myself to tell him I was the cause of the epidemic. At least not yet. But I filled him in on what was going on with the shamblers and how dangerous things were getting, then told him I wanted him to leave town for his own safety.

When I finished, he crossed his arms over his chest and gave me a defiant Jimmy Crawford glare. "Nope."

I shook my head in disbelief. "Dad, didn't you hear a single thing I just said? Contagious disease that turns you into a zombie. And not the cool kind like me!"

"I heard you," he said. "But I ain't leaving, and you can't make me."

I threw my hands up in exasperation. "Actually, I *can* make you. I'm stronger than you, remember?"

"But you ain't more stubborn!" he declared with a satisfied smirk. "And you're out of your damn mind if you think I'm leaving when you might need help."

I saw it then—the flash of bone-deep fear and worry. My annoyance vanished. Only a few weeks ago, he thought he'd lost me forever. How could I expect him to go off on a frickin' vacation?

"You're right," I said. "I'm sorry. I *was* out of my damn mind." I seized him in a hug. He returned it with just as much gusto.

"Glad you understand," he said gruffly.

"I do." I pulled back and gave him a serious look. "But can we compromise? Can you stay at the Tribe's lab?"

He made a face. "That place ain't the most welcoming. And it ain't exactly a hotel."

"It's not a fleabag dive, either! You'd have a room to yourself. Meals. Security out the ass."

He eyed me. "Same as jail. I ain't goin', and that's final."

I sighed. There was no convincing him when he was like this. "Okay, fine. Stay here, but don't go out! I mean it. And you need to wear mosquito repellent anyway, and lock the doors and windows, just in case."

My dad grumbled under his breath but nodded. "I'll get the shotgun out, for even more just in case."

"Since when do we have a shotgun?"

"*We* don't have a shotgun. *I* have a shotgun. Twelve gauge. Did a favor for a buddy of mine, and he gave me it."

"Huh." I flopped onto the sofa. "Okay then. Do you have shells for it?"

"A box of number six."

Nowhere near the stopping power of double-aught buckshot, but enough to do damage. I was all for saving the shamblers, but not if my dad was in danger.

"That'll do." I glared at him. "Just make sure you're shooting a shambler. When Mr. Cleg down the road gets drunk, he looks like one. Go for the legs. It's pretty tough to actually kill them." Not to mention I still clung to the hope they could be cured. "And if it gets really bad out there, I *will* drag your butt to the lab."

He smiled and settled beside me. "Kinda nice you worryin' about me."

"You're my *dad,* dummy." I let my gaze linger on his face. Though he'd only recently turned fifty, he looked at least a decade older. His thin hair was streaked with grey, and lines crowded around his eyes and mouth, helped along by decades of smoking, drinking, and stress, as well as an old back injury and a lack of anything resembling exercise. "I worry about you," I added quietly. "Not sure I could handle losing you." I grabbed his hand. "Dad. I . . . I might live a really long time. That is, I'm not going to die of old age." I took an unsteady breath. "Dad, you could become . . . like me. I could—"

"Angelkins." His voice was soft and calm. "No."

My chest tightened. "What do you mean, *No*? Dad, you wouldn't have to ever worry about cancer or heart disease or arthritis or even a cold!"

A gentle smile curved his mouth. "Baby, I don't want to be immortal. Don't need to be. I already done my best thing ever: I made you."

My lower lip quivered. "B-but I don't want to lose you."

"It's gotta happen eventually, either way, Angelkins. A man ain't s'posed to outlive his kids."

"If we're both zombies you wouldn't," I shot back.

"Don't you sass me, girl," he said. "I'm trying to be all dramatic and shit, and you're spoiling it." He *tsked* under his breath, lifted a thumb to wipe away the tears that spilled down my cheeks. "I can't explain it, baby. I just know it ain't right for me. Look, knowing that I'm gonna die is what lets me appreciate bein' alive. But what happened to you, gettin' turned into what you are . . . well, it was a real gift, because god knows you deserved it. You didn't get to *live* during your first twenty years. But I know you better'n anyone else out there. And now that you got the chance to really live, you're gonna squeeze everything you can outta the rest of your life, whether it's ten years or ten thousand."

Sniffling, I swiped at my eyes. "Fine," I said. "But you have to promise me that you're going to take really good care of yourself from now on. Just because you're mortal doesn't mean you have to take a running start at death."

"Sure thing, baby." He patted my arm indulgently.

"I mean it." I gave him a fierce look. "I want you to get regular checkups with the doctor, and quit smoking—for *real*—and eat better, and hell, I want you to start exercising. More than walking to the mailbox and back."

His eyes glistened. "I'll do it. For both of us." He paused. "And mostly 'cause I'm pretty sure that if I don't, you'll turn me zombie out of spite."

I managed a wobbly grin. "You're goddamn right I will. And you'll never hear the end of it. Forever."

He wrapped his arms around me and heaved a sigh. "I guess I better get my ass into a gym."

"They won't know what hit them." I gave him a long squeeze, memorizing everything about him for the millionth time, then released him. "Is it okay if I play the game for a while?" I was pretty sure Andrew expected me to play it.

"Hell, it's yours, ain't it? Just watch out for the weirdos." He snorted. "There's one feller who kept following me around. Asked me to join him for a drink in the tavern. But he slunk away when I told him to fuck the hell off." He let out a snicker. "Guess he thought I was a lady."

"Can't hardly blame him. Look at that fur bikini—" My eyes snapped to the headset, and I gave myself a mental forehead smack. Of course! Weirdo guy had to be Andrew! People talked to each other in games all the time. I had no idea if people could eavesdrop on those conversations, but even if it was possible, there was no way anyone would think Andrew and I would communicate this way. "I'll be careful," I solemnly promised.

"Alrighty, then I'm going to head over to the Y and see if they can work with what I got." He struck a muscle pose and made a show of kissing his puny bicep.

"Better take care of those guns," I said, laughing.

He dropped a kiss onto my forehead then snatched up his keys. "Got .22s now, but I'll have .50 calibers before you know it!" He strode out, singing *Bat out of Hell* at the top of his lungs.

Good thing Mrs. Grady across the street was going deaf.

Chapter 20

I waited for Dad's truck to pull out of the driveway then made a pass with the bug scanner through the living room, kitchen, and hallway. It would be kind of awful to finally—hopefully—talk to Andrew in a—hopefully—secure setting, only to have the bad guys listen in.

Once I finished the house, I scanned the game console itself. Twice. Nothing. Excellent. I grabbed the headset and controller and plopped onto the floor.

Then got right back up again to find the directions on how to use the friggin' controller. I soon located them between the sofa cushions, along with a crumpled dollar bill and an empty cigarette packet. Nothing toxic. If not for my dad's housecleaning girlfriend, there could have been anything from petrified corn chips to dirty boxers down there. Go, Gina!

After a few minutes of reading instructions and fiddling with the controller, I unpaused the game and got the hang of walking Momzombique around.

A couple of beetle things scuttled past, but I ignored them and turned a slow circle, taking stock. "Crap," I muttered. "I should've asked Dad what the weirdo looked like."

People wandered about hawking various goods. Beggars begged, and shady figures skulked. I got the feeling they were part of the game and not other players. My hunch was confirmed after I deliberately walked into a man dressed like a baker, and his reaction was to give me a hearty greeting and say, "Baguette for you today, Swordbearer?"

A red-haired man with bulging muscles lounged near the door of the Wayside Tavern. He wore shiny silver armor and flowing purple cloak, and didn't look at all like the other "townspeople." He was also facing in my direction.

A quick check of the instructions revealed how to talk to other players. I cleared my throat, adjusted the mic, then toggled the button. "So, uh, come here often?"

"About time you got here," a voice that was definitely Andrew's grumbled. The muscled fighter turned and strode down the street. "Follow me."

I did so—after a couple of false starts and one instance of getting stuck in a corner and yet another peek at the instructions for how to climb steps. Eventually he led me into a ruined stone building and down into a cellar so convincingly squatty I ducked my head where I sat in my living room. A single guttering torch lit the room. On the wall opposite the stairs, a dark passageway loomed beyond the rusty bars of a gate. Distant screeches echoed in stereo.

"Are bugs going to come out of that?" I asked. I tried to point toward the barred gate but only succeeded in drawing my sword.

"I killed them already. I didn't want to be disturbed once you finally showed up. I assume that was your father, earlier?"

"Yeah. Sorry about that. This game is pretty cool. Did Saberton make it?"

"No," he said, the withering look clear in his voice if not on his character's face. "We don't make video games. And even if we did, it would be too obvious for me to use it for this."

"Right. Gotcha." I did a slow turn to take in the basement. "So, no one can listen in on us here?"

"On the street, other characters might be able to hear us. Not that any of them would have context or care about our conversation, but there's no point in taking chances. It's safer down here. And we need to talk." He made an unintelligible noise. "Would you please stand still? It's distracting."

"Seriously? It's not like I have to look at you." But I went ahead and faced him. "And yes, we really need to talk. You know what's going on here, right? The shambling zombies?"

"I've seen the news coverage, but I'm sure there's plenty I don't know."

I gave him the rundown—including Kristi's offer to help—all the while wishing Andrew's muscled dude had facial expressions so I could judge how the info was being received. "What is Saberton saying about all this?" I asked once I finished.

"Not a word. And before I address the Charish issue, are you certain those men in the swamp were Saberton?"

"Positive. Rosario identified one of them as a Saberton security dude. Harlon Murtaugh. He didn't recognize the other one, though, and didn't get a good look at the divers."

"Any distinguishing features on the second one? If I have ID on both I can see what project they're assigned to."

"Oh man. I'll try. Redhead, skinny but with muscles. Um. Nowhere near as tall as Murtaugh."

"You suck as an eyewitness, but I'll see what I can do. Now, about Kristi Charish."

"She's completely vicious, evil, and without morals?" I supplied helpfully.

"Yes, that's a given. But she's also a solid forward thinker and not to be underestimated. She's had spies and informants throughout Saberton for at least the past couple of years. Did you know she's on the Saberton Board of directors now?"

"Are you shitting me? How the hell did *that* happen?"

"Part of the deal my mother made with Charish to get her back with the corporation." He snorted. "Stupid move on her part because Charish all but controls that boardroom now. She has extortion down to an art. And her gift for analyzing situations and exploiting them to her advantage is unparalleled."

"You mean she knows the best ways to screw everyone over."

"Well, Charish is a sociopath through and through, so for the most part she doesn't *care* if people get screwed over in the process."

"Sure. For the most part. Except for people she hates. Like me."

He chuckled. "True. She really does despise you."

A dark spot on the wall behind Andrew shifted. Or had it? Maybe it was just an effect of the flickering torch.

"You wrecked her plans more than once, Angel. She doesn't forgive or forget."

"But do you think she would—" The dark shape moved, leaped. "Shit. Watch out!"

My warning came an instant too late. The camouflaged spider-demon thing pounced on Andrew and chomped its fangs into his head. Blood spurted, then Andrew flickered and vanished, leaving an impressive stain of blood on the floor.

"Dammmmn. The graphics in this game kick ass!" I crossed fingers Andrew would respawn soon so we could continue our chat.

Unfortunately, the spider-demon wasn't satisfied with killing Andrew and sprang toward me. By some miracle, I remembered which button to push to swing my sword and managed to slice two legs off with one swipe. Plus-six Sword of Deadly Hacking for the win!

Another swing cut a huge gash in its side, but the spider-demon scored a hit to my leg with a venom-dripping fang. My heart indicator went from green to yellow.

"Ha! Can't kill me that easily, sucker!" I jumped and avoided another fang slash. The spider came back around, and I did a power swing-jump and slash combo by pressing both the A button and right trigger.

It was Andrew's shitty luck that he chose that moment to respawn—right in the path of my power swing.

"Well, that was a pain in the—" was all he managed to get out before my sword sliced through him. Once again his health indicator went from green to black, and he vanished.

"Hope he has another life," I muttered and repeated my power swing on the spider—far more effective now that Andrew wasn't in the way—and the spider screeched and blew apart in a cloud of angry red sparks.

Stupidly pleased, I stalked the perimeter of the cellar to make sure there were no more nasties.

Andrew shimmered back to life. "Could you perhaps not kill me this time?"

"Maybe you should play the game a bit and level up so you don't get slaughtered when somebody steps on your toe."

He drew his gleaming sword and brandished it. "Try that move now, hon."

"I'll kick your ass another day." I snickered and sheathed my sword. "Do you honestly think Kristi could set her hatred of me aside in order to help us with this cure? And, if she's a sociopath, why would she *want* to help us?"

"Oh, that's easy. Because she can cover herself in glory. If she does indeed succeed in finding a cure, all sorts of doors will open for her, even bigger and better than Saberton. In other words, yes, she would gladly tolerate you lot for an opportunity of this magnitude."

"Ugh. Okay."

"I know. She's a horrible excuse for a human being, but she's a brilliant scientist."

"Ugh. And she works for your mother. Double ugh."

"I'm trying to change that. The board can vote a CEO out. I have a few members who would gladly cut the legs out from under my mother." He blew out a frustrated breath. "Unfortunately, Charish currently holds sway, and it's to her benefit to keep my mother as CEO. They have very similar *visions* for the future of the company."

"Triple ugh!"

"I know. I'm working matters as carefully as I can."

"Is everything going all right for you? Are you safe?"

"So far so good," he said. His tone was light, but he couldn't hide the ever-present stress that colored it.

"Your sister has been really worried about you."

He was silent for several seconds. "I know. Thea has been giving me reports on her. And you. It's how I knew you were coming back home."

Huh. Interesting. And impressively sneaky if Naomi was unaware. "But it would be too dangerous for you to try and make contact with her, since your mother would be expecting it."

"Precisely. A bit less of a risk contacting you since I hate you and everyone knows it."

I laughed. "Fair enough. Now then, how do I get in touch with you if I need to tell you something?"

"Hang something blue in your bathroom window. When you get a call from a telemarketer saying you've won a cruise to Argentina, that's the signal I'm here and can talk."

"A cruise to Argentina sounds awesome."

"Then you should start saving your pennies, because telemarketer cruise wins are fiction."

His character vanished, effectively ending the conversation. Though I was tempted to stick around and kill more beetle-dog-spider-things, I needed to get to bed.

There were real monsters to deal with tomorrow.

Chapter 21

In my previous life, I'd have taken a Xanax to help me sleep, but that option wasn't available to me as a zombie. Instead, I was forced to do stuff like count my breaths and consciously relax. But relaxing was pretty tough to do with the world on fire, especially when I was the one who dropped the match.

Finally, sometime after 2 a.m., I managed to doze off.

Only to snap awake at six. Morning light glowed around the edges of the blackout curtains. In the distance, a rooster crowed. Miss Paisley's, most likely. She lived near the end of the road and always gave away tons of eggs to family, friends, and neighbors. Except for us. We'd been a part of the egg krewe until three years ago when my dad—drunk—nearly ran her over while she was out walking her dog. That was bad enough, but when he got out of the truck and called her a dried-up stick, and her dog a mangy flea magnet, we were officially crossed off the free-eggs list for good. Which sucked, because yard eggs were a billion times better than store bought.

A text buzz from my phone cut my egg-musings short, and I snagged it from the nightstand. The number seemed vaguely familiar, but my frontal lobe wasn't awake enough to release the info.

<Good morning, sunshine! Be at NuQuesCor at 8 a.m. sharp so I can get blood samples from you and start fixing this mess! :-) K.C.>

Kristi Fucking Charish. The text had come in at 6 a.m. on the nose, which was what woke me. Bitch. And a smiley face? I gave the phone my middle finger then dialed Marcus's number. No way was I going to reply to Kristi before confirming this wasn't a setup. I was ready and willing to help find a cure, but not if it meant getting locked in a cage and experimented on. Besides, if I had to be awake, then so did Marcus.

To my surprise, he sounded wide awake when he answered—which told me he'd been up for a while. We'd dated long enough that I knew it took him an hour and a pot of coffee to not sound sleep-fuzzed.

"Hey, Marcus. I got a text from Kristi saying to meet her at NuQuesCor this morning. Will any Tribe people be there? I'd rather not go on my lonesome, if you know what I mean."

"Dr. Nikas has been there all night, along with Tribe security." In the background, a door opened and closed, followed by the sound of footsteps on tile.

A bit of my tension eased. "Gotcha. What about the people who usually work there?"

"We're only taking over half of the third floor. NuQuesCor regularly conducts highly classified projects, so the employees are used to not asking questions." Fatigue threaded through his voice, but it wasn't physical—more likely his weariness of being a figurehead, of being responsible without actually being responsible. "And to smooth the feathers of the displaced workers," he continued, "we're sending them to a week-long conference in Puerto Rico." He paused. "Hawaii was too expensive."

I silently prayed a week would be enough. "That was your idea, right? The conference thing?" I couldn't see Pierce giving a crap about smoothing feathers.

"Sure was," he said, tone a bit brighter. Another door opened, followed by a rising *thwup-thwup-thwup* sound. "Sorry, Angel," Marcus said, raising his voice over the noise. "I'm headed to NuQuesCor right now. I'll see you soon." The *thwup-thwup* grew louder and faster, then he disconnected.

Damn, he got to ride in a helicopter. Too bad that little perk couldn't make being Tribe head worth it.

I thumbed in a reply to Kristi's text: <I have to be at work at 8 but can be at NQC by 7>

Her reply came as I pulled myself out of bed.

<7 doesn't work for me. I'm occupied with other matters

until 8. Can you come on your lunch hour? I suppose we can hold off on the critical work until you pry yourself free>

I could practically hear her long-suffering sigh. Nice guilt trip, bitch. And it worked, which was even more annoying. Grumbling curses, I texted Allen.

<Might be about an hour late. Trying to clean up mess from other day> Hopefully, he'd read into that and understand what I meant.

<Do what you need to do but don't dawdle please. Cutting 2 as soon as you get here. Messy. Like other day>

Messy. Two dead shamblers. Damn it.

<10-4>

I returned to the Kristi convo. <Fine. I'll be there at 8 on the nose but HAVE to leave by 8:30>

<Your generous assistance is greatly appreciated!>

Ugh. I liked her a whole lot more when she was her normal, nasty self.

I shuffled to the kitchen, surprised to see my dad flopped on the sofa watching the morning news.

He gave me a bright smile. "Morning, baby. There's fresh coffee in the kitchen."

My eyes narrowed as I took in his bloodshot eyes and haggard features—as well as the controller and headset resting at the far end of the couch. "Did you stay up all night playing *Swords and Swagger*?"

"Um." He shifted. "Yeah. Y'got me. I heard you talkin' on the phone, so I changed it to the TV real quick."

My mouth twitched as I poured a cup of coffee. "And you might've gotten away with it except for one tiny detail."

Dad heaved a sigh. "I ain't never awake this early."

"Uh huh. You ain't never awake this early." I added cream and sugar, stirred. "Bad guys get caught when they act out of character. But you made coffee, and that's all that matters for now."

He snorted. "You hang around cops too much. I can't get away with shit around you no more. Not that I meant to stay up 'til the crack of dawn. See, I went online last night and found a discussion forum all about *Swords and Swagger*. Learnt how to make a character. So I created me a guy barbarian and then had to level him up so I could do the cool shit."

"*Had* to." I shook my head. "I don't know which is weirder:

you playing a video game all damn night or that you joined an online forum."

Dad chortled and went back to watching the news. But my amusement faded as I rummaged in the pantry for something more nutritious than Pop-Tarts. Kristi Charish was being nice and pleasant. That was definitely out of character.

"Goddammit!" my dad roared, startling me. "Fuck you, you fucking bitch!"

"What the hell, Dad? What'd I do?" I grabbed a towel to wipe up the coffee that had sloshed from my mug.

"Not you, Angelkins. Come see this goddamn shit! It's her! That piece of shit fuckstain cunt!"

I left the spilled coffee where it was. Dad only ever used the c-word for one person.

And there she was on TV. Lovely, perfectly stylish, and . . . blonde? She'd always been auburn before. I checked the crawl at the bottom of the screen to make sure it was really her. Sure enough, it read "Dr. Kristi Charish—noted neurobiologist." Guess she wanted to make a whole new start, now that she was a bigshot at Saberton. What sucked the most was that she looked fucking amazing with blonde hair. Fuck her. I was hands down the better blonde.

Her voice grated through me. *"It is my solemn duty to volunteer my expertise and services in this time of world crisis. I will find the cure."*

"Occupied with other matters, my ass," I growled under my breath. People were dying, and there she was puffing herself up in interviews, all fake altruistic and shit. That was definitely *in* character.

"Why's that bitch involved with any of this?" he demanded.

I sighed. "We're in deep shit, and she offered to help Dr. Nikas. Common ground to stop the spread of the zombie epidemic."

"She ain't right in the head." He jumped up, face flushed and hands balled into fists. "Tell me right now you ain't goin' nowhere near that good for nothin'—"

"Dad! I *have* to."

"Let them other zombie hot shots deal with her. You don't have to be around her."

"I do," I blurted. "This shambler mess is my fault." Somehow saying it out loud to my dad made it worse. And better. He would never blame me. "Long story, and it wasn't on purpose, but I'm the source of the infection, which means I'm needed for samples and stuff."

His body slumped in a sigh. "Damn, Angelkins. When you gonna get cut some slack?"

"Soon, I hope." I gave him a wobbly smile. No need for him to worry more than he had to. "There's some serious brain power happening when Dr. Nikas and Kristi work together."

"You ain't fool enough to trust her, right?"

"Not in the slightest. It's like having a cottonmouth in your sleeping bag. It's fine and dandy while it's cozy and warm, but it can bite you in the ass at any time."

He gave a grudging nod of approval. "Don't you let your guard down for one second, y'hear?"

"I swear I'll be careful." I nodded toward the game console. "I have some time before I have to get ready. How about we take Momzombique and your guy . . ."

"Barney."

I rolled my eyes. ". . . and Barney the Barbarian out on a little spider demon hunt."

"Hot diggety damn. Mebbe you can help me kill the Skeleton Spider!"

"It would be my greatest pleasure."

It took the better part of an hour, and each of our characters died twice, but we eventually fought our way to the lair of the dreaded Skeleton Spider and dispatched the foul beast. Dad whooped and hollered with abandon as we collected the treasure, but no amount of monster-killing glory could make me forget the ugly truth.

I was about to be Kristi Fucking Charish's lab rat.

Even though I'd been to NuQuesCor several times before, I still needed my GPS to help me navigate the convoluted route. Situated in the eastern end of the parish, it was a twenty-minute drive from my house. Less, if you drove like a bat out of hell.

Fifteen minutes later, I pulled into the parking lot and gazed up at the building that housed the biotech company. Three stories of white brick, with a scattered handful of windows to break up the monotony. Boring, stark, and functional.

Squaring my shoulders, I strode up the sidewalk and through double glass doors into a vast lobby that more than made up for the exterior—marble floors, burnished metal wall panels, artsy sculptures, and a number of comfortable seating areas. A dozen or so people mingled near a coffee stand—some in business clothes, and others in dressy casual with lab coats. A grizzled security guard sat within the circular desk in the center.

A fresh-faced young man in a tailored pinstripe suit approached from the direction of a curving staircase.

"Good morning!" he said, smiling brightly. "You must be Angel Crawford?"

"I am," I replied cautiously. "You work here?"

"No ma'am." His smile widened. "I work for Dr. Charish!"

"That's . . . awesome." No way could anyone fake being that cheerful. "Can you tell me where I need to go?"

"Dr. Charish's research suite shares the third floor with the NuQuesCor genetics program. They only have critical staff on duty and are restricted to the rooms on the east side." He whipped out a map. "For your convenience, I marked the way to Dr. Charish's main lab area."

"You mean Marcus Ivanov's research suite and lab area?" I said sweetly. "He's an owner. Not Kristi."

"Er, I . . . yes? That is, Dr. Charish—"

I snagged the map from his hand. "Mighty kind of you to mark this for me. What's your name?"

"Billy Upton, ma'am. It's a pleasure to meet you." He stuck out his hand.

"Likewise," I said and shook it.

"Here's your fob so you can get into the secured area once you're on the third floor." He handed me a lanyard bearing an inch-long nub of black plastic.

I slipped it over my head. "Thanks for your help, Billy."

"Anytime, Miss Crawford."

Bemused, I took the stairs to the third floor then followed the highlighted route on the map. The fob got me past a locked door and into the lab suite, where I navigated a maze of corridors, passing offices and break rooms and doors marked "Autoclave" and "Microscope/Fluorescence" and "Cell Culture." Lab coats and other protective equipment hung on hooks outside several of the rooms, including one bearing giant biohazard placards and "LEVEL 3 BIOHAZARD" emblazoned on the door in bright red letters.

Eventually, I reached a large room with multiple bays for

focused work. Three long tables took up the center of the room, with drawers and storage beneath. A sink and safety shower occupied one corner, opposite a large fume hood. Counters filled with every variety of analytical equipment ran along the left wall, while glass-fronted cabinets loaded with chemicals and supplies hugged the right. An enormous walk-in refrigerator took up a sizable chunk of the back wall.

Jacques worked to set up a second whiteboard for Dr. Nikas while four techs I didn't know held a quiet discussion over photos and paperwork strewn across the back table. The four wore identical starched white scrubs and lab coats, all male, all fit, and all thirty-something. Kristi's crew, and likely doing double duty as her eye candy.

Kristi had slipped a lab coat over the outfit she'd worn for the TV interview. She and Dr. Nikas conferred near a computer station, comparing information on the screen to that on a tablet she held. Beside them, Marcus fidgeted, seeming stressed yet oddly energized. Probably because he was finally *doing* something.

Brian, Kyle, and Rachel stood spaced around the perimeter of the room—out of the way, but close enough to intervene at the slightest threat. Two men in dark suits with obvious shoulder-holster bulges occupied the gaps between the Tribe security people. One had a black eye and a bandage across the bridge of his nose. Average height. Medium build. The other stood at least six-foot-five, broad-shouldered and intimidating. His nose looked like it had been broken half a dozen times, and his dark hair was cropped close, exposing a wicked scar where his left ear used to be.

Kristi's muscle.

The two stepped toward me. Kristi glanced up as they moved. "Stand down, boys. Believe it or not, Angel is invited." She bestowed a winning smile upon me. "My bodyguards. One can never be too careful." She passed the tablet to Dr. Nikas. "I'll be with you in a tick, Angel."

"Whatever," I muttered then gave the two thugs my own brilliant smile. Black Eye seemed familiar, though I'd been around so many Saberton security people it wasn't surprising. He hadn't been out in the swamp for the gator hunt, so I'd most likely seen him at Saberton New York.

Marcus came over to me. "C'mon. You have to see the pen."

"The what?"

"You'll see," he said with a wink then led me out of the lab, down the corridor, and around the corner. Halfway down that hall, he pulled open a grey metal door and gestured for me to step through.

I did so, only to find myself face-to-face with a massive, milky-eyed alligator.

Well, not quite face-to-face since there was a chain-link fence between us. Plus the gator's face was several feet lower than mine, but it was still just as much of a shock. Especially in the middle of a friggin' research building. I had no idea what the room was originally used for, but it was the size of a basketball court, with the gator pen occupying the nearest quarter. An eight-foot-tall fence topped with razor wire surrounded a broad swath of grassy turf with a shallow pool at its center—temporary home for two twelve-foot zombie gators and half a dozen smaller specimens, ranging from three to six feet.

"This is . . . impressive," I finally said.

Marcus chuckled. "Crazy, huh? These were here when Dr. Nikas arrived last night."

"Very crazy. Saberton caught all the zombie gators?"

"Not Saberton. Kristi's people. And there might still be more infected ones out there. No way to know for sure."

I frowned. "So Kristi was already setting up to work here."

"Her people were, at least. Her plane didn't land at the Tucker Point airport until around midnight."

The other gators began to trundle toward us. The one already by the fence let out a weird growl-moan.

"They seem to like you," Marcus said.

"This is taking the zombie mama thing to an uncomfortable extreme," I said, though I couldn't take my eyes off the big gator.

Kristi's voice sounded through the intercom, crisp and annoyed. "Angel Crawford to the central lab. Now."

I made a face. "The wicked witch desires my presence."

"Mustn't keep her witchiness waiting." He turned to leave but stopped when I didn't follow. "Angel?"

I crouched. All of the gators were now clustered on the other side of the fence from me, eerily still, and milky eyes on me. "Hey there," I murmured.

In unison, they opened their toothy maws and sent up a wavering chorus of unnatural growly-moans.

Marcus wrapped his hand around my bicep and hauled me

up. "That's just plain creepy. Let's go before they decide to rush the fence."

I shrugged out of his grip. "They won't."

"Riiiight. C'mon, zombie-gator whisperer."

Oddly reluctant, I backed out of the room then double-timed it to the lab.

Kristi gave me a sour look as we entered. "Finally. I didn't expect you to go scampering off, considering you're at the heart of this whole debacle. I need your blood." She pointed to a chair.

I could hardly refuse since she was right about the debacle/heart thing. Plus, Dr. Nikas gave me a subtle nod, which helped my nerves. I took a seat and stuck my arm out as Jacques approached with a handful of collection tubes and a pint bag. One of Kristi's techs followed him, carrying a tablet and tube rack. Thick black hair curled in the vee of his scrub shirt and ended in a precise shave line, as if his collar bones marked the border of a demilitarized zone. The name embroidered above his pocket was Harold Frost. Hairy Harry? I bit the inside of my cheek to keep a straight face. *Hunky hairy Harry had happy huge hopping healthy hares. Hardly horrible.*

Jacques had taken my blood for Dr. Nikas more times than I could count, so I heaved hairy hares out of my mind then settled back and relaxed while he slid the specialized needle in.

"Hey, Kristi. What's the deal with your guy in the lobby?" I asked after the third tube. "He seems way too nice to work for Saberton."

"You mean Billy? He doesn't work for Saberton. He works for me. Isn't he sweet? He's terribly young, but I enjoy having him around. Like a breath of fresh air."

I blinked. That was the last thing I ever expected Kristi to say. And she sounded utterly sincere, too.

Sincere, my ass. It wasn't in her nature. "Let's get to the tougher questions," I said, voice hard. "Why did you have Beckett Connor killed? And why were your thugs out in Mudsucker Swamp?" My hands clenched. "I know that's how you got those gators. Your people tried to kill us. I had to take out one of the divers before she could finish off Pierce."

Kristi grew somber. "Those weren't my people you encountered in the swamp. The gentlemen here"—she gestured toward her bodyguards—"captured those specimens last night. And I certainly did not have Deputy Connor killed."

"Bullshit!" I bared my teeth. "We ID'd the bald man who was in the swamp and at the hospital. Harlon Murtaugh, who works for *Saberton*."

"Saberton, perhaps. But not *me*." She made a sound of disgust. "I'm here independent of Saberton."

Bullshit again. "I have it on good authority that you're trying to take over the Saberton Board of Directors."

Kristi rounded on me. "Because those single-minded idiots only care about weaponizing the zombie parasite. They're stuck in a rut of one defense contract after another when there are a multitude of potential medical applications." She made an angry sound. "And the farm equipment? A move of pure desperation, and a waste of time and resources."

"*You* tried to weaponize the parasite by making zoldiers." I was vaguely aware that everyone had stopped working to watch the heated exchange.

She lifted her chin. "And it was a failure, which is why I moved on. As should Saberton."

Pierce entered, effectively ending the argument, though not my tension. What the hell was he doing *here*, around people who might have known the real Pierce Gentry? There was a damn good reason we were maintaining the fiction that Gentry had always been a zombie. If Kristi or anyone else at Saberton figured out Pietro had actually killed the real Gentry and taken over his form, it would open up an enormous can of worms as far as *how* he'd done so, and might lead Kristi or others to find out about mature zombies and their abilities. I didn't want to think what she might do with that information.

Then again, Pierce wasn't the sort to sit back and hide. He couldn't stand being out of the loop in any way, and probably felt coming here was worth the risk in order to make his own assessments.

I could only hope it wouldn't blow up in his face.

Kristi swept an appraising gaze over him and let out a throaty laugh. "Why, Pierce Gentry, you naughty boy. I thought I'd never get to see you again."

He folded his arms over his chest and glowered. "I guess this is your lucky day."

"And to think, you were a zombie the whole time you worked for Saberton. That's absolutely *hysterical*." She did a little golf clap. "Congratulations on pulling off such a delicate undercover job for so long. I can't say Nicole is pleased with your little charade, though."

Pierce simply nodded—the safest reply considering Saberton CEO Nicole Saber and the real Pierce Gentry had spent the last couple of years in a torrid affair.

Kristi glanced my way as Jacques finished taking the pint. "Perfect timing. I need blood from other zombies as well so I can establish proper norms. Pierce, how about you go first? Just one little tube."

I held my breath. Surely he wouldn't let Kristi get her hands on the blood of a mature zombie.

A muscle in Pierce's jaw twitched. "You don't need anything from me. There are other zombies here."

One-Ear Guard snorted. "Pussy."

"*You're* a pussy!" I declared, leaping to Pierce's defense both figuratively and literally. Pierce was a lot of things—asshole, jerk, prick—but definitely not a pussy.

Kristi's eyes shone with amusement. "Now, now, Fritz, we should be more understanding of Pierce's anxieties."

"I don't have *anxiety*," Pierce growled.

"If you say so." Her lips pursed. "You've never suffered from shyness either, so I don't understand this whole tall-dark-and-brooding thing you have going on now."

Pierce exchanged a long look with Dr. Nikas, then he jerked his shoulders up in a shrug. "Fine. I'll give you a damn sample."

Kristi gestured grandly to the chair I'd vacated and gave him a sly look. "Remember that time Nicole asked you to take your shirt off in the middle of a meeting? You didn't even hesitate. Perhaps you'd be willing to give us a repeat performance? Far better than simply rolling up your sleeve."

"I was undercover and playing my part," he said but then, to my astonishment, he gave her a cocky wink and tugged his shirt from his waistband. "But I'll oblige if it'll shut you up."

Her smile widened. "Ah, yes. There's the Pierce Gentry we know and love so well."

I watched, unease rising. Maybe he didn't want to raise suspicion by acting *too* different from the original Pierce Gentry's personality. But why would he give Kristi access to mature zombie blood, even if she didn't know what she had?

Pierce pulled the shirt off, exposing chiseled abs and a powerful chest sprinkled with dark, curly hair, wide lats that tapered down to a narrow waist, and arms with the perfect amount of muscle. Whuf. Pierce might be over a thousand years old, but holy shit goddamn he looked good half-naked.

Jesus. I was salivating over *Pierce*. "Well, it's been weird," I said, slapping my confused libido down, "but I have to go."

"But Angel, dear," Kristi said, "I need more samples."

"Yeah, well, I need to get to work. Besides, Jacques already siphoned a whole pint of blood from me."

"And yet your body is made up of so much more than blood, isn't it?"

Dr. Nikas looked up from the tablet. "Blood is sufficient for our current needs, Kristi."

She sniffed but didn't argue the point.

I shot Dr. Nikas a look of gratitude. "I'll come back after work."

"Not necessary," Kristi said, waving in dismissal. "I only needed you here for the samples."

Dr. Nikas held up a placating hand before I could deliver a scathing retort. "Angel is an experienced lab assistant. I need her here."

"Fine. She can come." Her smile turned feral. "Besides, I suppose it would be more convenient to have you close by in case I need even more samples."

Dr. Nikas moved to me and took my hand. "Thank you for coming in so early." He pressed a folded piece of paper into my palm.

"No problem," I said and casually slipped the paper into my pocket. "See you later." I sauntered out, waved to Billy in the lobby, and didn't look at the secret message until I was in my car.

Jacques will switch Pierce's blood sample once away from the other tech. No need to fret.

I let out a sigh of relief. Silly me. I should have known Dr. Nikas would take care of things.

With that worry settled, I followed the GPS's instructions back to civilization, pulling over once as an ambulance screamed by.

My car rocked in the wake, and it suddenly clicked where I'd seen Kristi's black-eyed bodyguard before. The roadblock. He was the guy FBI agent Sorsha Aberdeen arrested. So how the hell was he out and about now? And why had Sorsha been after him?

I didn't have any answers, but for the first time in the last few godawful days, I felt as if I finally had a lead. A thread to tug.

Maybe it would turn out to be a dead end, but at least I could take some action. Sorsha Aberdeen had arrested Kristi's bodyguard for a reason, and I intended to find out why. ASAP. I needed to ask a cop with access to the right info. And I knew just the one.

Chapter 22

Unfortunately, ASAP would have to be after the autopsies of the two shambler victims. When I arrived at the morgue, the bodies were waiting—along with Dr. Leblanc and two doctors I'd never seen before.

"Angel," Dr. Leblanc said. "This is Dr. Yolanda Lafferty and Dr. Bernie Reid from the CDC."

I did the polite nice-to-meet-you thing then excused myself and ran to the bathroom. With the door locked, I Googled both names. Not that I was completely devoid of trust, but I was completely devoid of trust.

I breathed a sigh of relief as both appeared to be exactly who they said they were. I didn't know whether having the CDC here was good or bad for the Tribe, but their not being obviously Saberton was a definite plus.

After sending a quick <CDC is here!> text to Dr. Nikas, I scurried to the cutting room to prep the bodies.

I unzipped the first bag to reveal the face of a teenaged boy—Nigel Copper. Sandy blond hair lay dank against his skull, and his forehead bore a scattering of acne. Heartsick, I opened the second bag—Tristan Copper—and found a young man with similar features but clearly a few years older. Dark stubble covered his jaw, and a gorgeous tattoo of a wolf's head was a spot of color on the pale skin of his upper arm.

My stomach churned. These were the brothers Allen had told

me about. Only twenty and seventeen. How could they be dead less than twenty-four hours after being infected?

After a moment to recover my composure, I got the older brother onto the cutting table and made sure all the tools were at hand and ready. Dr. Leblanc came in with Dr. Lafferty and Dr. Reid, and the autopsy began.

Other than some medical lingo, neither of the CDC docs were big conversationalists, which was fine with me. I did my morgue tech duties with quiet efficiency—being careful *not* to drop any brains this time—and kept my eyes and ears open for anything odd or interesting.

As the autopsy proceeded, I picked up the gist of what happened. The older brother had showed symptoms yesterday and bit the younger. The parents didn't know what was going on and took them to an urgent care clinic where both brothers received steroid shots. In the process, both parents were bitten. By the time all were transported to the hospital, the brothers were comatose, and the parents were symptomatic. Antibiotics, an antiviral, and an epinephrine drip were administered during the hospital stay, the same as for other patients showing shambler-symptoms. But by morning, the two young men were dead.

"Mosquito bite," Dr. Lafferty said, pointing to a tiny bump on the side of the older brother's upper arm. She exchanged a significant look with Dr. Reid.

"This is Louisiana," I pointed out. "Mosquito bites aren't exactly rare." I kept my tone light, but inner me huddled in the fetal position. If this shit could be transmitted via mosquito, we were fucked.

Dr. Lafferty's mouth pursed. "Mosquitoes are vectors for a good number of diseases, including several varieties of encephalitis."

By the time we started on the autopsy of the younger brother, inner me was rocking and gibbering in a corner. Both victims had a mosquito bite. To my frustration, Dr. Lafferty excised both bites for analysis, leaving no sample for Dr. Nikas. Dammit.

The presence of a few bites doesn't mean mosquitoes are spreading the shambler epidemic, I told myself, but the flimsy self-reassurance didn't ease my worry one bit.

After finishing up the second body, Dr. Leblanc and the CDC doctors left to review results in the main office. Allen returned, and while he helped me get the bodies sewn up and put away in the cooler, I gave him a quick rundown of the brothers, the steroids, and the bites—both mosquito and human.

"I'll get samples of these two for your people," he said as we heaved Tristan Copper W/M 20 YOA onto the shelf. "Let's hope to god they supply some answers."

"I'll ask Philip to swing by for them," I said. "Dr. Nikas will want the samples sooner rather than later."

"Have him contact me, and I'll make the arrangements."

I shoved a laden gurney to the side. "I need to go to the Sheriff's Office to talk to Ben Roth. Is it okay if I do that now?"

"As long as you make it snappy. No telling how many more of these encephalitis cases will come in." He glowered at the crowded cooler. "I need to light a fire under the asses of the funeral homes so we can move out some of our guests."

"I'll be quick," I promised.

He stalked off. I shucked my protective gear, grabbed my keys, and pushed open the back door.

And yanked it shut again at the sight of a dark green Chevy Impala pulling into the lot. Special Agent Sorsha Aberdeen. Shit. Last thing I needed was to be sucked into a conversation with her.

Hide? Except the only place to hide in the morgue was the cooler, and she might go in there to look at shambler bodies. Besides, I still needed to talk to Ben, and skulking in the cooler didn't fit with Allen's "make it snappy" order.

Flee. That could work. Keys in hand, I sprinted up the hallway toward the front of the building. At the door to the foyer, I paused and cautiously peered out in case the wily FBI agent had decided to come around to the front.

No Sorsha. Only Reb on the phone at the reception desk. Thumbs in my pockets, I sauntered by, gave Reb a wave and smile, then continued out the glass double doors as if I was merely heading to Dear John's for a mid-morning latte. Once out of Reb's field of view, I broke into a run to the corner of the building then did my sneakiest sneaking around to the back, crouching in the bushes until I could see Sorsha's car parked beneath the morgue entrance overhang.

She was still in the driver's seat, talking on her phone, dammit. I stayed put, branches poking my butt, and glanced at my watch only six times. Maybe seven.

After four agonizing minutes, she climbed out of the Impala and knocked sharply on the morgue door. A few seconds later, Dr. Leblanc ushered her in.

The instant the door closed, I dashed to my car and got my ass out of there.

First thing I did was call Dr. Nikas and tell him about the mosquito bites and the details of the CDC visit. Did he cringe every time my name appeared on the caller ID? I couldn't remember the last time I'd phoned him with good news.

After I hung up, I made a quick side trip to BigShopMart to purchase a toaster, tissue paper, and a gift bag that proclaimed "Happy Engagement!" in bright gold letters. I felt a little guilty using Ben's engagement as an excuse to go see him, but at least it was a darn nice toaster.

The Sheriff's Office HQ was only a couple of miles away— barely outside Tucker Point city limits. The two-story building was painted a jaundiced yellow with dull beige trim around small windows. The green entryway might have been attractive on its own, but against the sick yellow it looked like a decomp.

I stuffed the toaster into the gift bag, shoved tissue paper over it and fiddled with the arrangement in an attempt to make it look nice. Half a minute later, I muttered, "It's the thought that counts," gave up, and headed inside.

After getting directions to Ben's office from the deputy at the front desk, I navigated my way upstairs and down a long hall to the back of the building. His door was ajar, and I peered in to find him parked behind his desk, scowling at his computer screen.

"Are they hiding you back here for a reason?" I asked.

He looked up, a broad smile replacing the scowl. "Hey, my Angel of Death! What brings you here?"

"Prezzies!" I set the bag atop the inbox on his desk.

His eyes filled with pleased surprise. "Aww, you didn't have to do that. You're the sweetest."

"You can open it if you want. Or, y'know, pull out that crumpled mass of tissue paper. No actual opening required."

He chuckled and obliged. "Oh, wow. A four-slicer with separate controls! How did you know we needed one? Neil and I both love toast, but we only have a two-slicer with wonky heating elements. Been meaning to replace it for a month."

"And you can do bagels in it, too," I said, delighted that I'd managed to strike gold with the spur of the moment excuse-gift.

"That's awesome." Beaming, he replaced the toaster in the bag.

"Hey. I meant to ask you the other day. A guy nearly ran me off the road Monday morning—same day that drowning victim came into the morgue. Then he got stopped at a roadblock a couple miles later and Abadie arrested him. What's the deal with that?"

"Why don't you ask Abadie?" Ben asked with a mischievous gleam in his eye.

"Cuz Abadie and I aren't exactly bosom buds."

"You mean he's a prick."

"I was trying to be nice." I paused. "But, yeah."

Ben grinned. "Well, lucky for you I know the deets since I got passed the case. What little there was of it. It was weird. FBI wanted our help nabbing a Reno Larson, then all they did was charge him with trespassing, criminal mischief, and reckless driving."

"Trespassing where?"

"Admin building for the hospital. You know the brick single-story out back?"

"The one for authorized personnel only?" A tingle started at the base of my skull, telling me this was important.

"That's it," he said. "Even with the lightweight misdemeanor charges, the guy's bail was crazy high—way more than anyone would have thought. But he was out twenty minutes after it was set. Didn't even get his car out of impound. Not that it could be driven with four blown tires."

"Huh. That *is* weird." Had Sorsha arranged to have the bail set high to try to keep Reno Larson in jail for a while? And why? "Did anyone search the car?"

"Uh huh. The FBI agent got a warrant, and she and I went over it from top to bottom looking for anything tying him to that building or what he was doing there." He shrugged. "Didn't find a damn thing. That car was clean. Barely any dirt on the floor mats even. Abadie thought he saw the guy ditch something small, but a search along that stretch of the highway turned up nada."

"Or maybe there's something hidden in the door or hubcaps."

"I wondered that myself, but the warrant didn't extend to ripping the car apart. And the agent was hardcore by the book. Didn't want to do anything that might invalidate the search." He nodded in approval at the adherence to protocol.

"Yeah, no point fucking up the case by breaking the rules, right?"

"Exactly."

Too bad none of this cleared up why Sorsha had asked Bear about me and my dad. Could it be connected to the Larson stuff? Or was she juggling two cases at once? "Is this Reno Larson thing the only reason why Agent Aberdeen is in the area?"

"She said it was part of a much bigger case her task force is working, and that she'd be in the area for a while."

Bleh. I glanced at my watch. "I need to get back to work. We've been a little busy the last couple of days."

He winced. "So I hear. Has anyone pinned down what's causing the outbreak?"

"The CDC is on it, but they haven't found out anything yet." That much was true. "But you might want to wear mosquito repellent, just to be safe. And don't let anyone bite you. Same goes for Neil."

In any other situation, he'd have laughed, but he simply dipped his head in a grave nod. "10-4. Thanks for the toaster."

"Thanks for the info about the roadblock guy."

I exited the Sheriff's Office, musing over the conversation. Law enforcement had to stick to the terms and limits of warrants, otherwise any evidence they collected could be considered invalid and useless for getting a conviction. But I wasn't trying to get a conviction or find official evidence. I wasn't limited by pesky legalities.

With my plans for tonight set, I returned to the morgue.

Chapter 23

Ten minutes before my shift ended, I collected my things and watched the clock tick down. According to Allen, Sorsha's visit to the morgue had been simply to get an update on the shambler cases. No questions about me. And no new shambler deaths. But there were nine new cases at the hospital, which left me itching to get to NuQuesCor and do my part to help end this whole disaster. Maybe I wasn't as smart and educated as Kristi, but I could damn well wash beakers, sterilize equipment, and pipette the hell out of all sorts of shit.

The instant the clock ticked to 4 p.m., I grabbed my things and quick-timed it to my car, worry following me. If the infection kept spreading at the current rate, where would the patients go? Tucker Point Regional Hospital wasn't a large facility. And the shamblers needed to be quarantined and restrained and—

A hand grabbed my arm.

I shrieked and dropped my bag, even as the hours and hours of practicing the *ippon seoi nage* shoulder throw kicked in. I seized my attacker's wrist, pivoted, yanked, and bent in perfect-enough form to send him sailing over my shoulder.

The man let out a surprised yelp and landed in a heap before me. "Fuck me, Angel," he gasped. "What the hell?"

I stared for a second before recognition clicked in. "Kang?" He looked a good fifteen years older—an easy disguise for a mature zombie. "Why'd you jump out at me like that? You scared the shit out of me!"

Groaning, he clambered to his feet. "I did not jump out at you. I merely touched your arm."

"Grabbed. You *grabbed* my arm." With an exasperated huff, I found my keys and unlocked my car. "Get in before someone sees you. Jesus. What were you thinking?"

"I was thinking you asked me to wake up," he said with asperity as he climbed into the passenger seat. "And, I wanted to thank you for giving me a way to escape that place."

"You're welcome. Don't make me regret it."

Tense, I drove away from the Coroner's Office and didn't relax until I was sure no one was following us. For all I knew, Pierce had eyes on me in case Kang tried to do exactly what he'd just done and make contact with me.

I flicked a quick glance at Kang. "Are you doing all right? I mean, after I woke up from being regrown, it took me a couple of weeks before I could walk without looking like I was three sheets to the wind."

He chuckled softly. "I've picked up a few tricks here and there."

"Ha! I knew it." I grinned. "You were awake the whole time, and got used to your new body while pretending to be in a coma."

"Not quite the whole time but close enough. As far as I can tell, I woke about a day after I came out of the tank. Ariston was in the midst of a rather tense conversation with a man whom I quickly identified as Pietro in a new form. It didn't take me long to suss out it was in my best interest to feign unconsciousness."

"In other words, you were pretending yesterday when you said you didn't know who Pierce was."

He winked. "Seemed the right move."

"Heh. And Pierce was *sooo* insistent he could tell if you were faking it."

"Pierce," Kang said as if trying out the word for the first time, "isn't as phenomenal as he likes people to think he is."

I cocked an eyebrow. "And you are?"

Kang shrugged. "I've never made claims to greatness."

"Fair enough," I said after a moment's thought. Until Pierce told me how old Kang really was, I'd assumed he was as ordinary as any other zombie "When you were faking unconsciousness, did you hear everything I said to you?"

He sobered. "I did. And I don't have a solution for your shambler issue—at least not one that you'll like. Around fifteen hundred years ago in Constantinople, I saw zombies that were *wrong.* Aggressive, but not from brain starvation, and seemingly devoid of humanity."

I turned onto a side street. "How were they cured?"

"They weren't." Kang winced. "The infected—and anyone who'd been bitten—were driven into a house which was then set on fire."

"Oh." I passed a strip mall then drove into the alley behind it and killed the engine. "Yeah, that's not an option."

Kang gave me a long look. "Other than the current shambler crisis, you seem to be doing well."

"I am. I've had a few setbacks, but I got my GED last year, and I'm taking classes at Tucker Point Community College."

"That's good to hear," he said. "I confess, when I briefly woke up in the tank, I was quite shocked to see you alive and well. And even more shocked when I discovered you were welcome in the heart of the Tribe's lab."

I snickered. "A lot's happened since you got your head chopped off."

"Yes, I caught up on much of the news via Pierce, albeit unwittingly on his part." Wicked glee briefly lit his eyes. "I can't help but find it damn funny that you've become such a . . . valuable asset."

I bristled. "You don't think I can be a valuable asset?"

"Don't be silly. That's not what I think at all." Kang lounged against the passenger door. "I knew from the beginning Marcus was the one who zombified you. Pietro was pissed when he found out Marcus had turned someone without consulting him first." He chuckled. "And absolutely, utterly furious when he learned what kind of person you were."

"Drug addict, high school dropout, felon, loser," I supplied cheerfully.

"Model citizen, indeed." He cocked his head. "He wanted to have you killed. In fact, before I got my head chopped off, I didn't expect you to live much longer. But then you went and stopped the zombie killer and saved Marcus's life, yes? I suppose at that point Pietro could hardly claim terminating you would be for Marcus's own good."

I remained quiet for a moment as I sorted through my churning thoughts. Pietro hadn't gone so far as to have me killed, but he'd thrown me to the wolves when Kristi Charish needed a test subject.

Yet he'd also sent a helicopter to save me and my dad from raging flood waters, and then loaned me enough money to rebuild our home and our lives. *And* he'd paid me rather handsomely for doing various work for the Tribe. In fact, I'd recently discovered that my entire debt had been forgiven—payment, perhaps, for saving zombies from being exposed to the public.

"I think Pietro-Pierce and I are good now," I finally said.

He regarded me, forehead slightly creased as if trying to solve a riddle. "He doesn't trust many people. But he trusts you. Or your intentions, at least."

I met his eyes. "I just want zombies to be safe."

"And that's what he sees in you. It's all he has ever wanted."

"That's why he formed the Tribe, right?"

Kang let out a dry chuckle. "Yes, for better or for worse." He shook his head. "I'm still not convinced it's a good idea."

I snapped my fingers. "Because it draws attention."

"Precisely. And 'attention' is seldom kind to those who are different, much less a potential threat."

"Sure, but there are huge advantages, too," I said. "It's a community that helps each other out. It's a safe place, a ready supply of brains, and the latest in zombie health care."

"I agree." A light smile played about his mouth. "There are pros and cons. I have yet to decide which way the balance tips."

I fell silent while various thoughts ticked over in my mind. Kang was over two thousand years old. Of all the amazing cities and communities around the world, why had he settled *here*, in Nowhere, Louisiana? Surely not because he was Pierce's zombie-daddy.

"You're here to keep an eye on Pietro and the Tribe!" I cried, pleased when Kang nodded. "Wait. The Tribe's been around for hundreds of years, and you still haven't decided whether or not it's a good thing?"

"No. The Tribe as you know it has only been around for a

couple of decades. Before then it was a small group of perhaps four or five. Often it was only Ariston and the man you currently know as Pierce. It was only when Francis Coleman became Pietro Ivanov and gained his holdings, investments, and influence that he was able to organize and expand—helped considerably by technological advances in communication and transportation."

"Francis?" I snickered. "I can't picture Pierce ever being a *Francis*."

Kang smiled. "Francis was a decorated marine during the conflict in Vietnam."

"Hold up." I glared at him. "You mean the Vietnam War that happened in the twentieth century, right? Because you burned me once before, making me think you were talking about a recent war instead of an ancient one."

This time he laughed. "Yes, in the twentieth century. He saved fourteen U.S. soldiers by taking out a Viet Cong ambush and then literally carrying the wounded men to safety. Quite the badass."

I cocked my head. "Who was he before he was Francis?"

Kang pursed his lips in thought. "I believe he went by Clarence . . . Clarence Ambrewster."

"Jesus, that's worse than Francis."

"Clarence was equally badass in World War I *and* World War II."

I frowned. "He sure does love fighting."

Kang's expression shadowed. "He is skilled in the various arts of war, and as a zombie he is unusually suited for such a life. Throughout history, a good soldier has always been able to find a job." He paused. "Not to mention, a battlefield is an excellent source of brains."

I shifted to face him. "What does Pierce want from you? I mean, he's been nuts over whatever it is, but obviously you don't want to tell him."

Kang sobered. "It's complicated."

"Try me."

He remained silent long enough for me to worry he might bolt to avoid spilling the beans.

"Have you ever heard of a zombie referred to as *mature*?" he finally asked.

"Actually, yes. Dr. Nikas told me about them. It's how Pietro Ivanov became Pierce Gentry."

"Yes, precisely. And you know it has very little to do with age, right?"

"I think I remember him saying that."

"Good. That saves us a great deal of explanation." He looked up as if deciding how to proceed. "And you're probably aware that a mature zombie has a far higher level of abilities, such as heightened senses."

I nodded. "Like how Pierce can smell lies, and how Dr. Nikas can taste what's wrong with someone."

"Right. A mature zombie has a greatly reduced the need for brains and gains the ability to reshape himself into the form of another by consuming their fresh brain, as you saw for yourself when Pietro became Pierce. Of course, we didn't know the *how* of it—DNA reconfiguration—until a few decades ago when Ariston's research unraveled that part of the mystery." He took a deep breath and blew it out in a sigh. "Maturation is like an evolution, where host and parasite become one entity. Indistinguishable. And . . . a very long time ago, I figured out a way to trigger that evolution and *force* the zombie organism to quickly complete the process."

"Pierce wants to know how to do it!" I said. "But I'm guessing you're about to tell me why forcing it is a bad idea."

His shoulders sagged, as if bearing the weight of two thousand years of existence. "I met Pierce—known then as Sulemain—over twelve hundred years ago. We became lovers, and a year or so later, I turned him. He—"

"Whoa!" My eyes widened. "Pierce is gay? Or I guess bi. Holy shit!"

Kang laughed. "No, he has always preferred women." A sly smile lifted a corner of his mouth.

I gasped. "You were a woman?!" I grinned as he nodded. "Were you smokin' hot?"

He let out a snort of mock disdain. "Of course I was. I'd hardly take the form of a hag."

More questions burned to be asked, but I made myself focus. "Okay. So you and Sulemain were doing the lust and thrust, and you force-evolved him. Then something went wrong, big time. Am I right?"

Old grief filled his eyes. "Sulemain was a soldier, accustomed to killing when necessary. Yet he was also a good man—a tender and considerate lover with the capacity for great compassion and loyalty. We'd been together nearly seventy years before I forced the change, and I've regretted it for over a millennium." He massaged the center of his forehead as if trying to physically ease the pain of an old memory. "Sulemain's entire personality changed. Almost overnight, he developed a hair-trigger temper and a greatly increased capacity for violence. Not bloodlust or berserker . . . but cold-blooded and aggressive, terrifying to be around, even for me." He met my eyes. "I couldn't be with him anymore, although I have always monitored from a distance. It took *centuries* for the hyperaggression to fade such that he regained a measure of his old humanity."

That explained a lot. "When you pretended to fall asleep again, he went off on Dr. Nikas and punched a wall."

"That incident was a pale shadow of his former belligerence. It was after Sulemain rescued Ariston from the mob that change for the better began. Ariston was . . . is . . . a wellspring of calm. For everyone."

I smiled. "I've felt the effect about a zillion times."

"Ariston helped Sulemain regain balance, became a touchstone for the man Sulemain needed to be."

"Did you force-evolve Dr. Nikas, too?"

He shook his head. "After the disastrous result with Sulemain, I vowed never to force completion again. Ariston matured naturally after about two and a half centuries as a zombie."

"Is that about when most zombies do the maturing thing?"

"Most zombies never mature," he said to my surprise. "It takes the perfect match of person and parasite. There's no way to predict, but yes, if it happens, it's usually after a couple hundred years."

"If a zombie doesn't mature, what then? Do we just go on living like we are?"

"The relatively few zombies who manage to avoid death by accident or injury can potentially live several hundred years before they lose the ability to repair damage. At that point, they begin to swiftly age and die within a year or so."

Huh. And here I'd been thinking I was immortal. "Several hundred years isn't a bad haul."

"Not at all." Kang shrugged. "For that matter, I'm sure that even an evolved zombie has a limit to his life span, though clearly it's longer than twenty-two hundred years plus change."

"I can't even imagine living that long."

"It hasn't always been glamorous," he said, face an unreadable mask.

Two thousand years. How much tragedy had he seen? "How many mature zombies are there in the world?"

"A dozen, maybe less." He shrugged. "Who knows? There aren't all that many zombies in the first place, and only a scant few of them mature—with no known rhyme or reason. Through the years, I've encountered six others. None as old as I am, and none younger than Ariston."

"Kristi Charish has a theory that the zombie parasite controls its own population. Maybe it applies to mature zombies, too."

His eyes narrowed. "The doctor who wants to be queen dictator?"

"That's the one." My mouth tightened. "Over a year ago, she was trying to create zoldiers—zombie soldiers. I was kidnapped to be used as her test subject. She had one of her men shoot Philip Reinhardt, then gave me the choice of making Philip a zombie or watching him die. I couldn't let him die, so I turned him." I rubbed my arms. "The very next day they brought in another 'volunteer' and shot him, but the instinct wasn't there for me like it had been for Philip, and that man died in my arms."

"Because it doesn't work like that. A variable amount of time is required between turnings—weeks to months—which is why you couldn't save that second man."

"Found that out the hard way. Kristi told me it was because of a population control mechanism with the parasite, due to brains being a limited resource. I suppose that explains why there are so few zombies."

Kang regarded me with calm, ancient eyes. "Is that truly what controls our population?"

I made myself consider the question. Even if each zombie made only one new zombie every six months, the population would triple each year. Given our long lifespan, after a thousand years or so, we should have zombies stacked halfway to the moon—which obviously wasn't the case.

"It's not the parasite controlling the population," I finally said. "It's us. We choose when to make a new zombie." In fact, as long as I'd been with the Tribe, the only two new zombies created were Philip and Andrew Saber—both by me. "We're not indiscriminate. We know about the limited food supply. We know that more zombies means more chance of being outed and killed. For self-preservation, we don't go around making zombie babies every time we can, but only when we need or want to."

He gave me a sage nod. "We're not driven to create more zombies. Ever. There's no zombie hormones that make us bitey. We turn people we care about in order to keep them from dying."

"The instinct I had when I made Philip and Andrew into zombies came after I decided I needed to turn them. To save them."

"Exactly. We can lay dear Dr. Charish's hasty theory to rest. Plus, she didn't know about mature zombies, who need far less brains."

"So what does it all mean?" I asked.

He laughed softly. "It means we are both parasite and person."

I cocked my head. "Dr. Nikas once told me that the parasite isn't really a parasite. Said calling it a 'mutualistic symbiont with parasitic aspects' was a somewhat better description."

"It's a union that creates something entirely new." He shook his head. "We're still mysteries, even to ourselves."

Less of a mystery every day, thanks to Dr. Nikas. And, though I hated to admit it, Kristi Charish. "Speaking of mysteries, I have a burning personal question. Were you born a woman?"

"I was," Kang said. "Though I often took a male form, for mere survival. Throughout much of history, a woman without a husband or family to protect her often had a poor outcome."

I tried to imagine myself as a man. What would it feel like to have a dong flopping around? And just how itchy was ball itch? "So Pierce started out as Sulemain," I said. The name definitely fit him. "What was your original name?"

His eyes darkened. "I don't remember. The parasite protects memory to a vast extent, but . . . I never thought I would live this long. I didn't think to remind myself of certain details, and I've been more people than I can count." He forced a smile. "I've gone by Kang or a variation thereof for several centuries now. Makes it easier to remember who I'm supposed to be."

"Damn. Sorry." My phone buzzed, saving me from the awkward moment. "It's Bear. Nick's dad. I'd better take this." I hit the answer button. "Hey, Bear—"

"Angel," he gasped. "I'm at the bowling alley. My people . . . they turned. They turned shambler."

Chapter 24

"Call nine-one-one! And what do you mean they turned? Your survivalist group?"

"I called already! They're backed up. Dispatcher said it would be twenty minutes or more. It's six of us here. I don't know what—" Someone yelled in the background. "Jesus! Can you just fucking get here?"

"I'm only a block away. Hang tight." I disconnected then started the car and zipped to the bowling alley, narrowly avoiding crashing into an SUV as it careened out of the parking lot at breakneck speed.

I drove right up to the front and bailed out. A teenage girl huddled by an ancient Honda Accord, her shirt emblazoned with "Alvin's Alley."

"Don't go in there!" she gasped. "They went nuts. And someone shot Gussie." She hiccupped a sob.

Kang dashed for the door. I dragged the girl to her feet. "Get in your car and go."

"I can't! I left my purse inside."

I shoved my keys into her hand. "Then get in mine and lock the doors. And if you steal it, I swear I'll hunt you down and do horror movie shit. Now move!"

She scrambled toward my car. I sprinted into the bowling alley then flinched at the sound of a gunshot. Across the room a plastic sign shattered.

"Stop shooting," I roared even as Kang leaped over the snack bar and ripped the pistol from the owner's hand—who promptly fled out the front door. With the immediate threat under control, I took stock of the situation.

Alvin's Alley was twelve lanes of wholesome family fun decorated in a vaguely 70s retro theme, though with modern computerized scoreboards. It wasn't fancy, but it was clean and safe. Except for today.

On the floor beside the nearest bowling ball return, a man with dreadlocks moaned and slavered in a pool of blood.

Bear stood at the far end of lane six beside a baby-faced man I recognized as one of Bear's sales associates, Clark. Together they slung pins at two husky black dudes—the Rucker twins. In the next lane over, a woman with orange hair shambled toward them down the oiled surface.

"Don't kill them!" Bear shouted, distressed.

"We won't," I called back, hoping it was true. But how to stop these new shamblers?

Dreadlocks Man let out a howl and dragged himself toward me, legs apparently useless. In a blur of zombie speed, Kang snatched a towel from the snack bar and bounded to his side. Hopefully to stop both Dreadlocks Man's advance and the bleeding.

The door banged open, and Nick rushed in. "I heard the call on the scanner!"

"Four shamblers!" I hollered. "Don't get bit!"

Using his belt, Kang strapped the folded towel over the wound in Dreadlocks Man's back. Clark let out a moan and crumpled.

"Shit!" Bear jumped away to the next lane as Clark staggered to his feet, breathing noisily, and eyes dead.

"Make that five shamblers," I said. Damn, he sure turned fast. And Bear was seriously outnumbered now.

"Nick! Bowling balls!" I dodged past Kang and Dreadlocks Man to seize one up. "Knock them down!" I hadn't been bowling since I was a kid but I wasn't worried about form. With a shout of triumph, I slung the ball down the lane toward Clark.

Then cursed as the ball sailed into the gutter. Okay, maybe form did matter.

Nick sent a ball right down the center of his lane, knocking the woman on her ass. I tried again, achieving yet another gutter ball. "Fuck!"

He hit a button on the scoreboard, and rails rose up along the sides of the lane. "Kiddie rails. Try it now."

Great. I sucked that hard. But with the rails keeping the ball from the gutter, I managed to knock Clark off his feet.

"Bowling for zombies!" I whooped.

Nick took down Rucker One, but the woman was already clambering up.

"We need to restrain them," I said, aiming for Rucker Two. "Kang, look for duct tape or rope or something."

"There's duct tape in my truck," Bear yelled. He fished keys from his pocket and winged them at us.

Kang shot up and snatched them from midair in one fluid move then sprinted out the door. Nick and I continued to sling bowling balls at the twins, the woman, and Clark, while Bear played keep-away and tossed pins.

Kang raced in with three rolls of duct tape on each arm. Of course Bear would have a shitload of duct tape. A survivalist's best friend.

"Bear and Nick, keep them knocked down." I grabbed a stool from the snack bar. "I'll pin shamblers while Kang duct tapes them."

"I can help," Bear said.

"No! Doesn't matter if Kang and I get bit."

Bear's gaze snapped to Kang as he realized Kang was a zombie. Nick's did, too, with an added look of bewilderment. The Kang he knew was not only supposed to be dead, but younger.

Nick shook it off and slung another ball at Clark. I ran to the woman and gave her a solid kick to the midsection as she pushed up to her hands and knees. She toppled over, and I jammed the stool over her torso, putting my full weight on it to pin her. "Kang! Tape!"

He was already in motion, wrapping duct tape around her legs with the easy grace of a spider binding its prey. Once her ankles were secured, I chucked the stool aside and helped him get her wrists and mouth bound.

We repeated the process with Clark without too much trouble, but my puny weight wasn't enough to hold Rucker One, who was nearly as big as Derrel the death investigator.

"I'll grab his feet," Bear said. "I won't get bit that way." He pushed forward and wrapped his arms around the thrashing man's legs, holding on like a bull rider. Nick bowled Rucker Two off his feet then sprinted down the lane to grab Rucker One's wrists.

"Nick, get back!" Bear roared.

"Shut up, Dad," Nick said through his teeth, clinging on for dear life as Kang bound the man in damn near an entire roll of duct tape.

Rucker Two staggered to his feet. Breathing hard, I tackled him behind his knees, sending him crashing to the lane. His head thudded against the divider, and he went limp. Crap. Still breathing, though.

We rolled him onto his back as he started to come to, and got him trussed up before he could do more than flail a bit. He had a goose egg on his forehead, but at least it wasn't bleeding.

"Need to get the wounded guy, too," I panted.

Kang loped over and took care of taping Dreadlocks Man in a flash.

"Gunshot with entry in the gut and exit wound in the back," Kang said. "Spinal cord, I'm guessing, otherwise he'd have been up as well. I'll stick with him."

Bear rounded on Nick. "I told you to stay back. Are you hurt? Did you get bitten?" He ran his hands over Nick like a pat down until Nick slapped them away.

"I'm not hurt! Are you?"

"No, I'm fine." Bear gazed around him, agonized. "My people. Angel, are they going to be okay? They've been part of my survivalist group for over a decade."

"We're going to do everything we can," I told him. "A . . . specialist came down from Chicago. Dr. Kristi Charish. You might've seen her on the news—"

"The same Kristi Charish who locked you up in a cage?" He gave me an incredulous look. "You're working with her?"

Shit. Forgot I'd told him all about her right before I rotted apart. "We are. I fucking hate her, but she's the best chance we have of finding a cure."

The sound of rapidly approaching sirens put an end to the conversation. I raced to open the door for two paramedics and a frazzled Tucker Point city cop, Seamus Hardy.

"We got 'em restrained," I said as they entered.

The older paramedic, his right eye nearly swollen shut, gave me a thumbs up. "Thank god. That last transport was rough."

"You didn't get bit, did you?" I asked.

"Nope. Clocked by her heel," he said. "What do we have?"

I gestured toward Dreadlocks Man. "He has a gunshot wound, and one of the Rucker twins got knocked out for about ten seconds. The others were trying to bite."

"Got it. More units are on the way." He rushed to Dreadlocks Man while his partner did a quick check of the others.

Kang remained crouched beside Dreadlocks Man, answering the paramedic's questions. Bear and Nick stood watch over the other shamblers, ready in case any of them broke free.

Hardy radioed in a report then looked my way. "All five got sick at the same time?"

"Close to it. Within about five minutes of each other. Fucking weird."

"Fucking scary is what it is." His mouth tightened. "We took so long getting here because the same thing happened across town not half an hour ago. Except it was a bunch of lawyers having their weekly meeting. One went down then three more followed. Total mayhem. Two paralegals and the head of the firm got bit, so they're freaking the hell out."

I hissed a curse. "The hospital must be bursting at the seams."

Hardy nodded. "Every EMT crew within a fifty-mile radius is on call, and the hospital is full. Emergency triage has been set up at the Tucker High gym."

My worry tripled. "How is that secure?"

"Restraints. Lots of them." He lifted his chin toward the downed shamblers. "The duct tape was good thinking."

I gave him a weak smile. "You know what they say. Duct tape and WD-40 can fix anything." If only.

The fire department and two other ambulances rolled up. Still reeling from everything Hardy had told me, I retreated outside with Bear, Kang, and Nick.

The first pair of paramedics followed us out, with Dreadlocks Man strapped to a backboard on their stretcher. Once they had him loaded up and were gone, I shared the new info with the others.

"The pattern has changed," I said. "They're turning shambler sooner. And how the hell can a whole group turn at the same time? This makes no sense."

"Dad, are you *sure* you weren't bitten?" Nick asked, voice quavering ever so slightly.

Bear showed Nick his arms. "I'm sure. Some bumps and bruises. That's all."

A sick thought occurred to me. "What about mosquito bites?"

"Nope. Nick already warned me. I'm swimming in DEET." Misery twisted his face. "I brought these guys to the bowling alley to stay inside and keep an eye on them. Fat lot of good it did."

The naked worry in Nick's eyes didn't ease. I understood it all too well. "I've come to a decision," I announced. "Bear, you and my dad are going to stay at the zombie lab until this shit blows over."

Nick turned to me with such a look of gratitude that my knees went weak. "Thank you," he breathed. "That's perfect."

Bear puffed up. "No way. I'm not going to run and hide."

"Shut up, Dad!" Nick clenched his hands. "If you love me at all, you'll do this for me. Be safe."

Bear drew breath to argue then blew it out. "Jesus Christ. Fine. I'll go. Wherever the hell this place is."

"Kang, you can drive Bear's truck," I said.

Bear scowled. "I can drive myself."

"Nope. Bad idea." I stabbed a finger at him. "Like it or not, we still have you on shambler watch. Turning shambler behind the wheel would be ugly."

"Shit. You're right."

"Damn straight I am. I'll call my dad and tell him he has to go. Y'all can swing by and pick him up, then zip straight to the lab."

Kang gave me a sour look. "I just left that wretched place."

"I never said you had to stay," I snapped. "Drop them off and come back, because god knows we need the help."

Kang lifted his hands in surrender and turned to Bear. "Do you need anything before we go?"

"Nope. Got a jump bag and a couple of changes of clothes in the truck."

Bear and my dad would be safe. For now, at least. Better than nothing. But I also needed to protect Portia, who'd managed to become deeply important to me in a short amount of time. I felt a sharp pang at the thought of that lovely, gentle woman turning into a slavering creature. And Jane! Had Pierce's stalking extended to protecting her?

"There's someone else I need you to pick up. Hang on." I stepped away and found Portia's number, shifted from foot to foot as it rang.

"Hello—"

"Portia, it's Angel," I said in a rush. "Please don't think I'm crazy, but the weird encephalitis is spreading. Look, I really want you to be safe from infection, so I'm sending a friend over to pick you up and take you—oh my god, that sounds skeevy as hell."

"I'm not sure I understand."

That was the nicest way I'd ever heard anyone say "you're a complete fucking looney." And how *could* she understand? The whole thing was insanity.

"I know it sounds totally bonkers, but can you please get in touch with Jane Pennington? She'll vouch for me." I hoped. "I'm calling her the instant I hang up with you."

"Actually, she's right here with me."

"For real? Can I please talk to her?"

There was rustling, and then another familiar female voice. "Angel?"

No need to be vague with Jane. "The sick people are infected with a mutated version of the zombie parasite, and it's spreading out of control. I want you and Portia to go to the Tribe lab. You'll be safe there."

"Marcus called a few minutes ago and said he would send a car for me as soon as I was ready. Victor agrees it's best. I came over to warn Portia to stay inside and use repellent."

At least Pierce was still looking out for Jane. Or maybe Marcus had taken the initiative. Jane's bodyguard, Victor, was great protection under normal circumstances, but he wouldn't be much help against the shambler disease. "It'll take at least twenty minutes for a car to reach you from the lab," I told her. "I can have someone there for you *and* Portia in less than ten." Bear's pickup was a crew cab and could fit five adults easily.

"Yes, that would be better," Jane agreed. "Especially for Portia." In the background, I heard, *Jane, what on earth is going on?* "Portia, I'll explain everything, but Angel is right. You'll be better off going to . . . a safe place." To me, she said, "Don't you worry about her, Angel. I'm relieved she's invited."

"You're the best," I said fervently and sent up about a billion prayers of gratitude. "See you both at the lab later."

I hung up, glad that particular concern was taken care of, though I'd have to deal with the "invited" part sooner rather than later. I didn't exactly have the authority to say they could go to the Tribe's lab. "Bear, before you and Kang go get my dad, I need y'all to pick up Jane Pennington and her neighbor, Portia Antilles. They live in Belle Maison Estates."

Bear frowned. "Jane Pennington the Congresswoman?"

"That's her. I'm texting you the address right now."

Bear gave a brusque thumbs up. "Let's roll, Kang."

They jogged to the truck and took off. Nick watched them go with a curious look on his face. "So . . . John Kang is back from the dead."

"Sure is. The serial killer's victims were all zombies, and Kang was one of them. We got his head back and re-grew him." I allowed myself a grin at Nick's reaction then turned away to call Marcus.

"It's getting worse," I said when he answered.

"I know. Shamblers are turning faster and succumbing in groups."

"It's really fucking bad. I'm sending Bear and my dad to the lab to be safe. They're picking up Jane and another friend of mine, Portia Antilles."

"Jesus, Angel. Your dad and Jane, sure, but we can't turn the lab into a refugee camp."

"Yes, we can!" I shouted. "If we're ever going to come out of hiding, we need human allies, and that means we have to be allies to them in return. Now, you have four non-zombies heading your way in the next hour, and I swear to god if you don't roll out the motherfucking welcome mat for each and every one of them, I will burn the goddamn lab to the ground."

"Cripes, Angel. Relax." He exhaled. "You're right. About the allies, not the burning. We'll take good care of them."

My anger subsided. "All right. Thanks. And I wouldn't really have burned it down."

"It's okay."

"I mean, it's concrete, and it would be really hard to—"

"Goodbye, Angel."

The line went dead. Now for the toughest call of all.

I started speaking the instant my dad answered. "Dad, you

have to go to the Tribe lab. Shit's getting worse, and Bear Gala-tas is coming to get you in about half an hour. Please don't argue with me about this. Please."

"I won't argue, baby," he said. "I can hear it in your voice. I'll be ready when your buddy gets here."

I shuddered in bone-deep relief. "Really? I love you so much, Dad."

"I love you too, Angelkins. You be careful out there, okay?"

"I will. I promise."

My hands trembled as I shoved the phone into my pocket. I sat on the curb, closed my eyes, and tried to find a brief moment of balance.

A stretcher clattered by. The last of the shamblers being loaded into an ambulance. As the unit roared away, a warm hand gripped mine. I didn't need to open my eyes to know it was Nick. He didn't try and pull me close or hug me. Simply held my hand, letting me know he was there.

Tears filled my eyes, and I let them fall, crying for the whole awful situation as well as for how much Nick meant to me. He was an important part of my life, more than I could have ever expected. Kind and supportive—a good, decent man.

An image swam in my mind—the memory of his face twisted with revulsion at the sight of my rotting body. Yet, here he was, unafraid to touch me.

My phone buzzed with a text. I pulled my hand away to thumb in my passcode.

From Dr. Nikas. <We are monitoring the situation. Do you have access to samples?>

I started to reply with a No, then remembered Dreadlocks Man.

<I can get you some blood-soaked carpet>

<That will serve quite well for now.>

I heaved myself up from the curb. "I need to get some of that bloody carpet for Dr. Nikas."

Nick stood. "I have a box cutter in my car." At my curious look, a corner of his mouth kicked up. "My dad is a prepper. It rubs off."

He retrieved the box cutter, and we headed inside. Hardy leaned against the shoe counter, talking on his cell phone. "Yeah, honey, I know I said I'd be home, but we're slammed, and I'm stuck until the crime scene techs are done here, and they're still ten minutes out. I promise I'll make it up to—" He went silent and listened.

"Crap," I whispered to Nick. "We can't exactly cut a hunk of carpet out of a crime scene." The blood was a dark stain on the worn green carpet, surrounded by discarded gauze and syringe packaging and other EMT debris. Nearby lay the bloody towel Kang had used to slow the bleeding. Taking the towel from the scene would be a really bad idea, but the sight of it gave me a better one.

"Change of plan. I'm going to snag a clean towel from behind the snack bar and soak up some of the blood with it. As soon as Hardy gets off the phone, keep him distracted. I should only need about fifteen seconds."

"Got it."

I made my way toward the snack counter as if looking for something I'd dropped. Nick sauntered toward where Hardy continued to try and reason with his honey.

"Look, baby, don't hang up on . . . me." Hardy lowered the phone and stared at it glumly.

"Hey, man," Nick said, "can you help me look for my badge? It must've slipped out of my pocket when we were wrestling with the Rucker twins." He gestured vaguely toward where pins and shattered plastic and debris littered the far end of the lanes.

"Sure thing." Hardy shoved his phone in his pocket. "Better than trying to talk sense into my girlfriend. You wouldn't believe what she just said to me!"

The two ambled down the lanes, with Hardy giving Nick an earful. I ducked behind the snack bar counter, pleased to find a neat stack of white bar towels on a shelf below the popcorn machine. I snagged one then searched for a bag, but only found a box of gigantic industrial garbage bags under the sink. No sign of anything smaller.

It would have to do. I peeled one open as I strolled out to where Dreadlocks Man had been shot, casually dropped the towel onto the blood-soaked carpet, then stepped on it with my full weight. Lifted off and stepped again then stuffed the bloody towel into the bag. I was about to close it up when scattered water bottles caught my eye in the area where Bear's people had been sitting. Nice Springs bottling company—water from my hometown. What if something in the water caused the shambling? It made about as much sense as anything else. Nick was still talking to Hardy, but they were coming back up the lane. I grabbed two of the bottles and dropped them into the bag, then rolled it up tight and headed outside.

"Shit. My keys," I muttered. I'd given them to the scared girl. Maybe she left them on the seat? I peered through the window then almost burst out laughing. The girl cowered in my backseat, eyes squeezed shut.

I tapped on the window, and she let out a screech.

"It's safe now," I said, raising my voice so she could hear me through the glass.

She shifted to peer out. "C-can you get my purse? I don't want to go back inside." Her lower lip quivered. "It's in the office."

I couldn't blame her. "Sure thing. Open the door first."

By the time I got my contraband tucked under the front seat, Nick was walking out. After hearing the story, he jogged inside, soon returning with a bright purple bedazzled clutch.

The girl scrambled out of the car, snatched the purse from him with a stuttery thanks, then dashed to a pale green Kia.

More saddened than amused, I watched her squeal out of the parking lot. She was probably still in high school. Too young to see people turn into monsters around her.

"Poor kid," Nick murmured. His hand clasped mine again. I squeezed it back then forced myself to release it, feeling as if I was tearing free a part of my own self.

"Nick." I swallowed. "I like you. A lot. But you don't know what you're getting into with me." He started to speak, but I shook my head to stop him. "You've seen me rot and fall to pieces. If I don't get brains, that'll happen again. I eat *human brains*, Nick. It's revolting. And you've never seen me when I'm hungry. I have a monster of a time-bomb ticking within me. I'm messed up, weird, and gross. You deserve better. I-I care about you too much."

Like a total coward, I spun away, climbed into my car, and shut the door.

"Angel!" Muffled.

I peeled out in an echo of the girl's departure and didn't look back. It was stupid. The whole thing was stupid, like those dumb teen-romance movies where I'd yell at the screen at how stupid they were being.

But this was reality. And the stakes were too high.

Chapter 25

On my way to NuQuesCor, I passed three mosquito control trucks spraying the ditches. Maybe it was pure coincidence that they were out in force—after all, this area was well-known for West Nile virus. But I suspected the CDC had a hand in it, as a precaution.

In the nearly deserted NuQuesCor parking lot, I fished the water bottles from the bag then stuck them back under the seat. I'd give them to Dr. Nikas later when Kristi wasn't around. At least he wouldn't be snarky if analyzing them turned out to be a waste of time.

I headed inside, garbage bag with bloody towel tucked away in my backpack. Instead of Billy, Kristi's security guy Reno Larson a.k.a. Car Chase Dude stood watch by the staircase, regarding me with a smirk as I crossed the lobby. For an instant, I was tempted to call him by name, then decided not to tip my hand that I knew anything about him.

Upstairs, Billy leaned against the wall outside the main lab door. "Afternoon, Miss Crawford," he said cheerfully.

"Hi, Billy, and you can call me Angel. Why are you stuck out here?"

"I'm a glorified gofer, ready and waiting for my next task." He grinned. "Wait, did I say glorified?"

I couldn't help but smile. "How long have you been out here?" Though he wore a dark suit like Fritz and Reno, he didn't have the bulge of a gun under his jacket. Apparently he wasn't part of her security team.

"About three hours now." He pondered dramatically for a second. "Or perhaps it's been three days?"

"You poor thing," I said with a laugh. "Can't you at least play solitaire or Bubble Popper on your phone?"

"No way, Miss Angel. If Dr. Charish caught me, she'd fire me like that." He snapped his fingers.

"That sucks. I'd be dead of boredom by now!"

"Money's good. I can handle it." He winked. "For now, at least."

"You're a better man than I am. Er, figuratively speaking." I grinned. "I'd better get to work. Catch you later, Billy."

In the main lab room, soft jazz music floated over the low hum of equipment. Kristi perched on a stool in front of a computer while One-Ear Fritz leaned against a nearby counter, arms folded casually over his chest, but eyes sharp and watchful. Jacques and a Kristi-tech with a glorious chest-length auburn beard sorted through computer printouts at the center table. On the far side of the room, Brian and Rachel conversed quietly while still managing to keep an eye on everything.

Kristi glanced up as I pulled the garbage bag from my backpack. "You have the blood sample? Good." She pointed at the bearded tech. "You there! Come take care of this."

"Where's Dr. Nikas?" I asked.

"He left about ten minutes ago by helicopter to return to his own lab. Being here, around new people, is hard on him." She stated it frankly with no hint of derision.

"Yeah, it is," I said, more than a little surprised by her show of actual empathy.

Beardzilla approached, wearing mask and gloves, and bearing a big zip bag marked with a biohazard symbol. I slipped a glove onto my right hand then lifted the towel out and dropped it into the biohazard bag. Though I couldn't catch the shambler disease, I didn't want to contaminate everything I touched later and endanger others.

The tech left the room with the bag while I stripped off the glove and shoved it into the medical waste bin. I started to throw the garbage bag in as well then thought better of it. Kristi was almost acting like a normal, feeling human right now, but I wasn't keen on giving her full control over the blood sample.

After checking that her attention was elsewhere, I stuffed the bag into my backpack.

"Is there anything else that needs doing?" I asked.

She swiveled to face me, gaze penetrating. "Tell me what happened in the bowling alley."

Damn it. I hated turning over any sort of info to her, but Kristi was supposedly an ally, and needed to know. Holding back a grimace, I related the events with the same kind of precise detail I used when briefing Dr. Nikas.

She listened without interrupting, lips pursed in thought. When I finished, she tapped her pen on the pad and gazed at the ceiling, as if mulling over everything I'd said.

"Go back to the wounded one," she said after a moment. "He was shot in the spine?"

"That's what I figured since he stayed down. His upper body seemed to work fine, but his legs didn't."

"Interesting. And they took him to Tucker Point Regional, I assume?"

"Yeah. And if the others aren't there, they probably ended up at the Tucker Point High School gym. Triage kind of thing."

"All right. Let's go." Kristi logged out of the computer and slid off the stool. "Billy!"

He opened the door and stepped in. "Yes, ma'am?"

"Would you be a dear and drive us?"

Billy practically snapped to attention. "Yes, ma'am!" He dashed out.

"Us?" I shook my head. "Where are we going?"

"To the hospital, of course." Kristi tucked her legal pad and tablet into a black leather briefcase. "I know it's hard for you, but do try to keep up with the conversation."

I gritted my teeth. "Why do you want me to go?"

"For your scintillating wit?"

A furious retort bubbled up, but I held it back. She wanted me to lose my temper. I wasn't going to play her game. "Be fucking straight with me or find another lackey."

She lifted her chin. "I need an assistant who's able to interact closely with the shambler patients, and I would rather not jeopardize a human, considering your kind aren't at risk of infection. Jacques has important work to do here." She gestured toward Brian and Kyle. "And these two, well, they don't fit the other requisite. My assistant for this also needs to have a smattering of medical experience, which I'm assuming your time in the morgue has given you."

It wasn't an insult or even a backhanded compliment—though she'd seriously underestimated Kyle. I wasn't quite sure how to respond. I shot a quick look at Brian, but he simply lifted one shoulder a fraction of an inch in a "might as well" gesture. Or maybe it was "you're going to die." Hard to tell.

"Um. Okay," I told Kristi.

"Dr. Charish," Brian said. "Mr. Griffin will be accompanying you." Kyle stepped forward.

Her smile turned icy. "I have my own bodyguards."

"Yes, ma'am, you do." Brian's expression grew fiercely polite. "It's not *your* body I'm concerned about."

Kristi hesitated, as if weighing whether this was a battle worth fighting, then closed the briefcase and slung the strap over her shoulder. "Let's go then."

To my surprise, a limo was waiting for us out front. Though not a stretch big enough to fit ten high school seniors on the way to prom, it still screamed elegance and money and "I'm important enough to have someone drive me around while I think about important things."

I really needed to get rich.

Reno pulled up behind in a sleek black Mercedes sedan. Overkill much with the bodyguards? Maybe Kristi thought I'd attack her the instant we were alone. As much as I hated her, I wasn't even tempted. She was so nasty her brain would probably taste rancid.

Fritz climbed into Reno's car while Billy ushered Kristi and me into the back of the limo. Kyle took the limo's front passenger seat, and Billy settled behind the wheel. Kyle's presence was a relief, for that little pinch of fear that Kristi was up to something horrible with her need for an assistant—me, of all people.

I braced myself for snark, veiled insults, or other nastiness from her, but she ignored me and worked on her notes and tablet. Relaxing, I watched her out of the corner of my eye, quietly envying her ability to look so effortlessly stylish yet professional. Then again, money could buy an elegant smart watch, perfectly tailored clothing, and bras that actually fit and made your boobs properly perky. Hair cut and colored by someone other than "Kutz 4 Y'all," and stockings that weren't sold at the grocery store. And shoes . . . she had on elegant little tan pumps with a sensible yet attractive three-inch heel.

"Are your shoes made of *alligator* skin?"

Kristi flipped a page on a legal pad. "I certainly hope so. They're the Manolo Blahnik Blixa alligator pump."

I pulled out my phone and Googled the name. "Four *thousand* dollars?!" That was more than my car had cost.

Kristi made a notation in the margin. "Four thousand six hundred. Before tax."

She returned to ignoring me and didn't speak again until we pulled up at the hospital, and then it was to say, "Oh, here already? Let's go, Angel."

Billy leaped out to open Kristi's door and give her a hand out. Then he sprinted around to my side, looking crushed when he saw I'd dared open my own door. He thrust his hand at me, and though I was perfectly capable of getting out of a vehicle on my lonesome, I took it. Didn't want to hurt the poor guy's feelings.

Kyle let himself out and followed us into the hospital, a silent, comforting shadow. Not so comforting was Fritz taking up the rear. At the information desk, Kristi offered the white-haired lady there a dazzling smile. "I'm Dr. Kristi Charish. I believe Dr. Ingram is expecting me."

Before the words were completely out of her mouth, a brown-skinned man with a receding hairline and impressive mustache burst through a set of double doors and rushed up to Kristi.

"Dr. Charish!" He seized her hand and pumped it. "When your secretary called to say you were on your way here to offer a consultation pro bono, well, you have no idea how thrilled I was. Having a doctor with your credentials and experience help us with this medical mystery . . . it's a blessing from above."

Huh. Some of the tapping on her tablet must've been to her secretary to orchestrate a grand entrance. I would have probably done the same. Cut through the bureaucratic bullshit with a few well-placed phone calls. But the way he referred to her as "doctor" sure made it sound like she was an MD kind of doctor. Never would have thought that. What kind of bedside manner did she have? Lethal?

Kristi extricated her hand, smile never wavering. "I'm given to understand a patient exhibiting LZ-1 symptoms came in with a gunshot wound. Is he still alive?"

LZ-1? What a boring name for the Eugene-caused illness. Thanks a lot, CDC.

"Yes, yes. It's the most unusual thing I've ever seen. Come. I'll show you." He gestured toward the double doors then leveled a frown at the rest of us as we moved to follow her.

"I'm Angel Crawford. Coroner's Office." I pointed to the logo on my work shirt. "I'm partnering with Dr. Charish in this medical mystery investigation."

Kristi shot me an exasperated look at my self-promotion from assistant to partner, but she could hardly correct me in front of Dr. Ingram.

"Yes," she said through her teeth. "Quite the partnership."

"And Mr. Griffin is my assistant," I said cheerfully with a tilt of my head toward him.

Kyle said smoothly, "It's good to see you, Dr. Ingram."

Dr. Ingram shook his hand. "It's been a while."

While Kyle impressed me yet again, Kristi rolled her eyes behind Dr. Ingram's back. "I believe you were going to take me . . . and my partners . . . to the patient?" She gestured to include Fritz in the partnership.

"Oh, yes. Right this way!" He bustled off toward the elevators, Kristi's heels *tick-ticking* behind him. Up one floor and down the first corridor, a hospital security guard stood beside the door to room 202. A computer-printed sign proclaimed *Authorized Personnel Only*.

Dr. Ingram distributed face masks from an equipment cart near the door then led our little troupe of authorized personnel into the room. Harsh fluorescent light from the fixture above the headboard brightened the bed, but left the corners of the room in shadows.

Dreadlocks Man growled and jerked against his wrist restraints as we entered. He was lying on his back which struck me as odd, since his worst wound was there. Kyle and Fritz took up positions on either side of the door, while Kristi, Dr. Ingram, and I eased closer to the bed.

"What's been done about his injury?" I asked.

Dr. Ingram shrugged helplessly. "Very little, to be honest. We've been unable to perform surgery due to the, er, violent nature of the patient and the utter ineffectiveness of sedation."

"So he's just lying there with a gunshot wound?" I asked, aghast.

His shoulders hunched. "Both entry and exit wounds have been treated and bandaged, but we can't even scan him to assess the extent of the damage."

Kristi nodded toward the mobile computer workstation near the foot of the bed. "I need to see his records, please."

Dr. Ingram typed in his passcode, waited, then did it again. "Sorry, the system has been glitchy since a crash day before yesterday."

"The day Beckett Connor was here," I said. "Tuesday, right?"

"Yes yes, he was the first LZ-1 case." He peered at the screen. "Quite a mess. Ah, I mean the computer system. Not the unfortunate Deputy Connor."

Kristi raised an eyebrow. "I've always found ReliaFile EMR to be extremely dependable."

"It is. I mean, it has been. This was the first major issue since it was installed years ago." Dr. Ingram clicked the mouse a few times. "Ah, here we are." He pulled up a set of records with the name "August Lejeune" at the top. The "Gussie" the girl at the bowling alley had referred to.

Kristi took over the computer, face intense as she scanned the info. "His blood counts are normal. No coagulopathy. Blood gases, urine. Normal."

"That's correct. It's . . . completely unprecedented. He has an epigastric entry wound and an exit wound at the level of T7. The bullet went right through his liver. He should be bleeding out internally, but there's no sign of it."

"He's not dying," Kristi breathed, eyes alight.

"Yes, he is," I pointed out with a scowl. "Maybe not from the gunshot wound, but this infection is killing people, and it will kill him."

Kristi closed the file. "I'm aware of that. However, you must admit this is a fortuitous development for the patient. Otherwise, he would likely be dead before a cure could be developed."

"I suppose, yeah." Her logic did little to counter the mercenary glee behind the words.

Lejeune let out a hair-raising growl that trailed off into "Hunnnnnnngrrryyyyyy."

Dr. Ingram sucked in a breath. "That's the first time he's spoken since he came in!" He started to lean close, but I grabbed his collar and hauled him back—right as Lejeune lunged to the limit of his restraints, teeth snapping.

"Hunnnnnnngrrryyyyyy," Lejeune snarled.

Dr. Ingram collected himself and tugged his lab coat straight. "I, uh, yes. Thank you, Miss Crawford. We've started putting protection masks on the LZ-1 patients but, as you can see, Mr. Lejeune becomes very, ah, aggressive whenever anyone approaches. We feared he might aggravate his injury or succeed in biting someone during an attempt to put a mask on him." He smoothed his hair down with trembling fingers. "There's not much to be done about his hunger at this point, but he's receiving adequate nutrition via IV for the time being."

Lejeune's breath hissed through his teeth. "Hunnnnnnngrrryyyyyy."

I had an ugly feeling it wasn't cafeteria food he was craving—unless they'd recently put brains on the menu.

Chapter 26

If Kristi could have skipped in her Manolo Blahnik alligator shoes, she would have. As it was, she came perilously close to prancing as we returned to the car.

"My god," she breathed. "Think of the possibilities." She gave Billy a nod and smile as he opened the car door for her.

I exchanged a look with Kyle then got in on the other side while he took front seat again. Lucky bastard.

"Tucker Point High School, Billy," Kristi said.

"You want to see the other shamblers," I said.

"Sharp as ever, Angel." She patted her briefcase. "I need samples, but it's also necessary for me to see a number of LZ-1 patients in person for direct assessment. Samples alone simply aren't enough. Not to mention, I want to test how this mutated parasite of yours—"

"Eugene."

"Excuse me?" She frowned at the interruption.

I gave her a bland look. "The mutated parasite is called Eugene."

Kristi held up her hand. "No. You and Ari can continue using that silly name, but I will not. LZ-1 serves perfectly well as a designation for both the condition and the mutated parasite that causes it."

"Fine," I muttered. "Why LZ-1?"

"It was the CDC's Dr. Lafferty who came up with it. Officially, it's LZ-1, an ordinary file designation. But to her, it's Louisiana Zombie." Kristi tittered, the sound grating on every single nerve in my body. "Of course, Lafferty thinks it's a little inside joke between us to reflect the mindless nature of the victims. Oh, if she only knew how close to the truth she was."

"Yeah. Hilarious." Kristi's reaction made me want to punch her right in that perky nose, but even I could admit calling it Louisiana Zombie-1 was kind of appropriate. "So what did you want to test?"

"How the mutated parasite—*LZ-1*—reacts to brains. Dr. Nikas and I agree that brains are the most likely and logical stabilizer for the shamblers, but without a trial, it's only a hypothesis. I don't expect to find a difference in response between shamblers and normal zombies, but that confirmation in itself would be valuable information. I have with me packets of ProSwoleGel—a perfectly reasonable protein supplement to administer, though I've altered some to fifty percent brains. No one will be the wiser."

"Kyle tried to feed brains to Connor, but he wouldn't take them. We would've tried again—"

"But the poor fellow died before you could." Kristi heaved an oh-so-sad sigh. "Terrible shame."

My shoulders tensed. "Dying kind of happens when you're *murdered*."

"It was indeed a far too drastic measure." She *tsked*. "Saberton."

I sneered. "Yeah, you would never kill anyone for your own purposes."

"Come now, Angel. Let's not dredge up old grievances when everyone is cooperating so nicely. You don't want to cause more problems, now do you?" Her smile turned vicious. "Wasn't unleashing LZ-1 on the world enough for you?"

Kyle cast a dark look at her over his shoulder.

Fuck this bitch. "Now you listen to me, Dr. Kristi Fuckface. I've been playing nice right along with the rest of the Tribe. And I'll continue to do so as long as a treatment or cure is in the works." I bared my teeth at her. "But it's a fucking two-way street. Bitchdoctor snarkiness doesn't fall under the play-nice umbrella. I'm not here for your amusement. I'm here for August Lejeune and all the victims in the hospital and the gym." I leaned in. "If it weren't for them, I'd crush your skull and eat your brain right here and now and worry about the indigestion later."

It was Billy's turn to glance back, though his look was more horrified than dark.

"My, aren't we testy today," Kristi said coolly, though the fury in her eyes betrayed her true feelings.

I gave her my best dazzling smile. "And proud of it."

She flipped a page on her legal pad and pretended to work. Annoyance wafted from her in an acrid wave.

Ha! I'd shut her up and gotten under her skin. Wasn't much, but I'd take it. Allowing myself a mental fist pump, I settled back into the cushy comfort of the seat.

A few minutes later, we piled out in front of the Tucker Point High School gym—the same gym where my dad and I stayed after the flood swept our house away, and not far from the football field where the mass fight scene for *High School Zombie Apocalypse!!* had been shot.

A deputy and a Tucker Point cop chatted near the double doors. Kristi, Kyle, Fritz, and I showed ID, but it was Kristi's name that earned us the *Yes, ma'am, right this way, ma'am* treatment. The deputy handed us surgical-type masks and waited for us to put them on before ushering us into the gym.

Déjà vu hit me as I took in the scene. Cots with people on them, like after the flood. But the similarities ended there. Then, the cots had been clustered in family groups, and refugees slept or commiserated or played cards. The smell of fresh coffee and hot pizza had filled the air, and soothing music had played over the PA. Now, the cots were numbered and lined up in orderly rows. Thirty-two of them. Four rows of eight. Around two thirds were occupied—far too many for my liking—and close to a dozen gloved and masked medical personnel tended equipment and the restrained patients. The heavy stench of blood, sweat, urine, shit, and disinfectant blanketed everything. Growls, moans, and wails were the only music.

About a third of the patients wore the plastic face shields Dr. Ingram had mentioned, designed to protect the people tending them from being bitten or spit at. Each occupied cot—and a few of the empty ones—had an IV stand and a mobile vitals monitor at the head.

A woman in black scrubs with sleek grey hair pulled back into a ponytail adjusted the IV flow for a patient in the nearest row. The doctor I'd seen on the news when the epidemic first went public. She made a final tweak, disposed of her gloves, and approached in brisk strides.

"You must be Dr. Charish," she said. "Dr. Ingram told me you and your associates were on the way over. I'm Dr. Maureen Bauer. Epidemiologist." Her tone was crisp and professional, with zero Dr. Ingram-style fawning.

"It's a pleasure to meet you." Kristi shook the other woman's hand. "Perhaps you could get me up to speed on what you have here?" Her manner was equally no-nonsense, a far cry from her I'm-very-important attitude at the hospital. Was that a conscious thing for her to change her bearing depending on who she was talking to? Or did she have a natural ability to adjust to fit the circumstances? Either way, I couldn't help but envy the knack.

Dr. Bauer swept her arm to encompass the gym. "We have two other doctors, four RNs, and four patient care assistants on duty now. More personnel and more equipment are expected to arrive by morning."

I gestured to the pale yellow mitten-sleeve things she had on. Like flexible arm casts, they covered her forearms and hands, leaving thumb and fingers free. "What are those for?"

She flexed her fingers. "Kevlar fiber sleeves. Best protection against bites. We found that the majority of the patients can't tolerate having their mouths covered. It sends them into recalcitrant status epilepticus, perhaps triggered by panic, and is relieved only by removal of the face shields."

"Excellent observation and workaround," Kristi said. "What can you tell me about LZ-1?"

"It's fatal," Dr. Bauer replied, expression grim. "We lost two yesterday and three this morning. Their deaths were all very sudden, as if their bodies simply gave out."

"Fascinating," Kristi said, then she and Dr. Bauer dove into an epidemiology discussion that sailed over my head by the second sentence. I gave up trying to comprehend it and headed for the first row of patients. Kyle remained within earshot of Kristi, much better able to absorb the conversation for Dr. Nikas. Hell, for all I knew, he was recording it.

Though Dr. Nikas couldn't come here to assess the victims, I could make my own observations and report back to him. Every medical worker was deeply engaged in patient care, and I did my best to stay out of their way as I walked slowly past the cots. Some patients were bound with standard medical restraints, but the rest with straps fashioned from duct tape. Great minds think alike.

There were several familiar faces among the patients without bite shields. Nurse Patricia's dead-white eyes tracked me. A barista from Dear John's snapped and howled as I passed. The Rucker twins lay on adjacent cots, moaning and writhing. A subtle flutter rose in my gut. I stopped and reached toward the foot of the nearest twin.

"Hey!" a man's voice called out.

I jerked my hand back.

"Glove-up before touching." The voice belonged to a portly assistant the next row over.

I bit my lip. "Sorry!"

He shook his head at my stupidity and resumed adjusting the restraints on his patient.

The click of Kristi's heels warned me of her approach. "Ooooo. Twins can be quite useful in research."

A sliver of unease crawled down my spine at the creepy elation in her tone. "I'm sure they're thrilled to be here."

She ignored my comment. "Dr. Bauer is on board with trying to nourish these poor souls with the ProSwoleGel. I'm going to take a quick peek at all of them, then you can administer it. For now, run along." She waggled her fingers in a shooing gesture then turned her back on me and strode toward the first cot.

"For now, run along," I mimicked, complete with an exaggerated derpy expression. Cuz I was mature like that.

Fritz joined Kristi as she peered at the first victim, ready to guard her precious body if the shambler got rowdy. In the next row, Kyle crouched beside cot twelve, attentive to everything around him.

A shambler behind me let out a piercing wail. I spun to see Dr. Bauer trying to check the pupils on an elderly woman. The patient wore a face shield, but it didn't stop her from lunging and trying to bite.

"Need a hand?" I asked. "Looks like everyone else is busy."

"I'd love a hand," Dr. Bauer said. "If you could hold her head still for a moment." Once I had the thrashing woman in my grasp, Dr. Bauer did the light shine thing with each eye, then gestured for me to release my hold. "Thanks for the help. You would think eleven staff for twenty-one patients would be adequate, but we're at the bare minimum for safety and maintenance. God forbid we fill the empty cots."

"Can't you call more workers in?"

"Screening is being done. We're not allowing anyone with children at home to work with these patients due to the uncertainties about transmission. Finger crossed, by morning we should have a decent pool from the surrounding parishes. But at the moment, we're fairly shorthanded."

"That's probably the right call, though," I said. "The part about workers with children."

A moan from the next cot over interrupted the doctor's reply. "Huunnngry."

It was Patricia, her eyes fixed on me and slightly less milky white than before.

"That's the first time any of them have spoken," Dr. Bauer said, frowning.

"One of them did at the hospital a little while ago." I went on to tell her about August Lejeune and his gunshot wound.

Patricia let out a keening wail. "Huunnngry!" She shuddered. "Braaaains."

Dr. Bauer gasped and put a hand to her mouth. "Oh dear god. It's true."

Not the reaction I expected. "What do you mean? What's true?"

Dr. Bauer dropped her hand to her stomach. "A paramedic told me about a woman he took to the emergency room an hour or so ago."

"One of these LZ-1 cases?"

"No, but connected. The patient—I'll call her Miss L—told the authorities her uncle had been bitten last night by a neighbor—number twenty-one over there—but the incident hadn't been reported because her aunt wanted to treat the uncle at home." Dr. Bauer let out a sigh. "No insurance and didn't want to lose everything to medical debt."

I winced. "All too common."

"Indeed. This morning Miss L woke up to her aunt's screams from downstairs. She went down with a gun and found her aunt with her head bashed in and her uncle . . ."

"Eating her brain?" I gently prompted.

"That's what Miss L said when the police questioned her. The uncle came at her, and though Miss L shot him multiple times, it didn't slow him down. He clawed her up, but she managed to shoot him in the head and run for help."

Great. The monsters were getting more monstrous. "Let me guess. No one believes her story," I said sourly. "Or if they do, they won't admit it."

"Of course not. That would be crazy." Dr. Bauer's gaze rested on Patricia. "But I'll be quite interested to see what shows up in the uncle's stomach contents during the autopsy."

"The Coroner's Office pathologist is Dr. Leblanc. I'm sure he'd be glad to share his findings with you." I had no need to find out what was in the uncle's stomach. I already knew.

"Thank you. I'll keep that in mind."

"Braaaains," Patricia rasped.

A moan of *huunnngry* came from a patient in the next row, echoed by one of the Rucker twins. Patricia repeated, "Braaaains."

Kristi approached, gazing thoughtfully down at Patricia. "Interesting. We'll see how they do with the ProSwoleGel."

Dr. Bauer looked around at the harried workers. "I'm sorry I don't have anyone to assist you."

"Angel has that covered," Kristi said. "We won't disturb your—"

An IV stand on the third row crashed to the floor.

"Arm's loose!" a nurse hollered.

"Excuse me," Dr. Bauer said and rushed over.

"I wonder how that happened," Kristi said as if she wasn't wondering at all. "Come on, Angel. Hop to it. We have testing to do."

Chapter 27

"There are twenty-one patients," Kristi told me as she headed toward cot one, where Fritz waited with her briefcase. "Each will receive a packet." She lowered her voice. "Six packets contain a proprietary blend of ProSwoleGel and brains. One is pure brains. And the rest, unadulterated ProSwoleGel. *You* will administer them, because *you* can't get infected."

She was only testing the brain-food on a few of the patients, yet feeding all of them, not only to have a control group, but also to muddy the waters if anything odd happened with the test subjects. Since they all supposedly received the same food, any bad outcome would be considered an isolated incident, and certainly not the fault of a well-known nutritional supplement.

At patient one's cot, I tugged on gloves for the sake of appearance. "How did you choose who gets what?"

Kristi retrieved her tablet from the briefcase Fritz held. "All you need to do is feed the patients the packets I give you. Let me worry about the rest."

I folded my arms over my chest. "It's not a complicated question, and I'm not feeding anyone anything until you give me a satisfactory answer."

"No need to make a scene." She glanced around as if afraid someone would notice my grievous insubordination. "I selected two males, two females, one of the twins, and the youngest. Satisfied?"

I shrugged. "It'll do." For now.

Kristi consulted her tablet. "Cot one gets packet eight."

Fritz dug around in the briefcase then passed me a packet of ProSwoleGel with "8" written on it in permanent marker.

As far as I could tell, it was the standard commercial ProSwoleGel packaging, similar to squeeze yogurt. I tore off the top, and the aroma of peaches with a hint of vanilla floated up, but not a whiff of brains.

Patient one was a thirty-something woman wearing a face shield, her once-manicured nails ragged and broken to the quick. As I crouched beside the cot, she yanked against the restraints and growled low. I murmured softly, telling her it was going to be okay and we were working to find a cure. The words themselves probably didn't help, but I hoped my tone might.

Gingerly, I lifted off the face shield, ready to pull back if she snapped. But she simply bared her teeth, cloudy eyes fixed on me.

"Braaaains."

"Well, I have some reeeeally nice protein gel for you." I held the packet close to her mouth, gave it a quick squeeze when she bit at it. A good dollop of the goopy gel landed on her tongue, and she noisily smacked and swallowed it down.

"Braaaains!"

It took only three more squeezes to get the rest of it into her, though it didn't seem to satisfy her hunger at all. Not surprising since I suspected she really wanted actual brains, and I knew all too well how sucktastic brain hunger was.

While Kristi made notes on the tablet, I replaced the face shield, then we moved on to the next cot. Patients two, three, and four were also picked to receive plain old protein gel, judging by the scent. Two and three were moaning "hungry" and downed their whole packet, but four didn't say anything and wouldn't take the protein gel. Connor hadn't ever said "hungry," either. Maybe if he had, he'd have taken brains? But it wouldn't have made any difference. Not with a deadly tranq in his ear.

Though patients lunged and snapped at the medical workers, not a single one of them showed the slightest aggression toward me. Odd, yet . . . not. With every cot, my drive, my *need* to find a cure increased, as if these were people I'd known my entire life. People who needed my protection and were deeply important to me.

A chorus of *Braaaaains Braaaaaaaaains Braains* followed me to patient five: Rucker Twin One from the bowling alley. He lay on an extra-wide, extra-long cot, yanking non-stop against his restraints.

"Armell Rucker," I said in a soothing voice. "It's gonna be all right." He wasn't wearing a face shield, which allowed me to see his rictus grin relax as I spoke. In my periphery, I saw Kyle watching from several cots away.

"Packet one," Kristi said.

This time, when I ripped off the top, the lovely scent of pure brains filled my nose. Not as tempting as fresh, warm brains straight out of a skull, but delectable nonetheless.

Armell's eyes stretched wide. "Braaaaaaaaaaaaaaaaaains."

"Yep, some good old protein gel for you." I jerked back as he snapped at the packet. "Easy there, darlin'. This is some good stuff, but you have to take it slow."

Or not. When he opened his mouth to let out a phlegmy growl, I seized the opportunity and squirted the whole packet in. Tongue working, he swallowed the brains down with a gulp, growl fading to a low moan that sounded way too much like pleasure. Eyes already clearer, his head lolled as he breathed out, "Braaaaaaains," in a long sigh, with an expression of pure shambler bliss on his face.

Pleased, I moved on to Armell's twin, Arkell Rucker. He took regular protein gel in the same no fuss, non-bitey manner as the first three, though with less satisfaction, to judge by his piteous moans.

Cots seven and eight were empty, so we proceeded to the next row for patient nine, who looked enough like Dr. Leblanc to make my heart lurch uncomfortably before I realized it wasn't him. When I opened his packet, I had no doubt it was the gel-brain blend. The concoction smelled of proteiny vanilla brains along with a subtle pungent quality, like dirty socks in a laundry basket. Not very appetizing, but then again I'd made some godawful mixtures in the past. Like the time I tried to make brain sushi. Or the disastrous guacamole incident.

Nine ate the mixture just fine, but then kept sticking his tongue out, as if he was trying to get rid of the taste. Different. I sniffed the packet and was about to take a tiny lick when Kristi snatched it from my hand.

"Would you behave?" she scolded. "We do *not* have time to

dillydally." Exasperated, she shoved the empty packet into the
briefcase and pointed to the next cot.

How the hell was she able to make me feel like a third grader
who'd been caught eating paste? And why was she being so
protective of the empty packets?

Kyle continued to shadow me from a distance as I fed the
next two patients ordinary protein gel. At patient twelve, I ripped
open the packet. Peaches. Vanilla. Brains. And a sharp, chemical
scent that reminded me of acetone and burnt sugar. I turned to
Kristi. "What the hell is this?"

She consulted her tablet. "Brains and gel."

"You do remember I have a much better sense of smell than
you, right?" I kept my tone low and even. "Tell me what the fuck
this is. There's something in here besides brains and ProSwole-
Gel. It's definitely not the same as the blend I gave to patient
nine. That one had a different smell."

"Angel, you're overreacting," she said, jaw tense. "Can we
please get back to feeding the patients?"

"I thought we were over the lie-to-Angel bullshit." I narrowed my eyes. She wanted me to shut up and not ask about the
ingredients. "I'm feeling a might bit peckish. Maybe I should go
ahead and down this packet of brains and protein." I lifted the
packet to my lips.

"Stop," she hissed. "Don't eat that. I'm testing two possible
cures! Use your head and imagine what that might do to your
recently recovered parasite."

My little bluff had worked, and now I knew what she was
really doing here. I lowered the packet. "Does Dr. Nikas know
you're testing cures now?"

She hesitated for only an instant, but it was long enough to
tell me he didn't. "Angel, we can discuss this later. Right now,
we have work to do."

There was no way Dr. Nikas would approve tests on live
patients sight unseen. I could always refuse to feed any more
patients, but that wouldn't stop her enlisting the help of Dr.
Bauer or even Fritz.

In a zombie-speed move, I snatched the briefcase from Fritz
and slung the strap over my shoulder. "I'll meet you at the limo."

Kristi grabbed my wrist. I stopped, looked down at her hand
then up at her face. "You don't really want me to make a scene,

do you?" I said, low and silky. "I'm *really* good at making scenes, and I have nothing to lose. Wanna try me?"

She released me and muttered to Fritz to stand down. I turned away and strode down the row toward the entrance. I still had the full-yet-open packet in my hand, and since I was tired of holding it, and feeling more than a little ornery, I shoved it into the briefcase and gave it a good squeeze.

Clickety-clickety-click. Her heels behind me. "Angel?" she said sweetly, for everyone else's benefit. "We need to discuss that procedure a teensy bit more."

I kept walking. "We can do it on the way back to NuQues-Cor."

Behind me, a mighty voice roared, "BRAAAAAAAAAINS!"

I spun to see Armell Rucker bucking so hard his cot was inching along the gym floor.

"BRAAAAAAAAAINS!" he bellowed, triggering moans and howls and hisses of *braaaaaains* and *hunnnnnngry* from what seemed to be every patient in the place.

Kyle angled toward me, and I shoved the briefcase into his hands. "Keep that safe and call Dr. Nikas."

With smooth efficiency, he grasped the handle and pulled out his phone. "On it."

Leaving that concern behind, I rushed to the swarm of nurses, doctors, assistants trying to hold Armell and cot in place. Kristi watched from a few yards away, expression a combination of curiosity and shock.

"BRAAAAAAAAAAAAAAAAAAINS!"

He fought the restraints, warping the cot frame with every fierce yank. Heart thudding, I shouldered in next to Dr. Bauer, grabbed Armell's head, and hung on for dear life as he thrashed. I tried talking to him to maybe soothe and calm, but my voice was lost in the racket of the other patients.

The cot frame gave way with a groan of metal and tipped to the side. One arm restraint came loose, and Armell swung the liberated limb, clocking a worker in the side of the head. It would only be a matter of seconds before he ripped completely free of the twisted frame. If that happened, a bullet to the head would be damn near the only way to stop him from hurting others.

No way was I going to let that happen. There had to be a way to calm him without anyone having to die. I scrambled back and looked around in a desperate search for a miracle.

My gaze stopped on patient four. That was it. I tore the face shield from her and hollered, "Status epilepticus!" like it was a magic spell.

Dr. Bauer looked at me as if I was crazy, then her eyes lit up in understanding. "Everyone! On the count of three, grab him and hold tight!"

On three, I dove into the fray. They wouldn't be able to hold Armell for more than a few seconds, but that was all I needed. With zombie speed, I fixed the shield over his mouth and tightened the strap. He clacked his teeth together hard then let out a bellow worthy of a bull elephant with a rosebush up his ass. A violent twisting move sent three people crashing back on their asses, but before I could rip the shield off as a bad idea, he went limp. A second later his fingers started twitching as his unrestrained forearm moved in a lazy arc.

"That's it!" Dr. Bauer cried, as if she couldn't believe the tactic had worked. "Get the restraints off and put him in the recovery position."

The cacophony of the other patients died back to earlier levels, with the occasional *braaaaains* or *hunnnnngry*, as if in sync with Armell's state.

Breathing hard, I sat back while four workers disentangled Armell from the wrecked cot and rolled him to his left side. "How long is it safe for him to seize like this?"

Dr. Bauer knelt beside him, checking pulse points. "We'll get him back on the monitor in a sec. For now he's breathing. All we need is enough time to set up his restraints again."

Within a few minutes the assistants had a new cot set up and restraints in place. They rolled Armell onto a blanket, then heaved him up onto the cot.

Dr. Bauer, armed with her Kevlar sleeves, cautiously removed the face shield while the assistants worked swiftly to tighten restraints. Armell sucked in a snotty breath and let it out in a low moan. No thrashing. No biting.

I rested my hand on his shoulder. "There you go, sweetie. It's going to be all right." But what the hell? My intuition told me it was no coincidence he turned into a zombie berserker not long after eating pure brains. Which meant my hopes that brains could be a shambler stabilizer were now dust.

On the other row, a patient abruptly let out an eerie, piercing whistle-cry that didn't sound like it could come from a human throat. Number nine—the one who reminded me of Dr. Leblanc. His back arched and his head thrashed as if he'd been doused in burning oil. He screamed then. Loud. Guttural. Horrific.

A second later he collapsed to the cot and didn't move again. His heart monitor went from normal looking blips to a wavy line, like a series of steep hills and valleys close together.

Dr. Bauer raced to his side. "Code on nine! Sustained V-tach. Move it, people, move it!"

I stayed beside Armell, hand still on his shoulder, staring in shock as the medical team scrambled in organized chaos. Too much like Connor. Sharp orders flowed together in my ears, but the team reacted and acted smoothly with chest compressions and ventilation and medications.

Only a few minutes ago, I'd given that man Kristi's dirty-sock-smelling cure trial. I glanced over and saw that she hadn't moved from her spot. She watched the team work on patient nine, forehead puckered and mouth tight as she slowly pulled on gloves. Definitely didn't look happy.

I dragged my attention back to the frenzy of activity around cot nine.

Charging to one-twenty joules. Clear. Shock. More chest compressions. Epi.

I couldn't see exactly what was happening, but judging by the serious focus of the team, it wasn't good. I remained beside Armell, talking to him, soothing. There was nothing I could do for patient nine except hope for a miracle. But deep down, I knew he was gone.

I didn't even know his name.

V-fib. Compressions. Shock at two hundred. Cursing. Asystole.

More compressions. Epi.

Nothing.

Dr. Bauer stepped back, wiped her forehead with a sleeve. "Shit . . . shit. I'm calling it. Time of death 18:22."

Kristi started toward Dr. Bauer. I followed, stomach churning after witnessing the man's death.

Dr. Bauer's eyes were haggard over her mask. "The others we lost. No screaming. Nothing like this."

"I'm so very sorry to be brusque in this difficult moment,"

Kristi said, "but I need to take postmortem tissue and blood samples from the deceased immediately, along with random samples from some of the others."

Dr. Bauer waved a weary hand. "Take whatever you need if it will help put an end to this nightmare."

Kristi murmured a quiet thanks then gestured for me to follow her. At the end of the row she spoke through clenched teeth. "I need my damn briefcase."

"If it contains sampling equipment, sure."

Kyle glided over as if on cue, briefcase over his shoulder. To my chagrin, he passed the briefcase to Fritz then held his phone out for me. "Angel, there's a call for you. I'll help Dr. Charish collect the samples."

I took the phone with a nod of thanks. Kyle would not only collect samples, but also keep an eagle eye on what she was doing.

While the two of them got to work, I speed-walked to a far corner beside the bleachers, out of earshot of anyone except maybe Kyle.

"Hello?"

"Angel." Dr. Nikas's gentle voice, rough with tension. Kyle must have filled him in on everything, including Armell's awful reaction to pure brains and the death of patient nine. "Are you all right?"

Not "tell me what I need to know." Or "do this do that." I let out a shuddering breath. "Yeah. I was the one who gave that patient the gel stuff with the test cure, but I know it wasn't my fault he died." I had plenty of other shit to feel guilty about. No sense taking on guilt that didn't belong to me.

"Precisely." He sounded relieved that he didn't have to talk me off the ledge. Again. "You may have delivered the means, but his blood isn't on your hands. Kyle said Kristi planned to test seven patients with three of one cure trial, three of another, and one of pure brains. Your quick thinking and bold intervention to stop the trials likely prevented more deaths."

"Thanks, doc. But it doesn't change that she used me, and an innocent man died." I shot a furious glare across the gym at Kristi. "I really want to wring her neck. Now would be a really sweet time."

"I know." He sighed softly. "I can't make this right. Nothing can bring that man back. I can only ask that you give me a chance to deal with Kristi myself tomorrow, after analysis is complete on the samples Kyle took from the open packets. And, after I have the full story from you, along with whatever information I can get from her. She has little trust for us, with good reason, but I need to hear her rationale for conducting these cure trials without consulting me. We need her, but I can't abide games—especially those that kill. Will you give me that time?"

Anger and heartache still roiled within me, but I couldn't deny Dr. Nikas. "Of course," I said. "I won't do anything stupid. Not on purpose, at least." I grimaced as a thought occurred to me. "How will Pierce take this? Kristi's supposed to be open and honest with you. Will he try to default back to the zombify-and-enslave plan for her?"

"Quite possibly, but I will handle him." His voice sounded infinitely weary, I suspected from centuries of being Sulemain-Clarence-Francis-Pietro-Pierce's rock and solace. "I told Kyle to return her briefcase and to not allow any more feeding. You did right in taking it, but I cannot have a meaningful conversation with her if we keep it from her."

"All right," I said and tried not to grumble. "I don't like it, but I understand. And I trust you." Besides, she could mix up another batch of the cures-that-kill if she wanted to, so there was no point taking the packets from her. "I'll be at the Tribe lab later this evening."

"Good. I will see you then. Take care, Angel. And thank you."

By the time I returned to the cot area, Kyle and Kristi had finished taking samples. While Kristi thanked Dr. Bauer, I said a last goodbye to Armell, and then we departed without fanfare.

As soon as we were in the limo, Kristi raised the Plexiglas partition between us and the front then gazed out the window, forehead creased in thought.

I managed to tolerate the silence for all of thirty seconds. "What exactly happened back there? A man *died*."

"I'm quite aware," she replied tightly. "I don't need some backwater hick to enlighten me."

"How about having a civil conversation? That's really tough for me at the moment, but I'll give it a shot for the good of the team."

She remained silent for at least a full minute before finally speaking. "All right. It seems consumption of pure brains may trigger a short period of calm followed by extreme violence, aggressiveness, and strength in LZ-1 patients. Whereas brains processed with protein gel do not. I can't draw a definitive conclusion based on a single case. The *one* cure trial I was able to complete on patient nine yielded some data, the extent of which will be determined after analysis of his blood and tissue samples."

"Yielded some data?" I sputtered. "You killed a man!"

"He wasn't supposed to *die*. That was an unfortunate outcome."

"Jesus." I tossed my hands up. "What the hell happened to make you such an unfeeling bitch? Did mommy not hug you enough?"

Kristi's eyes snapped to me. "Oh, do you want a sob story? Maybe some tragic tale of neglect and abuse?" Her lip curled. "Well, you won't get it. I had a perfectly ordinary middle-class upbringing in middle America with two middle-aged parents who wanted me to be happy—in their own middling way. Sent me to college where I graduated in four years, summa cum laude, with degrees in biology and chemistry. I told my parents I wanted to be a doctor, a researcher. Their reply? 'That's too much for you to take on. Go to nursing school first.'" She snorted. "Would they have said that if I'd been their son?"

"Doubtful," I agreed. Kristi had a couple of decades on me, and breaking out of gendered roles was even harder back then.

"You have no idea what it's like to not be taken seriously, to command the most expertise and have your opinions and ideas casually dismissed, only to watch a male coworker put forth the same ideas and be lauded for it." Her hands clenched. "To be passed over for advancement and opportunities because you're not *friendly* enough, or you don't *smile* enough. To be forced to toady to morons in charge of funding and project approval."

Pure venom filled her eyes when I laughed.

"Trust me," I said. "I know what it's like not to be taken seriously. People assume that because I'm not as educated, I must be stupid." I sneered in derision. "You do it to me all the time. Hell, you're the worst! According to you, I'm just a backwater hick who'll only get in the way while the smart people work." My chin went up. "I grew up with *nothing*, and yeah, I dropped out of high school—after my abusive mother committed suicide in prison. My god, I'm such a loser, right? At least I'm trying to *get* educated."

"You might have a point," she said grudgingly.

Why did that feel like such a damn victory? "Dr. Nikas takes you seriously."

She nodded once. "Yes, he does. He's a decent man who's far too hard on himself."

"That's something we can agree on," I said, somewhat off balance by our sudden if tenuous rapport. "Why didn't you tell him you were going to test possible cures?"

She touched her forehead, as if sensing a headache coming on. "It was a last-minute decision. He'd already left for his lab, so exhausted I hated to bother him, especially for what I truly believed would be trivial tests."

I didn't buy into her compassion, even though she came across as sincere. "Here's an idea," I said. "Bother him about anything and everything. He's super dedicated and would rather hear all the details. Work *with* him, not at odds with him."

"I do enjoy working with him." Her lips pressed thin. "When it's of my own volition, that is." She leaned toward me. "You know what's worse than not being taken seriously? Being *taken*. Forced to work, first for your precious Tribe, then for Saberton after they 'rescued' me from Pietro and took me straight to their Dallas lab, whether I wanted to go or not."

"Dr. Nikas hated that you were a prisoner," I said quietly. "He threatened to leave the Tribe if it ever happened again." No way was I going to tell her about Pierce's proposal to turn her into a zombie.

Kristi sat back and crossed her legs. "Did he now? He *should* leave the Tribe. He'd be far better off." She pulled out a legal pad and began perusing notes, signaling an end to the conversation, and leaving me with plenty to mull over for the rest of the return trip to NuQuesCor.

Chapter 28

It was twilight when we arrived back at NuQuesCor. Since I was heading to the Tribe lab next, Kyle passed me the packet samples for Dr. Nikas then continued inside with Kristi.

I spent a good chunk of the drive puzzling over Kristi's statement about Dr. Nikas. Why would she think he'd be "far better off" away from the Tribe? She was well aware of his paralyzing fear of crowds. Maybe she wanted him to come to work for Saberton? Though I couldn't imagine any incentive that would convince Dr. Nikas to defect to the enemy.

My worry shifted to how my dad, Jane, Portia, and Bear were handling being thrust into the world of zombies. Especially Portia. The others already knew about zombies and had come to terms with the fact that brain-eating monsters walked among them and could actually be pretty nice people. But I'd thrown Portia into the deep end.

Not that I regretted my decision. I'd rather have her be freaked out and hating me than see her duct-taped to a cot. Still, once I reached the Tribe lab, I tucked the water bottles from the bowling alley into my backpack then practically ran inside.

After I turned the protein packet samples over to Reg, I found Bear sitting in the central rotunda, face puckered in worry.

"Angel!" He lunged up from the chair. "Any news?"

"I checked on your people about an hour ago. They're stable." A safe answer. Better than telling him that some of his people were restrained in the high school gym, and one of them had gone berserk.

"Yeah? Okay. That's good, I guess." He started a nervous pacing. "I told the rest of my group to get into their bunkers and keep in touch with each other and give health updates."

"That sounds pretty solid." I paused. "Why didn't Nick just have you get in your own bunker? I assume you have one."

"Oh, I definitely have one. But Nick probably knew I wouldn't stay in it and would instead be checking on the others."

I smiled. "Was he right?"

"One hundred percent. But now he's still out there, with all that shit going on."

"Nick knows all of the safety protocols," I reassured him.

Bear scowled. "Everyone in my survivalist group knew them, too. Didn't help my people at the bowling alley. I fucking worry about him."

"So why are you telling *me* you're worried?"

Bear stopped pacing. "You're right. You're fucking right."

"Of course I am. Go call him right now. But first, where are the others?"

"The Congresswoman is in the conference room making a zillion phone calls, pulling strings to get more medical staff and supplies down here. Your dad is in the media room, and Miss Portia went off with that tall doctor guy."

"She did?" My pulse quickened. "Why? Was she hurt? Or was she really freaked out about the zombie stuff? Or doesn't she know yet? Is she—"

Bear held up his hands. "Angel, stop! She's fine. We broke the news to her on the way here. Figured it was better for her to find out from us before she was in the thick of things."

"How did she take it?"

"Utterly disbelieving at first, as expected. Then Kang . . . well, let's just say he convinced her zombies were real."

"Nuh-uh. No 'let's just say.' What did Kang *do*?"

"Weirdest thing I've ever seen." Bear whistled low. "First he got *old*, like he was in his eighties. Then a knife slash kind of wound opened up on his arm and closed right back up. And then he went back to looking normal forty-something. I could tell she was a believer when she started asking him questions—really technical stuff on how it worked. Kang finally told her she should talk to Dr. Nikas."

I relaxed. "She's in good hands then."

"Sure seemed that way to me."

He stepped away to call Nick. I made my way to the media room, where I found my dad playing *Swords and Swagger* on the big screen TV.

I gaped. "You brought the PlayBox *here*?"

He startled then faced me with a mulish expression. "Well, y'gave me a half hour's notice, and I remembered that this place ain't exactly a fun house."

"Okay. Wow." But I had to admit he had a point. "Well, you know how I said it might've been from someone with the Tribe? It turns out it was from Andrew Saber—the guy I turned into a zombie when I was in New York."

"What, like a weird ass Mother's Day gift?"

I snickered. "Not quite. He had to go into hiding because there was a chance his mother—Nicole Saber of Saberton Corporation—had found out he was a zombie. And he's using the game as a way to communicate with me."

"So I guess I shoulda left it at the house." He grimaced. "Sorry, baby. I'll get it all unplugged so you can take it back."

"Nah, keep it. I'd never get it set up right in a million years. But if I'm not here and need to get a message to Andrew or talk to him, you have to do it for me."

He groaned. "Guess it serves me right for bringing it along."

"Sure does." I grinned and kissed the top of his head then went to the research wing.

I found Dr. Nikas in the computer room seated beside Portia. Before them, amorphous blobs flowed across a monitor screen. Portia said something that made Dr. Nikas laugh, a warm sound that sent a wave of delight through me. I couldn't remember the last time I'd heard him really laugh. Nearby, Marla lay flopped on the floor, with Portia's big dog, Moose, beside her.

Dr. Nikas looked up as I entered. "Angel, I was just showing Dr. Antilles some of our research."

She smiled and put a hand on his arm. "Please, call me Portia."

His own smile turned radiant. "And you must call me Ari."

I bit my lip. "Portia, you're not freaked out?"

"I admit I had a few qualms, but Ari has been showing me how the organism utilizes prions. It's quite fascinating." She stood, probably sensing that I needed to talk privately with Dr.

Nikas. "But I'd best go see if Jane needs anything." She politely excused herself and left, with Moose padding behind her.

He watched her go, smile fading.

"She's really nice, isn't she," I said.

"Indeed she is. A remarkable woman."

"You don't look very happy about it."

He looked away. "She is also a very sick woman."

I sank onto a stool. "Please tell me you mean sick like 'Whoa, dude, that kick flip was *sick*!'"

"Alas, no. Unless I'm mistaken, she has advanced pancreatic cancer."

Tears stung my eyes. "Well, that sucks." Understatement of the century. Dr. Nikas could smell sickness, so I had no reason to doubt him. Dammit. I should have fucking hugged her at the coffee shop. "Maybe she'd be willing to be turned?"

The lines in his face deepened. "It's much harder to turn someone successfully when they have late-stage cancer."

I frowned. "But Kyle had advanced lymphoma when Brian turned him."

"Kyle beat enormous odds. I don't have enough data to make a definitive statement, but I would estimate less than a fifteen percent chance of success with metastasized cancer. And if the turning fails, death is immediate."

I silently railed at the unfairness of it all. I had a feeling Dr. Nikas was doing the same. "How much time does she have?" I asked, pleased that my voice only wobbled a little.

"Perhaps six months. Without reviewing her test results or, er, tasting her, I cannot be certain."

I squared my shoulders. "Okay, we'll deal with that once the current crisis is over." I refused to let myself believe the current crisis might last much longer. "I couldn't get the bowling alley carpet, but I got some blood on a bar rag and gave it to Kristi. Since you weren't there, I saved the bag so you have some to work with." I handed over the bag and the two bottles. "This is what Bear's people at the bowling alley were drinking. Nice Springs. Maybe the shambler disease was spread through the water? I know it's a longshot."

"It is a longshot, but it wouldn't be a shot at all if you hadn't had the presence of mind to collect the bottles." He gave me a proud smile that lifted my spirits. "Now, why don't you tell me everything that happened."

With supreme effort, I managed to keep it all from tumbling out in a torrent, and instead carefully thought through each event to include any details that might be important.

Dr. Nikas listened attentively until I finished. "I've already spoken to Bear Galatas to get his account of events. I am deeply disturbed and quite baffled at the report that people are turning within minutes of each other. It implies another factor in the transmission that I've yet to even consider, much less isolate." Fatigue washed over his face. "This shambler epidemic is like nothing I've ever seen before." He shook his head. "I'm missing something, and I've no idea in which direction to look."

"You seriously need to stop being so hard on yourself." I stood and planted my hands on my hips. "Even Kristi says so, and if the two of us agree on something, you know it has to be true!"

A puzzled smile touched his mouth. "Did she?"

"She did." I paused. "She also said you're pretty much the only dude who takes her seriously. As odd as it sounds, I'm fairly sure she respects the hell out of you, despite the fact that you're a nasty, icky zombie."

A chuckle escaped him. "Strangely enough, that's quite heartening."

"Yeah, well hold onto that good mood, 'cause now it's time for me to give you the full briefing on Kristi and the gym."

"Yes. I do need to hear it." His expression turned bleak, and I had a feeling it was both for the patient who died as well as the failed cure trial. He listened attentively while I rattled off every aspect I could remember. By the time I was done, I wanted to call Portia back in and get him to smile and laugh again, but right now her being terminal might just make him sadder. "Do you need help with anything?"

He patted my shoulder. "Not at the moment. You should go home and get some rest."

"I'll be at NuQuesCor bright and early."

"As will I."

I reluctantly left him to his work then checked on my dad in the media room—only to find Portia, Jane, and Bear in there as well. Jane's zombie bodyguard, Victor, sat unobtrusively in the far corner, reading a paperback with Moose sprawled at his feet. Jane held the second game controller, and the others shouted encouragement as she and my dad slaughtered a variety of monsters in the ruins of an ancient castle.

I sat next to Bear. "Did you talk to Nick?"

"Uh huh. He told me he respects my position and my concerns, but he wants to be where he's needed. He's doing good out there. Hard to argue with that. Gotta say, I'm really proud of him."

"Did you tell him so?"

He chuckled. "Yes, I did. You've taught me a thing or two about that."

"Glad to hear it. If it helps, I worry about Nick, too."

"I know. Y'all are really good together. You take care of each other." Before I could fumble out a response to his statement, he rose to investigate a tray of sandwiches that someone had thoughtfully provided for the human refugees.

I waited until the gamers finished the level then told my dad I was returning to the house to get some sleep. After the expected, "You be careful, y'hear me?" I started to leave then stopped by the armchair where Portia sat, bare feet tucked beneath her.

Trusting my gut, I bent and gave her a hug.

Startled, she returned it then gave me a curious look as I straightened. "What was that for?"

"Kinda felt like you need one."

A warm smile spread across her face. "Thank you. I suppose I did."

Feeling somewhat lighter, I continued on out to my car.

The cool thing about hugs was giving one meant you got one, too.

Chapter 29

My good mood faded during the drive home, growing nearly as dark as the sky. It didn't help when I passed a mosquito truck spraying its payload of malathion. Then another. And when I turned onto my road, a mosquito control plane zoomed low overhead, dousing everything below in a fine mist of chemicals.

Fatigue gripped me as I pulled into my driveway, and I sent up a silent thanks for Dr. Nikas's stay-awake mod. At some point after midnight, I intended to break into the impound lot to search Reno Larson's Camry, and it wouldn't do to fall asleep in the process.

I still didn't trust Kristi. Sure, she'd shown an unexpected human side in the limo, but so what? Didn't excuse all the shit she'd done.

Except . . . except some of her arguments made sense, like the part about her trying to find more medical uses for the parasite. And her zombie-soldiers project had indeed gone bust, even before I escaped and she was forced to blow up the abandoned factory.

Kristi claimed she was working independently from Saberton. Maybe Andrew had information as to how true that was.

Either way, I still had threads to pull, and one big shiny one was currently sitting in the St. Edwards Sheriff's office impound lot. Wherever the hell that was.

Bear's pickup was parked in front of my house, and it took

me several seconds to realize Kang must have driven here after dropping off the humans at the lab. Made sense, now that I thought about it. Where else would he go? Oooh, maybe he'd be up to helping me with my little mission? A second set of zombie hands sure would come in handy.

Kang was on the couch when I stepped in. He bolted upright, hand closing on a baseball bat beside him.

"Oh, it's you," he said, relaxing his grip.

"It *is* my house, y'know." I dropped my bag on the coffee table. "You must have been deep in dreamland not to hear my car, or me clomping up the steps."

He smiled wearily. More than weary, I realized. His eyes were dark pits in his face. "I figured I'd be more use after a little rest," he said. "I was wiped."

"You look like you still are," I said. "Get some serious sleep. I'll change the sheets on my dad's bed."

"That's not necessary."

I pinned him with a glare. "You might be ancient, but you just re-grew. One little nap isn't enough. Push too hard too fast, and you'll regret it. And if you mean changing the sheets isn't necessary, you don't know my dad."

He lifted his hands in surrender. "I suppose I can use more sleep."

It took me no time at all to remake the bed with fresh sheets, though probably not to Gina's standards. With a grateful nod, Kang unabashedly stripped to his skin and crawled into bed.

I flicked off the light and closed the door to just a crack. Time to connect with Andrew. Pawing through my dresser drawers yielded a bright blue T-shirt with a giant extended middle finger emblazoned across the front—a holdover from my loser-and-kind-of-a-jerk phase.

After turning it inside out to hide the rude gesture, I hung it in the bathroom window. That's what Andrew had told me to do if I needed to talk to him. Well, he'd said hang something blue, not specifically an inside-out obscene t-shirt. Not that it mattered. How would anyone be able to see it, considering it was full dark? And besides, the bathroom window faced a patch of woods and—

My phone rang. No way.

"Congratulations!" a robotic voice announced. "You've won an all-expense paid cruise to Argentina!"

Crap. The response to my signal had been a jillion times faster than I expected. And what the hell? Did he have a camera trained on my house? I hurried to call my dad.

"Hey, time to be Momzombique," I told him. "I need you to ask Andrew something. Do you have a way to write it down?"

"No, I ain't got no way to write it down," he grumbled. "Hang on." I heard a muffled, "Any of y'all got a pen and paper? Angel needs me to deliver a message!" More rustling then, "Okay, shoot."

"Ask Andrew if Kristi really is working projects on her own, apart from Saberton, and if Saberton really is as focused on defense contracts and weaponization of the parasite as she says they are, and if she really is as fed up with it as she claims. She says she wasn't involved in our swamp encounter with Saberton or Connor's murder, but I'm not sure whether to believe her. Tell him to do a check on a guy named Harlon Murtaugh."

"Dang, girl, slow down! I got 'If Kristi is working' . . ."

I repeated my questions much more slowly until he had it all. "Write down his response, too, please? Then call me back."

"Got it."

I hung up then trudged to the living room and booted up the computer. Dreading what I might discover, I went online and searched the local news. I was the source of the shambler epidemic, so it didn't feel right to hide from the consequences.

Sure enough, the top story was about a band who was in the middle of their set at a local bar when they started turning shambler, one right after the other. Shaky video taken by a bar patron accompanied the story. I watched, nauseated, as bar-goers screamed and tried to flee, tripping over chairs and each other to evade the shambling bass player and lead singer.

I stopped the video and leaned close to the screen, peering at an out-of-focus blob behind the bass player. Making the video full-screen simply made it a larger out-of-focus blob, but going back a few seconds and slowing the playback to a crawl earned me a clear shot of a water bottle at the base of the singer's mic stand, along with another on its side by the snare drum. Nice Springs Water.

Fingers trembling, I copied the link and texted it to Dr. Nikas. <Same brand water bottles by band members! Could be a link somehow!!!>

A moment later: <We tested the water in the two bottles you

brought but found no trace of Eugene or any possible deriva-
tives. I'm sorry but the presence of the water bottles is most
likely a coincidence.>

My spirits plummeted through the floor and into the dirt below. So much for a breakthrough.

My phone rang, forcing me to stop moping.

"Hey, baby," my dad said. "Me and Andy had a nice little
chat. He said Kristi has a good many projects of her own and,
um, aw-ton-uh-me."

"Autonomy. Means she doesn't have to answer to anyone."

"He'll see if he can get hold of payroll records and check if
Harlon Murtaugh or anyone else is getting paid for projects they
ain't supposed to be working on. But it may take a while."

"Anything is better than nothing."

"Andy said he can't vouch for what she might or might not
be fed up with, but Saberton's starting to come 'round to the
point of letting go of the defense contract crap."

Hmm. It didn't support her claim that they were still focused
on the defense stuff, but it didn't contradict it, either. Not the
definitive answer I was looking for, though still useful info.
"Thanks a million, Dad."

After an exchange of "love you"s, I hung up, feeling not
quite as morose. Sure, the water bottle thing had been a bust, but
we weren't out of leads. Dr. Nikas—with the *help* of Kristi—
would figure shit out, then the shamblers would be cured, and I
would never have to exchange a civil word with Dr. Kristi Charish ever again.

But the subject of helping Dr. Nikas reminded me of my idea
to find someone to help him who had the necessary medical
credentials, experience, and knowledge, who was also willing to
be turned into a zombie. How hard could it be?

Very, I soon realized, after a Google search for "dying neuro-
biologists" yielded a handful of articles about already dead neu-
robiologists. Fine. I'd let the Tribe accountant deal with that
particular job opening. "Wanted: Neurobiologist. Ideal candi-
date is near death. Perks—not dying. Salary—negotiable. Socio-
paths need not apply."

I was still too restless to go to bed for the needed two hours
of sleep, so I texted Justine.

<you free to chat?>
Her reply was swift. <hell yes>

Relieved, I pulled up the video chat program.

"You look like shit," she said once it connected.

"So do you," I said, eyes narrowed. "What happened?"

She shook her head, dark hair swinging about her face. "Nope. You first. I saw the news tonight about the LZ-1 encephalitis. Are you okay?"

"Yeah, I'm fine." Physically at least. How could I tell her that I was the source? "It's just been kind of crazy and exhausting. I'm assisting the people who are trying to find a cure, as well as working my usual morgue job. I sent my dad out of town."

"What about you?" she demanded. "You're actually handling the bodies, aren't you? What if you get sick?"

"I won't. We have plenty of protective gear." I hesitated at the worry on her face. "And the lead researcher says that because I'm recovering from mono, my immune system is ramped up high, so I have a crazy low chance of getting infected." It was a steaming pile of bullshit from one end to the other, but, hey, she was an English major, so with luck she wouldn't know enough science or medicine to notice the giant gaping holes in my argument.

To my relief, her expression relaxed. "Okay, good," she said gruffly. "Not sure I could find anyone else who'd get my sense of humor."

"There is no one else."

"Probably a good thing."

"Damn straight. And now it's your turn to spill. What's wrong?"

Justine pulled a face. "My ex-girlfriend called, wanting to get back together. She's gorgeous and funny, but also over-the-top jealous. The last straw was when I found a digital recorder behind a bookcase in my apartment. She'd planted it to find out if I was talking to other girls." Justine snorted. "And the only women I talk to regularly are my mom, agent, and you."

"That's crazy." I rolled my eyes. "I mean, you're awesome and cute, but I just don't swing that way."

"It was pretty nuts." She sighed. "Once upon a time, I was head over heels for her, but I can't go back to that kind of insecurity and nonstop suspicion."

"No kidding!" I said. "I guess I'm lucky I don't have any psycho exes. One is a loser—well, was a loser. Can't really call him that anymore since he's starting to get his shit together." Never thought Randy would ever settle down with a real job, but the aviation repair stuff sure seemed to suit him. "And with my other ex, we flat out didn't work as a couple. But he's a good guy, and I'll always care about him."

"Aww, that's the sweetest."

"Ain't it though?" I said with a thick southern drawl, making her giggle.

"Has Nick asked you out yet?"

My smile vanished. "I . . . kinda broke it off with him."

"What?! Why? What did he do?" She shifted forward, her face that of a woman ready to come right through the screen to my defense.

"No! Nothing. He's the best. It's me."

She slowly sat back. "Do you not like him anymore?"

"No! I mean, yes I still like him. A lot. I'm just . . . it's not healthy for him to be around me."

"Uh huh." She folded her arms over her chest. "Do you have leprosy?"

I scowled. "Suppose I did have leprosy. It would be best for him to stay away, right?"

"No, because leprosy is curable now, which I know all about because I had a bit part in a documentary a few years ago. See, it's actually called Hansen's disease—"

"You're not helping!"

Justine smirked. "Oh, I think I am. Answer me this: does he still like you?"

I slumped. "Yes."

"And would you give up if he told you he was ending things for your own good?"

"No. I'd fight for him. You're right about everything." I stuck my tongue out at her.

She did a victory fist pump. "Of course I am!"

I let her gloat a bit more, then we shifted the conversation to lighter stuff.

Eventually we said our usual "bye 'til later!" and signed off. I was tired enough to sleep now, but while I was at the computer, I looked up the address of the impound lot. Turned out the St. Edwards Parish Sherriff's Office didn't have the need or the space for an impound lot of their own, therefore they and every other police agency in the parish rented space from Big Bubba's Towing.

The address told me I'd driven past the place about a zillion times on my way to and from the Tribe lab, though I couldn't picture it for the life of me. Then again, tow yards weren't usually all that scenic, and therefore unlikely to draw my attention.

I shut down the computer, set my alarm for midnight, and got my zombie ass to bed.

Chapter 30

My alarm went off at midnight. I immediately activated the stay-awake mod since I knew too damn well that if I waited, I'd fall right back to sleep.

Ten seconds later, a warm rush flowed through my body, washing away every trace of fatigue. I sprang out of bed, feeling as if I'd slept a solid nine hours.

I dressed quickly in black fatigue pants, long-sleeved black shirt, and sneakers, then I dug my balaclava out of my underwear drawer and stuffed it into a thigh pocket. It said something about my life that I even owned a balaclava. It wasn't as if South Louisiana ever got cold enough to need one.

In the other thigh pocket went a brain packet along with a dozen more to keep in my car. A quick rummage through the kitchen junk drawer turned up a big flathead screwdriver, a box cutter, a pair of dollar store gardening gloves, and a multitool—all of which found homes in my various pockets. That should be everything I'd need for the search of Reno's Camry.

After a quick breakfast of grits and brains, I checked on Kang—verifying he was still asleep and okay—then headed out.

It wasn't until my GPS told me I'd arrived that I realized why I had zero clue what the place looked like. Big Bubba apparently wasn't too keen on visitors. On the left, a tiny sign about the size of a piece of notebook paper, marked a gravel driveway, beyond which was a good-sized chunk of property surrounded by a six-foot chain-link fence. The gate was secured with a heavy chain and padlock, and within the perimeter fence, a lighted area glimmered beyond sparse trees. The impound lot, I hoped.

I made a quick check of the GPS map then continued past the Big Bubba's entrance and turned left onto a rough gravel road that skirted the property. A quarter mile down, I took another left onto a narrow road that paralleled the back side. A deep ditch ran between road and fence, spanned by a second driveway that led to another locked gate. Best of all, about a hundred feet past the driveway was a stand of pines snugged up against the fence, thick enough to keep anyone from seeing my car.

Bubba's property looked to be about five acres. The impound lot sat near the center, a fenced enclosure lit by a lone streetlight which left everything beyond its glow in shadowy darkness. Perfect for my needs. A dirt track meandered between the perimeter and impound fences, probably going all the way around to meet up with the front entrance drive. Dozens of junk cars filled both corners, and two rusted shipping containers huddled against the fence on the left.

I pulled off the road just past the first pine, killed the engine, then dug my trusty glass-punch tool out of the glove compartment. Yeah, I was a zombie, but I still had no desire to be trapped in my car if it ever ended up in one of the many waterways in the area. And for situations like these, a glass punch tool was quieter than a brick in case there was anyone within earshot. The punch tool went into the pocket that held the screwdrivers, then I pulled on the balaclava and climbed out of the car, locking it behind me.

With a running leap, I hurdled the ditch with ease, then crouched in knee-high grass outside the fence, watching and listening. Nothing in sight resembled a residence, but for all I knew, Big Bubba lived in the shipping containers. Not to mention, I'd watched enough TV to know that places like this always had a pack of vicious guard dogs—even though the only sign of life was a possum sniffing around the rusted shell of a minivan.

I scaled the six-foot fence and dropped to the other side then picked my way across the uneven ground toward the impound lot. Countless hunks of steel, old wheel rims, axles, and who knew what else lay covered in a treacherous tangle of grass and weeds. Watching my step, I crossed the dirt track and another twenty feet of tetanus booby traps to the impound lot fence—a formidable twelve feet of commercial grade chain link. At least there wasn't any razor wire or spikes.

After reaching the top, I climbed down the other side instead of jumping—partly because of the height, but mostly because the inside of the fence was lined with cars.

I reached the ground between an LTD and a Kia then took stock. In addition to the cars around the perimeter, more were parked in a line down the middle of the lot. All told, there were twenty or so vehicles of a variety of makes and models, including an odd little three-wheeled car and, right smack in the middle, a shiny red Camaro with a dealer sticker still on the window. Two Camrys, but only one was silver, not to mention having four blown tires and a deflated airbag.

Pleased, I tugged on the gardening gloves. No point leaving fingerprints all over the car I planned to turn inside out.

I pressed the point of the punch tool against the bottom corner of the passenger window, and was rewarded with a shower of safety glass. Time to get serious. I wasn't constrained by pesky shit like probable cause or the limits of a search warrant. There was no one to stop me from slicing carpet or removing door panels.

And I did. For nearly an hour I sliced and ripped and pried. Yet even though I uncovered every secret hidey hole a car interior could possibly have, I came up empty. The same with the wheel wells and undercarriage. Nothing.

Crossing mental fingers that the trunk would yield something useful, I hit the release latch. The trunk interior was clean and empty except for a plastic bin that held a fire extinguisher, road flares, and a first-aid kit. I gave Reno grudging props for his roadside emergency preparedness, but none of that told me why he'd been at the hospital admin building, and why Sorsha had been watching him. I changed the blade on my box cutter then slashed at the lining, dug through the spare tire well, and even sliced open the spare tire itself. Nada.

I held my frustration at bay with effort. I'd tugged this thread hard and so far had nothing to show for it. Great. Found Reno's car. Tore it apart. But I—

The sound of tires on gravel cut my pity party short. Headlights of an approaching car shone through the trees. With only seconds before the vehicle made the curve, I scrambled into the trunk and pulled the lid shut to barely a crack so I could see who was coming.

To my everlasting annoyance, a battered green pickup stopped right outside the impound lot gate. A man stepped out— at least six feet tall and skinny, with a potbelly that made him look nine months pregnant. With twins. Impressive, in a grossly disproportioned way. I eyed him as he fumbled with the key for the gate lock. Long, stringy hair. Dingy flannel over a grubby white t-shirt. Stained jeans.

Potbelly Guy wrestled the lock open and pulled the gate aside. "C'mon, babydoll." He waved for the passenger to join him.

A woman with painfully red hair climbed out. She wore a crop top, exposing a midriff that had never known a situp. A black mini skirt at least two sizes too small strained over lumpy curves.

As she stepped around the pickup, I got a good look at her face. I clamped a hand over my mouth to hold back a chortle. Carol Ann Pruitt who, back in the day, had tried to steal my then-boyfriend Randy away from me. And this past fall she'd tried to bust my skull open with a pool cue during a bar fight, only to end up on the floor after I laid her skanky ass out with one brain-fueled punch.

"Bubba baby, why'd you bring me way out here?" Carol Ann whined. "It's creepy."

"Come on, I got a surprise for you." Bubba held out a hand for her. Pouting, she took it and allowed him to lead her into the yard.

"Now you gotta close your eyes," he said, grinning—or as much as a body could grin with only a scattered handful of teeth in his mouth.

Carol Ann giggled and squeezed her eyes shut. "You gonna do something nasty to me?"

"Aww baby, all sorts of nasty." Bubba led her around to the front of the Camaro—directly across from where I was hiding. "Okay, you can look now!"

She let out a gasp. "Oh my god! Is it yours? It's so gorgeous!" She rushed forward to stroke her hands over the sports car.

"Nah, ain't mine, but that don't mean we can't have some fun on it." He patted the hood and leered.

"On it?" Carol Ann's face puckered. "You mean we can't drive it?"

Bubba shifted uncomfortably. "Well, no. Not this one, anyhow. I could get in a heap of trouble. But, um, next time I get me a hot car in, I'll make sure your purty little ass gets in the driver's seat."

Carol Ann squealed and threw her arms around his neck. "You're the best, Bubba!"

Or maybe she'd said "the best Bubba" because she was hedging her bets. Either way, she seemed plenty satisfied with his offer. She did a little jump and wrapped her legs around Bubba's waist. Or mostly around, since the size of his belly made the feat impossible. Not to mention, Carol Ann wasn't exactly petite, and Bubba didn't have a ton of muscle tone.

The result was Carol Ann trying to tighten her legs to hold on while Bubba staggered to keep his balance. He saved them from crashing to the ground only by turning and falling forward onto the hood of the Camaro, with Carol Ann flat on her back.

"Aww, yer so damn sexy," Bubba crooned as if placing her on the hood had been his intention all along. "You want me to fuck you right here? Would ya like that?"

Carol Ann giggled then shimmied out of her undies and tossed them aside. "What do you think, big boy?"

I pulled the lid closed just shy of latching since I had zeee-rrrooooooo desire to see those two banging away. Yikes. The sounds were bad enough. Bubba grunting, and Carol Ann making porn star noises, mixed with the melodic tones of flesh slapping wetly against flesh.

At long last, Bubba let out a guttural cry, which seemed to be Carol Ann's cue to fake her own orgasm, with wails and moans so loud the poor possum was likely traumatized.

The noise finally trailed off to hard breathing and "Oh, baby, that was so good" from both. I dared a peek out again in time to see Bubba stuffing an utterly enormous wang back in his jeans. *Big* Bubba indeed.

For her part, Carol Ann didn't seem to care about her underwear and simply tugged her miniskirt down to its previous barely decent length. Yet my hopes that they'd leave crashed and burned as Bubba climbed onto the hood and stretched out beside Carol Ann. When he lit a joint and passed it to her, I had to choke down a shriek of frustration.

The two lay back and traded the joint back and forth, looking at who the hell knew what since the streetlight was too bright to see any stars. I couldn't even try and search inside the trunk while I waited for them to finish their post-fuck pot. It was too dark, and if they heard me fumbling around, not only would I be busted, but I'd have a much harder time escaping. Thank god the stay-awake mod kept me from drifting off out of sheer boredom.

Finally, the two stumbled off the Camaro and to Bubba's truck. I waited until the sound of the engine faded into the distance before climbing stiffly out of the damn trunk. Ugh. Bubba's little tryst had killed nearly an hour.

I resumed my search, ripping carpet out, and even pawing through the first aid kit. Still nothing. I was coming to the reluctant conclusion that Sorsha and Ben hadn't found anything because there wasn't anything to find.

Shit.

Dejected, I sat in the slashed driver's seat. Maybe I was going about this all wrong. What if nothing was hidden in super-secret places, because there'd been no time for that? Ben said that Reno might have ditched something small before the road block. Which meant it was a move of desperation. But what if there'd been something else not as easily ditchable? If there was, he'd have hidden it within easy reach of the driver's seat.

Pretending to be Reno, I scooched forward to where I could reach the gas pedal. Then, keeping one hand on the wheel, I tested to see how far I could reach, adding a couple of inches to make up for my shorter arms.

My hand brushed the CD player, and my pulse quickened. My less than stellar background meant I'd been witness to a car stereo theft or three. Though I was nowhere near as speedy as the hooligans I'd once hung around, I wasn't worried about reselling this particular stereo, so the big flathead screwdriver and a little brutality helped remove it in right under a minute.

I pried open the CD tray, making a little noise of delight at the sight of a small white card within. A punch card with no punches. Double Dime Diner—buy ten sundaes, get one free.

I flipped it over and found a series of letter and numbers. The tingle in my fingers told me this was important, but what the heck was it? Not a zip code or phone number. Address? Website? Order confirmation number? Whatever it was, it was a clue.

Reno had stuffed it into the CD player since it was too light to throw far. Too much chance it would fall onto the road and be found by the pursuit.

I took a picture of both front and back of the card then pocketed it and my phone.

Headlights flickered through the trees as someone turned off the highway and pulled up to the outer gate.

Nuh-uh. No way in hell was I getting trapped for another front row seat to the Bubba and BigBoy show. I bailed out of the car and sprinted toward the Kia by the fence. In a mighty, zombie-speed leap, I planted one foot on the hood, sprang to the roof, then launched myself high on the fence to cling like a spider on a web.

The heavy clatter of a diesel engine told me the newcomer wasn't Bubba unless he'd changed vehicles, but I had no intention of waiting around to find out for sure. I clambered to the top of the fence, threw my leg over, then thought better of jumping the twelve feet. Instead, I maneuvered to hang by my hands to make the actual drop a more reasonable five feet or so. Easy peasy. I pushed off from the fence with my feet and let go.

The ground gave way under my right foot with an awful screech of metal. Fiery pain raked up my calf. I flailed to stay upright but crashed sideways.

Crrraaaack. I might have screamed. I definitely fainted.

Muffled country rock music thumped. I opened my eyes to a cold, grey world. Dull pain throbbed in my right leg. I was lying on my side, lower leg wedged at an unnatural angle through a slab of rusted metal covered in weeds. Car door maybe. I shoved up onto one elbow, squinted for a better look. White bone poked out of an ugly gash mid-calf.

Shiiiiiiiiit. *It's okay it's okay. Parasite slowed the bleeding. Dulled the pain. Dulled the brain. Brains. Need brains.*

The scent of a fresh brain wafted over me. I inhaled deeply, zeroed in on it. Movement in the impound lot. I peered through the fence, between the Kia and LTD, to where a man unhooked a minivan from his tow truck. A low growl rose in my throat.

No no no no no no no no no. With numb fingers, I fumbled in my pocket for the packet of brains. Found it. Ripped off the top with my teeth. Squeezed the brains into my mouth. Squeezed some more. Sucked it dry.

A tinge of color returned to the cars, to the grass, to the man. The desire to crack a skull eased. A bit. I needed more brains. Had to make it to my car. Not that far.

How? Brain hunger made it hard to think. Brain fog from brain hunger. One step at a time. *Focus, Angel. Focus.*

The man was occupied with his business and would never hear me move over his music. My foot and half of my lower leg had gone straight through the metal scrap, getting gouged along the way then wedged in. The hard fall to the side had snapped both bones. Tib . . . tibia and fibula. Yes. Focus. And it was a compound fracture. Two jagged ends sticking out meant compound. Compound was bad.

Clenching my jaw, I grabbed with both hands below the break and twist-tugged. Then again. On the third pull, my foot came free. Bone grated on bone, and a wave of sickening pain cut through the brain-hunger numbness. I breathed like a pregnant lady in labor until it receded.

Woof. A heavy bark from inside the impound lot. *Woof.*

The possum scurried along between the fence and cars, passing right by me to hole up in an old tire a dozen feet away. A hulking brute of a rottweiler slid to a stop in the gap between the Kia and LTD. Locked eyes on me. Forgot the possum. *Woof woof WOOF.*

"Shh shh shh . . . nice doggie."

WOOF WOOF. If not for the fence, that sucker would be *on* my skinny ass.

"Rocko! Shut up!" Tow Truck Guy hollered. "Leave that possum be."

WOOF WOOF WOOF.

Shit. Staring down the bigass dog made him think I was a threat that needed to be dealt with. The last thing I needed was the guy coming over to investigate. I closed my eyes to slits, ducked my head, and went as still as possible.

Rocko rumbled a deep menacing growl. Better than barking for my predicament, though a shitload scarier. Here I was, rotting and being menaced by a rottie. I'd laugh if I wasn't so terrified.

"Dammit, Rocko," Tow Truck Guy shouted. The music got louder as he opened the passenger door. "Get in here, NOW!" He started our way.

The dog didn't move. I prayed for the shadowy darkness to

keep me hidden from human view. The scent of the man's brain raised a low growl in my own throat. Shit shit shit. I groped through the weeds. My hand closed on a baseball-sized rock, and I hurled it at the fence beside the possum's hidey hole. Either the dumbest or smartest thing I ever did. Could go either way.

Clang.

The possum popped out of the tire and fled the scary fence monster, letting out a stream of grunty screech-growls. Dog and master jerked their heads toward the sound—away from me.

Tow Truck Guy hollered at Rocko. "C'mon, ya dumbass beast. Possum's gone. Get yer ass in there!"

Rocko finally listened and bounded toward the truck. The dog jumped up into the cab and settled on the passenger seat. The man shut the door, then he and his fresh brain made their way to the driver's side. The door opened and closed, cutting off the source of the irresistible smell.

Breathing raggedly, I willed the skull-cracking urge to subside. Clenched my fists until the tow truck was long gone. Wasted time. Wasted brains. Stupid tow truck. Stupid dog.

Focus, Angel. Brains in the car.

It was hard to focus with the dull fog creeping in again. I half-crawled, half-dragged myself away from the impound lot and toward the perimeter fence. Only a hundred feet. I could do it. My leg thought differently, throbbed. I looked back to find it twisted a full ninety degrees below the break and threatening to pull loose. *No no no.* I didn't have enough brains in the car to completely regrow a limb. And how the hell would I drive without a right foot?

One step at a time, Angel.

Had to get to the car first. Brains were there. Yanked off the balaclava and sliced a hole in the top, then slipped it over the break like a sleeve. Stripped out of my shirt and cut off the bottom half. Kinda sorta got my foot turned the right way after an awful grating of bone. Forced my increasingly clumsy hands to obey and wrapped the t-shirt piece around the balaclava and break. Needed more. Stretchier. I struggled to wriggle out of my sports bra then gave up and sliced the front. Wrestled it off. Cut it in two. Rewrapped the t-shirt piece snugly. Used the bra to secure it above and below the break. That would be enough to keep my foot from falling off. Best I could do for now.

I pulled my shirt—now a crop top—back on and crawl-dragged for the perimeter fence line and my car beyond.

Or not. I collapsed in the middle of the dirt track, a godawful realization penetrating the haze of my thoughts.

The fence. Even if I could make it there, I'd never be able to climb it. No way.

And I was hungry. Soooo hungry.

I flopped onto my back and stared up where the stars would be. Like Big Bubba and Carol Ann. But I didn't have a Big Bubba beside me to carry me to the hood of my car. Brains in my car. No Bubba. Memory of a warm hand squeezing mine. Better than Bubba. Nick.

Nick! I scrabbled for my phone. Hit the speed dial with shaking hands mottled by rot patches. Shit. Answer answer answer.

"Angel?" Sleepily.

"Need . . . help." My voice sounded raspy and wet.

"Where are you? What happened?" No longer sleepy. Intense. Focused, like I needed to be.

Focus, Angel.

"Back of . . . Big Bubble's thing. Cars. Need brains. From my car . . . can't. Fence."

"Big Bubble's? I don't . . . Oh, Big Bubba's Towing on Cooter Mill Road?" Scuffling sounds in the background.

"Back of Bubbub. Car on lil road." I struggled to form the words. "Brains in glub . . . glove thing. Broken. Me. Help?"

"Tell me if this is right." More banging and scuffling. "You're at the back of Big Bubba's property. You're hurt and need brains, but there's a fence between you and your car. Brains are in the glove compartment."

"Don't come near . . . me. So hunnnnngry." It came out in a wet growl.

"I'm on my way. Fifteen minutes, tops. Don't hang up."

I fumbled the phone onto speaker. Laid it by my head. Stared up at nothing. Went still to conserve energy. Sounds dull. Vision dull. Pain dull. Nick's voiced droned on in a muffled blanket of comfort.

"Angel?"

"Didn't . . . hang up," I tried to say.

Light swept over me. And the scent of a human brain.

"I'm looking for you." His voice issued from the phone and from nearby.

I lurched to my hands and knees. Snarled. Eyes fixed on the dark shape beyond the fence.

The light swung back. Rested on me. "Angel, I have the packets. You're going to be okay."

Saliva filled my mouth, spilled over. "You're not. Stay . . . away." I crawl-dragged forward. Collapsed as rotted flesh shredded from my hand.

"It's too far to throw the packets." He climbed the fence and dropped down on my side. "I can't stay away, Angel. I won't."

I snarled, clawed at the ground to inch toward him. "Stay . . . back." The words were barely words, burbling through wet throat rot.

The luscious brain crouched twenty feet away, set the flashlight on the ground, pointed at me. I reached toward him, flesh trailing in strings from my fingers.

Something landed in the dirt in front of me. Not braaains. I growled.

Another something splatted in the dirt near my hand. The scent washed over me. Not warm. Not fresh. But brrrraaaaaaiiins. I grabbed it up. Squeezed it into my mouth. Let out a howl when there was no more.

But another open packet of not-warm brains landed. I sucked them down. Senses cleared a bit. "Nick?" I croaked as I snatched the first packet from the ground and ripped the top off.

"I'm right here," he said, voice calm and steady and soothing. He tossed another packet to me.

I scarfed down both packets before shifting to sit, bodily hauling my mangled leg in front of me. My leg below the break twisted to the right and angled off at forty-five degrees. Rot covered my fingers, but it was healing. Slowly.

Nick stood and approached.

I put up both hands. "Stay back! I . . . I'm . . . not whole yet."

"Would you please shut the fuck up?" He dropped to one knee in front of me then, with a crunch of bone against bone, skillfully pulled and straightened my leg.

I breathed through my teeth and sent up thanks to the universe that the parasite still had the pain dampened. "How can you even stand to be around me? I'm . . . gross."

Nick opened two packets at the same time and pressed them into my hands. "Angel, I swear to god, for someone so intelligent, you can be a real idiot sometimes."

I busied myself with consuming the last of the brains. Felt the tingle in my leg as the break repaired itself. And the tingle in my face as rot I couldn't see—but Nick could—healed. Finally, I said quietly, "You think I'm intelligent?"

"Yes! You're sharp as a tack. You learned the morgue computer system in three days. I struggled with it for a week when I started. You beat the odds and got your GED. You're in college now. You see things others miss. I could go on, but none of that's important right now."

I looked up at him. "What is?"

Nick's eyes met mine. "Rotting is pretty disgusting. I'm not going to lie. But you know what? I don't think *you* are disgusting. You still hang around me even though I poop. Pooping is pretty gross, right? I also fart, belch, and scratch my balls." He gave me a crooked smile. "I pick at scabs. And sometimes I even pick my nose."

I suddenly felt a billion times lighter. "But do you eat it?"

He winked. "There are no witnesses who could testify that I do."

I snorted a giggle.

"The point is, the gross stuff doesn't matter to me. *You* matter to me."

A warm tingly sensation chased away the last of the pain. "You matter to me, too."

"You okay now?"

I flexed my foot. "Yeah. I think so. How do I look?"

"Back to the Angel I know and . . ." He stood and drew me to my feet then wrapped his arms around me and pulled me into a kiss.

I melted into it, layers of stress and drama and pain of the past hour, the past *month*, falling away. His hands were warm and strong on my back, running up beneath my makeshift crop top. A wicked little part of me was glad my sports bra was tied around my leg, leaving my tits free for him to—Oh yeah. That.

He breathlessly broke the kiss about a year later and took my hand. "We'd better get out of here. I'm parked down by the gate."

"Dude, you reek of DEET, y'know?"

He laughed. "My new aftershave."

"I suppose I can tolerate it." I smiled. "For now."

We headed down the dirt track, hand in hand. He glanced at

me. "Had to break your window to get the brains. Sorry. I'll have it fixed."

I smiled, comfortable and happy. "If that's the worst thing to come out of this night, we'll count ourselves lucky."

His reply choked off, and he stumbled. "An . . . gel?"

"Nick! What's wrong? What—"

He gave a deep moan and collapsed in a seizure at my feet.

Chapter 31

I stared in shocked disbelief, heart pounding. "No! Oh no. Nick? Nick!" How could this be happening? He was wearing mosquito repellent, so it couldn't be a bite—

The kiss. That had to be it. Oh god. Not Nick.

Needed to get him somewhere safe. To the lab. I took deep breaths to calm the panic and willed myself into emergency overdrive. Hands shaking, I rolled Nick to his side. Dug keys from his pocket. Scaled the fence. Sprinted to his car by the gate.

Ram it right through the chained gate? No, wait. I dug through his trunk instead and came up with bolt cutters. Preppers gotta prep, right?

Cut the chain, kicked open the gate. Cranked the engine, peeled out down the dirt track toward where I'd left him. He loomed from the darkness in the wash of headlights, shambling with arms outstretched and lips pulled back in a snarl.

Slammed the car into park and left the lights on.

Cold knotted in my belly, and a sob rose. Stop it. No time for that. I had to move fast. I activated a dose of combat mod and counted down. *Five. Four. Three. Two. One.*

Sweet fire breathed through my veins. Night sounds of crickets and frogs amplified and resolved. My vision sharpened.

With my reflexes and senses at peak performance, I pulled the trunk release and bailed out of the car. Jumped up and down and waved my arms, hoping Nick would behave like other shamblers and try to pursue and bite. "C'mon Nick! Woooo. This way! Come at me, bro!"

His head swiveled toward me, eyes dead-white in the harsh light.

"That's it." I took a step toward the rear of the car. "C'mon."

He lurched forward with awkward, unbalanced steps.

I lured him until he was by the trunk then, in a blur of mod-enhanced zombie speed and strength no shambler could match, I tackled him into the trunk, stuffed his arms and legs in, and slammed the lid on him. Opened it again and grabbed the roll of duct tape I'd spied. Closed the lid. Pulled a long piece of tape off the roll, opened the trunk, wrapped Nick's wrists and hands. Slammed it again. Good. Good enough. No way was he coherent enough to use the trunk latch release on purpose, and with his hands wrapped he wouldn't do so accidentally either.

"I'm so sorry, Nick. We'll fix this. I promise." We had to.

I dove into the driver's seat. A three-point turn later, we flew down the dirt track and careened onto the road. In the rear view mirror, I caught a glimpse of my car near the stand of pines. It was only a matter of time before big Bubba discovered it—and that one of the impounded cars had been ripped to pieces. He'd put two and two together, and a world of trouble would come down on my head. But I'd worry about that later. After I saved Nick.

As soon as I hit the highway, I called the lab to give them the gist of the situation, and tell them we were on the way. *Followed a hunch at Bubba's place. Nick. Shambler. Ten minutes away. Help.*

And then I hauled ass, teeth clenched to keep me from breaking down and crying. Couldn't start bawling yet. I needed to see the road.

Thumpity-thump-thump. From the trunk.

Why did I have to go and call Nick to help me instead of Marcus or Pierce or Brian? Any one of them would have been a more logical choice than Nick to handle a hungry, injured zombie. It hadn't even occurred to me to call anyone else, but then again I'd been brain-starved and not thinking straight.

I cranked up the volume on the radio, tried to sing at the top of my lungs to drown out the thoughts and the thumps, but the words stuck in my throat. Fuck it. I didn't need to worry about hearing damage. I turned the volume up to the max, let the music pound me as the miles slipped by.

I tore into the parking lot and slammed on the brakes, shaking in relief at the sight of people waiting for us outside the lab. Kyle, Marcus, Rachel, Jacques—and of course, Bear.

Killed the engine and popped the trunk. Then couldn't hold back the sobs anymore. The combat mod had faded to nothing, leaving me weary and drained. Rachel and Kyle dragged the slavering Nick out of the trunk and held him down on a stretcher while Jacques secured medical restraints. I did nothing but shudder with big, snotty, chest-hurting sobs while the crew wheeled Nick inside, followed closely by an ashen-faced Bear.

My door opened, and Marcus was there, helping me stagger out. He didn't say a word, just steadied me enough to walk. I didn't need words. I needed the big gaping hole in my heart to heal, and that wasn't going to happen until we found a cure.

Marcus steered me through security to the medical wing. By the time he let me go outside Nick's room, my sobs had eased to sniffles.

Inside, Jacques and Kyle worked in smooth precision to transfer Nick to the bed and restrain him, then began setting up monitors and an IV.

Bear stood in the doorway, face stricken, holding himself back with an effort of will I doubted I'd ever possess.

"I'm sorry, B-bear," I choked out. "It's my fault. It's all my fault."

Bear spared me a perplexed look. "I know you're the source of this disease, Angel. That doesn't make *this* your fault."

"I'm the source, but this is different. I infected him . . . when I kissed him." My throat clogged. What the hell had I been thinking?

Bear turned to face me squarely and seized my upper arm. "Let me get this straight. You kissed Nick?"

I gulped and nodded. "And then he collapsed, like a minute later. I should never have—"

"Did you force a kiss on him?" His expression was stony, and his grip remained firm on my arm.

"N-no. He kissed me first." Fresh tears welled up at the memory of that glorious, perfect moment. It felt like I'd waited my entire life for it.

Bear sighed and eased his grip. "Fuck me. He finally made a move."

I blinked at him stupidly. "Huh?"

"That boy has been crazy for you since day one," Bear murmured, finally releasing me. His anguished gaze returned to Nick. Yet to my shock, he put his arm around my shoulders and pulled me to his side in a reassuring embrace—which of course started me crying all over again.

"Shh," he said. "It's going to be all right, Angel. Your Dr. Nikas and that Dr. Charish will find a cure for this shit." His throat worked as he swallowed. "I have to believe that."

I let out a shuddering breath. "Me too."

We both fell silent and watched the activity around the bed. Now that Nick was restrained and his IV started, Jacques and Kyle collected samples of blood, body fluids, and various tissues.

"Nick's mom and I divorced when he was four," Bear said after a moment, voice low. "She wasn't ready to be a mom. Never really wanted to be one either, to be honest. Her career was taking off, and it didn't leave much room for raising a kid. Nor did living in Podunk, Louisiana. She just moved to New York one day, and that was it. Didn't ask for custody."

"What about visitation?"

His shoulders lifted in a shrug. "When Nick was little, I used to take him to see her for Christmas and a couple of weeks each summer. But I stopped when he was nine. It tore him up too much to get his mom back only to have her ripped away again. Plus it was pretty clear she wasn't invested in being a part of his life." He shook his head. "She's not a wicked witch. I don't want to give you the wrong impression. She's an investment banker and travels all over the world. She's a huge advocate for women's rights worldwide—even started a micro loan program for women in poverty-stricken areas. Donated a shit-ton of money to build hospitals and clinics in Haiti. She's a good person, but she knew she was going to end up being a terrible mother."

"Nick never talks about her. I always assumed she was dead."

"Nope, still very much alive. Victoria sent child support without fail, and far more than was required. She set up a bunch of investment accounts for Nick. Hell, his retirement was set by the time he was fifteen. She paid for that house he lives in. Sends lump sums every now and then." He snorted. "As Nick got older, I half expected him to send it back with a nicely worded 'fuck you,' but I guess he's too practical—and too kind—for that. He squirrels it away and sends her a thank you note. Every. Single. Time."

"That's . . . kind of heartbreaking."

As if agreeing, Nick moaned long and low.

Bear gave a sad nod. "I feel the same way. I never wanted to be a single dad, but I sure as shit wasn't going to abandon him the way his mom did. I just wish I'd done a better job."

"What? At raising him? Nick's a terrific guy."

"He is, but more despite me than because of me. I should've been more of a *dad* than a father and really listened to him." His breath hitched. "I know you saw that black eye I gave him right before Mardi Gras. I swear to god, that was the first and only time I ever laid hands on that boy."

The agony in his eyes was all too real. "I believe you," I said softly.

Bear tightened his arm around my shoulders. "You've been a real gift to my family, Angel." He lifted his free hand to wipe his eyes. "No matter what happens, you'll always be a part of it."

"Goddammit, Bear," I muttered as the fucking floodgates let loose in my tear ducts. Then I had to compose myself as Jacques came over to us.

"Dr. Nikas left for NuQuesCor shortly before you called, Angel," Jacques said. "He's aware of Nick's condition and will return to assess for himself, if you'd like."

I managed a watery smile. "I think he'll do Nick more good if he continues his work there." I glanced up at Bear and got a nod of agreement. "Please give Dr. Nikas my thanks, and if you need any help here, I could use something to keep me busy."

"I will convey your thanks," Jacques said. "And I'd welcome the help processing these samples from Nick and inputting the data."

Bear patted my shoulder. "I'll stay here with Nick and will let you know if anything changes."

I threw my arms around Bear in a hug then followed Jacques to the histology room. Jacques immediately busied himself with prepping slides, and I moved to do likewise.

Yet now that I wasn't freaking out quite so much about Nick, I noticed that Jacques wasn't as placid and collected as he usually was. In fact, he looked downright upset—hands trembling as he worked, and face bearing an actual grimace. And I didn't think it had anything to do with Nick.

"Jacques? What's wrong?"

A slide slipped from his grasp to break on the tile floor. He looked down at the pieces then up at me. "I—" He tightened his hands into fists then took a deep breath and relaxed them, shoulders sagging. "I made an error, and I'm not sure how."

"What are you talking about?"

Jacques stooped to clean up the broken slide. "Yesterday, during the blood draws, Dr. Nikas instructed me to switch the tube labels on Pierce's blood and one of yours. Which I did."

"Right. Dr. Nikas told me you'd do it. Once you made the switch, Pierce's tube had my name on it, and mine had his. I'm guessing you pocketed his real blood, and Kristi was left with a tube marked as Pierce's but was actually mine."

"That was the plan, yes. And I followed it." His brow creased. "I couldn't take Pierce's real tube immediately with Dr. Charish's tech there, but I did so it as soon as I could."

"So . . . what was your error?"

"When I arrived here and removed the stopper from what was supposed to be Pierce's tube, I instantly realized that it was your blood, not his."

I blinked. "Wait. How did you know?"

"The scent," he said, matter-of-factly. "I've been working with blood samples for over a century and have developed a keen nose for such."

"Maybe you just grabbed the wrong one," I said, packing my tone with all sorts of reassurance. It was unnerving seeing Jacques upset like this. "The important thing is that you got the labels switched. As long as Pierce's blood isn't marked as his, it should be okay. Kristi would have no way of knowing it was mature zombie blood, right?"

Jacques nodded slowly. "The factors are subtle, even with a complete DNA analysis."

"And does Kristi even know about mature zombies?"

"No," he said with zero hesitation. "That information has always been kept from her—as from most."

"Then everything is most likely totally cool," I said brightly, despite the pinprick of worry that I couldn't shake. "What did Pierce say about it?"

"'What's done is done.'" He let out a breath. "I can only hope that all is indeed . . . cool." But a whisper of doubt remained in his eyes as he returned to work.

I dove into slide preparation, focusing on accuracy and precision in a semi-successful attempt to keep the bone-deep worry for Nick at bay. When we finished, I headed to the media room. I couldn't be with Nick. Not yet. I knew I was being a coward, but I would totally lose it for real if I had to keep seeing him being so . . . not-Nick. My Nick.

Though I fully expected the media room to be empty since it was 5 a.m., the sound of laughter and voices drifted into the hall. To my surprise, Victor and all the humans except Bear were present, listening to Rosario recount some humorous event.

Annoyance raced through me that they could be *laughing* at a time like this. Yet in the next instant, my ire drained away. It wasn't their fault shit was so borked. Besides, sometimes you had to laugh to keep from falling to pieces.

My dad saw me and scrambled to his feet. "Angel! Is Nick okay?" He hurried to wrap me in his arms.

"He's . . . stable," I said. "Why are you all awake?"

"We heard about Nick," Jane said simply. Beside her, Portia nodded.

I sniffled at the unexpected show of support. "Thanks. Bear's with him now."

Portia smiled warmly. "Dante here was telling us the story of how he got shot in the derriere."

Rosario chuckled and gingerly shifted position on the very fluffy cushion beneath his wounded ass. "Yes, I was about to describe how you ran across the spit of land and launched yourself into the water with a psycho-manic war cry." He cleared his throat then let out a keening and ridiculous ululation, causing everyone to burst into laughter.

Even me, though I attempted to glower. "That is *not* what it sounded like. It was more of a—" I shrieked a screeching *eeoooeeeeoooeeeeeeleeleee* that had Rosario lifting his hands in surrender.

"Dear god, please never make that noise again," he pleaded. "Haven't you hurt me enough?"

"Me? I didn't shoot you in the butt."

Rosario grinned. "Not the butt, yet you have shot me."

I realized he was referring to the incident before Mardi Gras, when both he and Judd had been after me, though for different reasons. "You *deserved* to be shot then. And I barely nicked you. Besides, it was your fault I ended up spending the night in the swamp only to have Judd show up missing half his head."

Rosario whistled. "That shit was weird. A couple of minutes

after you took off, he climbed his feet and staggered away in the same direction. I couldn't do much though, since I was busy trying to stop the bleeding from where you shot me, plus I didn't have another dart."

"Hang on," I said. "You didn't think there was something completely *wrong* when a dead man with most of his skull missing got up and walked off?"

Rosario gave me a shrug. "Honestly? My first thought was, 'Oh, I guess he was a zombie this whole time.' I didn't really know a lot about zombies back then. Judd seemed like he was going after you, but he was moving pretty slow, and you had a good head start." His mouth quirked. "And, you weren't exactly my favorite person at that moment. And then after I crashed the four-wheeler, I was on so many pain meds I didn't know what was real!"

Laughs and shudders swept the room.

"Is Dante telling his I-got-shot-in-the-ass story again?" Rachel said from behind me, voice weary but touched with humor. She stepped past me, though not before giving me what sure felt like a comforting pat on the shoulder.

She went over to sit beside Rosario, closer than casual friends would sit. Or even close friends. And the look they exchanged said quite clearly they'd be banging buddies if not for Rosario's injury.

"They were riveted by my tale," Rosario told Rachel with a grin. "Until Angel re-created her war cry."

"Oh, that's what the sound was!" Rachel smiled at me, and not in a mean way. "I thought Dante was whining again about having his bandages changed."

Of course everyone thought that was hysterical, myself included. Rachel launched into an amusing story of her own, regarding Brian and a loose cow. She was getting to the good part with the emu when I felt a touch on my arm. Marcus.

He did a little head tilt to indicate he needed to talk to me. About Nick, most likely. I left the media room and followed him a short distance to an unoccupied office.

He remained silent until he'd closed the door then asked, "Are you okay?"

"Physically, yes," I said. His expression was unreadable. "Are you . . . mad?"

He sat on a corner of the desk and folded his arms. "You said you were following a solid hunch, but I don't understand why you went out there on your own. We're slammed, but I could have sent someone to be your back up. I expected better judgment from you."

My mouth worked soundlessly for a few seconds before I could form actual words. "Better judgment? I didn't *plan* to fall onto a rusted car door and break my leg! Maybe someday you can tell me what it's like to have everything in your life go exactly according to plan, where nothing unexpected happens, and nothing ever goes wrong."

"Angel, I—"

"No!" I stabbed a finger into his sternum. "You listen to me, Captain Controlling. It wasn't just a hunch. It was a goddamn *lead*, a good one that I dug up and followed. And I even found something! But hey, I guess I should check with you and the Tribe every time there's a possible decision to be made, because obviously I'm too stupid to think for myself, and I need someone to hold my fucking hand!"

"Fuck." Marcus stood and seized my arms, jaw tight. "Angel, I don't think you're stupid."

"But you think I have poor judgment," I shot back, voice quavering. That one stung, because I knew all about stupid, shitty choices. I'd made a whole lot of them in my day, but thought I was past all that.

Marcus sighed and squeezed my hands. "I'm sorry. I shouldn't have said that, because it isn't true at all. You're right. You pursued a hunch that turned into a solid lead, just like any good cop would do. And you had every reason to believe this would be a simple in-and-out operation."

I eyed him. "And?"

"And . . . I don't expect you to check with the Tribe every time you make a move, because you're competent and careful."

"That's more like it."

His mouth twitched in a wry smile. "I hope you realize how hard it is for me to say that."

"I'm actually surprised your head didn't explode." Our dating relationship had been chock full of his well-intentioned controlling behavior.

Marcus winced. "I deserved that."

"Nah, you've redeemed yourself about a million times over

by putting up with this Tribe shit." I took a deep breath. "And now that we have all the other stuff sorted out, I admit it would have been a smart move to at least let Brian know where I was going in case shit went south. As it was, no one knew."

He inclined his head. "No argument from me on that. Apart from my being a controlling prick, it's not about asking permission—it's about keeping the team in the loop. And you *are* a valued member of the team."

"Y'all have my back as much as I have yours." The old loser me would have labeled checking in as control. I knew better, but it felt as if it was only now fully sinking in. "It's cool. Next time I have a premeditated bit of criminal activity in mind, I'll give Brian a heads up."

Marcus smiled. "Good deal. So, what was the lead that took you to Big Bubba's, and what did you find?"

I gave him the rundown about Reno and the car chase, my talk with Ben Roth, and Agent Aberdeen's involvement. "This was in the CD tray," I said, handing him the Double Dime Diner punch card. "But I have no idea what the letters and numbers could mean."

Marcus frowned at the card. "I got nothing," he said after a moment. "Sorry."

"No worries. Might not even be related to our current drama." I took the card back. "Now I have an unrelated personal question for you."

"Shoot."

"Whaaaaat is the deal with Rachel and Rosario? You and Rachel were an item, and then you weren't, and now she and Rosario are making goo-goo eyes at each other. Also, Rachel was actually *nice* to me, which is beyond comprehension. Am I in a coma and having a totally unrealistic dream?"

"Rachel has had a change of heart about you," he said, shrugging as if that explained everything.

"Yeah, that's the creepy part," I said, eyes narrowing. "Why? She's always hated my guts, convinced I'm going to blow up the Tribe or worse."

"Only a few people know the whole truth about why you had to be regrown," Marcus said. "The story that was circulated was somewhat vague, but the gist was that you suffered severe unexpected side-effects from a mod you used during the rescue in

New York." A smile tugged up one corner of his mouth. "Which is true."

"But hardly the whole truth," I pointed out. V12 was, indeed, the mod I'd legitimately used in New York. But the whole addiction thing afterward was my own damn fault, leading to my dramatic disintegration on Mardi Gras.

"And as for why the side-effects progressed to the point of deterioration," Marcus continued, "it was leaked that you took a larger than usual dose in order to save the Tribe from exposure. Which is also true."

"Whatever. And she *bought* that?"

"Somewhat. Rachel can be a real sucker for selfless acts of valor, but she wasn't really sold until Dr. Nikas had a talk with her." He shrugged. "I don't know the details of what he said, but I gather he gave her a bit of a scolding—gentle, but no less scathing—and suggested she reconsider her outlook and her opinion of your worth and loyalty."

"Oh man, a scolding from Dr. Nikas is the worst because he's so darn nice." Tears pricked my eyes just thinking about it. I'd been on the receiving end of a scolding or two from him. "So . . . why did you and Rachel break up?" I asked, totally casual-like. "I mean, y'know, not to pry or anything. Really."

His eyes crinkled in humor. "Right. Not prying at all. It was mutual and amicable." He paused. "Okay, I was the one who broke it off, but she was totally cool and mature about it. It felt a bit odd to be so new in this position and already dating an employee. Especially with the age difference. Plus, I felt like I needed to pay more attention to my work here." A wince flashed across his face.

His "work" here was a sore subject, and now wasn't the time to prod it. "Age difference?" I said. "How old is she?" Rachel looked like she was in her twenties, but that didn't mean a whole lot when it came to zombies.

"About seventy years old," he said. "She was an army nurse during the Vietnam war. One day she was in a medivac chopper with two wounded men and a third soldier. The chopper got shot down, and Rachel was hurt pretty badly. So was the soldier. But then—"

"Ooh! This is Pierce, right? No, wait. He was Francis back then."

He gave me a sour look. "You're ruining my story."

"It's a little predictable," I said. "The soldier was Francis-Pietro-Pierce, and he turned Rachel, and she's been with him ever since."

Marcus heaved a sigh. "You're leaving out all the tension, and the horror when she sees him eat the brains of the dead pilot. But yes, he turned her yadda yadda."

"Wait a sec. I thought Rachel hated Kyle because, back when he was a Saberton operative, he killed her father? How is that possible if she's seventy-something years old? Did Kyle take out a ninety-year-old dude? He's only been a zombie for a few years, so it's not like he was working ops half a century ago."

"She hates him. That's for sure." He sobered. "But the man Kyle killed was actually Rachel's son, who was nine years old when her unit was deployed to Vietnam—and in his fifties when he died."

"Ouch," I said. "I can't even imagine what it must be like to have your kid die—no matter how old they are. I guess I should get over my own dislike of her."

"I think you'd like her, Angel," Marcus said. "And I'm not just saying that. She's a survivor. Like you."

The unexpected compliment warmed me all the way through. "Thanks."

"Speaking of surviving, I know you probably want to stay here with Nick, but I think you should go to NuQuesCor when we swap out security people."

I started to protest then sighed. "You're right. The best thing I can do is help Dr. Nikas."

He chuckled. "That was easier than I thought it would be. I didn't even have to point out that you'd get to ride in the helicopter."

"Oooooooooooooooooooo!"

"Be out back in"—he checked his watch—"half an hour."

"Will do!"

"Oh, and you might want to consider a change of clothes first. Maybe even a shower?"

I looked down at my raggedy crop-top shirt and bloody, ripped pants. "You make good sense."

"I do try."

Chapter 32

I took a super-quick shower to wash off blood and muck then changed into my last pair of clean jeans and a borrowed scrub top. Reno's Double Dime Diner punch card—with the mystery letters and numbers—went into my jeans pocket, and the ruined fatigue pants got tossed into the trash.

My phone rang as I was shoving my toothbrush into its travel case. My house landline, which meant it was Kang. "Hey, dude. What's up?"

"Just had a visitor."

I narrowed my eyes. "Like, a knock-on-the-door kind of visitor? It's not even six a.m."

"Exactly like that," he said. "An FBI agent who wanted to talk to both you and your dad."

Fuck. "Lemme guess. Special Agent Sorsha Aberdeen?"

"That's her. She flashed her ID when I opened the door."

Double fuck. "What did you tell her?"

"That you weren't here, and I hadn't seen you since last night, and that, as far as I knew, your dad was out of town."

Fuckety fuck fuck fuckshitfuck. "Did she tell you what she wanted to talk to us about?"

"Nope. Didn't leave her card, either."

She wanted to see me in person, not just have a phone chat. And what the hell did she want with my dad? "Did she ask who you were?"

"Uh huh. I told her I was Seojun Kang. Your house guest. Seojun is also the father of John Kang, but I didn't need to tell her that part."

"Jesus, what if she'd asked for ID?"

"She didn't. But I got it covered. Chill."

Chill? Ha! But then I reminded myself that Kang had been around for a couple thousand years and surely learned a thing or two about survival. "Okay. Sorry. Thanks for the heads up."

"Anytime. I owe you." He hung up.

The phone call reminded me that I hadn't told Allen about Nick. I sent a quick text.

<Nick is sick. Same mess. Neither of us will be in. Too much to do. Sorry>

His answer came back seconds later. <Do what you need to do. Keep me posted>

I shoved the phone into my pocket then returned to Nick's room. My zombie baby Philip stood on duty outside the open door.

"Hey, ZeeBee," I said. "What's up?"

"Shambler watch," he replied. "Just in case."

Bear's whole group had turned, which meant there was still a chance he would, too. "Yeah." I sighed. "Best to play it safe."

"I'm sorry you're going through this," Philip said quietly. "I know Nick is special to you."

"He is." I blinked back tears. "Thanks."

"Any time, ZeeEm."

I gave him an affectionate punch in the bicep then stepped into the room.

Bear sat by the bed in a comfy chair that someone must have brought in for him. Nick thrashed and growled in the restraints.

"Any change?" I asked, already knowing the answer. Nick hadn't miraculously recovered since I was last in here.

"Maybe. I don't know." He rubbed his eyes, expression bleak. "Sometimes I think he recognizes me. Probably wishful thinking."

I gave his hand a squeeze. "I'm about to leave for NuQuesCor. I can be more useful there, helping Dr. Nikas work on a cure for this shit, and I want to be close by in case they need more samples from me. I hope you aren't mad I'm going."

He covered my hand with his. "I know you're as gutted by this as anyone, and you won't stop till you dig up the answers. I don't think Nick will—"

"Annnnngelllll." Nick rolled his head toward me. "Annnnn-gelllll."

"He knows you!" Bear leaped to his feet. "Nick! We're right here."

I touched Nick's restrained arm. "It's going to be all right."

Nick shuddered and moaned, burbly and wet. "Annngelll . . ."

I brushed my fingers over his cheek, braced for him to snap at them. But instead, he went still, milky eyes on me. He breathed out a long sigh. "Annngelll."

"Look at you pining for me," I said, throat tight. "I'm going to tease you about this later, once you're back to yourself." I reluctantly withdrew.

Nick jerked against the restraints again and howled. The sound tore at my heart.

"I'll be back as soon as I can," I told Bear, struggling to keep my voice even.

"You can't go now." His eyes held desperate hope. "Look how calm he was with you."

"I don't want to go. But I have to." I nodded toward Nick. "For him. For a cure." The thought of leaving Nick like this punched holes through my gut, but I couldn't stay here when I could be trying to save him.

Bear sat heavily and scrubbed his hands over his face. "Sorry. You're right."

"It's okay. I get it. Make sure you eat, please?"

"Will do," he said, though I wasn't convinced. "Take care of yourself, Angel. You hear me?"

"Loud and clear."

After a final heart-wrenching look at Nick, I returned to the media room and found Portia, Jane, Victor, and my dad still there.

"Y'all need to go back to bed," I said with asperity.

"I have too much on my mind to sleep," Jane said. "Besides, I have work to do. My constituency is in an uproar."

"I don't think I could sleep either," Portia added. "And I'm used to early hours."

"Well, I ain't," my dad said, pushing to his feet. "It's past my bedtime."

"I'm about to head over to NuQuesCor with the fresh security team to help Dr. Nikas," I told him.

"You do that," he said. "But you be sure to wake me if you need anything."

"I will." I kissed his cheek before he toddled off to wherever he was sleeping.

"Angel," Portia said. "Do you think it would be possible for me to go with you? I have extensive lab experience, and though it's not my field of study, I'm sure I can be of use."

Hell, she'd be useful for making Dr. Nikas happy, if nothing else. "Let me check with Marcus, but I'm all for it." His office was only a corridor away, but I saw no need to expend that much energy.

<Can Portia come to NQC?> I texted. <I like her. Dr N likes her. You should say yes.>

<Yes. Fine.> he replied, and I could almost hear him roll his eyes.

"Marcus says yes," I told Portia. "If you need to take anything with you, grab it. We leave in about five minutes."

"Be right back," she said and strode quickly off.

I glanced at Jane. "Could you make sure Bear eats?" I asked. "He's pretty stressed, and I have a feeling he'll forget."

"You can count on me."

"That was never in doubt," I said, smiling. "How's it going with your district?"

She winced. "There's a lot of fear. Marcus has set up a camera and microphone in the conference room so I can make a statement, then I'm being interviewed by Brennan Masters for the news." Her forehead puckered.

"You don't look too happy about it."

"I'm not." She met my eyes. "I represent those people. Why am I holed up in here while they're vulnerable? Because I have connections? It doesn't sit right with me, but Marcus and the security chief are adamant."

The security chief was Pierce Gentry. Of course he'd be adamant about protecting Jane. "None of us want to see you hurt," I said. "Besides, you need to keep yourself safe so you're around for your people and . . ." I stopped. Made a face. "And nothing. You're right. I'd pitch a fit if I was forced to stay in lockdown when I wanted—needed—to be out *doing* something, especially for people I care about. Who are we to tell you where to be?"

"Thank you, Angel." She stood. "After I finish the interview,

I need to make some public appearances. I'm going to talk to Marcus right now. I have Victor for protection, and I'm sure he and Mr. Gentry and I can come to a satisfactory arrangement."

"Sure," I said with a snort. "After Gentry tells you all the reasons you can't leave."

Jane smiled sweetly. "I've spent enough time in Congress to be quite adept at dealing with bullshit."

"You go, girl!" I said with a grin. Pierce didn't stand a chance against her.

She and Victor headed out. Portia stepped aside to let them pass then entered, carrying an elegant dark leather briefcase. "Ready when you are."

"Let's ditch this place." I led her through the lab and garage then out the back of the building, where a helicopter crouched on a bare patch of ground. Kyle, Rachel, and Brian waited nearby.

Brian stepped toward us. "Dr. Antilles, may I help you in?"

"I would be most grateful," she replied, pure class and elegance. I took mental notes on how she carried herself.

Kyle and Brian both helped Portia get settled and buckled up, then Brian plugged in her headset and showed her which channels were for public or private conversation.

Brian gestured for me to climb in. "We'll be relieving Dan, Raul, and Pierce."

At the mention of Pierce's name, Rachel gave Brian a measuring look. Rachel wasn't one of the people "allowed" to know Pierce was Pietro, but now I wondered if she'd figured it out on her own. More power to her.

I took the seat facing Portia's, glad that I'd paid attention during the headset instructions. Brian took the front seat by the pilot—a no-nonsense middle-aged woman.

This was only my second time riding in a helicopter, and the first had been a vastly different experience. It had been a military-style chopper, manned by Tribe people who knew how to handle the brain-starved injured zombie they'd plucked from raging floodwaters. There'd been no plush seats, or passenger headsets to block out the loud rotor noise.

Not that I cared. The chopper had saved my dad's life and that was all that mattered.

Kyle sat beside me, and Rachel across from him. The pilot secured the doors then settled in the cockpit and started the rotors. I put my headset on as the noise level rose, then gawked out the window as the ground dropped away. Portia's face shone with delight as she took in the early morning sky and the view. Ahead of us, the sunrise was a slash of fire along the horizon.

I pulled the punch card out of my pocket and frowned down at it, hoping that the answer would miraculously come to me in a fit of brilliance. TPR1064638. TPR . . . Tupperware? Hell, maybe Reno wanted to upgrade his food storage containers.

Kyle tapped me on the wrist then held up three fingers. When I looked at him stupidly, he pointed to the headphones.

Oh. Right. I switched to channel three.

He nodded toward the card. "Why do you have an EMR number?"

"It's the only clue I salvaged from the Big Bubba mission. What's an EMR number?"

"Electronic medical records. TPR plus seven digits is Tucker Point Regional Hospital."

Excitement raced through me in a tingly wave. "So this is a person's medical file?"

"I suspect so," Kyle said. "Normally only an admin or a doctor assigned to the patient can access the records, in which case all that's needed is the patient's name and date of birth. They would rarely, if ever, use the patient number to pull up the records, though it's not out of the realm of possibility."

"What could one of Kristi's people—namely Reno Larson— do with the number?"

"If he located or created a back door to the EMR database, he'd be able to access the file with the patient number, possibly without leaving a trace."

I thrust the card at him. "Can you find out whose record that is?"

He waved the card away. "I have it memorized. I'll make a call after we land."

I did a little jiggy dance in my seat then joined Portia in watching the scenery go by. Whose medical record would Kristi want, and more importantly, why? She sure hadn't gone about getting it in a legitimate way. But Reno's high-speed flight from the cops had happened before Douglas Horton became the first shambler case, which meant it was probably something completely unrelated to our current crisis.

The pilot began a gradual descent a few miles from NuQues-Cor, low enough for me to see people below tip their faces up to watch us fly past. The cars seemed to crawl along the highways compared to us.

One of the cars made a turn onto the road that led to NuQues-Cor. No big deal except that it was a dark green Chevy Impala.

"Kyle, that might be the FBI agent—Sorsha Aberdeen . . ." He didn't respond, which meant he'd returned to the main channel. I waved at him and pointed to my headset. Portia didn't need to hear any of this.

Kyle switched back to three, and I repeated what I'd said. He nodded then tapped Brian on the shoulder and held up four fingers.

I was tempted to switch over and listen in, but decided Kyle would simply pass along my observation. There wasn't much we could do about Sorsha except be on our toes.

The helicopter dropped lower and circled the ugly white lump that was NuQuesCor. A limo was parked out front, with a black sedan behind it. Reno exited the sedan as Billy gave Kristi a hand out of the limo's backseat. She shaded her eyes and looked up, then gave us a cheerful wave.

I flipped her off. She wouldn't be able to see it, but it made me feel better.

The pilot touched down gently on the roof then let the rotors wind down. I hopped out once the doors were open and helped Portia out. "Have you flown in a helicopter before?" I asked her.

"No. Never. That was delightful!"

I returned her smile and tried not to think about bucket lists and whether "helicopter ride" was on hers.

Brian escorted us to the stairwell and downstairs to the LZ-1 research suite. Portia's eyes were bright with interest as she took everything in.

We had a few minutes before Kristi made her way up here, more if she stopped at the coffee stand downstairs for a chai latte. And maybe that car hadn't been Sorsha's. After all, surely there were plenty of dark green Impalas. On a somewhat remote back road. Headed toward NuQuesCor. *Plenty*. Really.

Raul and Dan greeted us as we entered the main lab. Though they looked alert, it was clear they were bored out of their minds. Not too much excitement on the night shift. Fritz leaned against a counter, coffee in hand, and murmured a polite "Good morning."

Reg sat in one of the work bays, poring over data. Beside him was a large whiteboard filled with Dr. Nikas's unique shorthand. He glanced up with a distracted "yo" then returned to his work. In the next bay, Beardzilla had his head down on the table, fast asleep, and Hairy Tech sat and stared, eyes bloodshot. Had Kristi given them any down time?

Nearby, Pierce and Dr. Nikas stood with their heads together in discussion. Whatever the topic, Dr. Nikas looked stressed.

Yet at the sight of Portia, he brightened like a kid who got a pony on Christmas. He left Pierce scowling at the interruption and strode toward us. "Dr. Antilles. Portia. I am so very delighted by your offer of assistance."

"I truly hope I can be of use, Ari," she said with a warm smile.

Dr. Nikas seemed to remember there were other people in the room. "Ah, Pierce Gentry, may I introduce Dr. Portia Antilles."

Pietro had known Portia via Jane, but *Pierce* was meeting her for the first time. "Dr. Antilles. It's a pleasure to have you here."

"The pleasure is mine," Portia replied, shaking his hand.

Pierce's expression flickered for the barest instant, then he gestured to a nearby chair. "Would you care for water or coffee?"

"Coffee with a little sugar would be lovely. Thank you."

Like Dr. Nikas, he could smell her cancer, I realized, and he was being extra-nice because of it. I'd never ever seen him offer to fetch coffee for anyone before.

"Coffee, one sugar, coming up." Pierce smiled and glanced at Brian who nodded and strode off. Okay, still the Pierce I knew and loved.

I couldn't imagine what it would be like to sense illness in other people, whether you wanted to or not. Horrifying, most likely. Sure, there'd be times when you could catch a disease early and get the person timely treatment. But there would also be situations like this, where the person was dying and there wasn't a damn thing you could do about it, apart from a horribly slim chance of successfully making them a zombie. And turning wouldn't be an option for most people since we had to be selective about who we zombified. Too many zombies, and bad shit would happen. It was like not letting more people into a lifeboat because it would sink. What a terrible burden that must be.

I stepped close to Pierce and murmured softly. "I think Agent Sorsha Aberdeen might be on her way here."

Pierce gave a micro-nod. "Brian notified me before you landed. The best thing we can do is not arouse any suspicion."

"Does that mean you're leaving?" I asked. "After all, she might have questions for a man who used to work in New York for Saberton then abandoned it all to live in the Deep South."

Pierce glowered. "Yes, I've already considered that. And yes, the most prudent course of action is for me to leave with Raul and Dan. Just be polite, and don't give her any info she doesn't need."

Holy shit. Pierce was actually removing himself from a potentially sticky situation. "I'm so proud of you," I said and pretended to wipe away a tear.

"Fuck off, Angel," he said amiably and headed off to where Raul and Dan waited by the door.

The scent of fresh brains wafted over me. Rachel with a container full of chunks. She locked eyes with Fritz, lifted a piece, and made a show of slowly slurping it down, tongue darting out to lick her lips clean of dripping brain juices.

Fritz made a "yuck" face but surprised me by offering her an ever-so-slight wry smile. Giving her props for successfully squicking him out.

Brian returned with Portia's coffee which she accepted gratefully.

As Raul, Dan, and Pierce left, the elevator down the hall dinged. A second later, I heard the *thap-thap* of Kristi's shoes. Wedges rather than heels today, perhaps.

"Good morning, Pierce!" Kristi caroled in a way too cheerful voice.

Pierce's reply wasn't loud enough for me to hear, but Kristi laughed. "Oh, you're always such a grump in the mornings!"

The door to the stairs banged shut behind Pierce and the other two men.

Kristi entered the lab, giving a little poke to the sleeping Beardzilla on her way past. No sign of Reno.

"Nice to see you here bright and early, Angel," she said sweetly. She swept a measuring look over Portia. "And who is this, Ari? A new lab assistant?"

Portia set aside her coffee and stood, elegant and classy as fuck. "I'm Dr. Antilles." Her tone was cultured and smooth with a hint of polite indulgence. "And you are?"

Kristi hesitated, clearly expecting somebody to jump in and introduce her. When no one did, Kristi stuck her hand out. "Dr. Kristi Charish. A pleasure to meet you."

Portia shook her hand then released it and turned away to study a sheaf of printouts on the counter.

Kristi's expression tightened, but she pivoted away and dropped her briefcase heavily on a table, then became very interested in data on the computer. If she was trying to make Portia feel bad by ignoring her, she was failing miserably. It was clear Portia didn't give a genteel fuck, and outclassed Kristi in the snubbing department.

I masked a grin then busied myself with loading prepped samples into the centrifuge and restocking supplies. After a few minutes, Kristi shut the computer off and grabbed her briefcase. "If anyone needs me, I'll be in the cell culture room," she announced then sailed out of the room with Fritz in her wake.

Portia glanced after Kristi and sighed. "I was terribly rude to her."

"You didn't see me stopping you," I said with a wink.

She chuckled. "Yes, everyone tensed when she entered. I suppose I assumed she's a . . . difficult person to work with."

"Difficult is a nice way to describe her," I said. "Also, bitchy, heartless, snide, arrogant—"

"Angel." Dr. Nikas gave me a Look. "Dr. Charish is, perhaps, all of those things, but she and I have already made a number of advances together."

Rachel lowered her hand from her ear. "Kyle says Agent Aberdeen has entered the building."

I glanced around, only now realizing that Kyle had slipped out. "I think I'm going to go check on the gators." Avoiding Sorsha at all costs was the best tactic for me. She'd asked around about my dad and me then knocked on my door before dawn, and it wasn't because she wanted to play patty cake. I sure as hell didn't need to get arrested or detained. Not with Nick—and everyone else—needing a cure.

Not to mention, I had no idea how much she knew about zombies, or whether she believed we were monsters who needed to be exterminated. But I had an ugly feeling she knew I was a zombie. If so, my presence might make her suspect that others here were zombies, too. Hopefully, if I stayed out of sight, it wouldn't even occur to her to wonder.

Except I also really needed to know why the hell she was here. She was one big horking unknown. Did she already know I was in the building? Did she suspect the Tribe of evildoing? Or

Kristi? We'd all done our share of illegal shit. Hell, I'd *killed* people.

No matter what her reason for being here, I needed to snoop *and* stay out of sight. Easy. Sure.

I sprinted to the gator room and closed the door behind me then sent a quick text to Kang.

<I'm at NQC. That FBI agent just showed up. I'm ducking her>

<That sucks. Good luck ducking. Keep me posted>

The larger of the two big gators lifted his head, cloudy eyes flicking open.

"Hello, sweeties," I murmured as I crouched by the fence. Biggie plodded close and pressed his snout against the chain-link. I stuck my fingers through the gap and stroked his nubby hide then glared, anger rising, at the sight of a four-inch square of scaly skin missing from the base of his tail. Below it was a ragged strip, as if the square had been cut then ripped free, taking more hide with it. The wound seeped blood, though the edges showed signs of healing—not as much as in a regular zombie but more like keeping the status quo.

Scowling, I rubbed Biggie's snout. "Who did that to you, big guy?"

He snorted and growled low.

The other big gator bellowed and turned its head my way.

I beckoned it over. "If your buddy is Biggie, then you must be Tupac, right?"

Tupac snorted then splashed out of the pool and toward me, followed by the smaller gators. The entire group lined up side by side along the fence, snouts pressed against the chain link. All but the smallest two bore wounds like Biggie's. Grrrr. "Are y'all okay?"

They opened their mouths in unison and joined their gatory voices in a growly warble, eerie yet strangely familiar. I peered into their gaping jaws. Not a single one had a missing or broken tooth in the front. The snaggle-tooth gator that bit Douglas Horton was still out there somewhere.

I moved down the line, petting each for a moment, only to have them fall silent at my touch, one by one.

"All right," I said and withdrew my hand from the littlest one at the end. "Y'all need to back away from the fence now. We don't want Kristi to see this and wonder what's going on." I waggled my hand, and the gators turned and lumbered away. I should have been shocked, but I wasn't. Of course they listened to me. In a convoluted way that made irrational sense. After all, I was their mama. Grandma? Revered Ancestor?

Without thinking, I tipped my head back and growl-sang a long warbly note. The gators answered with a soft moan-song of their own.

As their weird crooning died away, another sound intruded from down the hall. Coming this way. *Thap-thap*. Kristi. And another set of steps. No-nonsense.

Sorsha Aberdeen? Shit. If I left the way I came in, I'd run right into them. There was no place to hide unless I wanted to brave the razor wire defense around the pen and trust that my babies would hide me.

Which left a hard sprint to the door on the far wall.

I reached it even as my zombie hearing told me the two women had paused to talk right outside the door. The only word I caught was alligators, but the second voice definitely belonged to Sorsha. Craaaap. I shoved my fob against the lock and prayed it would work on this door.

The lock clicked. I yanked the door open and darted into what seemed to be a small library with a computer work station—thankfully unoccupied—then pulled the door closed behind me, just as the Kristi-Sorsha door swung open. Pulse racing, I listened to make sure there was no alarmed cry of, "Aha! Someone fled through that door over there!" or the equivalent.

Nope. Just murmured conversation. Crap. Now I wanted to know what they were saying. I pressed my ear to the crack between door and jamb and willed my darling little parasite to give my hearing a boost.

"I don't understand," Sorsha said. "How are these alligators connected to the outbreak?"

"It's quite straightforward, really," Kristi said, managing to sound only a little pompous. "The first case to present was Beckett Connor, who suffered a minor alligator bite the day before he died. When I heard that, I sent my people into the swamp to bring back any infected alligators they could find. These specimens weren't hard to spot. Look at the color, the eyes. Obviously they were infected with LZ-1 or a related strain."

"Obviously," Sorsha replied, tone impossible to read. "Have you determined anything from studying them?"

"Ah, well, I've only had the specimens since yesterday, and there are many other avenues to explore."

"I see. This is all very interesting." Sorsha paused a long moment. "The whole affair reminds me of . . . zombies."

"Yes, isn't it fascinating?" Kristi trilled a laugh. "The parallel to movie zombies has certainly crossed my mind."

"I'm well aware of the 'Louisiana Zombies dash One' designation for LZ-1, Dr. Charish. Amusing." She didn't sound one bit amused. "I'm more interested in whether you've seen anything zombie-like before. Anything at all."

Shit. What was Sorsha's angle?

"Before this?" Kristi laughed again, but it verged on nervous. Not her typical smooth-operator style. "Movies, once or twice. Not my cup of tea, really."

"Mm-hmm." Pages flipped. "What can you tell me of the other researchers here? Ariston Nikas? Has he been helpful in your research?"

Helpful? I ground my teeth. It made him sound like he was Kristi's assistant.

Not that Kristi did a damn thing to dispel that notion. "Ari has been an absolute godsend," she gushed, and I could practically see her putting her hands on her chest and batting her eyelashes. "His assistance has allowed me—"

"Um, lady?"

I whirled and landed in a fighting stance. A slender black man around my age stood in a doorway on the other side of the room. He wore a lab coat over jeans and a Star Wars t-shirt, and carried a coffee cup. And he was shorter than me, which took a lot considering I was barely five foot three.

"You're not allowed to be in here," he said, though he didn't seem too bent out of shape about it. He took a sip of his coffee. "This is a secured area. If someone else sees you, they'll ask me why I didn't call security. So you should go." He waggled his hand at me exactly as I had done to the gators. "Or I'll have to call."

"I can't leave the same way I came in," I said, straightening from the silly fighting stance.

He cocked his head. "Were you sneaking around in the LZ-1 suite, too?"

"No! I work over there, but I, er, didn't want to run into my supervisor."

"Supervisors." He gave a nod of commiseration. "That's why I like the night shift." He lifted his chin toward the door to the gator room. "What's in there? Rumor has it alligators were brought in, but the sounds aren't like any gators I've ever heard. Creeps me out all night."

"Details are, um, classified." I offered him a helpless shrug. "Sorry. Nothing to worry about, though. I promise."

"Says the tricksy eavesdropper," Short Guy said, his voice colored with humor. He hooked his thumb over his shoulder. "Skedaddle, Ninja Girl. Out this way. The exit to the LZ-1 suite is down the hall to the left."

I breathed a thanks as I passed. The corridor was deserted, but quiet voices drifted from somewhere. Following his directions, I escaped to our lab area then paused in the corridor, listening carefully for Sorsha or Kristi.

No sign of either one. If I was lucky, the two were off making someone else's life miserable instead of mine.

I scurried back to the main lab room. Beardzilla and Hairy Tech worked, heads down, at the back table. Brian was doing his hourly sweep for listening devices as part of his normal security protocol. Dr. Nikas jerked his hand away from Kristi's computer, looking guilty as hell.

"Oh. It's only you, Angel," he said quietly.

I moved in close and kept my voice low. "What are you doing?"

He slipped a thumb drive into his pocket. "Keeping tabs on Kristi's work and progress. Everything in the lab is kept on the local computers—no cloud or outside server—to protect the zombie information. Her data is encrypted, but we can unravel it."

"Smart. You don't trust her."

"Never again." He looked a little sad at that, but then he straightened. "And I wanted her most recent activity safely acquired before I confront her over the gym death and her lack of communication."

"Good plan," I said. "Do you have results from the protein packet samples yet?"

"Jacques should have them later this morning, then I will meet with Kristi."

"If you need someone to watch your back, or even just to supply loads of moral support, I'm here for you."

He gave me a warm smile. "That hardly needs to be said."

I flushed, warmed by his unwavering trust in me. "By the way, I overheard the FBI agent ask Kristi if she'd ever seen anything zombie-like before. Seemed like an odd question to ask a scientist. Made me a little uneasy."

His brows drew together. "Troubling, indeed. We'll see what comes of this visit."

With any luck at all, Sorsha would leave after talking to Kristi. "On a related note, when I went to check on the gators, I noticed most of them have wounds." I described the odd injuries. "What's that all about?"

He frowned, perplexed. "We took small snips yesterday. Nothing at all like what you saw. I don't know what need she would have for more and larger tissue samples. She did not confer with me before taking them."

I glowered. "That's because Kristi thinks she thinks she's hot shit and in charge."

Dr. Nikas sighed. "I'll have a word with her about that as well."

"You need to start making a list," I said. "Like Santa, except it's allllllll of Kristi's naughtiness."

He cleared his throat, quickly squelching the ever-so-brief flash of amusement in his eyes. "Jacques called a few minutes ago with a report on Nick's condition. He's stable," Dr Nikas added quickly before I could freak out and imagine the worst. "There's been no change, which in our current scenario is good. However, I believe we can dispose of the theory that you infected Nick via saliva."

"You mean kissing? How do you know that wasn't it?"

"Jacques found a mosquito bite on Nick's left arm."

I shook my head. "That doesn't make sense. Nick was friggin' smothered in DEET."

Dr. Nikas spread his hands. "Unfortunately, even the best repellent cannot offer perfect protection."

"But he had on a long-sleeved shirt," I said.

Sympathy filled his eyes. "He could have been bitten anytime in the last forty-eight hours."

"Something's not right. The cases in the morgue each had one mosquito bite. The majority of the shamblers in the gym only had one mosquito bite. Nick has one bite. What are the odds of that many people getting only one bite if there are mosquitoes around?"

Dr. Nikas exchanged a glance with Portia, but it was Rachel who spoke.

"What are you saying, Angel?"

I looked around the room as I tried to make sense of my thoughts. "I'm saying . . . maybe the mosquito bites aren't mosquito bites."

Chapter 33

Well, that got everyone's attention. I gulped as the enormity of what I was suggesting hit home. But if there was any chance it was true, I had to keep going.

"What if someone is deliberately spreading the zombie epidemic using tiny little darts or something?"

"The CDC found traces of *Aedes albopictus* saliva at the bite locations of the deceased," Dr. Nikas said gently.

"Seriously? How do they know it's albopeck, er, mosquito spit?"

"The presence of certain enzymes."

"Oh." So much for that theory. "Maybe—" I paused to seize another thought before it flitted away. "Wait. I know it's a stretch, but if I wanted to intentionally spread the zombie disease and make it look like mosquitoes were doing it, I'd make sure that my little infectious darts or needles or whatever came with a side of skeeter spit."

Dr. Nikas's brows drew together. "That is a fair point. I'll ask Jacques to excise the bite area on Nick and test for Eugene and LZ-1."

I blinked. "They're different?"

"To the CDC, all cases are LZ-1 since they don't know the cause and haven't yet discovered the parasite. We, too, assumed Eugene was the universal pathogen until yesterday when I analyzed blood samples from the gym and the blood you recovered from the bowling alley."

"Okaaaaay," I said. "In other words, LZ-1 is new but kind of the same?"

"Correct. Eugene is the parasite mutation found in the cases we can trace directly back to you. Judd Siler from your bite. Douglas Horton and Deputy Connor from the alligators that consumed Judd's remains. All other cases show a variation of Eugene." A faint smile tugged at his mouth. "I would name it Eugene junior, but I fear that would sow confusion with outside authorities. Therefore, I have adopted their blanket designation of LZ-1 to use in reference to the new strain."

Damn. Eugene junior had more zing. EJ-1? "But doesn't a different mutation make it even more likely that someone purposefully caused the LZ-1 epidemic?"

"It raises many questions." He patted my shoulder. "We will see what Nick's mosquito bite shows."

"Thanks," I breathed, warmed to my toes that he was taking my concerns seriously—or at least seriously enough to run more tests to prove me wrong.

Dr. Nikas typed in a text message to Jacques.

"You know," Portia said, head tilted, "just as a thought experiment, Angel's deliberate inoculation theory could potentially explain how groups of people turned shambler within minutes of each other."

Dr. Nikas took a step toward her. "You think all could have been inoculated with LZ-1 at the same time?"

"Not necessarily. You tested the water bottles for traces of LZ-1 and Eugene." She said the name with no hesitation or scorn which made me love her all the more. "But what if the water contained a stimulant—a hormone perhaps—that could radically accelerate LZ-1 activation in someone already infected."

The look on Dr. Nikas's face was pure adoration. "Inoculate a group of individuals minutes to hours before, then trigger them all at once via an activator."

"That makes sense, even to me," I said. "Like soaking a sponge with gasoline. Nothing happens until you drop a lit match on it, then bam. Stick 'em with LZ-1 whenever, then the victims drink the activator water and they go shambly within minutes."

"Or leave them be and they eventually turn anyway." Dr. Nikas got that faraway look in his eyes that told me he was already leaps and bounds ahead and working through possibilities. "It's quite likely the stimulating substance would be harmless to people who had not been inoculated, meaning entire cases of water bottles could be treated."

"Yes!" Portia said. "That would eliminate the need to ensure only inoculated people drank the water."

"And the victims who turned in groups yesterday were all together and drinking bottled water," I said. "The bowling alley, the band. I'm betting the lawyers had bottled water in their meeting, too."

"I have already confirmed the lawyers had Nice Springs water," Dr. Nikas said as he sent another text. "The bottles you collected from the bowling alley are at the Tribe lab. I've asked Jacques to run full analyses on them as well."

"Wait one sec." I pulled out my phone and called Bear. "Hey, it's Angel. When you were at the bowling alley, did you drink any bottled water?"

"They were giving away free bottled water, but I had a Coke Zero. Never opened my bottle. Why?"

"Not sure yet. If Jacques comes in to check you for a mosquito bite, don't give him a hard time, okay?"

"I checked myself, but hard to see everywhere. I'll behave."

"Good deal. How's Nick?"

"No change," he said, voice a bit rougher.

"We're going to get the cure, Bear. I promise." I held back a sigh of frustration. "I gotta go now. I'll let you know when we have something." I hung up and shoved the phone into my pocket.

"Let me guess," Portia said. "He didn't drink the water."

"Nope," I said. "And he hasn't shambled. Yet."

Dr. Nikas sent another text then looked up, expression sober. "Very disturbing. If this hypothesis proves to be valid, it means that an organization or individual might truly be coordinating a deliberate spread of this terrible disease."

"But?" I said. Dr. Nikas didn't have his we-have-the-answer face on.

He remained silent for a long moment. "Frankly, I'm baffled. Though your hypothesis has merit, I believe it would be impossible to develop a specifically altered strain of Eugene in the few days since Douglas Horton and Deputy Connor succumbed."

"But it *did* alter," I said.

"Given the three-plus weeks since Judd's demise, natural mutation could account for it. The only other option—purposefully directing the mutation to a desired, stable outcome—is a time-consuming challenge with no guarantee of success." He shook his head. "Additionally, whoever created it would be foolish to release LZ-1 into the wild without also having a cure at hand, lest they fall victim themselves. And developing a cure would take even more time."

"So it's not possible?"

"I simply don't see how in such a short timeframe," he said. "Yet, I don't have the answer, either, which is why I asked Jacques to run those tests. Science is about gathering data and being willing to accept the results."

I forced a crooked smile. "Is it wrong for me to hope a bad guy *is* responsible for the epidemic since that would mean a cure already exists?"

"It's not wrong, Angel," he said, eyes warm with understanding. "And I can't deny that the hypothesis fits except for the timing."

"But why would anyone start an epidemic on purpose?" I asked then immediately shook my head. "Duh. If they'd already developed the cure, an epidemic would mean treatments. Pharmaceuticals. Money."

"Greed and the lust for power have been the driving forces behind any number of heinous acts," Portia murmured.

"Indeed," Dr. Nikas said. For an instant it looked like he wanted to take her hand, then he pulled his gaze away. "We'll know more once Nick's bite and the water are analyzed."

Fighting an evil organization or person to get the cure was something tangible I could do. To help all the victims. To help Nick. I couldn't fight nature or science. My chest tightened, and stupid tears welled up.

Dr. Nikas took my hand. "I believe we're close to a cure here, Angel."

Not close enough, I wanted to scream. Instead I nodded, not trusting myself to say anything without bursting into full blown tears. He was doing everything he could. We all were.

I gently tugged my hand free then stepped away to make a call.

"Hey, Dad," I said, voice thick.

"You okay, baby?"

"No. I mean, yeah, I'm okay. I just wish we were on the other side of this shit, with Nick and everyone else fixed up and healthy again."

"I get it, Angelkins." The nickname wrapped around me like a warm hug. "You're out working your tail off while your boyfriend's in trouble. It's rough. But if anyone can come through this after wrasslin' that sickness into the dust, it's you."

My *boyfriend*. Nick and I hadn't even had time to talk about what we were to each other. But it felt right. "I'm doing my best, Dad. I really am."

"I know you are, baby. I seen you in action. Wish I could be more help with all this, but I ain't as smart as these other folks."

I scowled. "First off, you are smart. You don't have the same experience and education, that's all. Huge difference. Second off, you are helping. You're staying safe so I don't have to worry, and I bet you're keeping people's spirits up, too."

"You know what I mean." He sighed. "I wish I could *do* something. I wanna stay busy so I don't fret so much about you."

"Yeah. I get it. Well, I started out washing dishes and beakers and stuff. Everyone there kind of pitches in when it comes to keeping the place clean, so how about you sweep up or whatever."

"I can do that! It'll be just like at the bar but with less dead bugs."

"A lot less! Hey, could you ask Rosario something for me?"

"Hang on. Let me get a pen and paper."

"Nah, this one's easy. Ask him if he told Kristi about seeing Judd walk off into the swamp after being killed with the tranq."

"Okay. I think I got it."

"Thanks. You can text me what he says."

We exchanged "love you"s and hung up. I returned to sorting project results, feeling much lighter.

My phone buzzed with a text about five minutes later.

<Yes he told her but not sure she believed him>

"Hey, Dr. Nikas?" I said. "What if someone had *weeks* instead of days to create LZ-1 and a cure?"

He gave me a puzzled look. "How so?"

I related what Rosario had said about seeing Judd walk off, and that he'd told Kristi. "What if she put two and two together and figured out Judd was some kind of zombie variant. Then used that info to start working on the LZ-1 mutation? Hell, she could have sent people into the swamp to find Judd's remains."

Portia looked thoughtful. Dr. Nikas ran a hand over his hair in a rare show of consternation. "Three weeks could be sufficient for a researcher of her caliber."

"There's a problem with that," Brian said. "We've been watching Dr. Charish closely in Chicago, and she hasn't set foot in a lab in the last three weeks."

Rachel cocked her head. "But she could have relayed the Judd info to Saberton R&D for them to do the work."

"That's true," Brian said. "We know there's a leak or a bug in our organization that we haven't pinned down yet." A look of aggravation swept over his face. "So let's assume that Monday, Saberton found out about Horton waking up and shambling in the morgue. Not only could that have triggered their gator hunt—and, thanks to the leak, they knew precisely where to go—but it also presented the perfect opportunity to debut their new LZ-1 toy, especially after Connor collapsed the next day. A case untraceable to Saberton that served to muddy the waters."

Rachel's brows knitted. "Why would Dr. Charish work with us against her own people?"

"I don't think she considers anyone 'her own people,'" Brian said with a snort.

"Yeah," I said. "Kristi looks out for Kristi. Right now, she's eating up being in the limelight as the star researcher working toward a cure. Maybe she even wants to beat Saberton at their own game and release a cure before they do, to undercut them. Be celebrated as a hero like Jonas Salk. You can bet your rosy red—"

Reno shoved the door open and entered. Kristi followed, eyes on a printout, and went straight to her usual stool.

"Ari, have you seen the analysis of the blood samples from the patient who died at the gym?" she asked, eyes on the reports. "The glutamate numbers are through the roof."

"Yes," he said. "And I have no explanation for it. I'll check the latest cultures."

Portia looked up. "I'll stay here and finish the extrapolations."

"That would be quite helpful," he said, as warmly as if he'd told her the heavens were in her eyes. He turned and exited the lab, pausing only to gently touch Reg's shoulder and ask if the tech would accompany him.

Reg responded with a nod and smile then left with Dr. Nikas.

Kristi's mouth pursed in a frown as she put the printouts aside and logged on to the computer.

I sidled up to her, ignoring the dirty look Reno gave me. "Hey, Kristi," I murmured. "Why'd you cut on the gators?"

She didn't bother to look up. "Samples."

"Taking out chunks of hide is pretty fucking harsh."

"They're already healing. Zombie-gators, remember?"

"That's not the point!"

"Sacrifices must be made to find a cure," she said as if lecturing a child. "If you aren't prepared for that, I suggest you excuse yourself from this research facility. Especially before I have the brains removed from the little ones later."

Whether she was serious or just fucking with me, her comment succeeded in stoking my zombie-mama protective instinct to volcano-hot. I leaned close and snarled, "Better damn well clear it with Dr. Nikas before you mess with those gators again." I knew he would never hurt them unless there was no other way to the cure.

She swiveled the stool to face me, fire in her eyes. "Those alligators are *mine*."

No, bitch, they're mine. I met her gaze with my own inferno. "If you hurt them, I'll make sure you get to spend time with them up close and personal."

"Oh, goodness. Am I supposed to be scared?"

"Only if you're smart." I straightened. "What did that FBI agent want?"

Kristi smiled smugly and turned back to the computer. "Agent Aberdeen was interested in my process and progress."

"*Your* progress?" I sneered. "You're not flying solo here."

"Don't get your panties in a twist, Angel. It's merely a turn of phrase. I was the one she was interviewing."

"Then why'd you let her think Dr. Nikas was your *assistant*?"

She slanted a look at me. "Eavesdroppers often mishear things."

"You said he was a godsend because of his assistance. What did you say to counter that?"

"If you don't know, then obviously you weren't included in the conversation."

I clamped down on a heated retort as Dr. Nikas returned without Reg, but with another sheaf of papers. He dropped them on the desk beside Kristi, and I stepped away. Just as well. I needed out of that conversation before I ended up slugging her pert little chin.

While Dr. Nikas and Kristi conferred, I busied myself with necessary scutwork—fetching printouts, sterilizing supplies, and even making coffee. At one point Rachel passed me a handful of brain chips, telling me that I needed to keep my strength up. After I gladly accepted them, she casually offered Fritz a chip.

"No thank you," he said, expression stern and serious. He flicked a quick glance toward Kristi then added quietly, "I wouldn't want to have a . . . *brain fart*."

Rachel pressed her lips together to hold back laughter and gave him a slow "you win" nod. He replied with a "damn straight" dip of his chin and went back to being a mean, tough bodyguard.

Around twenty minutes later, Kristi slid off the stool and gathered up her papers. "I'll be in the microscope room trying to get to the bottom of this," she announced and snapped her fingers. "Techs. With me."

As she stalked off, Hairy Tech and Beardzilla leaped up as if their chairs had turned into cactuses and hurried after her with Fritz following.

The sound of Kristi's wedges faded down the hall, but before I could celebrate her departure, I heard her say, "Agent Aberdeen, back so soon?"

"I never left," came the gravelly reply. "There are still a few people I'd like to talk to."

"She means me!" I gasped and looked around wildly for an escape. Hide under a table? Yeah, that would totally fool her—if she'd gone completely *blind* in the last half hour.

The only other door was the walk-in fridge. "Don't tell her I'm here!" I dashed into the fridge, pulled it closed to a thin crack, and peeked out.

Sorsha opened the lab door with Kristi on her heels.

Kristi looked flustered. "I'm happy to make time to answer—"

Sorsha stopped abruptly and pivoted to face her. "No need. I'll find you after I've spoken to Dr. Nikas." With no further warning, she shut the door in Kristi's face. I closed myself in the fridge before she could see me, even as I silently celebrated the glorious snub.

Too late, I realized I should have grabbed a lab coat on the way in. The fridge was kept at thirty-four degrees, like the cooler at the morgue. Fine and dandy for a few minutes, but who knew how long Sorsha would stick around.

I could barely make out her voice, but no matter how much I strained my ears and begged my parasite for help, the words remained unintelligible. The cold of the fridge raised goose-bumps on my arms, and I bounced in place and hugged myself in a pathetic effort to stay warm. I was a delicate southern flower, and anything below fifty degrees required a parka.

I jerked as my phone buzzed. My dad. I'd call him back as soon as Sorsha left. I sent it to voicemail, but a few seconds later it buzzed again. Crap. Maybe something bad had happened?

No, this time it was Portia's number. Puzzled, I hit answer, then remained silent as the sound of voices came through clearly.

"—appreciate your cooperation," Sorsha was saying.

"It's no trouble at all." Dr. Nikas. "As you can see in this chart, there are a number of phases associated with the progression of LZ-1."

Portia had called and left the line open so I could hear what was going on! What a marvelous, clever woman. I did a happy-boogie that warmed me up for about three seconds, then I went back to bouncing, hugging, and listening. Sorsha was being very nice, and everyone else was being super cooperative, using the "be accommodating and maybe she'll go away faster" tactic.

A phone rang in the lab. "Would you excuse me one moment, Agent Aberdeen?" Dr. Nikas said.

She murmured assent.

"I see," he said after a few seconds, I assumed to the caller. His voice was grave, so I doubted it was good news. "I will review the details shortly. Thank you."

"Is everything all right?" Sorsha asked politely.

"Ah. Yes. Everything is fine," he replied in a tone that oozed not-fine. "A young intern of mine had a hypothesis concerning an entirely unrelated subject. And I've just learned that there is evidence to support it."

Oh, man. Dr. Nikas was a terrible liar. Could he be talking about me and my mosquito bite hunch? If so, did that mean he'd confirmed LZ-1 was being deliberately spread?

"Speaking of young interns," Sorsha said, "I was under the

impression that a Miss Angel Crawford had been working with you here. Is she around?"

Fuuuck!

"Oh dear, she just left," Portia said, a billion times more convincing than Dr. Nikas. Then again, it wasn't a total lie. I had indeed left the room.

"Ah. That's too bad. I'll have to catch her later."

Gah! Did she mean literally?!

"Dr. Nikas," Sorsha said. "I'd like you to give me an idea of what you're doing to counter the LZ-1 epidemic."

"Certainly." He launched into an exuberant explanation of the progress of the disease and the search for a way to treat it, masterfully steering clear of anything zombie-related.

When Dr. Nikas referred to the chart and started an explanation of the LZ-1 signs and symptoms—which I figured would take at least a minute—I put Portia's call on hold and listened to my dad's voicemail.

"Hey, Angelkins. I guess you're busy. That's okay cuz I can tell you here just as well. I'm level nineteen now with Barney the Barbarian! And Andrew found me in the game—cuz last time I told him I was this guy and not your Momzombique gal. Anyway he said that this Harlon Murtaugh character has worked for Kristi here and there on Saberton's dime and was doing stuff for her just a coupla weeks ago, but he don't know if he's working for her right now. It ain't much, but I figured it can't hurt to pass it along. Shoot me a text so I know you got this. Love you."

Hot damn. Confirming any sort of connection between Kristi and Baldy was more than I had before. I texted back. <u did good dad. Thanks.>

I returned to Portia's call as Dr. Nikas was winding up his explanation of the *hunnnnnngry* phase. I expected Sorsha to ask him about zombies like she had with Kristi. But though she bombarded him with questions about LZ-1 and his research, she never once brought up the subject of zombies. Was that good or bad?

"And how do you like working with Dr. Charish?" Sorsha asked.

"Her assistance has been most helpful in this endeavor," Dr. Nikas replied without hesitation.

I let myself chortle since no one could hear me. Her assistance! Ha!

"No," Sorsha said. "How do you *like* working with her? Personally."

"Oh. Ah . . ."

I sent Dr. Nikas a thought-wave of think-on-your-feet-good-liar juju while Sorsha remained silent.

Dr. Nikas cleared his throat. "We have very, um, different . . . personalities. But she is brilliant and our work together can be—"

"Different how?"

Poor Dr. Nikas. He was used to the calm sanctuary of his lab.

He sighed as if resigned to his fate. "Dr. Charish can be self-absorbed, calculating, arrogant, snide, heartless, and willfully cruel. I can only hope I am none of those."

I grinned and did a fist pump. He'd used all my adjectives except bitchy and added a few of his own. Go, Dr. N!

"And yet you're still willing to work with her?" Sorsha asked, voice reflecting nothing more than mild curiosity.

"Dr. Charish is also clever, innovative, highly educated, and experienced," he replied. "I can think of no other who is equal to the task we currently face."

"I see," Sorsha said. "Would you give me a layman's explanation of the work you and Dr. Charish have done, specifically with the alligators?"

"There has been very little work as of yet," he said. "But if you will step over to this terminal, I will show you what I can."

Kristi had certainly been doing some work. Nasty work. Andrew's info on Harlon Murtaugh's connection to her brought me right back to my suspicion that she was involved in this entire mess. Sure, I had no real proof yet, and sure, Brian had a solid point about Kristi not being able to sneeze without the tribe knowing. But Murtaugh's presence at the swamp and hospital meant the LZ-1 disaster had to be the work of either Kristi or Saberton—or both. Plus, Saberton and Kristi were the only ones in the world besides Dr. Nikas who had the kind of zombie research experience needed to pull off an epidemic like this. But there was no way Kristi would stand back and let Saberton get the glory for a cure without her. Which meant it *had* to be Kristi at the helm.

Except Brian said he'd seen her get off that jet when it landed at Tucker Point Airport night before last—well after the Saberton gator hunt and after shamblers started shambling.

That didn't rule out her involvement, but it was a factor that had to be considered.

The back of my neck prickled, and it wasn't goosebumps. Randy had been repairing a private jet the other day. How many jets could a tiny airport like Tucker Point get in such a short time? Kristi supposedly arrived Wednesday midnight. Randy's repair had come in on Monday.

I put the call with Portia on low-volume speaker so I could keep monitoring it, then texted Randy.

<Hey. That jet u were repairing. Where was it from?>

<how the fuck should i know>

He had a point. I tried another tack.

<What time did it come in Monday?>

<4 or so>

<Did u see who got off?>

<bald guy and some brown hair lady>

Hmm. The bald guy could be Harlon Murtaugh. Then again, there were a lot of bald guys around. And Kristi was unmistakably blonde.

<ok. What about a jet that came in Wednesday midnight?>

<wtf is this about>

Dammit. <pls trust me. I need to know>

<u lucky. i was finishing up work on the monday jet when other jet came in. blond lady and a big dude missing an ear got off>

Kristi and Fritz, just like Brian said. I sighed. Maybe Kristi really wasn't—

<then brown hair lady left on the monday jet but wasn't same>

Huh? <Wasn't same what?>

<looked almost same but different>

Huh? <WTF r u talking about?>

< brown hair lady on monday was a rude bitch. i thought the wednesday brown hair lady was same lady but she was real nice>

I took a few seconds to parse his meaning.

<r u saying u thought the brown haired women were the same person except she was an a-hole the first time?>

<yeah and just a little different. dunno>

I thought furiously for a moment. <Was blonde nice or bitch?>

<super nice>

Holy shit.

<Thanks millions!> I realized now that the phone line had gone dead. Sorsha must have left, and so Portia had hung up. Perfect timing. I burst out of the walk-in. "She has a double!"

Brian sighed and pinched his nose. Portia gave me a pained look and whispered, "Battery died. Sorry."

Someone cleared their throat behind me.

I winced then composed myself and turned to Sorsha. "Agent Aberdeen! So nice to see you. Sorry I missed your arrival. I use the fridge as my quiet spot to meditate, y'know?"

She looked unconvinced. Probably my shivering and blue lips gave me away. Or maybe it was the ridiculous lie. Either way, she appeared unsurprised to see me.

I stood as tall as my not-quite-five-foot-three would allow. "I know you're after me and my dad, but I don't have time for this. Someone really special to me is sick and I need to—"

"I'm not after you," she said. "At least not to arrest or detain, at this point."

"Huh? Then why'd you show up at my house?"

"Because of this." She held up a thumb drive. "The medical records of one Angel Beatrice Crawford."

"What the fuck?"

She glanced at the door to make sure it was closed. "Reno Larson tossed this from his vehicle Monday morning."

"When Abadie was pursuing him!"

Sorsha nodded once. "Detective Abadie noted the general location, and last night I recovered the drive."

"The EMR number," I breathed and fumbled the card out of my pocket. "Reno had this."

Sorsha took the card and scrutinized front and back. "May I hold onto it? I'll give you an evidence receipt."

"Er, that's cool. You keep it." Best not to lay official claim to the item I'd stolen from an impounded car I'd trashed.

"I have questions," Rachel said.

"As do we all," Dr. Nikas murmured.

Rachel turned to me. "Beatrice? Your initials are A-B-C?"

"Yes, and you have no idea how many times my dad sang the damned alphabet song to me when I was little." I glanced toward the door to be extra-super-sure it was closed and noted that Kyle had slipped in at some point. "Reno works for Kristi," I said to Sorsha. "Do you think he was getting my file for her?"

She regarded me. "Why would Dr. Charish want your medical records?"

Rachel raised an eyebrow. "Why would *anyone* want your medical records, Angel? No offense."

"I have no freaking idea!" I gave a strained laugh. "Unless Kristi's super interested in the times my mom brought me to the ER because I was so *clumsy*." I maintained a smile even as my gut tightened at the old memories.

"And the time you overdosed," Rachel said with a slight shrug.

Dr. Nikas twitched at that, and I mentally crossed fingers Sorsha hadn't noticed. But surely she wouldn't be able to make any connection between my overdose and my becoming a zombie. But what could be so important about the overdose incident for Kristi to go to such lengths to see my records?

I dug my hands through my hair. "Well, whatever the reason, Kristi didn't get them. So it's all good."

Kyle spoke up. "The hospital computer system crashed the day of Deputy Connor's death."

I tensed. No, not all good. Kristi had been after my medical records, and Reno had failed her. She wouldn't have given up. "Harlon Murtaugh was there. He's—"

"I know who he is," Sorsha interrupted. "Excuse me. I need to make a call." She moved to the other side of the room and pulled out her phone. "Agent Garner," she said quietly. "There was a system crash at the hospital on Tuesday, during Connor's stay. Crawford said Murtaugh was there."

"Likely not a coincidence," Garner replied, his tone calm and easy-going despite the circumstances. No stupid door to block my zombie hearing this time—or that of the other zombies in the room.

"My thought as well. Another attempt at Crawford's records."

"Agreed. I'll get the cyber people on it to confirm," he said. "Charish made another call to Saberton ops five minutes ago. Gallagher's on standby if you need backup, and I just dispatched a team from Baton Rouge. But Charish is feeling the pressure, so act at your own discretion. Keep it contained and a lid on the weirdness. The ball's in your court."

Dr. Nikas exchanged a worried look with Brian, while I tried to appear cool and collected. How much *weirdness* did she know about?

The barest hint of a smile touched one corner of Sorsha's mouth. "Thank you, sir."

Brian stepped out of the room, phone to ear. Calling Pierce, I was certain.

"How did you know Reno was going to steal my medical records?" I asked Sorsha after she hung up.

Sorsha folded her arms. "I didn't. He was a person of interest, and I had eyes on him. When he gained access to the hospital admin building, I attempted to detain him, but he fled, leading to the pursuit."

"What does—"

Sorsha cut me off with a brusque gesture and leveled her gaze at Dr. Nikas. "What connection does Dr. Charish have with the decapitation murders two years ago? The serial killings."

Shiiiiiit! Kristi had coerced Ed Quinn into killing zombies and delivering their heads to her. If Sorsha was sniffing close to her about that particular fucked-up shitstorm, what else did she know? I was starting to regret that Pierce wasn't here with his experience in talking his way out of sticky situations. This was flypaper, honey, and road tar all mixed up into one giant mess.

Dr. Nikas cleared his throat. "Connection? With the killings? I, er, wasn't a suspect identified?"

"Yes, but that's not what I asked." Sorsha watched him, expression placid and intimidating at the same time. "How is Kristi Charish connected to the murders?"

This time I sent him some of my lie-through-your-teeth juju. I certainly had plenty to spare.

"I prefer not to answer that question."

No one moved. Or breathed. The only sound was the hum of a printer and the *tick-tick* of the wall clock.

"Fair enough," Sorsha finally said. "For now."

I released my breath and tried to steady my voice. "Does Reno's theft of my medical records somehow tie in to why you're asking about Kristi and the serial killings?"

She swung her attention to me. "It's funny how so many threads can weave into one big tapestry."

I swallowed to work some moisture into my throat. "Sooooo have you figured out a link between Ed Quinn's victims . . . and Kristi?"

Her eyes rested on each of us in turn before she spoke.

"I believe I have."

Chapter 34

Everyone remained silent. No way would any of us come out and say, "You know about zombies then, right?" And sure, Sorsha clearly knew something about zombies, but I had no clue how much. I had an ugly feeling she suspected I was one, but what about the others?

Finally, I couldn't stand it any longer. "Well?"

Sorsha leaned against the table behind her, a casual pose that looked more like a cat preparing to pounce. "I have reasons to believe Dr. Charish was conducting, or intending to conduct, experiments on the victims' remains—namely their heads. Not long after Quinn was identified as the killer, Dr. Charish had contact with a Walter McKinney, a.k.a. William Rook, who is wanted on more charges than I can count, and who is believed to have committed murder and kidnapping at Dr. Charish's behest." She lowered her head, eyes on me.

"That's right," I said leaning against the table behind me in a doomed attempt to copy her stance. "Last year he kidnapped my dad to get to me."

A tiny little mock frown puckered her forehead. "And why is that?"

"Why do you think?" I challenged and mock-frowned right back at her.

"I'm asking the questions here," she replied evenly.

"Well, I just asked you a question, so apparently I'm asking them, too!"

Behind her, Kyle gave me a warning head shake. Yet I didn't miss the ever-so-slight flicker of amusement in Sorsha's expression. I allowed myself an instant of triumph then pressed what little advantage I had.

"Look," I said. "I overheard you asking Kristi about zombies in the gator room. And back before Mardi Gras, you sure seemed fascinated by my zombie makeup." Which had been my actual rotting flesh. "Not to mention, you were awfully interested in the *Zombies Are Among Us!!* documentary that supposedly showed real zombies."

Satisfaction filled her eyes. "And what do you know of real zombies?"

I threw my hands up. "Are we seriously going to keep beating around the bush? I know you know!"

Brian eased back into the room, tucking his phone away. Sorsha took a step toward me, almost eagerly. "And what do I know?"

I bared my teeth. "That I'm a zombie. Woooooeeeeeooooo I'm a monster. Look at me!" I raised my hands like claws and widened my eyes comically. "Big scary brain-eating monster!"

Dr. Nikas sank onto a stool, looking a little pale. Brian made a pained grimace. "Jesus Christ, Angel," he hissed.

Sorsha didn't act the least bit surprised or disbelieving, confirming my hunch that she'd known all along. "I never said you were a monster," she said mildly.

I dropped my hands and glared. "What am I to you, then? A menace? Do you think zombies need to be wiped out or detained—for the safety of others?"

"I don't support genocide or unlawful incarceration."

Man, she was good at evasive answers. Yet it sounded like she was fine with zombies—or anyone—as long as we didn't break any laws. That looked great on the surface, except for one pesky detail: I'd broken a shit-ton of laws, both minor and major, from defiling a corpse all the way up to murder. So, yeah I was probably still fucked.

Except that she seemed to be focused on Kristi at the moment, and that was all right by me.

"Fine," I said coming to a decision. "You want to know the truth about the serial killer?"

"Angel!" Brian took a step toward me.

"Can it, Brian," I snarled. "Do you seriously think she won't figure it out? Hell, she knows most of it already!"

Dr. Nikas nodded once. "It's all right, Brian. Angel, go on."

I gave him a grateful look then returned my attention to Sorsha.

"Yes, Ed Quinn murdered those people, and yes, they were all zombies, but he was manipulated and brainwashed by Kristi to think zombies had killed his parents and that all zombies were murderous monsters." I went on to explain how Kristi had learned about zombies over a decade ago from Ed's parents, and after they died, her lies convinced Ed that his parents had been zombie hunters, and that he needed to avenge them and honor their legacy by collecting zombie heads. "Kristi wanted those heads for her own research," I said. "But she also wanted a real live zombie test subject. Me."

Sorsha considered my words. "Interesting," she said after a moment. "When you came out of the cooler earlier, you mentioned something about a double. Of whom were you speaking?"

"Kristi Charish," I said. "I think she's been here since Monday. A jet came in to Tucker Point Airport that afternoon with one passenger—a brown-haired woman. Kristi is blonde. No obvious connection, right? Wednesday at midnight another jet arrived, with a blonde woman who looked like Kristi and a man who fit the description of her bodyguard Fritz. In fact it probably was Fritz. Soon after that, a brown-haired woman departed on the first jet. However, my source at the airport says that it wasn't the same woman who arrived Monday. I believe Kristi came in on Monday, wearing a brown wig, then her double arrived Wednesday midnight, pretending to be Kristi, and then put on the brown wig and left on the first jet, her job done. Which means Kristi was here *before* the LZ-1 epidemic began."

Brian shook his head, but I spoke before he could. "I know you had eyes on her, Brian, but how close were they?"

He hesitated. "Apparently, not close enough."

"That matches my own intel," Sorsha said, surprising me with the nugget of information—and annoying me that she'd known all along.

"Fritz Colton has been working for Dr. Charish for the last month," Brian said. "He's a top notch freelance security pro who's always with her public persona—whether Dr. Charish herself or her double—in Chicago. That consistency strengthened the deception."

I wrinkled my nose. "And gave Kristi the freedom to do her LZ-1 lab work, with no one the wiser."

Sorsha regarded me. "And how are you connected to this epidemic, Angel?"

The safe answer would've been that I was merely helping to find a way to save the victims. But I had a feeling Sorsha would know I wasn't telling the whole truth.

"I'm the source," I said, squaring my shoulders. "For the original strain, that is. Everyone who's been infected after Deputy Connor has a mutated strain: LZ-1. The original strain happened when I . . ." I grimaced. No need to go into the whole bit about my addiction. "My zombie parasite got damaged." Yeah, that was good enough. "Anyway, Judd Siler was hunting me because he knew I was a zombie. I bit him and got away, but he tracked me again the next day and got shot. I ran to the swamp because I thought Marla was on my trail. But then Judd came after me—dead. I mean like half his head was missing. So I, uh, dispatched him—total self-defense, y'know? And then I guess the alligators ate his remains and ended up infected."

"Who is Marla?" Sorsha asked.

"A German Shepherd. She . . ." A thought was banging around inside my brain, evading my efforts to pin it down. "She's a cadaver dog—wait. Dr. Nikas, what did Jacques tell you when he called?"

Dr. Nikas rubbed his face with both hands. "That upon close examination, the puncture point in the bite on Nick is larger and far more precise than that of a typical mosquito, and that it carries traces of both inert and activated LZ-1 as well as *Aedes albopictus* saliva. Damning enough on its own, but Jacques's subsequent analysis of the water bottles revealed the presence of certain proteins that can stimulate LZ-1 into full activation. If Nick's presumed bite is representative of those on the other victims, I cannot help but accept that these are, in truth, inoculation sites."

Sorsha's eyes widened. "You believe it's being deliberately spread?"

Dr. Nikas dipped his head in a sober nod. She typed a text message.

Rachel muttered a curse. "So Dr. Charish and Saberton—"

I jerked a hand up. "Wait." That damn thought was still bouncing around like a coke addict in a mosh pit. "Just, wait."

Sorsha had been in town during Mardi Gras because of the *Zombies Are Among Us!!* short film. A film containing real zombie clips that Kristi had given Rosario—her then-lover and patsy—to pass on to the studio. Rosario, who'd nearly outed me with Marla at the Zombiefest, where the short film had premiered to promote the movie *High School Zombie Apocalypse!!*—the movie that starred Justine, who had an ex-girlfriend sneaky and paranoid enough to bug her apartment. Sneaky. Kristi could teach a masterclass in sneaky. She was the kind who would . . .

"Kristi bugged Marla!" I gasped.

"The dog?" Sorsha asked with disbelief.

Brian shook his head. "Angel, we scanned her along with everyone else."

"But how thoroughly? I mean, Kristi is smart enough not to use something that would be found on a superficial search. And maybe it would show up on an x-ray or something, but Marla would probably have to be sedated for something like that, and who would even think a deeper scan would be necessary on a *dog*?"

Brian didn't look convinced. "Dr. Charish had no way to know that Rosario and Marla would be brought into our fold."

"Ah, Dante Rosario is with your lot?" Sorsha asked. "I'd wondered what happened to him. I thought he'd been disappeared permanently."

"Yeah, he's with us now," I said then looked to Brian. "And you're right, Kristi had no way to ever think that he and Marla could possibly end up with us. She'd have bugged the dog to keep tabs on *Rosario*."

Rachel bristled. "Rosario told me how often he had to check in with her. That sounds exactly like something she would stoop to."

Brian rubbed the back of his neck. "And then she got unbelievably lucky when Marla came into our lab."

"It explains how Saberton beat us out to the swamp," I said. "And how Kristi could have known about Douglas Horton and Deputy Connor. Marla stuck by Dr. Nikas a lot while—Oh shit." I looked to Dr. Nikas in growing horror.

The blood drained from his face. "If so . . . she knows *everything*."

Everything we'd ever talked about. Including mature zombies. And the fact that Pierce was actually Pietro. "That's why she wanted you-know-who's blood." No wonder she'd cajoled Pierce into giving her a sample. "Oh, fuck. The switched blood tubes! She knew about you-know-who being you-know-what, so she watched closely enough to spot Jacques switch you-know-who's blood for mine—then she had Hairy Tech switch it back so Jacques ended up with my blood instead of you-know-who's."

Dr. Nikas sighed. "And that recently acquired knowledge explains why she wanted your medical records." He paused and flicked a glance at Sorsha, clearly unwilling to say more in her presence.

I turned to Sorsha. "Hey, Agent Aberdeen, would you possibly consider yourself an ally to our kind?"

Her brow lowered. "As an FBI agent, I'm an ally to anyone who's been victimized."

I waved my hands. "No no no. I mean you, personally. I know the feds have all sorts of restrictions and guidelines."

One side of her mouth tilted up slightly. "Actually, the task force I'm operating under allows its agents a good deal more leeway in dealing with *special* circumstances. However, speaking for myself. . . at this time . . . yes, you can consider me to be on your side. An ally."

I glanced at Dr. Nikas and got a micro-nod, which I interpreted to mean his nose told him Sorsha was telling the truth.

"Awesome. Right back at you," I said to Sorsha, then pivoted to face Dr. Nikas. "Why the hell did Kristi want my medical records?"

"Because you have certain mature zombie factors, such as your ability to use a control bite, that might have been caused by your, ah, unique blood chemistry at the time of your turning."

I made a face. "Drugs. The many *many* drugs I was on. But why would she care about that?"

He rubbed his mouth. "She hates us, but she envies us. And now I believe I know what her true purpose has been all along. I recently came across considerable research she had done on telomeres. I thought little of it until now, but I believe she is seeking a way to gain the benefits of being a mature zombie without having to, well, be a zombie first."

I stared at him. "She wants to be immortal." And Dr. Nikas probably "came across" that research by snooping in her files. Good for him.

"Is that possible?" Sorsha asked, surprised.

"Whether or not it is," Dr. Nikas said, "if Dr. Charish is attempting it, she must believe so."

"Jesus," I breathed. "She's a fucking psycho lunatic. She released this epidemic . . . but that means she has a cure, right?"

He met my eyes. "I would be shocked if she did not."

"Then whatever she was testing at the gym had nothing to do with a cure. But it could have been part of her immortality research." My stomach clenched as another thought occurred to me. "She started the epidemic to have an unlimited supply of test subjects. She won't miraculously come up with the cure— and bask in the glory—until she's done with them." I gritted my teeth. "And immortal."

"Indeed," Dr. Nikas said, eyes distant. "With this new insight, I believe I know her process now. I had been assuming a . . ." He trailed off then strode to the whiteboard and began scribbling notes. Portia went to the computer near him and pulled up the latest cell culture data.

The lab phone rang, but Dr. Nikas was already too absorbed to pay it any mind.

Brian picked it up. "This is Archer." He fell silent. "I see. Thanks." He replaced the phone in its cradle. "Jacques says that Nick has begun moaning for brains."

My gut dropped to my toes. How much longer did he have before his body simply gave out? I turned to the others. "We have to stop her. Confront her. Get the cure *now*. If she figures out we know what she's up to, she'll make sure we never get it."

"I agree," Sorsha said. "She's already spooked by my presence, and I've been in here with you long enough to make her worry. Last thing any of us need is for her to destroy data." She began to text another message. "I'm informing my supervisor of the new development. I'll also let my partner know what's going down, but he's at least twenty minutes away."

"What about the backup team Agent Garner sent from Baton Rouge?" I asked. "Are they driving or coming by helicopter?"

She gave me a long look. I gave an innocent shrug. "I have really good hearing."

"Of course you do," she said drily. "Driving. Also at least twenty minutes away."

Rachel eyed Sorsha. "What about local law enforcement."

"Too risky," Sorsha said quickly. "Potential biohazard, right?"

In other words, Sorsha was keeping the situation confined to her task force—and a lid on the weirdness. That fit our zombie leave-us-alone agenda perfectly.

Kyle spoke up. "We have enough personnel to confront her. Fritz and Dr. Charish are currently in the microscope room with two of her techs. The other two techs are right next door in histology. Both rooms are along the hallway around the corner, which means that Reno Larson, who has stationed himself outside those two rooms, has no line of sight on this lab or any of the other rooms along this corridor."

Sorsha folded her arms over her chest. "Poor tactics on his part."

"Quite," Kyle replied.

"Rachel and I need to stay with Dr. Nikas," Brian said. "Top priority."

Sorsha's eyes flicked from Kyle to me as if assessing her resources. "Unorthodox joint operations are not unheard of in my task force. We know how to . . . adjust the paperwork."

What the hell other weirdness did they deal with? Not that I minded. "What's the plan?"

"Charish has two bodyguards and four lab techs. If she resists—and I do expect resistance—it will be dicey, even with your special zombie abilities in play."

Of course she knew about zombie special abilities. "She also has Billy Upton," I pointed out.

"He's one of mine," she replied.

"No way! He seems way too sweet and innocent."

Sorsha let out a dry chuckle. "And he uses that to his advantage." Her phone buzzed with a text. She sobered as she read it. "Charish just made a call to Saberton security. Agent Garner believes she asked for backup and extraction."

"Which means we have to confront her right now!" I said, anxiety rising.

"It also means her backup might arrive before we're finished with her," she replied, mouth tight. "That tilts the odds that much more in her favor."

Except there was one unique zombie ability she didn't know about. "What if we had our own special backup right here?" I asked, smile growing.

She and Kyle regarded me with matching doubtful expressions.

Sorsha lifted an eyebrow. "And where is this special backup?"

I grinned. "In the gator room."

Her other eyebrow went up. "Are you trying to tell me you wish to use the alligators as backup?"

"Trust me," I said. "But we need to hurry. Let's go!"

"Hold on," Brian said. He opened a drawer and pulled out pint-sized packets of brains along with the normal smaller ones. "Tank up and stock up."

Kyle stuffed small packets into his pocket and ripped the top off a big one.

I did the same and gulped down the pint, half expecting the others to start a chorus of *Chug! Chug! Chug!* and a little disappointed when they didn't. I lowered the empty packet and let out a pleased sigh as the surplus of brains energized my muscles and tweaked my senses. Nowhere near as supercharged as with a combat mod, but the extra brains would give me the fuel I needed if this confrontation turned into a clusterfuck.

Once Kyle and Sorsha were ready, I opened the door a crack, pleased to see the hallway was empty, then I slipped out and ran as quietly as possible to the gator room, relieved to find Kyle and Sorsha right behind me.

Within, the gators were lined up along the fence as if they'd sensed me coming.

"Hello, darlings," I murmured. "Time to come out and play."

"Are you sure this is a good idea?" Kyle asked as I unlocked the gate. "You can't possibly have trained them in such a short time."

"I didn't train them." I pulled the enclosure door open. "I didn't have to. They know what I want and will do it for me."

Sorsha looked ever-so-slightly uncertain—the first time I'd seen her look anything but cool and composed. But when the gators stayed where they were, she relaxed a bit.

"I need Biggie and Tupac," I said, smiling when they lumbered forward and through the open gate.

The six-footers and the rest of the smaller ones moved to follow but stopped when I made a *tsking* noise. "No, I only need the grown-ups for this," I told them. "It might get danger-ous."

They stared up at me with forlorn expressions. I sighed. "Okay, y'all can come, but you have to stay out of the way." I crouched between the two big gators and rubbed their toothy jaws. "Let's get that bitch."

Chapter 35

"No hissing," I told the gators, voice low yet stern. "No bellowing. No noise, okay? We're being *sneaky*. Now let's do this!"

Head high, I started down the corridor, flanked by the two enormous reptiles. Man, if those bitches from high school could see me now!

snick snick shwuush snick shwuush snick snick shwuush

I stopped. Sighed down at my eager guardians. Claws and tails made more noise than I'd expected.

"I stand by my decision to use the gators as backup," I whispered to the others. "But Reno will hear us coming. Kyle, can you go ahead and take him out?"

"Consider it done." He loped noiselessly to the far corner, did a quick peek around, then disappeared from our sight. A second later my zombie hearing picked up a soft "oof," then silence.

After a brief, tense wait, Kyle reappeared and gave us the all-clear.

"Nice," Sorsha murmured.

I grinned. "Yeah, Kyle gets shit done."

I got my gator procession going again, striding with glorious, reptilian purpose to Kyle.

"What did you do with Reno?" I asked him.

"Supply closet and zip-ties."

"The techs in the histology room might hear us when we go

to deal with Kristi," I said. "We can help Billy take them out of action so they don't cause problems for us later."

Sorsha merely smiled. "If Billy needs the help, then by all means."

Once around the corner, Sorsha pulled the histology room door open. Both techs and Billy looked over at her. Sorsha gave Billy a single short nod then closed the door again.

Several soft thuds. Then nothing.

"I think he has it covered," Sorsha said.

"Niiiice," I murmured.

I slowed the gators as we approached the door to the microscope room. Kyle and Sorsha drew their guns. I took hold of the door handle, focusing on the gators and what I wanted them to do.

"On three," Sorsha whispered. "One . . . two . . . three!"

I yanked the door open and stepped aside. Biggie surged forward, with Tupac right on his tail, and Kyle and Sorsha following. I went in behind them, the smaller gators swarmed around my legs as I strode past computer stations and into chaos.

Shouts and curses. Gator bellows. The crash of glass. Within a few frenzied seconds, Fritz, Kristi, Hairy Tech, and Beardzilla were at bay against the far wall, hemmed in by the scanning electron microscope and the gaping jaws of man-eating zombie gators.

"Hands where I can see them!" Sorsha barked. The techs hurried to comply, and even Fritz had his gun drawn, but took his finger off the trigger and slowly lowered it to the floor. Kristi shot him a murderous glare and began rapid-fire texting on her phone.

"Drop the phone, Dr. Charish," Sorsha snapped.

Kristi made one more tap then set the phone on the counter. "What is the meaning of this?" she demanded.

"You're being detained for questioning, Dr. Charish," Sorsha said, keeping her gun on the four detainees while Kyle gave them each a quick but thorough pat-down—removing an impressive number of weapons from Fritz's person.

"This is ridiculous!" Kristi cast a quick glance at the wall clock. Checking to see how long until her reinforcements arrived?

She sputtered with fury as Kyle zip-tied her hands behind her back, but she was smart enough not to resist. In short order, Kyle had all four detainees restrained and seated in a row in front of their gator guards. He retrieved Kristi's phone from the counter then passed it to Sorsha with a murmured, "Passcode locked." Sorsha nodded and slipped it into a pocket.

"I'll be filing a complaint with the director of the FBI, Agent Aberdeen," Kristi spat.

"You go right ahead and do that, Dr. Charish." Sorsha gave Kyle a head tilt toward the hall, and he took up a position in the doorway to keep an eye out for trouble.

"Turn over the cure, Kristi," I ordered. Gator growls echoed my words.

She widened her eyes in shocked innocence. "The cure? Are you mental? Ari and I are still working to find it!"

"Cut the crap," I said with a sneer. "I always knew you were evil, but I never thought you'd create a deadly epidemic for your own benefit. You started working on LZ-1 right after Rosario told you about Judd shambling. And you've been using a double to throw off the Tribe's surveillance."

Kristi gave a little sniff. "Having a look-alike isn't a crime. But spying on me is! You zombies are the criminals." She glared at Sorsha. "They're the ones you should arrest, Agent Aberdeen."

"I'll be sure to look into it," Sorsha replied with zero inflection. She holstered her weapon then stepped back and began texting, managing to keep an eagle eye on the detainees while her thumbs flew over the phone screen.

"Obviously the Tribe had good reason to spy on you," I told Kristi. "And I know you bugged Marla. It's how you knew where to go in the swamp, and why you wanted my medical records, as well as a certain person's blood."

"I beg your pardon?" Her lips quivered as if holding back a laugh. "Did you seriously just accuse me of planting a listening device in . . . in a *dog*? Oh my, that is rich!" She met my eyes. "I didn't bug the dog, Angel. I didn't need to. I put the pieces together because I'm *smart*." She snickered with a nasty edge that clearly said *And you're not*. "Pierce Gentry was my informant in Saberton. Then, not only did he suddenly stop sending updates, but he inexplicably defected to the zombies' side. Because, by some strange twist of fate, he'd actually been a zombie all along? And, by some insane coincidence, this all happened in the same timeframe when Pietro Ivanov miraculously escaped the New York lab—except, oh no, he then died in a plane crash." She rolled her eyes. "I'm boggled that anyone bought that ridiculous story. I went back to Gentry's latest physical exam and had no trouble confirming he most definitely had not been a zombie. It didn't take much for me to conclude that Pietro had the means to change forms—an ability I'd seen no evidence of in all my years of zombie research. Of course I wanted his blood!"

Fuck. That made sense. And now Sorsha knew what mature zombies could do. And that Pierce Gentry used to be Pietro Ivanov. I mentally crossed fingers she'd remain our ally and that the info wouldn't come back to bite us in the ass. "Well, what about the swamp and the gator hunt?" I asked, scowling. "Sure was convenient y'all found the accident site and made it there before we did."

Kristi tilted one eyebrow up. "Winds and tides. You know . . . science."

Crap. Same way Marcus had figured it out. "Yeah, well, how'd you find out about Deputy Connor's collapse? Or Douglas Horton coming back to life, so you even knew to look for gators?"

She flicked a glance at the clock. "That was indeed via a bug, though not in the dog. It was where your people never thought to scan—in your darling boyfriend's car." She gave me a mock-pout. "The poor thing. I hear he's feeling a bit under the weather. Along with all of his daddy's little survivalist friends. And Daddy, too, before long."

I held myself back with sheer force of will, but the gators bellowed and snapped in response to my homicidal fury. I took grim pleasure in how Kristi paled and squirmed back. She was spilling all the beans with an FBI agent present, which meant Kristi felt certain of a timely rescue. I felt certain she was going to lose a few teeth before this was done.

"One way or another, I'm going to wring that cure out of you," I said through my teeth. "Maybe I should let a gator have one of your hands? Or a foot? Maybe both. I don't think they've been fed yet today."

Tupac growled deep and ominous. Hairy Tech screwed his eyes shut, and the scent of hot piss hit my nostrils.

Kristi took a long look at the clock then bared her teeth in triumph. "You'll be far too occupied with other matters very . . . soon."

A heavy *whump* shook the building.

"What the hell was that?" Sorsha demanded even as the fire alarm started hooting.

Kristi batted her eyelashes. "I think your friends might need your help, Angel."

Kyle took off at a dead sprint toward the main lab.

"Go!" Sorsha told me. "I've got this."

"Don't let them leave!" I ordered the gators then raced after Kyle and activated a combat mod.

Kyle had likely done the same, besides having a good head start on me. By the time I rounded the corner, he'd already made it to the main lab door. He yanked it open, stepping back as smoke and an odd fog rolled out, then he charged in. Farther down the hall, Reg burst out of the cell culture room and sprinted into the lab after Kyle.

I poured on the speed and followed them in. The fog was already dissipating, and I realized it was a waterless fire suppression system, used in places where water would fuck up sensitive equipment and computers.

Not that it mattered. The computers were twisted, smoking heaps of plastic and metal. Cold nausea gripped me. Kristi had blown them up to destroy data.

I pushed back the sick fear and assessed the scene. Rachel was ripping apart the remains of a computer with her bare hands, blood running down her face from a long gash on her forehead. Brian had his back to me—with a dozen or more bits of shrapnel sticking out of it. He was trying to feed brains to Dr. Nikas, who had numerous gashes on his face and chest.

Dr. Nikas, who was cradling a bleeding Portia.

"Oh god, Portia!" I dropped to my knees beside her.

She coughed, pink foam bubbling at her mouth. "Ari . . ." she wheezed.

"I'm here, Portia," he said, face contorted in pain and grief.

Brian leaned close to me. "She was right by Kristi's computer when it blew. The charges were small, but the pressure wave hit her hard."

I nodded, sick. That was how explosions killed you—a wave of pressure that battered your internal organs. She was going to drown in her own blood.

"You have to save her, Dr. Nikas," I told him. Begged him.

"I don't know if I can," he said, agonized. "The cancer. The injuries. And . . . I will not without her consent."

"You have to try!" I took her hand, terrified at how light it seemed. "Please, Portia. Let him try and save you."

She coughed again and brought up blood. "I . . ."

"Portia!" I wanted to squeeze her hand but didn't dare. "You'd be a zombie, but you'd have a chance to live."

"Ari . . . ?"

"Yes, dear one?" He touched her cheek.

"Yes . . . give me . . . the chance," she whispered. "Give us the . . ." Her eyes lost their focus.

Brian shoved two open brain packets at Dr. Nikas. "You have to heal before you do anything else." He'd probably been trying to get the distraught man to take brains since the explosion.

Dr. Nikas took both packets and devoured the contents, eyes never leaving the dying woman in his arms. He pulled her close and placed a gentle kiss on her forehead then shifted to bite her trapezius. With a low growl, he gave a sharp tug to part the flesh then went still, breathing softly through his teeth.

What was he doing? Had he changed his mind about turning her? When I'd turned Philip Reinhardt and Andrew Saber, I'd slavered and shredded flesh like, well, a monster.

But when I'd tried to turn Kristi's next test subject, the instinct never rose. What if that was happening with Dr. Nikas? I clenched my hands together to keep them from shaking. Kang had told me my instinct failed because I'd recently turned Philip. But what if Dr. Nikas was exhausted and depleted from so much work? Or what if something else was wrong, and he couldn't save her?

Brian set Rachel's half-full container of fresh brain chunks beside Dr. Nikas. I unclenched my hands and forced myself to breathe. The next stage of turning required brains to help transfer and nourish the parasite. After I'd finished the rending-and-tearing stage with Philip and Andrew, I'd chewed brains then spat and bitten them into the numerous wounds I'd created. But Brian didn't look at all uncertain, which told me Dr. Nikas's behavior was normal. Maybe the process simply wasn't as gruesome for a mature zombie.

Dr. Nikas released his bite-hold on Portia's shoulder, still cradling her limp form close. He took a hunk of brain, chewed it, then clamped onto the wound again, all neat and tidy and controlled. If I hadn't known better, a casual glance would have made me think he held her in a lover's embrace.

But was he cradling a dying woman or one about to start a fresh life? Only time would tell. I looked away to give them a semblance of privacy as well as to distract myself. Kyle helped Rachel dismantle computers, removing hard drives and flash storage in the hopes of salvaging info. Reg gathered and organized scattered files with fierce efficiency.

"What's the situation with Dr. Charish?" Brian asked.

I turned to him. "We have her locked down and—" Long slivers of plastic were embedded in his left cheek and eye, injuries he'd clearly ignored while taking care of Dr. Nikas. "Dude, you've got something on your face." I licked my thumb as if ready to wipe off a bit of dirt.

He let out a strangled laugh. "Just need a little spit and toilet paper, and it'll come right off."

"Seriously, you need to do something about that," I said. "It's kinda freaking me out."

The building trembled again with a smaller *whump*. Kyle and I exchanged a charged look.

"Sorsha," I breathed. The computers in the microscope room.

"Go. I got this," Brian said in an unnerving echo of Sorsha.

I lurched up and sprinted back the way I came.

Smoke and fog seeped around the histology door and poured from the microscope room. At histology, I skidded to a stop and yanked the door open.

"You okay, Billy?" I shouted through the fog, barely able to see him stagger to his feet.

"10-4," he croaked.

I spun toward the microscope room even as Kristi Fucking Charish stepped out like a demon emerging from the bowels of hell, smoke curling around her, and heralded by unearthly gator growls and wet snorts. She held her briefcase in her left hand, and her right gripped a tranq gun. Zombie tranqs. Shit. This would be a really bad time to get dropped by one of the damn things.

"Perfect timing," she breathed and lifted the gun in my direction, finger tightening on the trigger. I scrambled to evade, but even my zombie combat-mod-enhanced reflexes weren't going to be fast enough to counter my forward momentum.

Kyle slammed into me, knocking me aside. I crashed into the wall then fumbled to grab him as he staggered, a tranq dart sticking out of his shoulder.

Except instead of going limp as if he'd been tranqed, he began convulsing.

I yanked the dart out, threw it aside, and hugged him close. "What the hell did you do to him, Kristi?" I yelled.

She dropped the empty tranq gun. "Well, I was hoping for you to be my test subject, but he'll have to do."

"To test what?" Kyle was jerking harder now. I lowered him to the floor then tried to pull his gun from his holster, with no success. *Fuck.* It was a retention holster, and I didn't know the right sequence of moves to get the gun free. "What's happening to him?"

"Behold the *other* part of my project," she said with a nasty smile.

"What, your stupid immortality shit?"

Kristi shrugged. "That one's not quite ready, but I'll crack it soon enough. This"—she lifted her chin toward Kyle—"is so I don't have to deal with you lot for the rest of eternity. My anti-zombie serum. Or, more precisely, a *real* zombie serum." She let out an ugly little chuckle, while I struggled to keep Kyle from hurting himself. "You fed a version to poor patient nine at the gym."

"You said that patient wasn't supposed to die," I said, voice shaking with rage.

"He wasn't. But I learned oh-so-much from him. Tweaked the formula." She checked her watch. "In a few minutes, the parts of Kyle Griffin's brain that make him a thinking, feeling person will be permanently disabled—devolving him into a true, traditional zombie. Mindless, obedient, and just intelligent enough to be trained for menial work. Won't that be nice?" She looked behind me as Billy stumbled out of the histology room. "Have fun with the new Kyle!" she sang and hurried off in her stupid wedges toward the roof stairs—probably to wait for a helicopter extraction.

Billy staggered up to me. "I'll get her."

"No! Check on Sorsha." I prayed that Kristi hadn't killed her. "I don't hear a chopper yet. Kristi can't go anywhere."

Billy glanced in the direction of the stairs then jogged unsteadily to the microscope room. "She's alive but needs a medic!" he hollered a few seconds later. "Calling now."

Kyle's convulsions calmed to tremors. One hand gripped my arm like a claw.

"Ang-gel," he stuttered.

"Dr. Nikas can fix this, Kyle," I said, struggling to keep my voice steady. "It's going to be okay. He can stop this before . . . before it causes permanent damage." Kristi had probably laced her serum with something that anesthetized the parasite so the toxin could do its nasty work. It was what I'd do if I was an evil psychopath neurobiologist. He needed a parasite stimulant. Now.

"Another combat mod," I said. "That may slow the effects of the serum down and buy you time." I reached for his mod port, but he pushed my hand away.

"No. I . . . I'm ready t-to go."

"Where—"

"I don't want . . . t-to be c-cured. Please. P-please."

My shoulders sagged as I realized what he meant. "Oh."

"P-p-please."

Brian had turned him zombie against his will and stolen death from him—a death Kyle yearned for. And last year, I'd promised him that, when the time came, I'd help him die.

It seemed a relatively easy promise to make back then, in the comfort of a posh New York hotel. But now I was faced with the reality.

"All right," I said, words barely a squeak. "I need your gun." It wasn't easy to kill a zombie, but a few ways were permanent.

The tremors were beginning to ease, but I suspected that meant the toxin was starting to do its work. "Retention holster," he slurred. "Twist right, tip forward and pull."

Tears spilled over as I twisted and pulled in the right sequence to remove his gun from the holster.

His grip on my arm loosened, and his eyes struggled to focus on mine. Yet his face was smooth with soul-deep relief. He'd been ready for this for a long time. "Thank you . . . Angel."

"Anytime, dude," I said, trying for humor but choking on a sob.

"It's been an honor . . . and pleasure to know you." A soft smile touched his mouth, and then he rolled facedown and tucked his chin to his chest.

"The honor and pleasure has been all mine," I gasped out past the tears. The gun was a Beretta M9—a model I was familiar with from training with him. I checked to make sure a round was chambered and the safety off, then pressed the muzzle to the base of his skull and looked away. "Goodbye, Kyle."

I pulled the trigger.

The sound crashed through the corridor, and brought Billy at a run. "What the hell?" Though he didn't reach for a weapon, he held himself loose and balanced, a ready stance like I'd seen in my *jiu jitsu* instructors. Billy knew how to handle himself.

I dropped the magazine and cleared the chamber, then set the gun beside Kyle's body and lifted my hands away from my body. "Are you going to arrest me?"

He took a slow step forward. "Why did you shoot him?"

"Because I promised him I would."

He searched my face. "I see."

"Do you?" I said. "Because if you're not going to arrest me, I need to chase down the bitch responsible for all of this." The distant *thwup-thwup* of a helicopter reached us. Kristi's extraction.

He nodded once. "Go do what you gotta do."

"I appreciate it." I activated my last combat mod and took off for the stairs, glancing into the microscope room as I passed. The computer stations were slagged wreckage. Sorsha was crumpled on the floor. Someone was huddled on the counter. The back wall was splattered with blood, and the gators were in a frenzy . . . feeding. On what—or who—I couldn't tell.

I tore into the stairwell, vaulted the steps three at a time and burst out onto the roof, teeth bared in a snarl.

Kristi stood on the far side, shading her eyes toward a helicopter that was still several hundred yards away. She startled as the door slammed open against the outer wall then shot me a furious glare. "You lost," she yelled. "Accept your fucking defeat already!"

"Like hell! Give me the motherfucking cure!"

She laughed, clearly enjoying the moment immensely. "Not until after your boyfriend is dead."

"Then I'll just have to take it from you!" I broke into a run even as gunfire spat from the helicopter door. Chips of concrete flew up around me, and a bullet whizzed by my ear. I kept my focus on my target and picked up speed, ignoring the jolts of pain as two bullets found their target. I was still able to run, so they didn't matter.

Her arrogant sneer crumbled as I rapidly closed the distance between us. Her eyes widened in mounting panic. She shifted her weight to evade even as I corrected for it.

I hit her low, knocked her off balance. Wrapped my arms tight around her legs and waist. Lifted her off her feet and kept running.

Kristi screamed and struggled as she realized my intent, but it was too late. A three-foot wall surrounded the perimeter of the roof, and I leaped, planted one foot on top of it, and pushed off to sail out into the open air.

I tucked my head against her chest. Her scream vibrated against my cheek. The ground came up fast. I yanked my arms back to avoid getting them crushed.

The ground slammed into us, cutting off Kristi's shriek. My Kristi-cushion went *crack cruuuunch pop*, and pain sliced through my ribs and right knee and ankle.

Slowly, I lifted my head, feeling the creak of bone and tendons throughout my poor abused body. I'd expected to land on the parking lot, but apparently I'd launched us off the back of the building to land on hard dirt just beyond a line of bushes. Didn't matter. The fall from a three-story building was enough. And probably best we hadn't landed in the parking lot, considering the lot would surely be filled with people from the evacuated building.

THWUP-THWUP-THWUP. The helicopter overhead, hovering. I forced myself to roll off Kristi to stare upward. The pilot, wearing headset and sunglasses, peered down at us, mouth set in a scowl. I braced myself for bullets to spit from the open door, followed by Saberton thugs rappelling down to finish me and rescue her.

But to my relief and glee, the door slid closed, and the helicopter zoomed off. Mission aborted.

I gave the departing chopper a shaky middle finger, then groped for a brain packet.

Kristi wheezed in a ragged breath and let it out in a moan. I gulped down the brains and welcomed the tingle of healing.

"You're dying, you psycho," I rasped then pushed up to one elbow and dragged her briefcase to me. Though it was locked, a little brain-powered force got it open.

But the only contents were a medical magazine with her face on the cover, and a list of celebrity agents. Nothing that could possibly be a cure, or even a hint toward one.

"Fuck you, you worthless sack of skin." I didn't regret taking Kristi for a short and fast flight. She never would've told me what the cure was. Not when she'd infected Nick and Bear and countless others on purpose. I only wished I could have drawn her end out more. Made her suffer. Because unless we came up with a miracle, Nick was going to die.

Something moved in my periphery. I jerked up to a crouch.

"It's all right, Angel," Kang said. He moved to Kristi's side, dropped to one knee, and peered into her face as she moaned and coughed blood.

"What are you doing?" I asked, eyes narrowed. "Don't turn her! Is that what you're going to do?"

Kang leaned close to her bleeding head and inhaled her scent.

"No, Kang, don't save her! She's the last person in the world who needs to be a zombie."

Kang got to his feet and pushed through the bushes, then picked up something I couldn't see at the foot of the building.

"Kang . . .? Please don't."

"Chill, Angel." He returned to Kristi.

And slammed a brick down onto her head.

I jerked back as blood spattered. "What the fuck?"

He brought the brick down once more to smash the skull open. I stared, uncomprehending as he tore pieces of skull aside and grabbed handfuls of brain to stuff into his mouth.

It wasn't until he gobbled down the third handful and his features began to shift that it finally clicked. "Whoa. Dude."

He smiled around another fistful of brain. I watched in awe as his skin lightened and his limbs grew slimmer. His torso narrowed at the waist, and widened at the hips. His—her?—jawline softened, the cheekbones became a touch more refined, and the eyes took on a Northern-European shape, with the irises shifting to blue. His black hair fell out, leaving him briefly bald before new hair sprouted and grew to a length similar to Kristi's— though scraggly and unstyled. And mousy brown streaked with grey. Ha! She'd never really been blonde *or* auburn!

"I need her clothes," Kang-Kristi said.

"You sound just like her. That's so creepy."

"I am her," he-she winked and slipped Kristi's wedges off. "Which means I'm on the Saberton Board of Directors."

"Holy shit," I breathed, fumbling to unbutton her blouse. "You totally are." It was brilliant. With our own Kristi Charish, and with the help of Andrew Saber, we could change Saberton from the inside. Except . . . "Shit, dude, maybe this wasn't such a great idea. Kristi is wanted by the FBI, and—"

We froze at the sound of running footsteps. This was going to be hard to explain. At least Kang-Kristi had no makeup and messy brown hair, and therefore didn't look exactly like Real-Kristi. And maybe whoever was approaching would assume Real-Kristi had smashed her skull in the fall rather than getting it bashed in with a brick?

Billy came running around the corner of the building and slid to a stop. He took in the woman in ill-fitting men's clothing, then the partially dressed dead woman on the ground, the smashed skull, the bloody brick, and the distinct absence of most of her brain.

His gaze finally rested on me. "Gotta say, this assignment sure hasn't been boring."

Chapter 36

Sirens wailed in the distance.

"Angel, get back upstairs and deal with the gators," Billy said. "I'll take care of . . . this." He waved a hand at the two Kristis.

"Take care of this how?" I asked with suspicion. "The mass-murdering Kristi is the one on the ground. The scroungy one is . . . new."

"I gathered as much," he said, manner still easy and friendly, though his eyes were guarded. "Trust me. You really do need to get upstairs before someone else dies."

Kang-Kristi swayed and sank to her knees, but gave me a thumbs up. Pierce had been forced to rest and integrate after his transformation from the Pietro-shape, but he'd been able to function for a while before completely collapsing.

"Go," she said. "I'm old enough to take care of myself."

"Well, pardon me for worrying about an old lady then." I cast one more uncertain look at her then raced for the front entrance. She was right. Her situation was as under control as it could be, given the circumstances. But I was the only one who could deal with the gators.

Several dozen people milled at the far end of the parking lot. The sirens grew louder. Fire department and paramedics no doubt, with deputies not far behind.

The building security guard at the main entrance waved me

right past. Billy must've given him a heads up that I'd be coming in.

The fire alarm was still hooting, and of course the elevators weren't working. I slid to a stop at the bottom of the stairs. Grey tinged my vison, my ribs were on fire, and an overall achiness screamed that I hadn't fully healed from the fall. "Okay, okay," I muttered to my body. "I'll be more considerate." I sucked down another packet of brains then climbed at a far more reasonable pace. Though I was still out of breath when I finally reached the third floor, the pain had faded.

Cries for help and the growl-bellows of gators echoed through the corridors as I ran through the LZ-1 suite. I found Sorsha, face covered in blood, sitting beside the closed door of the gator-filled microscope room. The short black guy from the genetics lab was on one knee beside her with a first aid kit, splinting her forearm. A thick lump of gauze already bound what must have been a nasty scalp wound.

Kyle's body was nowhere in sight, and the pool of blood had been somewhat wiped up, with a streak extending down the corridor.

"Hey, Ninja Girl," Short Guy said.

"Hey. Thanks for helping."

Sorsha's head lolled my way. "Billy texted that you've dealt with Charish."

"Er . . . yeah. She won't be any trouble." How much did she know? I wasn't about to fish for that info while Short Guy was here. "Are you okay?"

"I've been worse." Sorsha glanced toward the microscope room door as two male voices hollered for help. "Charish's techs. One was on the electron microscope, and I don't know where the other ended up. He was on a counter last I saw, and that wasn't going to last long."

That meant Fritz had been the gator food. Damn it. Even though he'd been working for the bad guys, he'd seemed like a basically decent guy. A pro. "Gators can climb," I said, "but the techs will be okay now that I'm here." I silently told the gators to leave the two high ones alone then touched Short Guy on the shoulder. "What's your name?"

"Travis Montague," he said as he tightened the last binding on the splint. "Finally got to use my First Responder training."

"I'm Angel. You did good, Travis. Would you mind going down to meet the paramedics and show them the way up?"

"You got it."

Sorsha grabbed his forearm with her good hand. "You are not to repeat, share, or otherwise disclose anything you've seen or heard here today. This entire situation is under federal investigation. Do you understand?"

"Yes, ma'am. I'm good at secrets. Part of my job."

"Thank you," she said and released his arm. "I'll contact you soon for a post-incident interview."

"Do you need my—"

"I'll find you."

"Alrighty then." He gave a nervous chuckle as he rose to his feet then winked at me. "See ya, Ninja Girl."

I crouched beside Sorsha and waited until I heard the outer door open and close. "Where's Kyle's body?"

"In histology," she said. "Billy took care of him."

Tears stung my eyes, and I blinked them back. "How did Kristi get past you?"

"While we were all distracted by the first explosions, she used her smart watch to begin a countdown for the rest of the computers, including the one by me in the microscope room. After it blew, I lost consciousness, but came to in time to see Fritz—still zip-tied—cutting Charish's ties with a knife he must have had very well concealed. As soon as Charish was free, she took the knife. But instead of cutting Fritz's zip-ties, she slit his throat and shoved him toward the alligators. The thrashing and blood distracted the gators, and she went right past them."

Poor Fritz. He'd been willing to sacrifice his life for his employer, only to have it taken in a totally fucked-up way. I shoved away the mental image of Kristi murdering him in cold blood and instead reveled in the fact that I'd taken her off the playing field for good. "I'm honestly shocked she didn't kill you," I said.

"I played dead, since I was in no condition to fight." Sorsha touched the bandage on her head. "There was plenty of blood from the scalp wound for the ruse to be convincing. Charish tried to get my gun, but I use a retention holster, and she gave up."

"Glad she couldn't get it," I said fervently. "She'd have shot you for sure." I pushed to my feet. "I'd best take care of the gators before they make too much of a mess."

"Too late for that," she said with a humorless chuckle.

We both looked up as the sound of a helicopter rattled the walls.

"Let's hope that's the good guys," I muttered.

I pulled the door open and stepped inside. The gators snapped and growled over an unrecognizable lump of gore—Fritz. Blood splattered the walls and equipment, and pooled on the white tile floor beneath the gators. The stench of shit and blood and sweat hit me in a putrid wave.

Hairy Tech clung to the top of the electron microscope, while Beardzilla lay atop the built-in cabinets. Both were flushed and wild-eyed. Understandably so.

"Angel! Watch out!" Hairy Tech shouted. "The blood . . . th-they went wild with the blood."

"It's going to be okay. Just stay where you are." I had to give him props for being worried about my own safety. It was possible none of the techs were aware of precisely how evil Kristi's schemes were. But I'd let Sorsha's special task force deal with that mess.

One by one the gators abandoned their meal and turned toward me. If gators could look guilty, they certainly did now.

"It's all right," I said to them as I approached. "I could hardly expect you to ignore a meal dropped at your feet, right? But now it's time to go back to the pen. Y'all did great." I crouched, and the gators swarmed me, pushing snouts forward for rubs and scritches.

"Jesus . . ." Beardzilla breathed.

"I'd stay up there if I were you," I told the techs. "Trust me, there's no place to run." Not that I really needed to say so. I had a feeling those two would have to be pried off their perches.

I gathered the gators and headed down the corridor toward their pen room, but stopped at the entrance to the main lab. Within, Portia lay cushioned on a pile of lab coats. Dr. Nikas sat beside her, holding her hand, head turned toward the script-filled whiteboard.

"You're alive," I shrieked and rushed into the room, belatedly telling the gators to stay put.

Portia smiled sleepily. "I am, aren't I. Amazing."

"It is. It is!" I dropped to my knees and tenderly seized her in a hug.

"I'm so glad you chose my pond to free your frogs," she said, words a little thick.

"You and me both!" I released her, only now realizing that Dr. Nikas was rattling off technical terms to Reg, who scribbled on a notepad. Not far away, Brian and Rachel sorted through salvaged computer drives.

Curses erupted in the corridor. Pierce.

"Why the fuck is the hallway filled with alligators?!" he shouted.

"Oops. I'd better put the kids away." I scrambled to my feet and ran out to the hall.

Pierce glared at the gators from a dozen feet away. "What the fuck, Angel!"

"Hi, Pierce! Boy, do I have a lot to tell you after I take these guys home." I rounded up the gators and started down the corridor. "Be right back!"

He muttered something, but even my zombie ears couldn't pick it up over the *snick* and *shwuush* of alligator claws and tails. I doubted it was, "Nice to see you, Angel."

I got them into their pen without incident and told them again how wonderful they were—and promised they wouldn't have to live cooped up forever. They raised their voices in eerie warbly growls that penetrated to my bones. I joined their song for a brief moment then returned to the lab, pretending not to notice the smears of blood the gators had left behind.

"Where's Kristi?" Pierce snapped the instant I stepped through the door.

"Dead," I replied, which earned me the attention of everyone in the room. I went on to explain how I confronted Kristi on the roof and then made sure the extraction team couldn't rescue her—by taking her over the edge with a flying leap.

I hesitated to tell the part about Kang since Rachel and Portia didn't know about the mature zombie ability to take on a new form. But, fuck it. The FBI agents knew, and Rachel was utterly loyal to the Tribe. And Portia . . . well, I had a feeling Dr. Nikas wouldn't be keeping secrets from her.

"But we still have a Kristi Charish." I took a deep breath and related how Kang ate her brain and took on her form, and how Billy said he would manage the whole Kristi-Kristi situation.

"Billy Upton?" Pierce said, eyes narrowing. "He's one of Kristi's people."

"Actually he's one of Sorsha's—"

"Jesus, Angel. You left that mess with the FBI?"

Though I wanted to yell at him, I calmly folded my arms over my chest. "Yes. Would you like to know why?"

"I would."

I kept my expression and tone super chill. "Because it was the right choice. Because Agent Aberdeen works with a special task force and already knows all about us. Because we need help—their help—to pull off the whole Kang-Kristi con and keep a lid on our secrets."

Pierce glowered for another few seconds then shook his head. "All right. I probably would've done the same in your shoes."

I resisted the urge to feign a heart attack at his decision to agree with me, and instead simply offered a cool nod. "But what sucks hard is that Kristi didn't have anything about the cure in her briefcase."

Pierce sighed. "I'm so sorry, Angel."

I blinked to keep back tears. Everything had been so chaotic I hadn't had time to really let it hit me. We had no cure, and Nick and the others were going to die.

"There's something else," I said, chest tight and aching. "Kyle is dead."

Pierce sobered. "What happened?"

I told him about Kristi and her new anti-zombie serum that turned zombies into mindless slaves, and how Kyle had pushed me out of the way and taken the hit.

Dr. Nikas disengaged from Portia, went to the whiteboard and wrote and erased, wrote and erased.

I told Pierce how I thought a combat mod might slow it down, and how Kyle had said no. That he was ready. Tears streamed down my cheeks, and I didn't try to stop them. I hadn't cried yet for Kyle, and he deserved my grief.

Finally, I told Pierce about the promise I'd made last year in New York, and then told him how I shot Kyle.

Shock amplified my grief when Pierce stepped forward and put his arms around me.

"You did the right thing," he murmured. "I was wrong to have Kyle turned against his will. Ari told me. Brian told me. I knew it in my heart. But despite what I did to him, Kyle was a faithful soldier, never giving less than his all. You were right to make the promise and to keep it."

Over by the whiteboard, Dr. Nikas said, "Reg, pull up the

analysis of protein gel sample two, again." Then after a moment, "Angel, forgive me."

I looked up and wiped my eyes. "What is it?"

"I'm sorry to disturb you." He had a dry erase marker in his hand and a blue ink smudge on his nose and cheek. "But this is important. I am on the verge of a breakthrough."

"You are?" I shoved away from Pierce. "What can I do?"

"Jacques sent the analysis of the protein packet gel that killed the patient at the gym. It had tranq components."

"That's right! She said she was testing it on patient nine, but he wasn't supposed to die. So she tweaked the formula—which is what Kyle got."

Dr. Nikas passed the marker to Reg and began preparing test tubes and solutions. "The non-tranq factors in the gel analysis are more mysterious, but your description of their purpose—to destroy higher brain function and create a mindless slave—brought the pieces together for me." He sent Reg to fetch a cold pack. "She *created* the LZ-1 patients as her test subjects. The formulation of the gel was tailored for LZ-1, so your interception of that packet has not only delivered to me what I believe to be the key to a cure, but also strips the veil from the misinformation Kristi had fed me."

Holy shit. The psycho woman created a killer epidemic not only to figure out how to be immortal, but to enslave zombies as well. "Whoa. Do you think the killer tranq in Connor's ear was the first serum test?"

He went still, considering. "It fits. There were non-tranq factors in the earwax sample as well. I do believe the purpose was to experiment, with murder as the result."

"And she was stringing you along on the cure?"

"Whenever I would get close to what I now believe is the right path, she would counter with a perfectly reasonable alternative. A detour rather than a roadblock." He took a small cold pack from Reg and placed it in the bottom of a beaker. "But I'm close to the answer, now, Angel." He handed me a test tube. "Will you give me a saliva sample?"

"Yes! Yes you can have all the spit you want!" I hocked up a loogie and spat it into the vial Dr. Nikas handed me.

He grimaced as he passed me another tube. "Saliva only, please."

"Oh. Sorry." I dutifully worked up a mouthful of only spit—mmm, fried dill pickles, seafood gumbo, braaaaains—and filled the tube.

He set the tube into the beaker as if my spit was the most precious liquid in the world, then turned back to the whiteboard and snapped out instructions. Reg leaped to follow them, his tall, angular form moving with surprising speed and agility.

A soft smile pulled at my mouth. Kyle's death had served his own purpose, yet he'd not only saved my life by letting the tranq hit him instead of me, but his selfless act would end up saving the lives of Nick and so many others. Kristi couldn't help but gloat to me, and in doing so, told me the effects of the serum.

Rachel had taken Dr. Nikas's place beside Portia, and Pierce was on the phone. Brian was gone.

But I knew why he'd left and where he was now.

I slipped out of the lab and down the hall. As I approached the corner, I heard a deep male voice.

"No, there's no one else you need to worry about. Agent Aberdeen is the only serious injury."

I stepped around the corner to see a square-jawed man in a dark suit standing beside Sorsha, while two paramedics tended to her injuries. One of them cast a dubious glance at the blood in the corridor—Kyle's and Fritz's—but apparently didn't feel there was any point arguing with the agent.

Agent Square Jaw pierced me with a measuring look as I approached. I ignored his appraisal and glanced into the microscope room as I passed. A fire blanket had been placed over what was left of Fritz, and all four techs sat zip-tied against one wall. At the far end was Reno, who sported a busted lip and a second black eye that I suspected were courtesy of Kyle.

"Agent Gallagher," Sorsha said. "This is Angel Crawford. She has been most instrumental in dealing with the situation here."

Gallagher gave me a curt nod. "Your assistance is greatly appreciated." His words were clipped and precise, as if he'd said them thousands of times before. He looked back at Sorsha. "And Dr. Charish?"

"Billy will brief you," she said. "The situation has taken an interesting turn."

"Yeah," I said. "I think Dr. Charish has had a change of heart." Literally.

"Don't worry, Angel," Sorsha said. "This isn't the first time we've dealt with and kept quiet . . . a weird outcome."

"Good to hear." I gestured toward the microscope room. "What about Reno and the techs and how much they know about, well, everything." I couldn't exactly come out and say zombies in front of the paramedics.

"My supervisor has a way of ensuring discretion."

I gulped and lowered my voice. "This isn't a deal where they just . . . disappear, is it?"

"Nothing of the sort. They'll simply be disinclined to speak about the issue of concern." She spoke as if it was a matter of fact.

Okaaaaaaay then. "Would you excuse me a moment?" I walked away without waiting for an answer then quietly entered the histology room, closing the door behind me.

Brian was on one knee beside Kyle's supine body. A blood-soaked lab coat had been wrapped around Kyle's head, to my relief. The exit wound for a shot like that would be gruesome. That wasn't how I wanted to remember him, and I was glad Brian seemed to feel the same way. This was his zombie baby—despite the turning being without Kyle's consent.

I put my hand on Brian's shoulder. He covered it with his own and gave it a light squeeze.

"You okay?" I asked.

"Better now." He looked up at me. "And you?"

"Better now."

He got to his feet and embraced me. "Thank you."

I didn't need to ask what for. "Come on. Let's get back to the others."

We stepped out to see that Sorsha had been loaded onto the stretcher.

"Good luck with—" I stopped at the sound of running foot-steps.

"Angel. Brian!" Dr. Nikas raced around the corner, Portia in his arms. "We have to get to the Tribe lab immediately!"

Panic shot through me. "Is something wrong with Portia?"

Dr. Nikas came to a stop. "What? No. She is yet unable to walk, and carrying her seemed most expedient. We must return to the Tribe lab to finish the cure."

"You found it?! You figured it out?"

"I believe I have," he said. "Come. There is no time to waste."

"Hold on a second," Gallagher said. "We need to take

statements—ow!" He glared down at Sorsha who had pinched his arm—hard.

"Let them go," she said. Firmly. "There are lives at stake. I'll get the statements later."

I breathed a thanks to Sorsha. Dr. Nikas took off at a run for the roof stairs with Brian on his heels and me bringing up the rear.

"What about Pierce?" I called as we bounded up the steps.

"He and Reg are staying here for the cleanup," Dr. Nikas said.

The helicopter waited on the roof, ready to go. At its door, Dr. Nikas thrust Portia into Brian's arms, then dug a syringe from his lab coat and jabbed it into my arm, straight through my shirt.

"Ow!" I said, even as he retrieved Portia from Brian and helped her into the chopper.

I climbed in after and got myself buckled in. I started to ask Dr. Nikas what he'd injected, but he was already deeply absorbed and furiously scribbling notes onto one of Kristi's legal pads. He didn't even look up when Brian buckled him and Portia in. As for Portia, she gave Brian a sleepy smile of thanks then leaned her head against Dr. Nikas's shoulder and closed her eyes.

Without pausing his writing, Dr. Nikas took her hand in his and cradled it close, a move so casually tender that I had to look away and hide my grin.

A yawn caught me by surprise, followed by a serious case of the sleepies. Maybe the stay-awake mod was wearing off? Or maybe it was whatever Dr. Nikas had jabbed me with. Either way, as the rotors wound up, my eyes closed.

"Angel. Angel!" I woke to Dr. Nikas shaking my shoulders. "Come. There is no time to waste." His voice sounded distant. Muffled. My head pounded as if I'd been drinking all night, back in my pre-zombie days. "Brian, help her, please."

Dr. Nikas carried Portia out. I fumbled with the seat harness only to have Brian unbuckle it for me. Somehow he managed to get me out of the helicopter without my weirdly numb legs giving way.

"Wha tha fuck iss wrong with me?" I slurred.

"It's from the injection he gave you," Brian said. "That's all I know." He wrapped an arm around my waist and fast-walked us toward the door. With the movement, an all-body tingle gradually replaced the numbness.

Jacques and Philip were waiting for us by the entrance. Dr. Nikas passed Portia to Philip then gestured for me to hurry after him.

It was a good thing the tingle was turning into an electric rush—like a super shot of combat mod—because Dr. Nikas sprinted into the building with Jacques. I disengaged from Brian and ran after them to the medical wing. Toward Nick's room, I realized as we turned onto his corridor.

Dr. Nikas burst into his room, with me a second behind him.

Bear shot from the chair. "What's wrong? What happened?"

On the bed Nick moaned, "Braaaaaains."

I didn't know the answers to Bear's questions, so I gestured to Dr. Nikas.

Who gestured right back at me. "Go on, Angel. Bite Nick. By now your parasite has synthesized the compound I injected into you. But you need to bite him *now*." He took my arm and not-so-gently pushed me in the direction of the bed. "Bite him, Angel."

Good thing I trusted Dr. Nikas with my entire being. Plus, I was willing to do anything to save Nick. "Er, anywhere?"

"As long as you break the skin and salivate."

As I moved to the side of the bed, Nick rolled his head toward me. "Annngelllllll."

I leaned down, cupped the back of his head with one hand, and tugged the hospital gown off his shoulder. Before he could snap at me, I pulled him close and bit down hard on his trapezius, tore until I tasted blood.

Nick howled. I made sure plenty of spit got into the wound then released him and stepped back, wiping my mouth with the back of my hand. He thrashed in the restraints, screaming and slavering.

"I don't think it worked, Doc," I said, voice shaking.

"Patience, Angel. It may take a few minutes."

Bear took my hand.

The minutes ticked by. I stole a glance at Dr. Nikas. He watched Nick, no sign of uncertainty on his face.

The screaming and thrashing stopped as if a switch had been thrown. Nick's eyes closed, and his head lolled to the side. Yet his chest still rose and fell, so whatever was going on, it hadn't killed him.

Bear's grip tightened on my hand. "Come on, Nick," he murmured. "Come on, son."

Nick's eyes fluttered open. I held my breath. Though his eyes were bloodshot, the cloudiness was gone. He blinked and focused on me.

"Angel?"

I threw myself at him, seizing him—carefully—in a hug while Jacques swiftly released the restraints. "You're okay? You're okay!"

"Yeah." He weakly hugged me back. "I'm okay. What happened? Where am I?"

"Long story. You went shambler, but . . . you sure you're okay?"

"Achy. Head hurts. Starrrrrving."

I fought down a burst of panic. "Hungry? For what?"

"Burger and fries maybe. But I'd probably eat anything you put in front of me and then some."

That sparked more hugging and crying, and Bear came in for hugs and tears as well. After a moment, Dr. Nikas tapped my arm. "Angel, we must go now."

"Go where?"

"To the gym."

"Oh. Right. Oh wow, am I going to have to bite all of those people?"

"I'm afraid so."

I clacked my teeth together and grinned. "Let's do this."

Chapter 37

Arriving in the helicopter caused the expected stir at the high school gym. Even better, Agent Gallagher and another member of the special task force were there to make sure we had full, private access to the gym. The medical personnel still got testy when we kicked them out, but at least we had authority on our side—for once.

I went up and down the rows, biting one patient after another—with a break between each one to rinse my mouth. Sponge baths simply didn't cut it for sweating, slavering shamblers. By the time I bit the last patient, the first ones were coming around. But I didn't relax until Bear's people from the bowling alley were awake and coherent again.

After confirming the recoveries were proceeding as expected, Dr. Nikas gave the okay for the FBI agents to allow Dr. Bauer and her team back in. She was understandably pissed off at being removed, but forgot her annoyance as soon as she realized the outcome of our secret visit.

Dr. Nikas gave her his contact info and said to let him know if anyone didn't fully recover, and then we headed to the hospital. We took a car rather than the chopper this time, with Brian driving and the FBI agents escorting.

"Aren't people going to wonder about all of the bite marks?" I asked Dr. Nikas. "And won't they be able to trace them back to me?"

"You were far too busy to notice, but by the time the patients regain their senses, the bites have healed. My formulation was designed to stimulate a healing burst from your parasite to repair bodily damage caused by LZ-1 and, fortuitously, the bite as well."

I silently thanked my precious parasite once again. *You rock!* "I just realized something. Kristi was going to destroy all zombies with her anti-zombie serum." I looked at him. "That's why she thought you should leave the Tribe. Because she respects you. She didn't want to destroy you as well."

"And had I survived the destruction of all zombies, I would have focused my entire being on destroying her." He gave me a smile. "Fortunately for us all, you have done so already."

"Aw, shucks. I'm just a destroy-your-enemies kind of gal."

That made him laugh, which warmed me to the toes.

At the hospital, I repeated my bite and spit routine with all twenty-two patients, ending with Bear's survivalist buddy, Dreadlocks. Mr. August Lejeune.

His eyes fluttered open as soon as I pulled back from the bite. "It's . . . you," he murmured. "You . . . were in my dreams."

"Er, I was?"

"Singing. Strange song." His eyes drifted shut again. "Ga . . . tors."

"What the—"

Dr. Nikas pulled me aside. "I suspect the telepathic connection carried over somewhat with the LZ-1, though likely as little more than subconscious or dream fragments. Fascinating."

I grinned. "You say fascinating. I say weird."

Yet weird or not, August was the last on my to-bite list. With all infected patients treated, we collapsed into the car.

"Now we must return to NuQuesCor. We have more work to do there," Dr. Nikas said.

"You mean the infected gators, right? Please tell me you don't expect me to bite them."

He laughed, happier and lighter than I'd seen him in . . . well, as long as I'd known him. "No, not only would that be awkward, your teeth couldn't penetrate their hide. We will have to do it the hard way."

The "hard way" involved me spitting and spitting and spitting into a flask. When I could spit no more, Dr. Nikas swirled the container and held it up to the light.

"Under normal circumstances, saliva without a bite would be inadequate to spread the parasite—or in this case, the parasite and its synthesized by-products, i.e. the cure." He doctored the saliva with various substances. "But you have been biting today. A lot."

"I get it. When I bite, it activates the parasite to come out and play?"

He chuckled. "Precisely." He made a few more tests and adjustments then poured the mixture into a hypodermic gun.

In the gator room, Dr. Nikas opened a small bottle and waved it around. My nose tickled even though I couldn't detect an odor.

Biggie and Tupac bellowed and splashed out of the pool toward the fence, the smaller ones racing after. But their attention was on Dr. Nikas, not me.

"What the hell is that?"

"A pheromone I hoped would attract infected gators."

I cocked my head as I worked through his statement. "Oh! To use in the swamp so we can make sure we find any that are left out there?"

"Precisely." He screwed the cap back onto the bottle. "We'll send an inoculation team out every day until we are confident all have been found."

Relieved, I entered the pen and got the gators lined up—and made sure they behaved themselves. With the help of Reg and Rachel, we got each and every one inoculated. As soon as we finished, we retreated beyond the safety of the fence to watch and wait and hope my spit cure worked.

For nearly a minute, nothing happened. Then, one by one, their hide shifted back to healthy dark green, and their eyes lost the milky film. Normal alligators, once again.

"Y'all were great," I told them. "The coolest pets ever." They probably didn't understand me anymore since our connection had been due to the disease. And I didn't *feel* them at the edge of my mind anymore. I heaved a sigh. "I'm going to miss having y'all around."

We headed for the door. "When will they be released?" I asked Dr. Nikas.

"This evening," he replied. "I'm assuming you wish to accompany them to the swamp?"

"Yeah! That would be—" I jumped at a bellow from Tupac. The gators were lined up along the fence, snouts pressed against the chain-link. I let out a squeal of delight and ran back to give scritches. "You still like me!"

Biggie let out a low growl-warble as I rubbed his snout. They didn't croon anymore, and the weird mental link we'd shared had faded, but it seemed they still considered me a mama of sorts.

"Well, you won't be in here much longer," I said and gave them one last round of nose rubs.

My phone buzzed as we finally left the room. Allen Prejean. Shit. I'd forgotten to update him. I paused to take the call while the others headed for the lab. "Hey, Allen. Dr. Nikas found the cure. Nick is better and so is everyone else. Sorry I didn't call sooner, but I've had kind of a hectic morning."

He laughed. "Yeah, I figured as much. The CDC guys are losing their shit because they want to know how it was treated and why they weren't kept in the loop. But most people are so relieved the epidemic is over that they're not paying the CDC much attention. Death toll seventeen, but it could have been so much worse."

Seventeen more souls to help throw your ass into hell, Kristi Fucking Charish. "Remember Special Agent Aberdeen? I suspect she and her boss will make a few calls and quiet the CDC down."

"That's good to hear. So will you be back at the Coroner's Office tomorrow?"

"Absolutely!" Weird that I was *eager* to get to work.

"Excellent. See you then."

I returned to the main lab where Rachel, Reg, and Pierce had finished gathering up everything that belonged to the Tribe, along with a plastic bin of partially destroyed computer parts.

"What's all that for?" I asked as I helped carry stuff to the helicopter.

"The drives are damaged but aren't destroyed," Pierce said. "There is still a chance we can retrieve data from them. I know a lady who did recovery work for the NSA. She's expensive as all hell, but if she could get back any more of Kristi's work, it would be worth it."

"But we already have a cure." I pointed to myself.

"It's not the cure we're interested in," he said. "Kristi was working on how to become a mature zombie—without having to be a zombie. That's how she expected to become, essentially, immortal. But Dr. Nikas has other ideas from the direction the research was going."

He climbed into the helicopter and buckled in. Silent, I followed and sat across from him, fastened the seat harness like an old pro and got my headset in place. I waited until we were in the air then tapped Pierce's leg and held up three fingers.

"Kang knows how to force maturity," I said once he was on channel three with me. "But he had a good reason not to tell you how he did it."

"I know," he said. "He was right to keep it from me for so long. But I don't want to use his technique. Trust me, I know how . . . uncontrolled I can get." He shook his head. "But now I'm hoping that Dr. Nikas can modify his technique. Adapt it to prevent the hyperaggression or any other unfortunate side effects."

"And you're hoping that Kristi's research might have answers."

"Dr. Nikas is, and therefore I am." He fell silent but didn't switch the headset channel.

"I don't always agree with your methods or, er, attitude," I said after a moment, "but there's no denying you want the best for the Tribe and all zombies."

He met my eyes. "I want us to be as safe and secure as possible."

"Exactly. Which is why you need to take back Tribe leadership." He started to protest, but I shushed him. "Look, after today's fun and games, pretty much everyone who matters knows you're Pietro—even the FBI. So it's not a security risk anymore. Plus, Marcus hates being a figurehead. For his sake, you should either let him *really* be the Tribe head or take over yourself. But you and Marcus both will be happier if you just take over."

He regarded me with a slight smile. "You think so?"

"I know so. Marcus wants to go to law school. He'd be more benefit to the Tribe as a kickass lawyer."

"You're right."

"Damn, dude. That's the second 'you're right' in one day. You need to pace yourself." I grinned. "But while I'm on a roll, you also need to tell Jane the truth about who you really are." I leaned forward as much as my harness would allow. "I *saw* you stalking her the other day. I was at the pond, and I saw you watching her house. I know you still love her, so you should *do* something about it."

"This time you're not right," he said with a laugh, then held up a hand when I opened my mouth to tell him he was full of shit. "I wasn't stalking her that day. She knew I was there." His smile widened at my perplexed expression. "Jane has known the truth since not long after I became Pierce. But since it would look bad for a respected Congresswoman to be seen in a relationship with a younger man so soon after her fiancé's death, we've been keeping the relationship secret. The day you saw me at the pond, I was waiting for her visitor to leave. When it looked like he was going to be there a while, Jane called to let me know."

"That's so awesome," I said with a happy sigh.

"Glad you approve. We figure we can start dating openly this fall."

"Well, in the meantime, your secret is safe with me."

"I know it is, Angel."

By the time we made it back to the Tribe lab, Portia was moving around under her own power. She greeted Dr. Nikas with a heart-melting hug and kiss, then the two of them headed toward his private quarters. I silently cheered them on, so happy for both of them, but extra-especially so for Dr. Nikas.

I then checked on Bear and Nick—who was already up and around. I gave Nick an enthusiastic greeting that raised his heart rate nicely, then returned to the media room and helped my dad pack up the play box.

"Bear is heading back to town soon, now that he and Nick are in the clear," I told him. "He'll give you a ride, if you want."

"Sure do, cuz I got me an appointment at four this afternoon."

"Appointment for what?"

His eyes crinkled as he smiled. "Gettin' me a physical exam. The whole works. And it turns out Gina works at the Y, and she said she'd be like a personal trainer to me for a bit so I can learn how to exercise right and not hurt my back and maybe make it better."

"Gina. Your girlfriend?"

My dad doubled over in laughter and slapped his knee. "Me and Gina? Nah. She ain't much more'n your age. Bartended a coupla years down at Kaster's where I do clean up, but ended up in a mess last month when her boyfriend left her and her kid. She also works the front desk at the Y and cleans houses. We hammered out a deal where she'd clean our place in trade for me watching little Carter while she cleaned other houses. Trying to make ends meet, y'know? Working three jobs."

"You're babysitting?" I grinned. "You rock! And she does a kickass job on the house." I looked him over. "And if she can get you to exercise and go to the doctor, she has my blessing."

"That was you, Angelkins, that got me seein' about my health and all."

"Then I'm damn glad I came down on you about it." I gave him a kiss on the cheek. "You keep on listening to me, and we'll be all right."

After Bear and my dad left, I hung out with Nick in the media room and filled him in on everything that happened, then we just kind of cuddled and relaxed and watched movies and did a whole lot of nothing, which was wonderful, zero-stress time.

My dad texted halfway through *The Fifth Element*.

<Your car was in the driveway when I got home. Note under wiper>

A picture was attached of a small piece of paper that read "Everything's cool with BB. Thanks for the help. B.U."

B.U. was Billy Upton. I smiled and texted a reply. <Thanks. Had to leave my car when Nick got sick, and my friend Billy was nice enough to deliver it to the house> And apparently he'd smoothed things over with Big Bubba, judging by the note. That was a load off my mind.

Later in the afternoon, Dr. Nikas examined Nick and pronounced him fully recovered, which meant that Nick could accompany me for the release of the gators.

That evening, with the help of Philip and several other Tribe security, I cajoled and encouraged the gators to climb into rolling cage-crates. Once we finally got them loaded in a box truck, we headed for the swamp boat launch we'd used for our gator hunt mission. Weird that it was only a few days ago. It seemed forever.

Philip backed the truck up to the edge of the water. We opened the truck doors and the crates, then I retreated to stand by Nick.

The little gators needed no convincing, and quickly flopped onto the ramp and waddle-slid into the swamp. Biggie and

Tupac went last, lumbering down with reptilian majesty to slip into the water. They turned to face me, eyes and snout visible above the surface.

"Oh, all right," I said. I shucked off my shoes and waded in until I was waist deep. Biggie and Tupac rubbed up against me like cats, rumbling the water until I finally pushed them away and bid them a laughing goodbye.

With that, they swam off, disappearing quickly into the gloom. I waded back to shore and Nick.

"I have the weirdest girlfriend ever," he said with a smile and kissed me.

"So I'm your girlfriend now?"

"Sure are," he said. "Let's go home so you can get out of those wet clothes."

Life returned to a semblance of normal-busy fairly quickly. Saturday, Brian reported that Linda Garrison, the Health Department doctor, had filed a police report, stating that a man fitting Harlon Murtaugh's description used threats against her family to force her to get him access to a patient—Beckett Connor. I passed the info on to Allen, who seemed relieved that she was not, in fact, a Saberton baddie. Sunday evening, I asked Jane if there was a way to get the warning signs replaced at the dangerous curve out on Highway 1268—where Spencer Leigh had died, and where Marcus had kept me from the same fate by turning me into a zombie. Jane made a few calls, and by Monday afternoon the new signs were in place.

It sure was nice having friends who could Get Shit Done.

On Tuesday, I borrowed a black dress from Naomi and attended Connor's funeral. Since he'd died in the line of duty, the attendance was massive, with every law enforcement agency in the parish in attendance. I even spied Special Agent Gallagher in the back, but had no desire to go over and strike up a conversation.

But I did give my condolences personally to Connor's mother. "I'm sorry for your loss," I murmured then silently added *I avenged your son's death and killed his murderer.*

With Justine's help, I finished my essay in English comp about the worst birthday ever, and didn't pull any punches. The professor loved it and would have given me an A except for the fact that I had a tendency to put commas in all the wrong places, and so I ended up with a B+.

As far as biology went, I asked Isabella Romero—the student who Professor Dingle had given such a hard time—if she wanted to be study partners. And when she had trouble finding a babysitter for her young son, my dad was happy to help out.

Kyle's body was cremated, as per his wishes, and we had a private ceremony for him at the lab. Everyone spoke and did their public grieving, then we broke out some of Dr. Nikas's zombie booze concoction—again, as per Kyle's wishes—and had a rollicking wake for a proper sendoff.

Bear, Nick, Allen, and my dad were there as well, because even though they hadn't known Kyle in life, they were grateful for everything he'd done for all of us. And Marla and Moose wandered around in doggie heaven, getting the pets and scritches they so very much deserved.

The party was just winding down when Pierce called me over. "Jane texted that Andrew Saber is holding a press conference in five minutes. Meet up in the media room."

Soon enough, Pierce, Dr. Nikas, Brian, and I were clustered around the TV. Andrew stood before a throng of reporters in the lobby of Saberton's New York headquarters. Appearing vibrant and confident, he announced that his mother had stepped down and that he was now CEO of Saberton.

I snorted. "Stepped down, my ass. More like shoved kicking and screaming, I bet. Good riddance."

Andrew went on to praise Dr. Kristi Charish for her stellar work to unlock the cure for the LZ-1 epidemic. He then revealed that, tragically, Dr. Charish had suffered a mild stroke immediately after casting her vote in the Saberton board meeting and would be taking a sabbatical from research. But the silver lining was that she would be at his side to help lead Saberton in a new, humanitarian and eco-friendly direction. He closed with a sappy promise of a brighter tomorrow, thanked the reporters for coming, and left without answering the shouted questions.

"Hot damn!" I said as Pierce muted the TV. "That was a brilliant move since Kang-Kristi doesn't know squat about research."

Pierce looked thoughtful. "Kang has well and truly ensconced himself in the Saberton hierarchy."

I poked him in the chest. "That's right, and you and Kang are going to put your centuries of differences behind you and work together to create a brighter tomorrow for all zombies. Right?"

He surprised me with a genuine laugh. "What do you say, Ari?"

Dr. Nikas smiled. "I say that we are in a golden moment of opportunity. And if you fuck it up, I will have *your* head in a vat until you come to your senses." That produced a round of laughter from everyone, including Pierce. But as it died away, Dr. Nikas sobered. "With Kang only masquerading as a scientist, the burden of research rests on my shoulders. I need more help."

"The Tribe accountant was looking into the possibility of finding a dying neurobiologist or the like who might be willing to be turned," I pointed out. "And you already have Portia."

"Both with excellent potential." He blew out a breath, and his shoulders relaxed. "There's no rush. We're in this for the very long haul."

We. Not just Dr. Nikas or Pierce or Brian. It included me as well. I had a potentially very long life ahead, and damn it, I really liked the idea of spending at least some of it helping the Tribe—*my* people—bring about an honest-to-goodness better tomorrow.

A gasp came from the direction of the door. Naomi stared at the TV where Andrew waved to the press as he entered an elevator and the words *Saberton CEO Nicole Saber steps down* ran along bottom. She burst into un-Naomi-like tears. I ran over to pull her into a hug. She'd been worried about her twin for weeks, and now not only was Andrew safe, but he was being the kind of man she'd always wanted him to be.

Dr. Nikas herded Pierce and Brian out while I guided Naomi to the nearest sofa.

I plopped down beside her and took her hand. "Your mother has been removed from power, and you'll be able to see Andrew again soon. He'll make sure of it."

She sniffled and swiped at her eyes. "It's like waking up from a nightmare. I'm not sure if it's real or not."

"Aww. It's for real, babe." I gave her hand a squeeze. "The bad shit is behind you, and your brother is ready to mend fences."

"Everything's falling into place for the zombies, too." She stole a glance at me. "You know what we need since we're at the beginning of a whole new era?" A sly smile tugged at her mouth.

"Chocolate?"

"Ice cream, silly!" she said then widened her eyes.

Together we shouted, "Chocolate ice cream!"

We raced to the lab's kitchen and spent the next half hour eating chocolate fudge ice cream, talking, and laughing. It felt *gooooood*.

Once we'd stuffed ourselves sick, she gave me a hug and left for her security shift. I wiped ice cream off my chin then made my way to the Head Room to change out the nutrient goo.

Humming, I put in my code, pulled the door open, and stepped in.

Dr. Nikas loomed in the semi-darkness beside the empty regrowth tank, one hand gripping his temples between fingers and thumb as if he had a headache.

I started to ease out of the room.

"Angel," he said. "Stay."

I slowly closed the door behind me. "Is something wrong?"

He lowered his hand. "Take a look in Adam Campbell's vat."

I peered through the glass lid into the crockpot of nutrient snot and its resident head. All seemed normal in a grey-skinned, severed head, horror show sort of way. "I don't—" Then I saw it: a little bud about the size of a jellybean sprouting from the neck stump. Just like with Kang's head. "He's regrowing! What changed?"

"Everything." Dr. Nikas put his arm around my shoulders and gazed down into the vat with me. "I spent this past week reviewing what we recovered, and what I stole, of Kristi's immortality work. She wasn't as close to a solution as she'd believed, but the direction of her research sparked a fresh line of thought, and I tested a new nutrient formulation on Adam. I discovered the progress only moments before you walked in."

"That's awesome!" I paused. "It is awesome, right? I mean, when I walked in you looked upset."

"Upset, no. I was a bit overwhelmed by the enormity of the implications." He gave my shoulders a squeeze and stepped away from the vat. "This discovery opens untried research paths. The way isn't clear yet, but I see the potential, the end result. Not with development of a brain substitute—which I have determined would never healthily maintain the parasite—but a way to quasi-mature zombies so the amount of brains required for sustenance would be greatly reduced."

My smile grew. "Like how you and Pierce and Kang need a lot less brains. That's brilliant."

"Research and development will likely take years, but I am certain it can be achieved." He shook his head. "I wonder how Dr. Charish would feel if she knew her legacy was not immortality for herself, but the trigger for a long-term lifeline for zombies."

"She would hate it from the very depths of her cold, black, shriveled heart."

"What a tragedy." He sighed. "If she had been open and honest with her findings rather than the cruel egoist she was, such marvels we could have accomplished."

"Yeah, but you're the real foundation of all this. You just need people around to spark your genius and keep you on your toes."

He gave me a warm smile. "Like you."

"Me?" I laughed. "I won't argue with the keeping you on your toes part, but I'm not much of an intellectual spark."

"Don't sell yourself short, Angel. You grasp concepts readily and often see solutions others may not."

I blinked. "I do?"

"Look at all you have accomplished over the past year and a half, the scrapes you've wriggled out of, the clever ideas you've put forth. You even keep Pierce honest, and that is no mean feat."

I squirmed, blushing. "I guess I'm a survivor."

"That you are. A survivor with intellect you don't yet appreciate. You proposed that the mosquito bites weren't really mosquito bites. You uncovered the link between the water bottles and shamblers turning. And remember how you said you thought the combat mod might have stimulated the anesthetized parasite in Kyle? I tested the process as part of my inquiry into Kristi's work, and you were right. You didn't know the specifics of how it would function, but you came to a solid conclusion worthy of a hypothesis."

I blushed more.

He regarded me, eyes deep and ancient and wise. "What do you want to do with your life? If you could have your heart's desire."

I started to blurt out a line about having peace and quiet, enough money to live on and keep my dad safe, a home. But that wasn't what he meant. He wanted to know my impossible, secret dream. Tears pricked my eyes. "I like my work at the morgue, and I love biology, and I love working here with you, but I wish it could be more—wish *I* could be more."

"In what way?" he asked quietly.

"Educated, so I could really help. Not just some classes in community college, but—" My old loser self tried to tell me I was making a fool of myself, that Dr. Nikas didn't care about my stupid fantasy. But I knew better. I wasn't being a fool, and Dr. Nikas cared for real. "I'd like to be a neurobiologist. I know it's kinda crazy. I just—"

"Angel, there is no reason to not live your dream."

"I'm just so far behind. I have the stubbornness to stick it out, but I'm already twenty-three and haven't even finished one college course."

He laughed, genuine and heartening. "Time is on your side, Angel. The Tribe will back you, and lord knows I will need help for many decades to come."

I laughed with him. Of course time was on my side. I was a zombie. I threw my arms around his neck. "Thank you for believing in me. No, not just that. For helping me believe in myself."

"You are one of a kind, Angel," he said, smiling as I released him.

My phone alarm beeped. "Oh, shit! I have to get to the morgue, but I haven't changed the gel in the head vats yet."

"Go. Reg will take care of it."

"He'll lovvvvve me for that," I muttered then brightened. "Ooo! Dr. Nikas. What do you think about getting Reg a cat? He was joking about it the other day, but I don't think it was really a joke. He could keep it in the living area and media room and stuff. It wouldn't be a bother in the lab. I could go to the shelter and find one that would be perfect for him. A surprise, y'know? But if you don't think it would be good idea, I understand."

His eyes brightened. "It is a splendid idea, Angel. Now, get yourself to work."

Beaming, I scurried out, mind whirling with the conversation. And the possibilities.

Me. A neurobiologist. Dr. Crawford! Now, wouldn't that be something?

Life continued to settle into a more normal routine. Andrew called Naomi, and they talked for close to an hour. Afterward, Naomi let us know that Kristi had been working on her own with regards to the LZ-1 epidemic, though using Saberton personnel and resources. She added that Andrew was already cleaning house of anyone who'd been involved in the nastier side of Saberton research and operations.

People continued to die in a variety of ways, both tragic and stupid, and made their way into the morgue. And I continued to judiciously harvest brains.

I had brains in my belly, and all was right with the world.

The FBI opened an investigation into Nicole Saber and her suspected ties to racketeering, fraud, kidnapping, and murder. Naomi and I celebrated with more ice cream.

Allen seemed pleased that Nick and I had finally progressed to dating. "I saw this coming when you first started working here," he said, smug.

And when Derrel happened to catch us stealing a quick kiss in the morgue parking lot, he gave me a bone-squishing hug and declared, "I told you it would all work out!"

A week after Kyle's funeral, I jerked awake to heavy pounding at the door. A bleary look at the clock told me it was 8 a.m. Ugh.

Grumbling, I tugged on a robe then shuffled out and opened the door. Nick stood on the porch with a backpack over one shoulder and a small cardboard box in his hands.

"Good morning, Angel," he said, far too cheerfully. "There was a package for your dad on the porch. You look especially perky this morning!"

I gave him a middle finger and then a kiss. "I got called out at 2 a.m. to scrape a motorcyclist off the highway."

Nick set the package on the table and gave me a more thorough kiss. "Then it's a good thing I stopped by Lagniappe Café and picked up beignets."

"Ooooo. Gimme!"

Grinning, Nick fished a large white paper bag from his backpack and handed it over.

"Oh man, they're still warm." I grabbed a plate from the kitchen then poured the beignets out, getting powdered sugar everywhere and not caring. This was how beignets were meant to be eaten—warm and covered with a shitload of powdered sugar.

"Fank oo," I managed around a mouthful of pastry.

"And once you're done, we can look through these." He pulled a stack of brochures and pamphlets from the backpack and set them on the table—away from the sugar. "College catalogs. TPCC is fine for getting your basics, but you're going to need doctorate-level education for the sort of research you want to do. That means, after a couple of years, you should attend a university with a strong undergrad biology program."

"Have I told you lately that you're the best?"

He chuckled and started to make coffee. "I think the kiss at the door covered that."

I licked my fingers and poked through the stack. "These are from all around the country." I looked over at him. "The thought of living somewhere else feels so weird. I've lived here my entire life. I *know* this place."

"I get it. Same boat for me." Nick started the coffeemaker then returned and fished a pamphlet from the stack. "That's in Florida. Excellent biology program, and it just so happens to be where I was accepted to med school."

I smiled up at him. "You decided to go for forensic pathology?"

"You helped me crystallize my goals." He kissed me. "Two more years as a death investigator, then I'll be ready."

"Watch out, Florida. Here we come!" I grinned then sobered. "Still, the thought of moving away is more than a little terrifying."

Nick bent down and kissed me. "You've faced down armed mercenaries and evil scientists. You jumped off a three-story building on purpose. I think you can handle this."

"Sheesh. All right. But you'd better help me study for the college entrance exams."

"You know it."

My dad's bedroom door opened, forestalling another round of kissing. As he shuffled into the kitchen, he gave Nick a bleary squint.

"Mornin,' Nick. Didja spend the night here?"

"No, sir. I brought beignets for you and Angel. Oh, and I brought in a package for you."

"No shit?" He peered at the label then ripped it open. "Hot damn! Andrew done sent me the *Swords and Swagger* sequel!"

I checked the package. Yes, definitely addressed to my dad. "I'm not sure Andrew will have as much time to play, being the CEO and all."

"Nah. That boy needs stress relief now more than ever." He headed to the coffeemaker and poured himself a cup. "It's such a purty morning, I think I'll have my coffee outside. Give y'all a bit of privacy." He winked at me then headed out to the back porch.

A mug smashed outside. "Jesus fuck!" my dad yelled.

I shot to my feet as he raced back inside. "Angel!" He gasped. "You got some visitors."

"Huh?" I ran outside then stopped dead at the sight of Biggie and Tupac happily sunning themselves in my back yard.

"Holy crap," Nick breathed. "They came all the way here? That has to be twenty or thirty miles!"

"Cole Bayou is at the back of this property," I said, dashing tears of laughter away. "I guess they made their way through the swamp and down a series of waterways to get here."

"That . . . is weirdly adorable." He pulled me close. "Angel Crawford, I love you. And I even love your very weird pets."

"I love you, Nick Galatas. And I promise they'll be outside pets only. Imagine the litter box!"

We kissed and the gators bellowed their approval.

Maybe believing in a better tomorrow wasn't so sappy after all.

Diana Rowland

My Life as a White Trash Zombie
978-0-7564-0675-2

Even White Trash Zombies Get the Blues
978-0-7564-0750-6

White Trash Zombie Apocalypse
978-0-7564-0803-9

How the White Trash Zombie Got Her Groove Back
978-0-7564-0822-0

White Trash Zombie Gone Wild
978-0-7564-0823-7

White Trash Zombie Unchained
978-0-7564-0824-4

To Order Call: 1-800-788-6262
www.dawbooks.com

DAW 201

Diana Rowland

The Kara Gillian Novels

"Rowland's hot streak continues as she gives her fans another big helping of urban fantasy goodness! The plot twists are plentiful and the action is hard-edged. Another great entry in this compelling series." —*RT Book Review*

"Rowland's world of arcane magic and demons is fresh and original [and her] characters are well-developed and distinct.... Dark, fast-paced, and gripping." —*SciFiChick*

To Order Call: 1-800-788-6262
www.dawbooks.com

DAW 176

Seanan McGuire
The InCryptid Novels

"McGuire's imagination is utterly boundless. The world of her *InCryptid* series is full of unexpected creatures, constant surprises and appealing characters, all crafted with the measured ease of a skilled professional, making the fantastic seem like a wonderful reality."
                                                            —*RT Reviews*

"The only thing more fun than an October Daye book is an InCryptid book. Swift narrative, charm, great world-building . . . all the McGuire trademarks."
                                                            —Charlaine Harris

To Order Call: 1-800-788-6262
www.dawbooks.com

DAW 143

C.S. Friedman
The *Magister* Trilogy

"Powerful, intricate plotting and gripping characters
distinguish a book in which ethical dilemmas
are essential and engrossing."
—*Booklist*

"Imaginative, deftly plotted fantasy...
Readers will eagerly await the next installment."
—*Publishers Weekly*

FEAST OF SOULS
978-0-7564-0463-5

WINGS OF WRATH
978-0-7564-0594-6

LEGACY OF KINGS
978-0-7564-0748-3

To Order Call: 1-800-788-6262
www.dawbooks.com

Necromancer is such an ugly word
...but it's a title Eric Carter is stuck with.

He sees ghosts, talks to the dead. He's turned it into a lucrative career putting troublesome spirits to rest, sometimes taking on even more dangerous things. For a fee, of course.

When he left L.A. fifteen years ago he thought he'd never go back. Too many bad memories. Too many people trying to kill him.

But now his sister's been brutally murdered and Carter wants to find out why.

Was it the gangster looking to settle a score? The ghost of a mage he killed the night he left town? Maybe it's the patron saint of violent death herself, Santa Muerte, who's taken an unusually keen interest in him.

Carter's going to find out who did it and he's going to make them pay.

As long as they don't kill him first.

Dead Things
by Stephen Blackmoore

978-0-7564-0774-2

Tad Williams
The **Bobby Dollar** Novels

"A dark and thrilling story.... Bad-ass smart-mouth
Bobby Dollar, an Earth-bound angel advocate for
newly departed souls caught between Heaven and
Hell, is appalled when a soul goes missing on his
watch. Bobby quickly realizes this is 'an actual, hon-
est-to-front-office crisis,' and he sets out to fix it,
sparking a chain of hellish events.... Exhilarating
action, fascinating characters, and high stakes will
leave the reader both satisfied and eager for the next
installment." —*Publishers Weekly (starred review)*

"Williams does a brilliant job.... Made me laugh.
Made me curious. Impressed me with its cleverness.
Made me hungry for the next book. Kept me up late
at night when I should have been sleeping."
                                        —Patrick Rothfuss

The Dirty Streets of Heaven: 978-0-7564-0790-2
Happy Hour in Hell: 978-0-7564-0948-7
Sleeping Late on Judgement Day: 978-0-7564-0889-3

To Order Call: 1-800-788-6262
www.dawbooks.com

DAW 207